THE PIRATES OF TARUTAO

BY
Paul Adirex

ARIES BOOKS

THE PIRATES OF TARUTAO, its story, including incidents and dialogues involving deceased and living individuals, are created by the author's imgination based on historical facts.

Published by Aries Books, 19 Soi Aree 1, Paholyotin Road, Bangkok, Thailand

Copyright © 1994 by Pongpol Adireksarn
Second Printing, April 1996

ISBN : 974-89046-9-5

Printed in Thailand by Amarin Printing & Publishing Public Co., Ltd.

"Greed causes wars and conflicts which are destructive to everyone concerned. The victors incur hatred upon themselves, and the defeated live in suffering. Winning over oneself by controlling greed is the best virtue."

A Buddhist Proverb

MAP OF SOUTHEAST ASIA

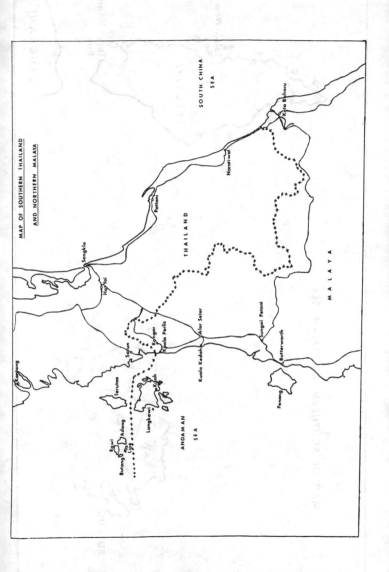

MAP OF SOUTHERN THAILAND
AND NORTHERN MALAYA

MAP OF SOUTHERN ANDAMAN SEA

LANGKAWI

Taloh Wow Bay

Taloh Udang Bay

TARUTAO

Pante Bay

Pine Bay

ADANG

LIPE

RAWI

BUTANG

PROLOGUE

"Tarutao? Why?" The Director-General of the Department of Corrections (DG-DOC) of Thailand asked. He looked across his desk at his deputy, who was making a report to him.

"Sir, you instructed us to find a large, uninhabited island as far away from Bangkok as possible, and set up a penal colony for pre-release vocational training of convicts," the deputy replied. "We've found the best island. It's Tarutao. It's ninety square miles, so it's large enough, and it's in the Andaman Sea, about three miles from British Malaya, and 700 miles from Bangkok. It's the southernmost island in Thai territory that met your requirements, and..."

The DG interrupted, "How far is it from our mainland?"

"About twelve miles, close enough to send supplies there regularly. It's also easy for our officials and the prisoners to get there," replied the deputy, who knew the reason behind his boss's question.

"Good, that's my main concern. This new prison must be able to accommodate at least three thousand inmates and three hundred guards and staff. Transporting supplies will be a major consideration. Cutting off transportation for a long period of time would be a disaster. You must be aware of that."

"Sir, I considered that the most important factor when I chose Tarutao. But the island also offers other natural benefits. Besides vast land, it has plenty of water, even a few waterfalls and several streams. Another favorable factor is that the sea around Tarutao is unpredictable and dangerous, affected by monsoons almost all year-round. The waters are also infested with sharks, which will discourage the prisoners from trying to escape by swimming to the mainland and nearby islands."

"Good. It's Tarutao then. Organize a team to build living quarters for our officials, the guards, and the prisoners." The DG paused and then gave his order, then asked another question, "When do you think it'll be ready?"

The deputy replied immediately. He had anticipated this question and planned his answer in advance. "It's now May 1937. It'll take me about one year to have the island ready. Labor is no problem, we have plenty of people. I intend to use prisoners from the nearby provinces. The weather, which we can't control, could be our biggest obstacle."

"Do what you have to and request any help that you need. Have Tarutao ready by June 1938."

Unknown to the DG and his deputy, neither of whom had ever set foot on Tarutao, the island possessed certain features which would make settling on the island more difficult than they had thought. In Malay, Tarutao means "old and mysterious." The name was appropriate because for millions of years since its formation, Tarutao had been left unsettled by humans.

Viewed from the sea, the island looked appealing and welcoming, the several high mountains and fertile land were covered with lush green rain forests. However, despite its appearance, there had never been a permanent human settlement on Tarutao. For centuries fishermen and merchant ships had used Tarutao only as a temporary shelter from the stormy seas of the monsoon season. They also sometimes stopped to procure fresh water from one of the several streams that flowed from the mountains. Fishermen occasionally set up camps along the beaches to dry and store their catches, but those few who dared to venture further inland never returned.

Legend had it that Tarutao was cursed. People who tried to settle permanently on the island usually became ill, suffering chills, high fever, and frequently death. Those who survived were plagued with chronic fever, frequent relapses, and occasional delirium. Although the natives had no name for this dreadful sickness, modern medicine calls it malaria, the scourge of mankind.

Tarutao's rainy, humid climate allowed malaria to thrive. The tropical rain forests and the mangrove swamps surrounding the island's shoreline were ideal breeding places for the mosquitoes that carried the malaria contagion.

In addition to mosquitoes, the streams on Tarutao were also infested with crocodiles. Visitors who chose to camp near the seemingly safe, beautiful streams, or wandered around at night, often fell prey to those ferocious reptiles.

The weather also discouraged a permanent settlement on Tarutao. From May to October, the western side of the island was buffeted by the prevailing southwest monsoon, which caused strong winds, high waves, and heavy rains in the Andaman Sea. The shipwreck debris that washed up on Tarutao's western shore bore evidence of the sea's cruelty during those six months. The eastern side, well protected from the southwest monsoon by the skyline of mountains, became exposed to the northeast monsoon from

November to April. These weather conditions made traveling across the sharkinfested sea to and from Tarutao difficult and unsafe.

The island was about fourteen miles long, and six miles at its widest part. The bays and beaches on the western side were welcome sights to sea travelers seeking shelter from the wind and the waves during the northeast monsoon period. Inland, there were mountains covered with dense jungles extending down to the edge of the sea. The northern side was a narrow tip lined with limestone cliffs dropping straight into the sea. The southern end had a long curved beach, its flat ground extending inland and sloping upward towards the mountains. The eastern shoreline, which faced the mainland, was covered with mangrove swamps, had one big bay and a few smaller bays which provided shelter during the southwest monsoon season.

As the Director-General instructed, the Department of Corrections sent an expedition and construction team in June 1937 to explore and prepare Tarutao for a permanent settlement to accommodate three thousand inmates and three hundred officials and guards. The construction of Tarutao Vocational Training Settlement (TVTS), as it was officially called to give it a less sinister and more appealing image, was completed one year later.

Within a year of June 1938, about two thousand prisoners were confined on Tarutao. Each group of prisoners was transported by train 560 miles from Bangkok to Kuan Niang station in Songkla province. From Kuan Niang the prisoners traveled fifty miles of dirt road to the city of Satun on the western coast. After a few days in the overcrowded prison in Satun, the prisoners were sent in small groups aboard two TVTS motor boats across the sea to Tarutao.

On September 18, 1939, a new and unique group of seventy prisoners was transferred from a Bangkok prison to Tarutao. They were political prisoners who had been arrested and imprisoned as the consequence of political turmoil in Thailand.

The revolution of 1932, during the reign of King Rama VII, abolished the absolute monarchy which had ruled the country for seven hundred years. Loyalists attempted a counterrevolt in 1933 but suffered a crushing defeat at the hands of the ruling military regime. The abortive revolt led to the abdication of King Rama VII in March 1934 and the mass arrests of about three hundred people, including members of the Royal family, high ranking military officers and civilian officials, journalists, and politicians. The trials took four years, and sentences were pronounced in 1938.

Eighteen people were executed by firing squad, and seventy were sent to imprisonment on Tarutao.

There were two prisoner compounds on Tarutao. The first, and the largest was located on flat land near the shore of Taloh Wow Bay on the eastern side of the island. It consisted of the administrative office of the TVTS, housing for two hundred and fifty guards and their families, and living quarters for two thousand prisoners. Five miles away, on the shore of Taloh Udang Bay at the south end of the island, was the second compound which housed one thousand prisoners. The two compounds were connected by a single dirt road built by the prisoners themselves.

The seventy political prisoners were put in an isolated area near the beach away from the common prisoners. Their area had no fence but its boundary was marked by red flags at intervals. At the entrance was a guard post manned by two guards armed with shotguns. A special detail of one police sergeant and six policemen were sent from Bangkok to guard the prisoners.

Political and common prisoners were given strict orders not to contact one another. Those who defied the order would be harshly punished. Unlike the common prisoners, the political prisoners were not in handcuffs or chains and were not required to do hard labor. But they were required to be at the roll call twice a day at six in the morning and six in the evening. If any political prisoner attempted to escape and was captured, the penalty was immediate execution by firing squad.

CHAPTER 1

A small group of men moved in single file slowly and quietly through the waist-deep stream. A half-moon lit the night, so they stayed close to the bank, concealing themselves in the shadows of the tall mangrove trees that crowded along the stream bank. The stream emptied into Taloh Udang Bay, and the men could see that from that point, it was open space across a wide sandbar to the whitecapped sea visible under the moonlight. The man leading the group looked up at the sky and whispered to the men behind him.

"We have to wait until those clouds block the moonlight before we can move across the sandbar. It's low tide now and I can't bring the boat in here to pick you up."

"How far is the boat from the sandbar?" whispered one of the men in the group.

The leader pointed out a spot across the sandbar, in the water, and replied. "From where the waves break we'll have to walk about six hundred feet to get to the spot where the boat is waiting. The water there is waist-deep."

The man leading the group was Mee, the only fisherman allowed by the TVTS to live on Tarutao. Mee and his small family had been living on the island years before it became a prison. His wife had died of malaria six years ago, leaving him with two daughters and a son. The older daughter had married a TVTS guard, and the two of them lived in the prison compound at Taloh Wow Bay. Mee lived at Taloh Udang Bay with his sixteen-year-old daughter and twenty-year-old son. He made a meager living selling his catches to the TVTS. But this evening, he was risking his life for a reward of five thousand baht (two thousand and thirty-two US dollars in 1939) in cash and the promise that his two children would be well taken care of. In exchange, he was to lead the five men behind him safely to the island of Langkawi, five miles across the channel.

Mee wanted his younger daughter to have a better future than her older sister, whose husband was only a prison guard. And he was clever enough to realize that in order for his wish to come true, his daughter would need a proper education and a good environment. Tarutao, with a prison and three thousand inmates, was no longer a suitable place for a young girl to live and grow up. The five men promised Mee that they would send his daughter to the best school in Malaya.

The five men desperate to leave Tarutao on this fateful night were political prisoners who had arrived at this island prison twenty-nine days ago. They were Naval Captain Praya Sarapai (Praya was a title given by a king to his loyal subjects); Army Colonel Praya Surapan; Louis Kiriwat, a newspaper editor; Chalam Liampetrat, a lawyer; and Khun Akani (Khun was another title given by a king), a railroad engineer.

Praya Sarapai, who had planned and led the escape, was a former assistant undersecretary in the Ministry of Defense. He was intelligent and well educated. His former position had taught him much about the neighboring countries and their relations with Thailand. He was aware that the extradition agreement between Thailand and British Malaya did not apply to political prisoners seeking asylum.

Praya Sarapai knew that Langkawi, an island belonging to British Malaya, was only five miles from the south end of Tarutao. If he could find a way to escape to Langkawi, he would be free. Since his arrival on Tarutao, Praya Sarapai had been planning his escape. He was quick to make friends with Mee and his family, and when he learned of Mee's ambitions for his children, Praya Sarapai recruited Mee to help with the escape.

Suddenly, darkness spread over the sandbar and the sea beyond it. A cluster of dark clouds had enveloped the moon, completely blocking out its light. Mee decided the time was right, and began to wade rapidly towards the sandbar.

"Hurry! We've got to go now before the moon comes out again," he urged. Silently, the five men waded after Mee to the other side of the stream, and climbed over the bank which led to the sandbar. Their luck held, and the dark clouds continued to hide the moon so that it was still dark when they left the sandbar and rushed into the sea. They followed closely behind Mee, the only one who knew exactly where the boat was.

When they were thigh-deep in the water, they heard welcome words from Mee. "The boat's over there!"

The prisoners looked up and stared hard ahead into the darkness. About one hundred feet away, against the dark shape of the island, they could see a long object bobbing in the water. By the time they reached the boat, the water was waist-deep. They could see two figures on board move toward the side of the boat as they approached.

Praya Sarapai felt a pair of strong arms pulling him up into the boat. He looked up and saw the smiling face of Mee's son, Lek. Standing behind Lek was his sister, Noi.

Lek greeted Praya Sarapai and said, "We were worried when you were late. We thought that something might have happened."

"We were waiting for the clouds to block the moonlight," Praya Sarapai replied while helping his fellow prisoners to climb up into the boat. "We're all here. Let's go," he said to Mee.

Mee, standing in the bow, replied without turning. "No wind!"

Mee's words made everyone's heart sink. The five prisoners listened attentively and looked around. Mee was right. There was no wind at all, and the sea was as smooth as a sheet of glass.

"That's strange! October is the height of the monsoon season, and there is no wind. It's impossible!" exclaimed Khun Akani.

"Well, we have no choice but to go ahead. There's no going back now," Praya Sarapai said forcefully. "Get out the paddles. If we have to paddle all the way to Langkawi, then we just have to do it. At least if there's no wind, there'll be no waves either, so it'll be easier to paddle."

Lek slowly pulled the anchor up, and the small sailboat began to move forward as Praya Surapan and Mee dipped the paddles into the calm sea. There were only two paddles on the boat, so Praya Surapan and Mee took the first shift.

"It's two miles from here to the big rock in the middle of the channel. That rock marks the boundary between Thailand and Malaya," Praya Sarapai said.

"Chalam, are you still certain that we'll make it?" Louis Kiriwat asked nervously. Chalam, a recognized astrologer, was the one who had decided on the most auspicious date and time to escape.

Chalam replied firmly, "I'm confident of my calculations. We're still free and alive. Just keep going. Everything'll be fine."

Half an hour passed as they headed southward in the dark. Ten minutes after Praya Sarapai and Khun Akani began their turns at the paddles, they heard a sound coming nearer and nearer.

"It's the wind!" shouted Mee. He got up and began readying the boat's single sail.

Moments later, the wind arrived, a welcome breeze against their faces. As the wind filled its sail, the small boat surged forward, cheered on by its desperate passengers.

They sailed on in the dark. The moon seemed to have disappeared forever behind the clouds. Mee and Lek assured the five men that they were heading in the right direction. The five men had no choice but to allow destiny to take its course, so they sat quietly, contemplating their unknown future.

Then Mee said, "We've reached Langkawi!" and pointed beyond the bow of the boat.

All the men could see was the dark shape of a large mountain about three hundred feet away, looming out of the darkness. But to the passengers of the small sailboat, it was the most pleasing sight they had seen for some time.

At daybreak, they landed on a beach near a fishing village on the western shore of Langkawi. It was October 17, 1939.

CHAPTER 2

The passenger/cargo ship, the MANILA STAR, made her way slowly up the Sarawak River as she approached Kuching, a regular stop on the five day run from Manila to Singapore. After the ship left the South China Sea and entered the wide Sarawak River, on her way to Kuching twenty miles upstream, the passengers, most Malays and Chinese, began to emerge from their cabins. Those who were disembarking at Kuching, the capital of Sarawak, a sovereign state on the island of Borneo, were getting their belongings ready. Others were enjoying the scenic wilderness which lines both banks of the river.

Among the passengers gathered on the deck, one man in particular stood out from the crowd.

He was six feet tall, which was considered very tall by the Asian passengers standing around him. He also differed from the other passengers in his dress and features. His well-cut, expensive khaki suit fitted his lean body perfectly. He wore a white shirt without a tie. His suntanned face and hands, indicated a long stay in the tropics. His rugged, attractive face was enhanced by alert brown eyes and neatly combed brown hair. His easy smile gave him an air of friendliness. People generally liked him at first sight.

His name was Collin Cunningham.

Cunningham and the other passengers climbed the steps to the open bridge, the highest deck of the ship. From there, they had a breathtaking panoramic view of their surroundings.

It was jungle everywhere. A sea of lush green jungle spread out as far as the eye could see. Along the horizon rose a skyline of mountains whose jagged high peaks almost touched the clouds. The only break in this green sea was the city of Kuching, which had just come into view.

Excitement shining in his eyes, Cunningham approached the front railing to get a better view, for the first time, of the city of his dreams. He was overjoyed to finally see Kuching, the city that had lured him from his home half-way around the world.

Nine years earlier, in 1930, as a sophomore at the University of Maryland, Cunningham fell under the spell of LORD JIM, Joseph Conrad's dramatic tale of a young Englishman living and working in the exotic islands of Southeast Asia. The book sparked what would become an obsession with Southeast Asia, as Cunningham read all the books that he could lay his hands on about the region.

Soon, his sole objective after graduation was to go to the Malay Archipelago to find Patusan, Lord Jim's fictional domain.

Cunningham's plans threw him into sharp conflict with his father, Sam, a self-made businessman who owned the largest hardware store in Rockville, Maryland. Sam Cunningham had never gone to college; he'd built his own business from the ground up, through hard work and shrewd business practices. But Sam also recognized that in order for his business to survive and grow, he would need a well-educated manager. So he demanded that Collin, the eldest of his three sons, go to college. Sam hoped that Collin, armed with a degree in business administration, would help him run the family business.

The conflict began when Collin joined the army right after graduation without consulting his father. After basic training, Collin was commissioned as a second lieutenant in the Ordnance Corps. The situation worsened after Collin requested an assignment anywhere in Southeast Asia. The Army responded by posting Collin to an American army base near Manila in the Philippines.

Sam Cunningham was furious, when, two weeks before he was to leave for Manila, Collin finally decided to tell his father about his commission and overseas assignment.

"Collin, how could you do this to me?! I send you to college to get a good, practical education, and you completely abandon your common sense."

"Dad, I won't be gone forever. There's nothing wrong with serving in the army. It's every man's duty." Collin tried to calm his father down. "I'll be back in two years, and after that I'll work hard for you."

"It was that book, wasn't it? That LORD JIM made you go crazy. Why this stupid obsession with Lord Jim? Why?"

"I just want to see the world, Dad. This is my only chance. I'll be doing it at the army's expense. The army will pay my salary, arrange my transportation and living accommodations, and look after my welfare. It's a strange and far away place, but I'll be safer in the army than I would be on my own."

"What so special about this character, this Lord Jim?" His father still blamed the whole thing on that book. "You told me once that he was your hero. Tell me, what happened to him in the end? Did he become a millionaire?"

"He let himself be killed by his best friend's father who blamed Lord Jim for the death of his son."

"And that's your hero?" exclaimed his father. "I don't believe it! If you ask me, any guy that would do a thing like that is a moron, not a hero! Do you want to end up like him?"

"Never, Dad. Lord Jim was a romantic and an idealist. But this is 1934, and I'm a realist. I'm a survivor, like you, Dad. I'll never let myself trapped in the situation like that. I don't want to be like him. I just want to visit the places that were mentioned in the book. Don't worry, I can take care of myself," Collin said confidently. "I'll be back after two years, or three years, at the most."

Five years had passed since that conversation, and Cunningham was still far from returning home, although he wrote to his parents occasionally. He had become attracted to the Orient, and as the days passed, found he enjoyed his time in the Philippines more and more. He decided that he had the right to pursue his own life, and was willing to accept the consequences.

After his first year in the Philippines, Cunningham saw an opportunity to make a fortune for himself. As an officer at the ordnance depot on the base, he learned about the procurement and distribution of arms, ammunition, explosives, and military related equipment. His files contained information about all the major arms and material suppliers in the United States and Europe. And he could see a time coming when his contacts with these suppliers would be very useful. Conflicts between nationalist movements and the colonial powers in Malaya, French Indochina, Burma, Java, Sumatra, and the Philippines were on the rise, and if those conflicts ever escalated into open revolts, the combatants were going to require a regular supply of arms and ammunition. Cunningham quietly prepared a list of potential customers, confident he was going to make a fortune.

Cunningham left the army in 1937 but stayed on in Manila. He went into business selling arms and military equipment to the owners of sugar cane plantations, mining companies, and others who needed arms to protect their business and personal interests. His business flourished, and Cunningham enjoyed the good life. He lived luxuriously, dress expensively, and socialized frequently with Manila's upper crust.

Then, in 1939, two events occurred which caused Cunningham to leave the Philippines.

The first event happened in the middle of September 1939 when Cunningham met a man named Tim Curtis at a social function. Curtis, who was British, was a deputy to the chief secretary of the Sarawak Government Service. Sarawak had been ruled by the British Brooke family as its Rajah since 1841. The country's greatest source of wealth was its oil, but it also traded in rubber, antimony, and pepper. Curtis sold those commodities to Manila-based American and European trading companies. Cunningham, with his charismatic personality and exciting occupation, charmed and fascinated Curtis. One day the Briton asked Cunningham if he would be interested in working for the Sarawak Government Service.

"Collin, I'm serious about that offer. Sarawak has been relying on the supply of technical and industrial goods from Britain and Europe. But now that Britain and France have declared war on Germany we've become concerned about their continued ability to deliver our supplies. Shipping goods to the Far East is going to be difficult because the sea routes between Europe and Asia will be harassed by German submarines. So, we've decided to look into suppliers who aren't at war and could be in a better position to provide with what we need. We think the United States will be our most important source, and we need someone like you with contacts with the suppliers there."

"Tim, I appreciate your confidence in me, but I have my hands full running my own business," Cunningham was diplomatic in declining the offer. "However, Sarawak sound like an exotic and a peaceful place to live. It's less hectic than Manila, I suppose."

"You're right about Sarawak. Have you ever read LORD JIM?" the Englishman asked.

Curtis's question piqued Cunningham's interest.

"Of course. It's always been my favorite novel. As a matter of fact, it was the reason that came out here. I was looking for Patusan, Lord Jim's domain."

"Then you have to go to Sarawak."

"Why? Is there a connection?" Cunningham asked, puzzled by Curtis's statement.

Curtis laughed before replying. "Patusan is Kuching, the capital of Sarawak. The book suggested that Patusan was somewhere in Sumatra, but actually it was Kuching that Conrad wrote about."

"Where did the name Patusan come from then?"

"Actually, there was a village called Patusan. It was the stronghold of a pirate chief up along the Batang Lupar River. It was raided and burned to the ground by the first White Rajah, Sir James Brooke. Conrad probably got the name Patusan from that village."

"Okay, you've just sold me on a trip to Kuching. But I have to tell you the truth, the job is only a secondary consideration."

The job in Sarawak, however, became a top priority when two weeks later, the second event occurred. Cunningham was working in his office, when two men in casual dress, but with a military air about them, came to see him. They told his Filipino secretary that they were old friends from the army and walked right into his office before the secretary could stop them.

Cunningham didn't know either of them, but they seated themselves in front of his desk without being asked. Before Cunningham could say or do anything, one of them spoke in an unfriendly voice.

"Cunningham, since we used to be in the same army, I'll be frank and brief with you. We've been watching your activities for about six months now, and we're not happy. The arms and equipment that you supplied to certain plantations have somehow fallen into the hands of a radical movement which is strongly anti-American."

Cunningham was about to interrupt, but the man held up his right hand and continued talking. "Let me finish first. We know that wasn't your intention, but for the sake of peace in this country we'd like you to cooperate with us."

"Which plantations?" Cunningham asked. "Can you prove any of this?"

The man gave Cunningham three names and handed him three sheets of paper. As Cunningham studied the papers, to his dismay he realized that the arms and equipment listed on those papers were indeed supplied by his company to the three suspect plantations.

"You mentioned cooperation. What do I have to do and

do I have any choice?" Cunningham asked, feeling angry with himself for not being careful enough.

"Yes. Two choices. Give up your business, or leave the country," the man replied in a firm voice. "There's also a third choice. You can do both. We'd like you to pick number three."

Cunningham didn't doubt the man's words. He understood the situation very well. The war had already begun in Europe. The threat of Japanese aggression in Asia was real, as evidenced by their recent invasion of French Indochina and their 1937 conquest of northeastern China. The US armed forces had every cause to be concerned about the situation in the Philippines. If sufficiently armed, the radical nationalist movement could revolt openly. The Japanese might then decide to take advantage of the situation by giving support to the revolt. Such events would seriously undermine the US presence in the Philippines and weaken US defenses in the Pacific.

Cunningham knew full well that the governing US authority would do anything to prevent such an occurrence. It would be wise for him to take the advice of these two men. He had made enough money to last him a wile without working. When he remembered Curtis's offer, he decided that the time was right to go to Sarawak.

From where he stood on the ship, Cunningham had a clear view of Kuching and the surrounding area. Kuching, nestled between the Sarawak River and the jungle, was a hundred times smaller Manila. The town itself stretched about seven hundred feet along the river. Rows of brick buildings extended inland for only about two hundred feet. None of the buildings was higher than two stories. It was the smallest capital city in the world, and the most isolated. Beyond and around it were jungles and mountains. It was in the wildest part of the wilderness, but to Cunningham, Kuching was the perfect, peaceful hideaway.

At last, he had found Lord Jim's Patusan.

Tim Curtis was pleased that the American had accepted his offer and welcomed Cunningham eagerly. Cunningham was put in charge of procurement of supplies from abroad and given a bachelor bungalow in the residential compound behind the Court House, which was also the administrative office of Sarawak. Despite the sharp contrast to his previous life of luxury, and his profitable, but sensitive, occupation in the Philippines, Cunningham was won over by Sarawak's slow pace of life and tranquil atmosphere. He welcomed the change to a simpler lifestyle. Content in his work and his new life, he grew indifferent to the war in Europe and Japanese aggression in mainland Asia. Sarawak was cut off from the rest of the world; it could have been on another planet.

Cunningham was genuinely happy. He fit in easily with the small western community. The thirty or so families, mostly British, included him in their social lives, and afternoon high tea with his fellow officials became one of Cunningham's favorite events. He also enjoyed his work, particularly taking supplies to the outstations in the remote interior. The only transportation into the interior was by boat, on rivers that wound through the most primitive areas in the world. He slept in Dayak longhouses, ate native foods, and was fascinated by the local customs and way of life. It was fun, it was great adventure, it was what he'd dreamed of since college.

In 1941, about eighteen months he'd first met Tim Curtis, Collin Cunningham's life took another hairpin turn.

Cunningham returned from a two week trip to Sarawak's

interior to find a message from Curtis asking him to come to his office.

"Collin, I've noticed that you've been enjoying your stay here. You've become a dedicated civil servant of Sarawak."

"I'm having the best time of my life. Lord Jim himself couldn't have done better," Cunningham replied, and both of them laughed.

But the American sensed that his friend was uneasy. "Is there anything you want to discuss with me, Tim?" he asked.

Curtis was silent for a few moments before he spoke in a low voice. "Collin, I was the one who asked you to come here. Naturally, I feel responsible for your welfare and I'm concerned about what will happen to you."

"Oh, come on, Tim," Cunningham interrupted impatiently. "Please say what you want to say. I'm old enough to take it."

"Only a handful of people, including myself, know this, but the Rajah has decided to give up his absolute powers and change Sarawak into constitutional monarchy. He'll make the announcement in March."

Curtis was talking about Rajah Vyner Brooke, the third White Rajah of Sarawak. The Brooke family had ruled this country for one hundred years, and during his year in Kuching, Cunningham had heard the extraordinary story of Sir James Brooke repeated endlessly. In 1841, Brooke came to Sarawak, which at that time was a territory of Brunei, to suppress a rebellion. As a reward, the Sultan of Brunei made James Brooke the Rajah of Sarawak. He became known as the White Rajah and was knighted by Queen Victoria in 1848. In Sir James Brooke, Cunningham found himself another hero, and another dream. Cunningham wanted to rule his own territory, like the White Rajah.

Cunningham knew that once the Rajah surrendered his absolute power, the transition to constitutional monarchy would still be a problem. Conflict among the various factions seeking power would throw Sarawak into turmoil. The peaceful, pleasant atmosphere and uncomplicated life that had captivated Cunningham would be over. It seemed the time had come for him to leave Sarawak and look for his own territory.

During that meeting, Curtis and Cunningham also discussed other developments which might affect his future stay in Sarawak.

"Collin, the war in Europe is intensifying, and it's starting to have s serious impact on this area. It's becoming clear that the Japanese occupation of French Indochina is part of a plan to use that area as a base to attack the East Indies which, as you know, includes Sarawak, Java, and Sumatra. The oil wells in Sarawak are major targets. They also want our rubber for their industrial needs."

Cunningham stared out the window for a few moments, and his face became still and somber. "You know, Tim, even though I served in the army and was involved in the arms business, personally, I don't see any point to war. People who want something should try trading for it instead of taking it by force." He shook his head. "War is destructive to everyone, even to the victor. The lives of millions of soldiers will be wasted, and millions of innocent people will die, or, if they're lucky, just lose their homes. No, sir, I'm certainly not in favor of war."

"Tell that to Hitler, Mussolini, and Tojo."

"Do you really foresee war in this area?" Cunningham asked.

"It's inevitable. Everyone's expecting it. The United States is pouring reinforcements into the Philippines. The British are busy building up defenses in Singapore and

Malaya. The Dutch are preparing to defend Java and Sumatra."

"But I don't see any defense preparations in Sarawak. What is the Rajah doing?"

"Well, as you know, we don't have a standing army. The Rajah has been trying to get the British to defend us, and actually, there was an agreement signed in 1888, which placed Sarawak under British protection. But most people, especially the British, seem to have conveniently forgotten all about it. It looks like the British are concerned only with the defense of Singapore and Malaya. Sarawak is not their direct and vital interest," Curtis said. As he continued, a note of bitterness crept into Curtis's voice, "Collin, if you want to leave here for the United States or someplace safer, I won't blame you."

"I appreciate your concern, Tim. But I think it's still too early to decide about leaving. The invasion may never come. Besides, we'll be busy during the next six months preparing for the celebration of one hundred years of the Brooke dynasty."

Cunningham tried to cheer Curtis up with this reminder that on September 24th, the whole country would celebrate the one hundredth anniversary of James Brooke's investiture as the Rajah of Sarawak. What he didn't tell Curtis was that he'd already thought about leaving Sarawak, but for a different reason. He had not yet decided on the date of departure because he still had no idea where he would go, but he knew he didn't want to go back to the United States and run his father's business.

Six months later, during the September 24th anniversary celebration, Cunningham met the Rajah of Alor Setar, a dignified man in his early fifties. The Rajah, who had been educated in England, was the ruler of Alor Setar, the capital of the state of Kedah in northern Malays. Cunningham was assigned to escort the Rajah during his stay in Kuching, and they became good friends.

One afternoon while they were having tea, the Rajah of Alor Setar invited Cunningham to visit his city.

"You'll like Alor Setar and Kedah state. It's as peaceful and beautiful as Sarawak. Although it's called the rice bowl of Malaya, it also has many rubber plantations. And I'm sure that there'll be plenty of opportunities for a good businessman like you. Have you ever given any thought to what you'd really like to do, Collin?"

"Frankly, Your Highness, I've always wanted a large plantation, one with rubber trees and fruit orchards. Something close to the sea, or a seaport, so I can export my products and import manufactured goods to sell throughout Southeast Asia."

"Hmmm, it seems like you've given your future a lot of thought. I think I might have just the place for you." The Rajah smiled when he saw a spark of excitement in Cunningham's eyes. "Have you ever heard of an island called Langkawi?"

"No, sir, I have to admit that my knowledge of Malaya is very limited. Where is it?"

"It's a part of Kedah state, it's in the Andaman Sea about ten miles from the mainland. Langkawi is a large island, lots of good land to settle and develop. The soil and the climate there are suitable for growing rubber trees and tropical fruit. And it has one of the best harbors on the western coast. The water is deep and the harbor is protected all year round. Kuah, which is the main town on the island, has been a popular seaport for decades." The Rajah smiled again as he noticed Cunningham listening attentively. No doubt he was assessing whether Langkawi was the right place for him.

Then Cunningham made up his mind.

"Your Highness, your Kedah state has just gotten itself a new resident. I'm going to Langkawi."

The old wooden ferry boat moved into the channel between a group of three islands on the left and Langkawi on the right. Once in the channel, the boat was protected from the unseasonable strong easterly wind. As the wind died down and the sea became calmer, the passengers began to emerge from the main salon where they had been cooped up for almost three hours during the crossing from Kuala Kedah, a coastal port ten miles from Alor Setar. The passengers, mostly Malays and a few Chinese, were scattered around the open upper deck and the bow enjoying the fresh air and scenery.

Collin Cunningham walked to the bow of the boat to get a clear view of Langkawi and the nearby islands. He sucked in the fresh sea air and welcomed the light wind against his face. He felt invigorated despite the heat of the early afternoon sun. Soon, though, he felt tired from the long journey from Kuching.

Ten days earlier, he'd said good-bye to Tim Curtis and left Kuching on a passenger and cargo ship bound for Singapore, a two day journey.

On December 2, 1941, Cunningham boarded a Singapore train bound for Alor Setar. The train ride along the five hundred and sixty miles of tracks passed through several towns, jungles, mountains, rubber plantations, and rice fields. It was picturesque, but tiring.

The train arrived in Alor Setar late in the morning of the next day. After checking in at a hotel near the train station, Cunningham went to the Rajah's home. The Rajah

was pleased to see that Cunningham had arrived safely.
As he had promised Cunningham in Kuching, he assigned
one of his aides to take the American to see the land on
Langkawi.

Cunningham had saved up a large sum of money from his
business in the Philippines and from his salary in Kuching.
He transferred all of his savings to a bank in Singapore
and drew out the equivalent sum in six gold bars, each
of which weighed 150 grams or .33 lbs. He had a special
belt made with leather pouches to contain the gold bars
for easy and safe carrying.

Cunningham had also changed his dress style in
Singapore to fit in with his new environment. He now
wore a Malay style shirt with the tail hanging over the
trousers. The loose tail helped conceal the belt strapped
around his waist.

As the ferry boat approached the landing at Kuah, the
captain abruptly reduced speed. Cunningham, standing at
the bow, momentarily lost his balance, and instinctively
grabbed the railing with his left hand while his right hand
clutched the belt underneath his shirt. Cunningham never
let the belt, which contained all of his savings, out of his
sight or his reach. During the rough crossing, when the
boat was rolling up and down through the waves,
Cunningham could feel the weight of the belt and its
content rubbing against his waist. He was grimly amused
at the thought that if the boat happened to capsize he was
willing to drown with the belt and the gold bars rather
than take them off his body and lose them.

From the bow of the ferry boat, Cunningham took a
good look at Kuah and the scenery on the island. The
first thing to catch his eye was the golden dome of a

mosque rising above a forest of coconut trees. Beyond the mosque, rows of houses lined the only street in town. Further in land, high-peaked mountains lined the sky, sheltering Kuah and its harbor from the northeast monsoon. Across the harbor from Kuah, another larger island with high mountains offered effective protection against the rage of the southwest monsoon.

Cunningham looked at the harbor with approval. The Rajah of Alor Setar was right when he said that Langkawi had one of the best harbors on the Malay western coats. This was the place he'd been looking for, Langkawi was going to be his domain.

The date was December 5, 1941, and Cunningham had found his Patusan.

CHAPTER 3

"Got some very bad news for you, Hawkins." The guard, dressed in a British army uniform, spoke through steel bars to a big man sitting in a cell at the army garrison guardhouse in Kota Baharu, the capital of Kelantan, a state in northern Malaya.

"What do you mean?" Hawkins, an army sergeant in a disheveled uniform, rose from his cot and moved his massive body closer to the steel bars. He stared down at the guard.

"I hear the military court has just sentenced you to be executed by firing squad in two days," the guard answered. As the guard walked away, a stunned Hawkins went back to his bed and sat down.

Sergeant David Hawkins of the Eighth Indian Infantry Brigade was the son of British army officer stationed in Delhi and an Indian woman. His father died when Hawkins was ten years old, leaving the boy with his mother in Delhi. When he turned eighteen, he joined the British Indian Army, for the past four years he'd been a sergeant with the Eighth Indian Infantry Brigade. His brigade had been in Kota Baharu for three months, guarding the British garrison against an anticipated Japanese attack.

Hawkins stretched out on the bed and stared at the ceiling, contemplating his forty-eight hour future. He seemed to have been born under an unlucky star. Although he came from a poor family, his darkly handsome good looks were a considerable asset, and a source of trouble. Wherever he went, women seemed to be attracted to his Anglo-Indian features, and he was equally attracted to them. Several times he had gotten himself into trouble with jealous husbands and boyfriends.

But this time he was in really deep trouble. He had killed a man. What was worse, the dead man was a rich and respectable Chinese businessman. He came home too early one evening and found Hawkins in bed with his naked wife. Furious, the husband pulled a pistol from a drawer and aimed it at Hawkins. Not thinking, Hawkins grabbed anything that he could lay his hands on and hurled it at the husband to throw him off balance.

Unfortunately for Hawkins, and the husband, he'd picked up a heavy pair of scissors. Its pointed ends went straight and deep into the husband's neck. He died without firing a single shot. At the time, Hawkins thought it most sensible to give himself up to the military police and plead self-defense. He was confined in the garrison guardhouse while the Chinese community in Kota Baharu demanded the most severe penalty for Hawkins.

"It's not a fair sentence. I did it to defend myself." Hawkins abruptly sat up on his bed and spoke to his cell mate, Corporal Peter Grant.

Grant had been caught breaking into the garrison ordnance depot to steal arms and ammunition. Resisting arrest, he'd seriously wounded two military police corporals. Grant was still waiting to be sentenced by the military court.

"The country is in a state of emergency now," Grant said. "I guess with a Japanese invasion expected any day, our commanders don't want to run the risk of rebellion by the local population. So the sacrifice of one sergeant to calm down the restless natives is worth it. They're not gonna listen to you, not in this situation."

"Well, I'm not gonna just lie down and die for them, and I'm not gonna let them shoot me, either. I'm gonna find a way to get out of here, because I'm too young to give up my life, and I have too much to do. What do you say, Grant? Are you going to stay around to find out whether or not they'll shoot you too?"

Grant smiled grimly. "If you've got a plan to break out of here, I'm with you."

"You bet I've got a plan. We'll act on it tomorrow." Hawkins said decisively.

The guard who brought them breakfast on the morning of December 6, 1941 was too careless. He was alone. He never thought that Hawkins and Grant would dare break out of the garrison guardhouse in broad daylight. He opened the cell door, bent down to pick up his trays, and walked into the cell holding a food tray in each hand. He did not suspect anything when he saw Hawkins, sitting on the bed, turned away from him. Grant, who was near the door, moved further away to a corner when the guard came entered.

The guard bent down and placed the trays on the floor. As he straightened up, Grant suddenly sprang at him from behind and pushed the guard into Hawkins's waiting arms. One blow from Hawkins's powerful fist on his chin knocked the guard unconscious.

Hawkins and Grant left the cell and walked quietly to the

door that led to the guardroom. Hawkins opened the door slightly and saw two guards busying themselves with newspapers and coffee. Hawkins whispered instructions to Grant, who nodded in agreement.

Hawkins opened the door wider and dashed out with Grant following closely. With incredible speed for a big man, Hawkins picked up a wooden chair and smashed the head of one of the guards. The other guard looked up in surprise as Grant hit him in the chin with his right fist.

Both guards fell to the floor, the one hit by the chair lay completely still. The other one was only dazed and was trying to get up. Hawkins stepped in and struck at the guard's head with the chair. This time the unlucky guard remained motionless on the floor.

"Grant, get the pistol and the wallet from that guard!" Hawkins knelt and took the pistol from the holster of the guard lying nearest to him. It was a Browning HP35 automatic pistol. He checked the magazine, and smiled when he saw it was fully loaded with thirteen 9mm Parabellum bullets. The guard's wallet contained several five pound notes, which Hawkins put in his own pocket. He rose and looked in Grant's direction.

"Hurry, Grant. We have to get out of here. Did you get all the guard's cash? Don't forget the pistol."

"Yes, I have everything. Let's go."

They moved cautiously to the door that led to the outside; they leaned against the wall and looked out a window. One of the army's staff cars, a British Morris 10HP four door sedan, was parked in front of the guardhouse.

"The key might be in the car," Grant whispered. "It's usual army practice to leave the key in the ignition switch."

"I hope so. Let's walk out slow and casual," Hawkins said.

Something on the wall that they were leaning on caught Hawkins's eye. It was the road map of Malaya. Realizing how valuable a road map was in this situation, he tore the map off the wall, folded it, and put it in his pants pocket. "Are you ready, Grant?" Hawkins turned around and looked at his cell mate.

"Anytime you are," Grant replied briefly.

"Let's go then."

Hawkins opened the door and walked casually towards the staff car. Grant followed right behind him. No one was nearby. Platoons of soldiers doing morning drill in the distance paid no attention to them. Since they'd only been in the guardhouse two days, both Hawkins and Grant were still in their army uniforms. From a distance, they looked like a couple of ordinary soldiers just getting into a car.

Hawkins got in the driver's seat and Grant sat next to him. Luck was with them. The key was in the ignition. Hawkins checked the fuel gauge. Another stroke of luck. The tank was almost full. Hawkins started the engine and moved the Morris slowly towards the main gate.

The two guards at the gate were not as strict about cars leaving the garrison as they were about those entering the garrison. When they saw a staff car approaching the gate, one of then raised the barrier and waved the car through. Hawkins and Grant were so tense that they unconsciously held their breath as the car passed through the gate. Hawkins gripped the steering wheel firmly with both hands to control his nervousness. Grant clutched the handle of his pistol while observing the guard's movement, but all went well. Then they heard another guard shout at them.

"Stop! I want to have a word with you."

Hawkins stopped the car and looked at the guard approaching the Morris. He noticed that the guard was walking casually and did not have his hand near the pistol in his holster. He glanced at Grant who was about to draw his pistol. Hawkins shook his head "no" almost imperceptibly, stopping Grant.

The guard reached the Morris and asked them, "Where are your caps, chaps? You know it's against regulations wearing uniforms without caps, especially when you're leaving the garrison. The brigadier is very strict about this."

Hawkins braved a smile and spoke casually. "Sorry, they're in the back seats. But thanks for the warning. We'll put them on. We're in a hurry to run an errand for the colonel."

The guard nodded and waved them on.

The Morris moved out of the garrison compound as the guard lowered the barrier to its normal position. Hawkins and Grant sighed in relief and looked at each other incredulously. They were now free.

Hawkins knew it would be suicidal to stay in Kota Baharu. Within a few hours the entire British army would be looking for them. All residential areas and every public place would be thoroughly searched. Reward posters with their photographs and descriptions would be plastered all over the city. It would be best for them to get out of Kota Baharu as soon as possible.

Hawkins stopped at a grocery store and sent Grant in to buy provisions for the long trip he had in mind. He was studying the map when Grant came out of the store carrying a big brown bag.

"Did you get enough provisions to last us at least three days?" Hawkins asked as Grant got in the car.

"More than enough. Have you decided where we're going?"

Hawkins nodded as he started the engine and moved the Morris onto the road. He handed the map to Grant and said, "We are now in the eastern part of the Malay Peninsula close to the Thai border." Grant looked at the map as Hawkins explained, "However, we can't cross the border on the road from Kota Baharu. Our troops on this side of the border and the Thais on the other side are now on full alert for the possibility of a Japanese invasion. They will guard both sides of the border very tightly. We'd never make it."

"How about going to Singapore?" Grant suggested.

Hawkins shook his head before replying. "Are you crazy, Grant? Singapore is our biggest base in Southeast Asia. We'll be arrested as soon as we set foot there. Besides, it's a long way to Singapore. It's too risky to drive all the way there."

"Where can we go then?" Grant asked. He studied the map closely.

"We really only have one choice, we've got to get into Thailand. We have to cross over a long range of mountains to the western side, then we'll also be close to the Thai border."

"Why Thailand? Why don't we go to India? You came from Delhi," Grant suggested.

"The authorities know that, and that's where they'll expect us to go. Every MP in India is going to be expecting us. Listen, Grant, why don't you just let me do the thinking?" Hawkins said impatiently.

"I just want to be helpful," Grant replied.

"I can't concentrate with you asking all these questions."

"All right. I'll keep quiet, but tell me what you've got in mind."

Hawkins said nothing as he tried to find the quickest way to leave town. He turned left at the next intersection, onto the road that led to a bridge over the wide Kelantan River. Once on the other side of the river, Hawkins followed the paved road towards the mountain ahead.

Hawkins felt much better now that they were out of the city without any incident. He smiled at Grant who had been sitting quietly.

"Cheer up, Grant. We're free and we're on our way to Thailand. From Thailand we can go just about anywhere. Burma or even all the way to China. We could even go to Vietnam, Laos, or Cambodia. Those three aren't British territories, so we'll be safe. They belong to France, and since France is now under German occupation, the French aren't going to bother with us; they have other things on their minds."

"And what can we do to earn a living in those countries that you've mentioned?" Grant couldn't resist asking another question.

"Haven't you heard? There's a war on. And where there's war, there's plenty of work for soldiers. We can offer our services to whoever needs them," replied Hawkins. He stepped down on the accelerator, and the Morris sped up the mountain road. Within minutes, Kota Baharu disappeared from sight.

Lieutenant Kevin Knox stood at attention in front of his brigade commander, Brigadier John Fitzpatrick, who was not in a cheerful mood. The brigadier was furious when he was informed that Sergeant Hawkins, who was to be executed tomorrow, had broken out of the guardhouse with another prisoner, and had wounded several guards in the process.

"Lieutenant, I give you all the authority you need to bring those two prisoners back here for the punishment they deserve," Brigadier Fitzpatrick said firmly.

The young lieutenant nodded confidently. "Yes, Sir. I'll take five men from my platoon, two sergeants and three corporals. They are well trained and reliable. They'll do the job," he said.

Brigadier Fitzpatrick also had every confidence in Knox, which was why he'd given the young man this assignment. Knox had been under the brigadier's command for three years, and was a typical product of Sandhurst, the British Royal Military College. Knox's education had emphasized that an officer must be fit morally, mentally, and physically to lead the soldiers under his command. The College's motto "Serve to Lead" indicated what the British Army expected of its officers.

Knox received his first commission as a second lieutenant in an infantry battalion stationed in Singapore from 1936 to 1938. Later in 1938, he was transferred to the Fourteenth Punjab Regiment of the Eighth Indian Infantry Brigade in India.

Knox was five feet ten inches tall and well built. Plain looking, he was the sort of fellow who could easily be lost in a crowd. However, he had a talent for boxing, which had earned him a championship at Sandhurst. Besides being a disciplinarian who had been indoctrinated and trained to follow orders to the end, Knox was intelligent and resourceful. He was a just and able leader who won the respect and confidence of all thirty-two men in his platoon.

"Lieutenant, do you happen to know either of them personally?" Brigadier Fitzpatrick asked.

"No, sir. We are in different battalions. And I don't think they know me and my men, which will be to our advantage."

"What do you think Hawkins will do?" the brigadier asked.

"From Kota Baharu, he has three alternatives. He can go to Singapore by the coastal road and try to board a ship from there. The second alternative is to drive across the border into Thailand at Sungai Kolok. The last choice is to cross over the mountains to the western side and get on a ship at Penang bound for India, Thailand, or Burma."

"Where do you think he'll go?"

"If I were Hawkins, I would take the third alternative. Singapore is far away. Going there is quite risky because of the threat of capture along the way or in Singapore itself. Going to Thailand through Sungai Kolok is equally risky because, as you're well aware, sir, we've set up set up several road blocks on that road. From the western side of the Peninsula, he'll have a choice of more destinations. There's also a fourth alternative: to stay in hiding here in Kota Baaru, but I don't think he'll do that."

"All right, then. Take your men to the western side. I'll notify our military units and the local police authorities in Butterworth, Penang, and Alor Setar to also look for them and give you all their cooperation. Keep me informed of the situation. Good luck."

Knox saluted his brigade commander and left the room.

The drive across the mountain range was uneventful. There were no road blocks on the one-hundred-mile paved road, and the few vehicles they passed, mostly buses, paid them no attention. From Kota Baharu, it took them nearly three hours to reach a small town called Baling on the western slope of the mountain range. From Baling, in the distance, they could see the island of Penang. After passing Baling, they stopped by the side of the road to have a brief rest. They ate their first meal of the day, sandwiches that Grant

bought from the grocery store, and then continued the
journey, with Grant behind the wheel.

The road from Baling sloped downward towards the
fertile, rice growing plain. The drive from Baling to Sungai
Petani took thirty minutes. They stopped to refuel at the
only gas station, which was located at a corner of the
intersection. Hawkins again looked at the map, then told
Grant to turn right onto the main highway heading north
towards Alor Setar, thirty-seven miles away.

"So you've decided to go to Alor Setar instead of
Penang," Grant said as he followed Hawkins's instruction
and moved the Morris into the highway.

"There are too many of our troops and MPs in Penang.
It's better if we go to Alor Setar and try to find our way
into Thailand from there," explained Hawkins who had a
keen drive for survival.

They passed a British convoy with truckloads of troops
heading in the same direction. No doubt they were
reinforcement units to strengthen the Jitra Line, a defensive
line to protect Alor Setar from attack by land. Just before
they reached the center of the city of Alor Setar, Hawkins
saw a small dirt road which veered off to the left. He
looked at the signpost which read, "KANGAR 30." He
told Grant to stop the car and again looked at the map
thoughtfully.

Hawkins pointed at the dirt road and said, "Take that
road instead of going into Alor Setar."

"Since we're in this together, mind if I ask why?" Grant
asked curiously.

"It's been almost six hours since we left the garrison.
I'm certain that Kota Baharu has radioed our military units
and police in this area to be on the lookout for us. They've
probably also sent a team after us. It'll be a big mistake

to go into the city. We'll be safer in the suburbs and away from the main roads. I know that our troops prefer to stay on the main highway and disregard the back roads. This dirt road will take us to Kangar, the capital of Perlis which is the smallest state in Malaya. There are no British forces in Kangar."

"How do you know all this?" Grant asked admiringly.

"They've trained me well," Hawkins said with a laugh.

"And what'll we do when we get to Kangar?"

"Actually, we're not going directly to Kangar. According to the map, before Kangar there's a small port called Kuala Perlis where we can find a boat to take us either to Langkawi or Thailand. I think the sooner we leave the Malay mainland the safer we'll be." Hawkins paused for a moment to think, and added, "We'll take our chances on Langkawi."

"Okay, whatever you say. You seem to know where you're going." Grant said. He concentrated on keeping the Morris on the road.

The British-built Ford WOA2 heavy utility truck, which had been converted into a personnel carrier, sped away from the Kota Baharu army garrison as soon as it was through the gate. There were six men in it. All were dressed in British army combat uniforms.

Knox sat in the front seat beside the driver, a British sergeant named David Brown. In the rear, four soldiers sat on two rows of seats facing each other. They were all Indians from the Fourteenth Punjab Regiment of the Eight Indian Infantry Brigade, one sergeant and three corporals.

The men from Punjab, a large province in northern India, were good fighting men. They made up a large contingent of the British Army in India. They had fought alongside the British soldiers and had distinguished themselves in many wars. Now the Punjab troops of the Eleventh and Ninth Indian Divisions again formed an important element in the British defense line in northern Malaya.

Knox, Brown, and Rachan, the Indian sergeant, were each armed with a Browning HP35 automatic pistol, the standard sidearm of the British Army. Each of the three Indian corporals, Prem, Chai, and Visnu, carried a Sten MK5 submachine gun.

Knox and his men were given strict orders by their brigade commander to bring Hawkins and Grant back alive. They knew that it would be difficult to do so. The two fugitives were armed and well trained. It was unlikely that they would give themselves up without a fight, especially Hawkins who knew that he would be executed if captured. Knox therefore had to find a safe and effective way to carry out his orders.

He was confident of his assessment of Hawkins's plan. When they crossed the bridge over the Kelantan River from Kota Baharu, they came to a fork in the highway. The right fork would take them to the Thai border, the left led to the mountain road that connected the eastern and the western parts. Knox decided to go left. Ten minutes later his choice was confirmed when they arrived at a small town called Pasir Mas. A traffic policeman told them that a British army staff car with two men in it had passed through town about two hours earlier.

Knox and his men traveled hard without stopping until they reached Sungai Petani. There Knox had to decide whether to turn left or right on the main highway. He decided to go to Butterworth first. It was only twenty-two miles away from the turn off at Sungai Petani, while

Alor Setar was thirty-seven miles away. If he could not find Hawkins and Grant in Butterworth, the gateway to Penang, he would return to Sungai Petani and then go to Alor Setar. By that time there should be reports from the military units and the local police in Butterworth, Penang, and Alor Setar about the two escaped prisoners.

Knox and his men arrived in Butterworth at five o'clock in the afternoon of December 6, 1941. They went straight to see the British commanding officer at the Bagan Ajam army garrison. The garrison was on the eastern shore overlooking the island of Penang, only two miles away across the channel and Knox had decided to stay there overnight. He was waiting for reports from the local and military police forces which were still pressing their networks of informants for the whereabouts of Hawkins and Grant.

"If they're not in Penang and Butterworth, then they must be in Alor Setar," Knox said to his men as they settled into the barracks. "I don't think they've crossed into Thailand yet. The road leading to the Thai border has been closed. So if they want to go into Thailand now, they'll have to trek through the jungle."

"Lieutenant, what's your plan if we encounter them?" asked Sergeant Brown. He had been in the same platoon with Knox for the past four years, and was among Knox's most trusted men.

"We have one advantage over them. They don't know that we've been sent to come after them. If we encounter them, act like we don't know who they are. Then I'll decide whether the situation will allow us to capture them without a gunfight."

"I hope we run into them soon," said the big Indian sergeant, Rachan. "I heard that the Japanese invasion may come any day now, and I want to be back in Kota Baharu in time to fight them."

"I'm also concerned about the invasion," Knox said. "The garrison commander here told me a reconnaissance plane spotted a large Japanese force in the South China Sea. It looks like several divisions with eighty landing crafts and a convoy of battleships are heading in this direction. I feel the same way as you do, Rachan, but we have our orders. We can't go back without accomplishing the mission. I'm confident that we'll find Hawkins and Grant wherever they are and take them back with us."

CHAPTER 4

The Andaman Sea, which was turbulent during the southwest monsoon season from May to October, was relatively calm the morning of December 7, 1941. At seven, a small sailboat with two passengers left the fishing port of Kuala Perlis. Hawkins and Grant were relieved that they'd been able to escape the mainland safely. So far, luck had been with them.

They'd arrived in Kuala Perlis the previous day intending to hire a boat to take them to Langkawi. However, darkness was fast approaching, and Hawkins and Grant felt uncomfortable sailing in unfamiliar waters at night. Both were landlubbers with very little sailing experience. So they decided to stay overnight in Kuala Perlis, a fishing village located at the mouth of the Perlis River, and hire a boat the next morning. After a simple dinner of fried fish and squid with rice at a local food stall, they went to sleep in the Morris.

The next morning Hawkins and Grant went to a pier where several small fishing boats were moored. However, since neither Hawkins nor Grant could speak Malay, and none of the fishermen they talked to could speak or understand English, they had difficulty hiring a boat to take them to

Langkawi. Impatience and frustration plagued Hawkins, until he came up with a simple idea. He took a roll of British five-pound notes from his pants pocket and held them in his hand. He pointed at the banknotes, then at one of the fishing boats, then to the big island beyond. It worked. The fishermen now nodded and smiled to show that they understood.

One of them stepped forward, apparently the owner of the boat that Hawkins had pointed to. He took a five-pound note from Hawkins's hand, pointed to the boat, and walked towards it. Hawkins shook his head in disbelief, put the rest of money back into his pocket, and motioned Grant to follow the fisherman to the boat.

When they were halfway between the mainland and Langkawi, Hawkins noticed another large island close to Langkawi on his right. He examined his map and saw the words, TARUTAO ISLAND, printed under the drawing of the island. There was a dotted line drawn in the space between Langkawi and Tarutao to mark the boundary separating Thailand and Malaya.

Hawkins decided he wanted a closer look at Tarutao. He turned around and motioned to the fisherman at the tiller to sail along the northern coast of Langkawi. When they reached a spot directly opposite the south end of Tarutao, Hawkins and Grant saw a cluster of buildings on the distant shore. It looked so peaceful and exotically beautiful with the green mountainous landscape of the island in the background that they assumed it had to be a sizable village.

On the spur of the moment, Hawkins made a decision.

"Grant," he said to his fellow fugitive, "I've decided on a change of plans again. Langkawi is still a British territory, if we go there, we won't be completely secure

and free. We'll certainly stand out among the local
population, and it won't be long before the British authorities
know we're on Langkawi."

"So you're thinking of going to that island instead,"
Grant interrupted. He nodded in the direction of Tarutao.

"You guessed it," Hawkins said with a smile. "It'll be
safer if we stay quietly for a while on that Thai island
instead of Langkawi. We'll move on when we want to."

Hawkins turned around, and gestured for the fisherman
to head straight to the village he saw on Tarutao. The
fisherman refused, shaking his head and pointing at
Langkawi. He said something in Malay which Hawkins
and Grant could not understand.

"What is he saying?" Hawkins asked.

"Maybe he doesn't want to go there because that island
is in Thai territory."

"I just want him to drop us off. He doesn't have to
stay with us," Hawkins said with growing frustration.

Hawkins continued to point towards Tarutao, and the
fisherman continued to refuse, repeatedly shaking his head
no and gesturing inexplicably with his hand. Finally,
Hawkins lost patience. He got up, walked over to the
fisherman, pulled out the pistol, pressed its barrel against
the man's chest, and pointed at Tarutao with his free hand.
The frightened fisherman decided that if Hawkins was
this determined to have his way, it was best for him to
do exactly what this big man with the gun wanted. He
nodded and turned the sailboat towards Tarutao.

That morning, as Hawkins and Grant set sail from Kuala
Perlis, Knox and his men left the army garrison in
Butterworth. Earlier, the military police in Alor Setar had
passed Knox a report that a British army convoy had
encountered a speeding army Morris staff car the previous

day at around four in the afternoon. It might be the car
they were after, Knox thought, because the police networks
in Butterworth and Penang had failed to report a Morris
with occupants matching the description of Hawkins and
Grant.

It took Knox an hour and a half to drive to Alor Setar.
To his dismay, the local military police informed him that
they had not seen the Morris or the two escaped prisoners
anywhere in Alor Setar. They were of the opinion that
Hawkins and Grant had not come into the city at all.

Knox studied the map he'd brought with him, and
decided to take a chance. Addressing his men he said,
"They must have gone to Langkawi. Since Hawkins is
half British and half Indian, he may want to go back to
India. If that's what he has in mind, aside from Penang,
the nearest seaport where he can get on a ship that could
take him to India is Kuah, on Langkawi."

"Langkawi is a large island covered mostly with
mountains and jungles," Brown said. "Hawkins and Grant
could hide out there for a while. It could take us a long
time to find them."

"If they're on that island, then we have to find them,
no matter how long it takes," Knox said firmly.

As Knox and his men were leaving Alor Setar for Kuala
Kedah to catch a ferry to Langkawi, Hawkins and Grant
were jumping out of the fishing boat into the knee-deep
water at Taloh Udang Bay on Tarutao. The fisherman then
hurriedly sailed his boat back to the channel and headed
back to Kuala Perlis. He wasn't going to ask his two
passengers whether they wanted him to wait for them. He
was glad to get rid of them, especially the big mean man
with the pistol. As far as he was concerned, he'd already
been paid, and how the two foreigners intended to get

from Tarutao to Langkawi was none of his business.

Hawkins and Grant walked up the wide stretch of the beach to the gathering crowd ahead. In the excitement of discovering a village on the peaceful island where they'd intended to take refuge, they failed to notice the strange composition of the crowd that stood quietly watching as the two men approached them.

As they got closer, Hawkins realized that the crowd was composed entirely of men. No women and children were visible. And they looked more like castaways than normal villagers. They all wore the same clothing: old brown shorts and T-shirts. Before Hawkins and Grant could confer with one another, a voice from the crowd spoke to them in perfect accented English.

"Welcome to Tarutao. You are our first visitors in two years. Who are you and where did you come from?"

Puzzled, Hawkins and Grant looked at each other and then back at the crowd. Then Hawkins answered, "We are British soldiers. Who are you people? We didn't expect to find anyone who could speak English so well on such a remote island."

The man who spoke perfect English laughed softly before replying. "I am Luang Mahasit. I was educated in England for many years. We are political prisoners. We've been confined here for two years. This island is a prison. Didn't you know that?"

The two escaped prisoners from Kota Baharu stood frozen in disbelief. Then Grant recovered and whispered to Hawkins, "You broke us out of the guardhouse just to end up in a prison? So much your changes of plans."

"Shut up. I'm not particularly happy myself," Hawkins whispered back.

Suddenly there was shouting in a language that Hawkins and Grant did not understand, and the crowd of prisoners parted as armed men in khaki uniforms approached. Hawkins and Grant found themselves staring at the business ends of several shotguns and rifles.

They stood perfectly still as the English speaking prisoner told the uniformed men about the two accidental visitors. He acted as the interpreter for both the uniformed men and the two foreigners.

"These are the guards, and they want to know who you are and what you're doing here. This is a prison and a restricted area," Luang Mahasit said in English.

"We are British soldiers from Alor Setar under an order to scout the islands in this area," Hawkins said. "We were going to Langkawi. Then we saw the buildings on this island. We thought this was a village so we decided to come up here to have a look. But it looks like we're stranded here because the fishing boat that we hired in Kuala Perlis has left us. Anyway, we'll have time to look around this island. Will there be a boat to take us back to the mainland or Langkawi when we are ready to leave?"

The political prisoner translated Hawkins' explanation into Thai for the guards. After one of the guards replied, Luang Mahasit turned to the two foreigners and said, "They've asked you to remain here while they report your presence to the director. They have two boats that run between the island and the Thai mainland, but you will have to ask the director yourself about having one of the boats take you to Kuala Perlis or Langkawi."

Knox and his men arrived at Kuah on Langkawi in the afternoon of December 7, 1941. From the landing, they walked to the Kuah police station, a one-story wooden building located across the street from the port. As Knox and his men walked into the station, the police chief, a chubby Malay in his early fifties, greeted them cordially in English.

"Welcome to Langkawi, sir. I am the chief of police here. What can I do for you?"

"We're looking for two British men. They escaped from the army stockade in Kota Baharu two days ago." Knox said. Brown showed the police chief photographs of Hawkins and Grant.

The Malay shook his head after looking at the photographs and said, "I haven't seen them. Not many Westerners come to Langkawi. There's nothing interesting here, just jungles and mountains."

"Have any foreign visitors arrived in the past few days?" Knox asked.

The police chief thought for a few moments before replying. "Yes, an American. He arrived two days ago, but he is with an aide of the Rajah of Alor Setar. He's the Rajah's guest. He's looking for land and has gone out everyday into the jungle and mountains. He can't be one of the men you're looking for."

"I don't think he is. But I would like to talk to him anyway. He might run into these two men while he is exploring the island. Where can I find him?"

"He's out somewhere on the island at the moment," the police chief said. "He stays at the Kedah state government guest house with the Rajah's aide. But he has to go to the restaurant at the Kuah Hotel for meals, because it's the only place you can find decent Western food. You'll also have to eat there. Kuah Hotel is also the only hotel on Langkawi, so if you're thinking of spending the night here, then that's the place for you."

"Thank you for your assistance," Knox said with a smile. "You've been very helpful."

After leaving the police station, they walked about one hundred feet up the street to the Kuah Hotel.

"That must be him," Knox said to his men as he watched a Westerner walk into the restaurant with a Malay man. "I'm going to go talk with him."

Knox left his table, and walked over to the table where Collin Cunningham and the Rajah's aide were seated.

"I am Lieutenant Kevin Knox of the Eighth Indian Infantry Brigade. I'm here on a special assignment. May I have a few words with you?"

Cunningham looked up at the British officer and smiled. "Please sit down and join us for dinner." He gestured to an empty chair. "We can talk while we eat. I hope you don't mind, but I'm so hungry from walking all day."

"Thank you," Knox said sitting down on a chair opposite the American. "I won't take a lot of your time. I just want to ask you a few questions."

"Sure, go ahead. What would you like to know?" Cunningham asked.

Knox told the American about his mission and showed him the photographs of Hawkins and Grant. Knox was disappointed to hear that the American had not run into anyone resembling the two escaped prisoners. As a matter of fact, he had not seen any Westerners while exploring the island.

"Thank you for answering my questions. I'll ask around tomorrow morning. If nothing positive comes up, I'll then take the ferry back to the mainland in the afternoon. Thank you again."

"You're welcome. Hope you get your men," Cunningham said.

Knox stood up and returned to his own table.

Knox, a light sleeper, woke to the sound of distant thunder. He sat up in his bed and looked out the window at the darkness. He heard the thunder sound repeatedly, but strangely, he saw no lightning. Turning on the flashlight he kept by the side of his bed, he looked at his watch. It was five in the morning, December 8, 1941.

Knox heard footsteps and people talking in the corridor outside his room. He got up, and with a pistol in his right hand, walked to the door. He opened it slowly and peered out. He saw Brown and Rachan talking to the hotel manager, who then turned, and hurried downstairs to the lobby. Knox left his room and went over to the two sergeants.

"Lieutenant, did you hear that thunder?" Rachan asked.

"It sounded like an explosion to me, sir," Brown added.

"Or bombing," said Knox, who suddenly had the uneasy feeling that something bad was happening. "Listen. There it is again." The thunder sounded again, it came from the direction of the mainland.

From the hotel's lobby, they heard the sound of a radio. Knox hurried downstairs followed by Brown, Rachan, and the three Indian corporals, who were in full combat uniform, submachine guns at the ready.

"Everybody, listen! The war has started! The Japanese have invaded!" The manager of the hotel shouted for silence as he turned the radio's volume knob up to its maximum setting.

Radio Penang was broadcasting a report from the BBC that the Japanese had launched a surprise air attack on the American naval base at Pearl Harbor in Hawaii. The attack on Pearl Harbor, which began at eight o'clock on the morning of December 7, 1941, was timed to coincide with Japanese attacks elsewhere. It was one o'clock in the morning on December 8, 1941, and several thousand Japanese soldiers had landed in southern Thailand and Kota Baharu in northern Malaya. Both Kota Baharu and Alor Setar were now under air attack.

"Is there anyplace from which we can see the mainland?"
Knox asked the hotel manager.

"Yes, there's a path behind the hotel," the manager
replied. "It leads to a lookout point, and it takes about
an hour to get up there. If the weather is clear, we can
even see all the way to Alor Setar."

"Let's go then. Please lead the way," Knox said.

As they left the hotel, they were joined by Cunningham
and the Rajah's aide, both of whom had heard the noise
and concluded that it was the sound of bombing and not
thunder. They reached the lookout on top of the mountain
at ten minutes before seven.

It was a clear morning, and the visibility was very good.
As they watched in horror, squadrons of warplanes, no
doubt Japanese, stormed over and around the city of Alor
Setar. Columns of black smoke covered the entire area.
After a devastating, ten minute attack, the planes left,
disappearing eastward towards the horizon. They were
returning, Knox believed, to aircraft carriers somewhere in
the South China Sea.

For two hours, the spectators on Langkawi watched and
waited to see whether the planes would return to inflict
more damage. Nothing further happened. Apparently the
scene they'd witnessed was the last sortie of the first round
of attack. Everyone was certain that there would be more.
The war had just begun.

The small group of men atop the mountain sat quietly
contemplating the situation.

Knox and his five men all had similar concerns. The
long awaited Japanese attack on Malaya had finally begun.
Their mission to find and capture Hawkins and Grant
suddenly took second place to their main concern: returning

to the mainland, and their regiment at Kota Baharu, as soon as possible. Hawkins and Grant could wait, thought Knox. This would be the first war for him and his men, and they didn't want to miss a moment of it. The outbreak of war with Japan was now uppermost in their minds.

Cunningham, on the other hand, was concerned about his personal quest for land. The outbreak of war, just when he had found his own Patusan, perfect for growing rubber and fruit trees, had shattered his dream.

Cunningham's other concern was the Rajah's safety. Without the Rajah's assistance, it would be difficult for him to claim the land and settle on the island. Therefore, he decided, he had to go back, find the Rajah, and sure he was safe. It would probably be best to bring the Rajah back to Langkawi with him. The island was not strategically important to the Japanese and didn't have a British military installation, so it would be a safe place to stay during the war. While the war raged on in the outside world, thought Cunningham, he would be developing his domain on Langkawi.

Cunningham, Knox, the Rajah's aide, and Knox's men went to the port in the afternoon to wait for the ferry from Kuala Kedah. They waited until sunset, but the ferry never came. Talking with the port master they were dismayed to learn that, under the present circumstances, he didn't think the ferry would come out again at all. There was no government boat on the island. Their best bet was to hire a fishing boat to take them back to Kuala Kedah. If the wind conditions were favorable, a sailboat could get there in about six hours.

Again, to their disappointment, they could not find a boat that was willing to go to Kuala Kedah. The news of the Japanese invasion of Malaya and the bombing of

Alor Setar had spread all over the island. None of the fishermen in Langkawi were willing to risk taking their fishing boats, their only means of earning a living, to the Malay mainland, which was now a war zone.

Eight days passed, during which Cunningham and Knox remained stranded on Langkawi. Disheartened, they listened everyday to Radio Penang's reports on the progress of advancing Japanese troops.

After five hours of resistance, the Thai troops in southern Thailand capitulated to the more powerful Japanese forces on December 8, 1941. The Thai Government then allowed the Japanese forces passage through Thailand into Malaya. On December 10, two of the finest battleships in the British Navy, the H.M.S. Prince of Wales and the H.M.S. Repulse, were attacked and sunk near Kota Baharu by about eighty Japanese torpedo bombers. Kota Baharu fell the same day, and British forces retreated along the eastern coastal road towards Singapore. The Jitra line, which was the defensive line for Alor Setar, broke on December 12, and Japanese troops began a ground attack on the city of Alor Setar itself. Penang was also bombed on the same day, and high casualties of civilians were reported. On December 14, Alor Setar fell, and Japanese troops advanced to Butterworth and Penang.

During the eight days Knox and Cunningham were stuck on the island, people from the mainland escaped the war-torn area by sailing to Langkawi. The scores of boats that brought the refugees to the island were scattered in Kuah's bay. Their owners refused to go back to Kuala Kedah, no matter how much Cunningham and Knox offered to pay them.

It was December 16 before they finally found a boatowner willing to return to Kuala Kedah. The owner had brought members of his family to Kuah and was returning to fetch the rest of his large family.

Kuala Kedah was not the same sleepy fishing village Knox and his men had set sail from only eight days ago. Since the invasion, it had gone from being a peaceful coastal port to a chaotic refugee camp as a maddened crowd of Malay and Chinese tried to flee from the Japanese invasion. People and their belongings sat around the several piers waiting to negotiate with the few remaining boatowners to take them safely to Langkawi, and even to Thailand.

After paying and thanking the boatowner, Cunningham, Knox and his men, and the Rajah's aide jumped to the pier from the boat. They tried to avoid being trampled by the oncoming crowd that rushed to the boat and inundated the owner with their offers.

They left the port area and headed to the place where Knox and his men had parked the Ford personnel carrier before boarding the ferry. Knox had offered to drive Cunningham and the aide to the Rajah's residence. They learned from the passing crowd that after Alor Setar had fallen two days ago, the Japanese had attacked Butterworth and Penang. Since the gunfire and explosions of the past two days had stopped, it meant that the fighting was over, and no doubt Butterworth and Penang had succumbed to the Japanese attack.

Knox asked several people about the British forces that were defending Kota Baharu and Alor Setar. He was told that the captured British soldiers had already been sent by train to Thailand. They were to be part of the work forces building bridges and railroad tracks into Burma.

Knox, his men, and Cunningham were at a loss as to where to go and what to do. They were now in enemy occupied

territory, and if discovered, they would either be shot or
captured. As professional soldiers, Knox, Brown, and the
four Indian soldiers felt humiliated. They'd been totally
confident in the superiority of British military might, and
never imagined that the heavily fortified Jitra line and Alor
Setar would fall so easily under the Japanese attack.

As they approached the Ford, which miraculously
appeared to be undamaged by eight days of anarchy,
several armed Japanese soldiers appeared from their hiding
places behind the Ford. The British soldiers and the
American stood frozen at the sight of the submachine guns
trained on them. A few more squads emerged from the
houses nearby and surrounded the eight men. Apparently
the Japanese had been waiting for the occupants of the
Ford to return.

Knox realized it would be suicidal to try and fight their
way out of the trap. The Japanese had them outnumbered,
and they would be cut down before they could even draw
their weapons. They wouldn't be going out in a blaze of
glory, resistance would only result in a massacre. They'd
be better off saving themselves and waiting for the chance
to fight the enemy some other day. So Knox raised his
hands high up to surrender. His men, Cunningham, and
the Rajah's aide followed suit.

A young Japanese officer, not much older than Knox,
stepped forward and pointed at Knox's pistol. Although
the officer spoke in Japanese, Knox understood the gesture.
He unbuckled the belt holding the holster and pistol and
gave them to the Japanese. The officer said something that
Knox did not understand and gave Knox a slight bow.
Brown and Rachan unbuckled their pistol belts and let
them drop to the ground, while the three Indian corporals
slowly unslung their Stens and placed them on the ground

at their feet.

The officer gave an order, and the Japanese soldiers approached the eight men, removed the weapons, and began body searches.

"It's mine! You can't take it away from me!" Cunningham yelled angrily.

Knox turned around and saw two Japanese soldiers wrestling the American to the ground as they tried to take a belt from around his waist. The American was fighting fiercely to protect the belt, which contained his life savings. Two other Japanese soldiers joined in the struggle and succeeded in pinning Cunningham to the ground.

Brown and the Indian soldiers looked at Knox, asking with their eyes whether they should help the American. Knox shook his head and stood still. He did not know why Cunningham was struggling so hard against having his belt taken away from him. He would not risk his life and those of his men for this American's silly act.

One soldier picked up the belt and opened the pouches. He shouted excitedly and showed six glittering gold bars to his commanding officer and fellow soldiers. The Japanese officer said something, and his soldiers laughed while nodding their heads.

"You dirty thief!" Cunningham yelled. He got up and lunged at the soldier who was holding the gold bars.

The enraged American forgot that he was surrounded by fully armed Japanese soldiers who could easily kill him. He also forgot that they were at war, and he could be shot as an enemy. Before Cunningham could reach the Japanese, Knox reacted, and tackled the American. Their bodies collided, Cunningham lost his balance, and fell down again to the ground with Knox holding him down.

"Collin, do you want to get yourself killed?" Knox

shouted at Cunningham. "Get a grip on yourself, show a little common sense. It's only gold. It's not worth dying for."

Looking at the Japanese with hatred in his eyes, Cunningham said, "You don't understand, that gold is all I have. It's my life savings. Without it, I can't buy that land."

Knox tried his best to console the American. "You still have your life. Save it. You'll have a chance to get it all back. You'll never get the gold and the land if you're dead."

The Japanese officer shouted a command. The soldiers surrounded the eight men, and with their submachine guns raised, gestured their newly captured prisoners-of-war to get up and walk to a waiting truck.

Slowly, Knox pulled Cunningham up from the ground. Rachan knew what Knox had in mind, and came over to help his platoon leader. He kept a firm grip on the American's arm. Sandwiched between Knox and the big Indian sergeant, Cunningham would be unable to break loose and attack the Japanese again.

They were put on a truck and driven to the Alor Setar police station, escorted by two trucks of Japanese soldiers. They were then ordered out of the truck and lined up in front of the station. Three unarmed Malay in police uniforms came out to meet the Japanese. A Malay speaking Japanese soldier acted as interpreter.

After a brief discussion between the Japanese officer and the Malay policemen, one of the Malay policemen spoke to the prisoners in English.

"You are now prisoners-of-war. We have been instructed to hold you in our cells until the order comes to transfer you to another place. Follow me."

The Malay policeman turned and led the eight prisoners into the police station as the Japanese officer and his platoon got in their trucks and drove away.

CHAPTER 5

Lieutenant General Tomoyuki Yamashita, commander of the Japanese forces in Malaya and Singapore, walked into Alor Setar's meeting hall. Instinctively, the large crowd assembled in the hall rose from their seats and stood in silence. As General Yamashita took his seat on a raised dais, he faced a crowd made up of the ruling sultans, rajahs, and high ranking officials of the four northern Malay states of Kelantan, Terengganu, Kedah, and Perlis, the Thai governors of the three southern provinces of Songkla, Satun, and Pattani, and representatives of the Thai government from Bangkok.

This meeting, the first since Malaya and Singapore had fallen under Japanese occupation two weeks earlier, was to inform local officials and rulers of the terms of the Japanese administration of Malaya. The British forces in Singapore unconditionally surrendered to Yamashita on February 15, 1942.

Sitting ramrod straight in his chair, Yamashita was every bit the soldier. After graduating from Hiroshima Military Academy with honors, he was commissioned into an infantry regiment and rose through the ranks to important positions and responsibilities. He had been the military attache to Switzerland, Germany, and Austria; commander of the Fourth Division in northern China; and inspector general of the Army and the Air Force. His present post was commander of the Twenty-Fifth Army.

The invasion of Malaya and capture of Singapore, the impregnable British naval fortress and symbol of Western might in Southeast Asia, was the most important task of Yamashita's career. The Japanese high command had expected this campaign to take one hundred days, but Yamashita had accomplished his mission in sixty-seven.

Yamashita was a tough, aggressive officer, he commanded his troops with strict discipline and treated his enemy with absolute ruthlessness. When the British forces in Singapore decided to surrender, the British commanding general, Lieutenant General Percival, asked for a twenty-four hour grace period before signing the surrender document. Yamashita's reply, through his American-educated interpreter, was blunt, "Then, in that case, we will continue the attack for another twenty-four hours." The unfriendly tone of this terse reply prompted General Percival to surrender unconditionally. The samurai ethic, which emphasized that the punishment for failure or dishonor was death, was deeply ingrained in Yamashita's character.

Yamashita looked directly at his anxious audience and spoke in an authoritative voice as the interpreter translated his words into American-accented English.

"I've summoned all of you here to officially proclaim the complete occupation of the Malay Peninsula by the Japanese Imperial Forces. We've taken over the administration of the whole of Malaya, but the four northern states, Kelantan, Terengganu, Kedah, and Perlis, which once were Thailand's protectorates and were ceded to Britain in 1909, will now be under the supervision of Thailand. The formal transfer of protectorate rights will take place in the middle of next year. I command all of you to cooperate fully with the authorities representing Japan and Thailand. Does anyone have any questions?"

Complete silence filled the large hall for a few moments. Then a man in the uniform of the Kedah state police stood up and bowed to the Japanese general. Yamashita nodded.

The policeman spoke nervously, "General, I am the chief of the Kedah state police. I have a matter before me that requires your attention. We have two British soldiers, four Indian soldiers, and one American civilian who were captured by your troops in our custody. They have been imprisoned in the Alor Setar police station since December 16 of last year, and we fear your troops have forgotten about them. Please decide what to do with them. They've become quite a burden to us."

After thinking for a few seconds, the Japanese general said, "All the enemy soldiers captured in this area have already been sent to the western part of Thailand to construct railroad tracks into Burma. We have no transportation to send just these seven men there. Singapore is already overcrowded with prisoners-of-war. Is there a prison around here that can hold these prisoners?"

A man stood up and identified himself. "I am the Governor of Satun province in southern Thailand. Twelve miles west of our coast in the Andaman Sea is an island called Tarutao which has been a penal colony since 1938. It's now holding three thousand inmates and sixty-five political prisoners. I'm certain that this island prison can accommodate seven more prisoners without any difficulty."

"Good. Then send them to this Tarutao." General Yamashita ordered.

"Gentlemen, I've received orders to transfer all of you to another prison. It'll be better than these small cells, I can assure you." The chief of the Kedah state police spoke to the seven men standing in their cells in the Alor Setar police station.

The Rajah's aide had been released on the third day of their capture. In an attempt to carry favor with the local population, the Japanese high command had ordered all Malay nationals released from any confinement. However, all foreigners from the countries that were at war with Japan would remain imprisoned.

None of the seven prisoners spoke. They listened in silence and gloom. In the two and a half months since their capture, they had been living under great tension, expecting that the Japanese would come one day, take them out and shoot them, or send them to a prisoner-of-war camp. But nothing happened. As a matter of fact, they had not seen a single Japanese soldier during their entire confinement, only the Malay police guards who took turns watching over them brought drinking water and meals to their cells. They were only allowed to leave their cells when they went to the toilets.

Until this Malay policeman showed up to take them to another prison, it seemed they'd been forgotten and left to rot in these tiny, smelly cells.

They were taken by truck to the Alor Setar train station. When they arrived, a middle-aged man dressed in some sort of khaki uniform greeted them with a friendly smile.

"I am the Governor of Satun Province in Thailand," the man said in English. He told them his Thai name, which was so long that none of the prisoners could remember it with confidence. The man seemed very friendly, and shook hands with each of the seven men.

"I'm to escort you to my residence in the city of Satun. From there, you'll be sent to a penal colony on the island of Tarutao. It is an open prison, so you won't be confined in a cell," he said.

"Who ordered us to be sent there?" Knox asked.

"General Yamashita himself, the commander of the Japanese forces occupying Malaya and Singapore," the Governor replied. "You should consider yourselves lucky that you're not being sent to build railroad tracks in the jungles of Thailand and Burma, or to the overcrowded prisoner-of-war camp in Singapore."

"I've lost track of the date. What day is this?" Knox asked.

"March 3, 1942," the Governor replied.

"I can't believe it! We've been living in those stinky cells for almost three months!" Sergeant Brown exclaimed.

"In a few days, you'll be enjoying fresh sea air and vast open space with mountains and rain forests," the Governor said with a smile of encouragement. "Please board the train now."

Knox and Cunningham were asked to sit together on a seat opposite the Governor. Brown, Rachan, and the three Indian corporals occupied rows of seats next to them. Behind them were four Thai policemen armed with submachine guns.

"How long will it take to get to your city?" Cunningham asked. He had been quiet all along.

"The train ride to Hat Yai, which is a large railway junction town in Thailand, will take three hours. From there we'll travel by car on a dirt road about sixty miles to get to Satun," the Governor replied. As the train rolled slowly out of the station, the Governor looked at Cunningham and asked, "I was told that you are American.

Why were you captured with the British soldiers? You are a civilian, aren't you?"

Briefly, Cunningham told the Thai about himself, including what the Japanese soldiers had taken from him. He clenched his fists and his face turned fierce with hatred when he mentioned the gold bar incident.

"You lost just six gold bars," the Governor said. "You're considered lucky compared to the other Westerners who lived in Thailand and Malaya. All of their property was confiscated. The men were taken from their families and were sent to build railroad tracks somewhere in the jungle. Those people have certainly suffered and lost much more than you did. Cheer up. All is not lost. You're still young. You'll have the opportunity to find wealth once the war is over."

The train trip took them through rice fields and rubber plantations, welcome changes after the boring confinement in the Alor Setar police station. The freedom of movement invigorated the seven prisoners, and lifted their spirits. Knox and Cunningham found that they enjoyed and appreciated the Governor's company, he treated them as if they were his personal guests rather than his prisoners.

The Governor told them that although Thailand had declared war on the United States of America and Great Britain on January 25, 1941, it was only to save the country and her people from the ravages of war. The Thais in general did not hate the Americans or the British, on the contrary, relations between the three nations had been very cordial for the past century. Throughout the modern history of Thailand, since the reign of King Rama IV (1851-1868), every ruling monarch and his government had relied upon the services of American and British personnel for modernizing Thailand.

In fact, the Governor had received his training in administration during his early years in the civil service under British advisors. Therefore, although their governments were officially at war with one another, the common citizens of Thailand generally sympathized with the Allied prisoners of war and tried to lessen their hardships whenever the opportunity allowed.

The Governor and the seven prisoners arrived in Satun just before dark. The kind-hearted Thai official had the prisoners stay at his home for two days. On March 5, 1942, the seven prisoners, escorted by the chief of Satun police boarded the ADANG, one of the motor boats belonging to the TVTS, and headed for Tarutao.

CHAPTER 6

"Director, the ADANG has returned. There are seven new prisoners. They're all foreigners!" A young man in a khaki TVTS uniform TVTS panted as he spoke to Khun Apipat, the director of the TVTS. He had run about a mile, all the way from the pier at Taloh Wow Bay where the ADANG had just berthed.

The director looked up from his desk at his clerk. "There was no mention of any foreign prisoners. The Governor's message just said to send a boat to pick up some prisoners. No details were given."

"The Satun police chief is with them," the clerk said. "They're coming to the office now to report to you."

Khun Apipat rose from the wooden chair behind his desk. He was a big man, almost six feet tall, taller than the average Thai man, who stood at about five feet five inches. In his late forties, he was solidly built and had a dark brown complexion. His immense size, cold eyes and stern face were not a welcoming sight to any prisoner. His physical features, combined with his reputation made him the right man for the right job as the warden of the most dreaded prison in Thailand.

Khun Apipat was born and raised in Ayuttaya, the

ancient capital of Thailand. In 1915, he embarked on a career with the Department of Corrections, starting out as a lowly clerk. However, the twenty-one-year-old was ambitious, intelligent, and keen to learn the bureaucratic process. He worked hard and was well liked by his superiors and fellow officials. Promotions came quickly, he became an aide to a DOC deputy, and accompanied his boss on several trips to inspect prisons in various parts of the country. A few years later, the former clerk was an expert on prison administration.

In 1930, Khun Apipat was appointed warden of the prison in Chiangrai, an important test of his toughness, survival skills, and administrative ability. Chiangrai, a province in northern Thailand bordering Burma and Laos, was one of the most rugged and undeveloped areas of the country. His superiors in the DOC respected his dedication to hard work and his strong leadership, which was sometimes demonstrated by a ruthlessness essential to success in the wilderness.

After five years of solid performance in Chiangrai, Khun Apipat was promoted to section chief in charge of property development at the DOC head office in Bangkok. His new job included managing the establishment of the TVTS in 1938.

When the first director of the TVTS was stricken with malaria and transferred to a less strenuous post in 1939, the DOC sought a replacement physically tough enough to endure Tarutao's cruel environment, but at the same time experienced in prison administration. Ruthlessness was another important qualification, the new director had to be able to keep thousands of inmates under control. Khun Apipat fitted the qualifications, and he had seniority, an important consideration because the director of the TVTS was a division chief, one rank higher than a section chief. Khun Apipat was promoted to director of the TVTS in May 1939.

Six months after his appointment, Khun Apipat experienced the first serious setback of his career. When seventy political prisoners were sent to Tarutao to be under his charge, he realized that they were not bandits or common criminals. Socially prominent, these men were educated, intelligent, high ranking, proud officers. They were leaders in their circles, but to Khun Apipat they were a burden, and potential trouble-makers.

Among them were three major generals, two army colonels, one naval captain, three lieutenant colonels, four majors, four captains, thirteen lieutenants, and fifteen sergeants. Given a chance, they would instigate riots, or lead the common prisoners in an open revolt. He didn't understand why Bangkok hadn't thought about these hazards before deciding to send the political prisoners to Tarutao.

Khun Apipat decided to keep the political prisoners separate from the common prisoners. He set up a camp in an area near the beach at Taloh Udang Bay, a decision which would prove to be his big mistake. At Taloh Udang Bay the political prisoners could look across the waters and see Langkawi, so temptingly close. Less than a month after their arrival, five political prisoners successfully escaped to Langkawi.

Khun Apipat was seriously reprimanded by the DOC and suffered a considerable loss of face. Fortunately, however, none of the escaped prisoners returned to Thailand and to stir up trouble for the government. Otherwise, his position and career would have been seriously threatened. Still, it took him two years to win over the rest of the political prisoners, who cooperated fully with him in exchange for leniency and a relaxing of the rules he had imposed on them. As a result, none of them attempted to escape, and Khun Apipat regained the confidence of his superiors.

Two uneventful years passed. Then last December 7, two British soldiers suddenly turned up on the island, claiming they were on a scouting mission for the British armed forces in Alor Setar. The next day, the Japanese invaded Malaya, yet the two soldiers were strangely unconcerned about returning to their regiment to fight the invading Japanese troops. When Khun Apipat offered to have a boat take them back to the Malay mainland, they asked instead to be allowed to stay on the island.

When Thailand declared war on Britain on January 25, the two soldiers gladly surrendered themselves, becoming prisoners-of-war on Tarutao. Khun Apipat didn't have the heart to turn them over to the Japanese, so he allowed them to stay on. Even though they obeyed his rules and didn't cause any trouble, their presence on the island still made him uneasy. And now another group of foreigners had just arrived, which made him even more uneasy.

Khun Apipat looked out his office window, and saw the Satun police chief heading towards the office. Behind him were three Westerners and four Indians. He felt uneasy because his knowledge of English, especially conversational English, was very limited. As the warden, he felt awkward about not being able to communicate with the seven foreign prisoners to show his authority at their first meeting. He hated feeling awkward. He turned around to the clerk who still stood at attention, and told him to inform the police chief to come in alone and to let the prisoners wait outside.

There was a knock at the door, and the police chief walked into the room with a friendly smile on his face. He and Khun Apipat had known each other for years, they'd been stationed in Chiangrai together. "Khun Apipat, how are you? I have new prisoners for you." The police chief handed the director of the TVTS a sealed envelope. "This is a letter from the Governor of Satun."

Khun Apipat opened the letter and read its contents. He frowned and said to the police chief, "They are prisoners-of-war sent here by order of the Japanese commander. One lieutenant, two sergeants, and four corporals, and one American civilian. Why Tarutao? This is neither a prisoner-of-war camp nor a concentration camp."

The police chief smiled and said, "Maybe that's why they were sent here. It was the Governor himself who proposed this idea to General Yamashita. Do you really want them to be sent to a concentration camp?"

Khun Apipat did not reply. He avoided looking at the policeman and continued reading the Governor's letter. The Governor emphasized that the seven prisoners-of-war were to be treated like the political prisoners because he considered them as belonging in a similar category.

Khun Apipat looked up at the police chief and said, "I don't mind keeping them here. My main concern is the burden of feeding the whole population of Tarutao, which includes my staff, the guards and their families, the common prisoners, and the political prisoners. Did you know that the common prisoners have gone from two thousand two years ago to three thousand today?"

"That's a lot of stomachs to fill," said the policeman, with sympathy. "Are you still receiving supplies regularly from Bangkok?"

Khun Apipat sighed. "Before the war broke out, there was no problem with supplies. But since the war, it's been hard, in the past two months, we've only received one shipment. I sent a telegram to the Department inquiring about the rest of the shipments. Their answer was that Bangkok was also having their own problems with supply shortages, but the Department would try their best to send whatever they had available. I'm really worried, Major. I have almost four thousand mouths to feed, and now you've brought me seven more. We'll be in serious trouble if the supplies are ever cut off."

"Oh, don't be too concerned, Khun Apipat," the police chief said, consolingly. "The people in Bangkok won't let you down. They know about your problem here."

"I hope you're right, but I only have a one month reserve of rice left. If the new shipment doesn't come within thirty days...oh, well, I'll go ahead and take those foreign prisoners to the Taloh Udang Bay compound now." Khun Apipat turned to his clerk and told him to get the transport ready. The young man bowed and left the room.

Khun Apipat and the police chief emerged from his office, and walked over to the seven prisoners. The police chief pointed at Khun Apipat and spoke three words in English to the prisoners. "Khun Apipat, Director."

Khun Apipat nodded at the prisoners and forced a smile, but didn't speak.

Since he was the highest ranking officer, Knox felt that he should assume leadership of the prisoners, so he stepped forward and introduced himself, his men, and Cunningham. Not sure what else to say, he fell into an uncomfortable silence. Lacking a common language, they could not express themselves or communicate effectively with one another, so they stood in awkward silence.

Khun Apipat's clerk came to the rescue with the news that the transport was ready. Khun Apipat sighed in relief, said farewell to the police chief, and gestured for the prisoners to follow him.

There were three ways to travel the five-mile dirt road between the Taloh Wow Bay compound and the Taloh Udang Bay compound: by walking, which normally took an hour and a half, by bicycle, and by buffalo drawn carts. The second and the third ways were privileges reserved only for Khun Apipat, his staff, and the guards. There were, however, a few special occasions when, with Khun Apipat's permission, prisoners were allowed to ride on the carts.

There was also a fourth way to get around, but it was rarely used. The TVTS had two teak boats, the ADANG and the RAWI, former fishing vessels about sixty feet long. Each was powered by twin Japanese-made marine engines and could reach the speed of ten knots per hour. The two boats had been purchased from a failed Japanese company which had tried to set up a fishing station on Tarutao. They'd been converted into work boats, and now carried the TVTS's personnel, prisoners, and supplies between Tarutao and the mainland.

Khun Apipat and three guards rode in the first cart. The guards carried shotguns. Knox, Cunningham, and Brown were in the second cart, and the four Indian soldiers rode together in the third cart. Four guards, also with shotguns, brought up the rear in a fourth cart. When he saw that everybody had boarded a cart, Khun Apipat ordered the convoy to move out.

Each cart's driver used one hand to hold the reins and the other to command the water buffaloes with a long bamboo rod. The driver of Khun Apipat's cart tapped the two water buffaloes twice with the rod, and the buffaloes started walking. The other drivers followed suit, and the whole convoy began moving.

Even though they were to be confined indefinitely and their future was unknown, the seven prisoners were in good spirits. They were fortunate not to have been sent to a labor camp, or a concentration camp. During their stay in Satun, the Governor had briefed them on Tarutao, the TVTS, and its director. He described conditions on the island, including the different treatments that political prisoners and common inmates received. So although they could not converse with Khun Apipat, they knew what to expect.

Cunningham was himself again, smiling and cheerful. Imprisonment on Tarutao meant he would be close to his dream land on Langkawi, and from Taloh Udang Bay he'd be able to see Langkawi everyday. He would also have time to put his shrewd mind to work, planning where and how to make enough money to purchase the land when the war was over.

The convoy left the office and moved slowly along a dirt road, passing rows of wooden houses which the foreign prisoners assumed belonged to the staff and guards. These houses looked too good and were too few to accommodate thousands of inmates. After the staff residential area, they came upon rows of long huts, each of which could sleep about one hundred people. These were no doubt the common prisoners' living quarters.

The common prisoners were kept at hard labor all day, so that they would be too exhausted to escape. There was no break for lunch because they were only given two meals a day, breakfast and dinner. They worked nonstop from eight in the morning to three in the afternoon. They ate dinner at four, attended a roll call at five, and were in bed by six o'clock.

Along the way the convoy passed several groups of common Thai prisoners cutting down trees, planting vegetables, burning garbage, cutting grass, and repairing buildings. The prisoners were undernourished and in weak physical condition. All were dressed in old and partly torn brown shorts. Only a few had T shirts on; the rest were naked from the waist up. However, none of the prisoners were in chains.

The common prisoners were so weak they would have been unable to work if they'd been chained. So the TVTS decided not to put chains on them. The seven foreigners hoped that conditions in the political prisoner compound would be better than those they saw in the common prisoner compound.

Guards in khaki uniforms, armed with shotguns and rifles, stood watch at intervals. The guards who directly supervised the laboring prisoners carried long, heavy rattan canes to enforce discipline. The bruises on the naked backs of most of the prisoners showed that the canes were used often.

After leaving the Taloh Wow Bay compound, the convoy was suddenly surrounded by dense jungle. The dirt road they traveled was lined with tall trees and reinforced with limestone rocks to ensure that it remained serviceable year round.

Up and down the hilly road the water buffaloes pulled the wooden carts, seemingly undisturbed by their heavy load. Stout and tough-looking, but docile, water buffaloes naturally possessed the endurance needed to survive Tarutao's rough terrain, high humidity, and frequent rainfalls.

They rode quietly for about an hour until, finally, they came to a clearing from which they could see several rows of huts and houses : the second prisoner compound at the south end of the island. The convoy crossed a wooden bridge over a stream and rolled past the cluster of wooden buildings which housed the guards. Directly opposite were long huts, the prisoners' living quarters.

They continued further for another thousand feet as the road curved around a bend and led to Taloh Udang Bay. The political prisoners' compound sat on the shore just above the beach.

Captivated by the raw, natural beauty of the bay, the seven foreigners stared in disbelief at their new home. The bay, with its long white sandy beach, formed an almost crescent moon shape. At both ends of the bay, densely forested mountains sloped downward, almost touching the sea. The breaks between the forests and the sea were lined with limestone cliffs and boulders of various sizes. Emerald colored waves thundered against the cliffs and boulders, spraying white foam high up in the air. Across the channel, Langkawi stood, its skyline of jagged mountains starkly visible.

If it were not for the grim fact that they were prisoners-of-war, the seven foreigners would have thought that they were on a holiday, touring a beautiful national park.

Tall coconut trees shaded a cluster of variously sized wooden huts with thatched coconut leaf roofs, giving the scene the look and feel of a picturesque South Sea island village. The atmosphere of peace and tranquility was totally different from that of the common prisoner compound. It was difficult to believe that this sanctuary could be part of a prison.

When they saw the approaching convoy, the men relaxing under the coconut trees began to get up and shout to alert the others. More men emerged from the bungalows.

"Lieutenant, look !" Brown exclaimed. He pointed at two men coming out of one of the bungalows.

Knox stared at the two men. "I can't believe it !" he said.

They were Hawkins and Grant.

Knox had never seen the two fugitives, but he had seen their photographs so many times that he would recognize them anywhere. He couldn't imagine how they came to be among the Thai political prisoners on Tarutao.

"Are those the men you were after?" Cunningham asked.

"Yes, they are," Knox replied. "So they didn't go to Langkawi as we expected. They came here instead."

"Quite ingenious, those two," Cunningham said with a soft laugh. "Hiding themselves in a prison. You would have never found them if you hadn't been sent here. Do they know who you are and that you are after them?"

"I'm certain they don't, we were in different regiments," Knox said. "But I think it's best that we all keep quiet about our mission. Collin, you won't tell them, will you?"

"No problem at all," Cunningham replied.

Knox then turned to Rachan and the three corporals in the cart behind him. He signaled to the four Indians by pressing his right index finger to his lips and pointing his left index finger discreetly in the direction of Hawkins and Grant, who were joining the waiting crowd. The Indians nodded, acknowledging Knox's instruction.

"They look like British soldiers to me, they're all in our combat uniforms, except for one," Hawkins said. He was surprised that the newcomers were Westerners.

"Do you recognize any of them?" Grant asked with

concern.

"No. They must be from another regiment or division," Hawkins replied. "But just to be on the safe side, let's stick to the story we told the people here."

"But what if they ask what regiment or battalion we're from? What should we say? It'll be embarrassing if what we tell them happens to be the regiment or battalion that they belong to."

"We'll let them introduce themselves first so we'll know what regiment they're from." Hawkins was shrewd enough to find a way out. "Frankly, I'm glad we'll have British soldiers here now. It won't be so lonely."

The new arrivals got out of the carts, and Khun Apipat gestured for Luang Mahasit to interpret what he had to say to the new prisoners.

"This is the Taloh Udang Bay compound for political prisoners and prisoners-of-war." Khun Apipat faced the seven foreigners and spoke to them in Thai, pausing to let Luang Mahasit translate his words into English. Then he continued, "You will be subject to the same rules and regulations that apply to political prisoners. You won't be required to perform hard labor for the TVTS. You'll be free to move around, but you must return for morning and evening roll calls. I won't ask you not to attempt to escape because where would you escape to? Everything from Burma to Sumatra, Borneo, and Java including Indochina, Thailand, and the Malay Peninsula is now under Japanese occupation. I hope you'll have the sense to realize that you're better off here on Tarutao than taking a chance with the Japanese. They might just shoot you on sight."

Khun Apipat then turned to the prisoners gathered in front of him and addressed them while Luang Mahasit interpreted for the foreign prisoners. "I have two concerns which all of you should also be aware of. First, because of the war, Bangkok is reducing our rations, so we're going to have to be careful in our food consumption. We must cooperate among ourselves in order to conserve food and produce our own food here for reserves. The second concern is malaria. So far we've been able to contain it because we have enough medicine and doctors. But if we face a shortage of medical supplies, then we may have a malaria epidemic on our hands. I have a feeling that the wars in Europe and Asia will continue for a long time and the longer the wars last, the seriously we'll be affected." He paused to look specifically at the seven newcomers, and said, "As a precautionary measure, I strongly advise all of you to take quinine tablets beginning after dinner tonight."

Khun Apipat looked directly at Hawkins and Grant while pointing at Knox and his men and said, "These newcomers are also British soldiers so you'll have more friends here. You can introduce yourselves later on. You'll have plenty of time to get acquainted." He then turned and pointed at Cunningham. "This is an American businessman."

When he finished his speech, Khun Apipat turned around, returned to his cart, and rode off.

Knox walked up to Hawkins and Grant and extended his right hand. "I am Lieutenant Kevin Knox of the Fourteenth Punjab Regiment in Kota Baharu. We were sent on a special mission to Alor Setar and were captured by the Japanese and sent here." He then introduced his men and Cunningham to Hawkins and Grant. They all shook hands with one another.

"How did you get here? Were you also captured by the Japanese? I didn't expect to find British soldiers way out here." Knox feigned curiosity as to how Hawkins and Grant ended up on Tarutao.

"My name is Hawkins. Corporal Grant and I were based in Alor Setar. Our regimental commander sent us to scout the islands in this area for safe places to retreat to in the event our forces needed to evacuate from the mainland. We hired a boat from Kuala Perlis and left a day before the Japanese attack. When we arrived on this island, which we didn't know was a prison, the boat abandoned us and we were stranded here. When Thailand declared war on Britain, we decided that it was best for us to surrender to the director of the prison as prisoners-of-war. We've been here ever since."

Knox and his men, including Cunningham, accepted Hawkins's story without further questions. Hawkins and Grant went back to their huts satisfied that the British newcomers did not know anything about them.

The seven foreigners then introduced themselves to Luang Mahasit who explained the life and activities on Tarutao and showed them to their quarters.

CHAPTER 7

"This looks like a pleasant little community," Cunningham said. He looked around the political prisoner area with approval as Luang Mahasit took them on a tour of the compound.

"We try to make the best of a bad lot. When we first arrived two years ago, the living conditions were almost unbearable. We all had to live together in one hut, and the food was so bad we couldn't eat it. It was horrible," Luang Mahasit replied. "So we decided to do something about our food and living quarters. There were seventy of us then, and we had a lot of experience in a variety of fields."

"Why the past tense? What happened? Did you lose someone?" Knox interrupted.

"After we'd been here about a month, five men managed to escape," the Thai replied.

"What happened to them?" Cunningham asked.

"We heard they went to Langkawi, and from there they sought political asylum on the Malay mainland. We haven't heard from them or about them again.'"

"So, how did you improve your living conditions here?" Cunningham said.

"Since none of us had to do any work for the TVTS,

we were free to do whatever we wanted with our time.
So we made a deal with Khun Apipat : we wouldn't try
to escape if the TVTS helped us improve our conditions.
Khun Apipat supplied us with the vegetable seeds, poultry,
materials, and tools that we asked for. We also have a
prince who is an expert in agriculture, you'll meet him
later on. With his leadership and expertise, we turned the
area around here into vegetable plots and poultry farms.
We even built ovens to bake bread, and we can make
preserves from the fruits that grow on this island. We are
quite self-sufficient in food production, but we still need
rice from the TVTS. We even have our own tailors,
shoemakers, and basket weavers."

"You must have read ROBINSON CRUSOE or THE
SWISS FAMILY ROBINSON," Cunningham said with a
smile of admiration.

Luang Mahasit laughed and said, "I did once, a long
time ago. But it's human nature to fight for survival. Our
fight here is not against other people, it's against starvation,
sickness, and poor living conditions. We've worked hard
together to achieve what we are enjoying today. We've
built several small bungalows so that we all don't have
to crowd ourselves into one big hut."

The Thai stopped talking as they reached a large hut.
Entering, the foreigners noticed some men lying on wooden
cots. Luang Mahasit pointed to a row of empty cots, and
said, "These will be your cots. Each cot has a mosquito
net for protection from mosquito bites and, of course,
malaria. If you want your own private bungalows, you'll
have to ask for materials from the TVTS and build them
yourselves, but some of us here can lend you a hand.
I'll leave you now to get settled in. We'll meet at dinner
which is served at four-thirty in the dining hall behind
this hut." Luang Mahasit turned around and walked out

of the hut.

After dinner, Luang Mahasit found Knox standing alone, leaning against a coconut tree. "Lieutenant, I was thinking that since you are an army officer, you might be interested in meeting some of our colleagues who once were high ranking officers of the Royal Thai Army," he said.

"Yes, I'd like that," Knox said eagerly. "I always enjoy learning about other soldiers' experiences."

Luang Mahasit led the British officer to a group of middle-aged men sitting in front of a bungalow, talking among themselves. Even in the shabby prison clothing, they looked distinguished. Luang Mahasit introduced them to Knox. When he learned that the group included three major generals, a colonel, and a major, all of whom outranked him, Knox stood at attention as though he was reporting to his superior officer.

"Lieutenant Kevin Knox of the British Army at your service, gentlemen. It's an honor to meet you."

Knox's gesture of respect and cordial words surprised the officers. They rose as one to return Knox's courtesy; their appreciation reflected in their eyes. They had been out of the military service for several years and tended to regard themselves old men, forgotten by the civilized world. Yet this young foreign officer had greeted them as if they were still soldiers.

One of the generals spoke to Knox slowly in English. "We are pleased to meet you, and we are deeply touched by your kind gesture. Because we are prisoners, no one has treated us with dignity and honor until you came. Thank you, Lieutenant."

The general took Knox's right hand in his and held it firmly for a few seconds. His colleagues smiled at Knox as, one by one, they silently shook his hand. Knox's gesture had been sincere, he had been raised to treat others with unfailing courtesy. He also understood Asian customs, especially those of the Chinese and Thai peoples, who held in high esteem those with seniority in age and rank.

Ten months passed, and the nine foreign prisoners realized that they'd no choice but to make the best of their time on Tarutao. They rarely received any news about the war or the outside world, and as they concentrated on making their lives on Tarutao useful and worthwhile, the war became less and less important to them.

Knox and Luang Mahasit became close friends. One week after his arrival, Knox walked past Luang Mahasit's bungalow and noticed that he was busy writing. Piles of books and papers surrounded him.

Knox went over and asked, "I hope I'm not intruding. May I ask what you're writing?"

Luang Mahasit looked up at Knox from his writing and smiled. "Not at all. As a matter of fact, you can be helpful. I am compiling English to Thai and Thai to English dictionaries. It has never been done before."

Knox was impressed. "That's quite an undertaking. I'll be glad to help if you think I can be useful," he said. "How long have you been doing this?"

"Oh, for several years. One nice thing about being imprisoned is that I finally have the time and freedom to concentrate on my work. I've been working on this project most of my life. You know, the five prisoners who escaped two years ago asked me to go with them, and I would have gone, too, but my work wasn't finished. I was concerned that if I were shot while escaping, or captured and executed, I would have wasted my life. Besides, I couldn't possibly carry all my books and papers with me. These dictionaries will be a very important link between future Thai generations and English speaking communities all over the world. So I decided to stay on to complete my work."

Luang Mahasit's selflessness amazed Knox. "I'd be honored to help."

Knox devoted the majority of his time to helping Luang Mahasit, and in doing so, he learned the unique Thai language, its alphabet, the different sounds, and various word usages. Knox also persuaded the other foreign prisoners to take Thai language lessons from Luang Mahasit, and within six months all nine foreigners could communicate adequately in Thai.

One day Knox observed two Thai prisoners, former army sergeants, practicing a different kind of boxing, one in which the boxers used their feet more than their fists. He watched in amazement as one man kicked as high as the neck and even the head of his opponent. And that was not all. The two sergeants also used their knees and elbows expertly against each other. A man could rapidly jab at his opponent's face two or three times with one of his feet before his opponent could dodge or guard his face with his hands.

Knox wanted to learn this foot-to-foot combat, so he asked the two sergeants to teach him this unique fighting style. He learned that one of the sergeants was a former boxing champion in his home province in northeast Thailand. The Thai sergeant was surprised and pleased that this young British officer wanted to learn the techniques of this style of boxing, called "Muay Thai" in Thai.

"It's difficult to learn to fight with your feet," the sergeant said. "You must practice a lot."

"I've got plenty of time. Your style of boxing really fascinates me. Please teach me," Knox pleaded.

"All right. You've got the build for it. I assume that as a combat officer, you know how to box."

"Only with my fists, and I also have hand-to-hand combat experience."

"Good. If you at least have a boxer's coordination, the training will be easier. Let's start with a brief history of Thai boxing, then some theory."

Knox sat down as the sergeant gave him a brief lesson. "The use of feet, elbows, and knees was part of a fighting technique developed during the time of King Naresuan the Great about three hundred and fifty years ago. At that time the Thais were constantly at war with the Burmese. This technique was also an effective defense. In those days, Thai soldiers held a sword in each hand. Since he didn't have a free hand, he used his feet to kick the enemy's legs out from under him, then he followed up with a fatal stroke from one of the swords. Thai warriors at that time were trained to handle the swords equally well with both hands."

"Ingenious! Why didn't we ever think of doing that?" Knox exclaimed.

"Maybe you are too much of a gentleman," the sergeant said with a smile. "We don't fight for sport. We try to kill the opponent as quickly as possible, anyway we can. Nonetheless, the basic principle of Thai boxing is more defensive than offensive. The idea is to counterattack with a fast, forceful, and decisive reaction. When your attacker's first blow fails, he'll be defenseless. That's the time to strike back. Please get up."

Knox got up and faced the Thai instructor. "Every man has two fists and two feet," the instructor said. "One could use either one foot or one fist at a time. But punching and kicking at the same time are awkward and ineffective.

It's also impossible to punch with both fists or to kick with both feet at the same time. Right?"

"Absolutely," Knox said.

"Now hit me with one of your fists, as hard as you can," the sergeant said. He moved closer until he was three feet away from Knox.

"What? Do you really mean that?" Knox exclaimed.

"Yes. The best way to teach is to demonstrate, not to talk."

As soon as the sergeant finished talking, Knox moved forward as fast as he could and aimed a right punch at the sergeant's face. The sergeant instinctively sidestepped to his left to avoid the blow, which missed his face by two inches. As the momentum carried Knox through empty space, the sergeant gently lifted his right knee up. It hit Knox right in the stomach, knocking him onto the ground.

The sergeant walked over to Knox and offered his hand to pull him up. Knox got up, massaging his stomach with one hand. He smiled at the sergeant and said, "You're too fast for me. I didn't expect the knee."

"But I anticipated your move," the sergeant said. "A returning blow from either a knee or an elbow is equally effective. Since I knew that you couldn't kick, I only had to watch out for your fists. Your left leg was forward, so I knew you had to hit with your right fist. I deliberately stood a little further away from you. Therefore, you had to leap from the ground to hit at me, which put you off balance.

"My point is that observing how and where your opponent stands is very important. If he stands close to you, watch out for his fists because he can't kick standing so close. On the other hand, if he stands further out, beware of the kick because he'll be too far away to punch effectively with his fist. It's a simple fact that a leg is longer than an arm. If he stands with his left foot forward, then he'll probably kick with his right foot. As for ourselves, we must always stand and move in such a way that our head and feet always form a triangle. This is the best position for both stability and momentum. These are the basics, learn them by heart, they should become second nature to you."

"When will I learn how to kick?" Knox asked eagerly.

"We'll begin kicking lessons tomorrow," the sergeant replied.

The next day the sergeant taught Knox how to kick, using a banana tree as a punching bag. Knox kept hitting at the banana tree with his feet, alternating right and left, until they became sore and the banana tree turned into pulp. The next day, the sergeant put Knox through the kicking exercise again with another banana tree. After six months, Knox was able to kick as high and as hard as his trainer. He also learned to effectively counter a kick with his knees, elbows, and hands.

Cunningham, on the other hand, was more interested in Tarutao's terrain, soil, and climate. Still relentless in his determination to build his own private domain, he dreamt of nothing but owning the largest rubber plantation and the best fruit orchard in Langkawi. The loss of the gold bars, his life savings, haunted him, and he'd vowed to himself that the war that had robbed him of all his wealth would one day pay him back.

Since his arrival, Cunningham had spent most of his time sitting on the beach at Taloh Udang Bay looking across the channel at Langkawi. Then one day, while was daydreaming about his plan, he was startled by a hand on his shoulder. He looked up and saw a distinguished looking, gray-haired man in his early fifties smiling down at him.

"I'm sorry if I've alarmed you," the man said in precise English and sat down beside Cunningham. "I've been observing you for a few days now. The way you stare out at the sea and sigh, one would think you are a heartbroken lover."

Cunningham could not resist laughing at the man's words. He smiled back and said, "I appreciate your concern, but it's not what you think. I'm not thinking about a woman. It's something else."

"If you think it'll make you feel better to talk about it, then I'm willing to listen. Maybe I can give you some advice. By the way, I am Prince Sittiporn," the man said offering his hand.

"Collin Cunningham." The American shook hands with the Prince.

"Now, tell me what makes you look so melancholy."

Cunningham told the Prince of his problem.

After the American had finished, Prince Sittiporn said to him, "I sympathize with you. I know how you feel because we political prisoners have also experienced the loss of our careers, wealth, and freedom. But we pulled ourselves together and made the best of a bad situation. I'm concerned that your obsession about this land on Langkawi will drive you crazy for nothing. My advice is that instead of waiting in vain for something that you cannot have right now, you should look at the land that you can walk on everyday."

"What do you mean by that?" Cunningham asked.

"Tarutao has plenty of land, and you have plenty of time to explore it. Besides, if you want to own a rubber plantation and a fruit orchard in the future, you're going to need to learn about plant cultivation. When the war is over, you'll be ready for the land on Langkawi. Do not despair, you can do yourself a lot of good."

"I appreciate your advice. But who's going to teach me?"

"I am," the Prince said.

Before his arrest, the Prince had been Director-General of the Ministry of Agriculture's Agricultural Promotion Department, and had also managed a successful vegetable and poultry farm near Bangkok. He was the man behind the political prisoners' success in becoming self-sufficient in food production. He had been devoting his time to experiments with the cultivation of several kinds of tropical fruits and vegetables on Tarutao. Cunningham became one of the Prince's assistants. He volunteered for the task of exploring different parts of the island and bringing back samples of plants and soil for the Prince to test and study. He recruited Hawkins and Grant to join him. The two fugitives eagerly welcomed the chance to be away from the compound and Knox and his men. They also found that they liked the American.

"Luang Mahasit, may I ask you some questions?" Knox asked. The two of them had been working on the dictionaries. The Thai scholar paused in his writing and looked up at Knox.

"I'll be glad to answer any question," he said.

"Does your name have a meaning?" Knox asked.

"Yes, it does. Actually, it's a title. My real name is So Settabutra. You see, under the absolute monarchy, officials and those who had served the King well for a period of time were awarded titles to be used in place of their names. I believe the system is similar to the titles of nobility granted by the English monarchs to their subjects. Your system begins with Baron, Viscount, Earl, Marquis, up to Duke. Our lowest title is Khun, then above that are Luang, Pra, Praya, and Chao Praya, which is the highest title given to a nonmember of the Royal family."

"Then the director's name, Khun Apipat, is his title, not his real name," Knox said feeling that he was learning something new everyday.

"That's right. His full title is Khun Apipat Suratan. It means great achievement in corrections service," the Thai explained.

Knox laughed and then said, "And all this time, I thought his first name was Khun and his last name was Apipat. What does your title mean?"

"My full title is Luang Mahasit Woharn, the man with great eloquence."

"You certainly deserve that title," Knox said smiling at him. "I'm also curious about the dogs I see running around in this compound. Whose are they?"

"They're ours. Originally, there were only a few dogs in the common prisoner compound. They belonged to the guards. After we arrived and began to produce our own food, there were leftovers after each meal. The dogs' keen sense of smell naturally led them here, where the food was plentiful. Because they were well fed, the dogs decided to make their home here with us. There are about forty now. Dogs are the most common pet in Thailand, and Thais are generally fond of them, so we allow them to stay."

"What breed are they?"

"They are the Thai breed."

"They look like the African Basenji," Knox said. In fact, the similarity was striking. The Thai dogs had short hair in a variety of colors : black, white, fawn, black with white markings, fawn with white markings, and white with black or fawn markings. They had wrinkled faces and heads, erect ears, and medium length tails, either curved or sickle shaped. Well muscled and agile, the Thai dogs were alert, keen, and devoted to their masters.

Most of the political prisoners' huts had two or three dogs living under them. They weren't just pets, they were also guard dogs. They would bark and growl at any strangers who came near the huts, even the TVTS guards. Knox found this amusing: in other prisons, dogs were used to control the prisoners, but on Tarutao they protected the prisoners from the prison guards.

It was also quite a sight to watch the forty dogs accompanying their masters when the prisoners marched to their daily bath in the stream about half a mile from the compound. The strange cavalcade was composed of an army of dogs at the front, seventy-four prisoners, including the nine foreign prisoners-of-war, walking in the middle, and the guards bringing up the rear.

Knox understood why the political prisoners appreciated the dogs' companionship. Some prisoners treated their dogs like their children. Aside from their fellows, the only other creatures on Tarutao that the prisoners could trust and regard as their kin were these noble Thai dogs.

CHAPTER 8

January was usually the most pleasant time of year on Tarutao. The climate was cool, humidity low, and there was no monsoon or rainfall. Normally, it would have been the perfect way to begin a new year, but to Khun Apipat, pacing back and forth in his office deep in thought, 1943 was shaping up as the worst year of his career. Bangkok and other industrial and commercial centers in Thailand had been targets of Allied air attacks, and considerable damage was reported. As the result, food and other commodities had become scarce, seriously affecting the resupply of Tarutao.

Before the war, shipments of rice, medical, and other supplies had normally come twice a month. As the war took its toll, resupply was cut back to once a month during the first half of 1942. In the second half of the year, resupply was cut back even further, and Tarutao was resupplied every other month. As the year ended, the situation continued to deteriorate. The rice reserves were low and decreasing every day. As quinine supplies dwindled, malaria began to spread among the common prisoners. The lack of doctors on Tarutao made the malaria outbreak even worse.

There had been two doctors on Tarutao before the war, but they were recalled when Bangkok came under periodic air attacks. The only remaining medical personnel Khun Apipat had were the doctors' assistants. They were common prisoners, well behaved, and smart enough to understand the doctors' instructions, but they hadn't been trained or educated to be qualified doctors or medics. And now they were confronted with hundreds of malaria-stricken patients. Without sufficient medical supplies and proper training, those assistants didn't have a chance against a malaria epidemic.

Khun Apipat's thoughts were interrupted by a knock on his office door. One of his deputies, Pradit, a thin man in his late thirties, entered. Pradit's face was sullen as he reported to Khun Apipat on the state of the rice reserves.

"Director, if we continue to feed the prisoners the way we've been doing, the rice that we have in stock will last only two more weeks. And if the next shipment is late again, we'll be in a very difficult situation."

Khun Apipat pondered the problem for a few moments, then said, "We just have to solve the problem ourselves until the next shipment arrives. I have an idea, we'll change the way that we've been serving rice to the prisoners. From now on serve them boiled rice mixed with fish, vegetables, and a lot of water. That way we'll save a lot of rice and fish. The water and vegetables are filling and will add weight. Right now, we can't afford to be too particular about the quality and the taste of the food because there are too many prisoners to feed. They're lucky we have any food at all to put in their stomachs."

"That's a good idea, but I'm worried that if we reduce the quality of the food, the prisoners won't have the strength to endure sickness, especially malaria."

Khun Apipat continued to talk as if he did not hear what his deputy had just said. "And also the desserts. Last year we had banana cooked with coconut milk, sweetened sticky rice, and boiled green beans alternating as desserts with each meal, and now they've been cut down to twice a week. Since our stock of coconut milk, sugar, and green beans is limited, we have to reduce dessert to once a week." Khun Apipat paused to think for a few seconds then asked, "How is the malaria situation?"

Pradit sighed and shook his head in despair. He told his superior in a tired voice. "Malaria is becoming a worse problem than the food shortage. As you know, we have limited supply of quinine tablets and they are reserved for the guards and staff. When the prisoners first arrived here, each of them was given a mosquito net. But now most of the mosquito nets have been torn and can't protect the prisoners when they're sleeping at night. We haven't received a new supply for about a year now. Without mosquito nets and quinine, malaria is spreading and impossible to contain. More and more prisoners are dying every day."

"How is the food situation with the political prisoners?" the TVTS director asked.

"So far the food shortage hasn't affected them yet because they're able to produce most of their own food," Pradit replied. "We supply them with rice, meat, and fish. They get eggs from their own poultry farm and they can grow enough vegetables for their own consumption. They're still eating three meals a day."

"In that case we have to reduce the amount of rice and food that we've been supplying to the political prisoners," Khun Apipat said. "From now on, we can supply them only two meals a day. Also, inform them that we can't get wheat flour for them to make bread anymore. There's no more on the mainland. They can't be immune to the situation anymore."

"Director, I have bad news about the political prisoners. One of them died of malaria yesterday, it was their first casualty. They're asking for more quinine tablets, and they'd also like to talk to you."

"I'll go to Taloh Udang Bay in a few days. They can see me then. What about the foreign prisoners, how are they doing?" Khun Apipat asked.

"They've adjusted to the conditions there. They eat the same food as the political prisoners and they get along well with them. So far they haven't complained about anything. All of them can now speak and understand our language. They're still young and strong, so physically they can endure the hardship. The British lieutenant and his men have been busy learning Thai boxing. The other two British soldiers and the American often go out exploring the island, but always came back in time for roll call," Pradit replied.

Khun Apipat nodded his head and dismissed his deputy.

"This is a very serious problem," Prince Sittiporn said to the gathering of political prisoners in the dining hall. "We have to do something about it. We can't just sit still and be killed one by one by either starvation or malaria. We've just lost one of our friends, and three more have been stricken with malaria. Honestly, I don't believe they'll survive without quinine. It's just a matter of time before malaria wins."

The meeting was called to discuss the situation after Pradit had informed them of the problems that the TVTS was having. The reduction in meals, the lack of wheat flour to make bread, the absence of a qualified doctor, and the complete depletion of quinine tablets for the prisoners were disturbing.

"What do you suggest we do?" a former army colonel asked.

"Since the TVTS can't do anything for us, we have to help ourselves," Luang Mahasit answered. "I believe that if we continue to live here on Tarutao, we'll all die of malaria. I suggest that we write a letter, or rather a petition, signed by all of us to the Prime Minister and the Minister of Interior asking them to transfer us to a place where there is no malaria epidemic. In a situation like this, I would prefer to be in a prison in Bangkok where we'd be near doctors and medical supplies."

A former general, sentenced to life imprisonment, got up and spoke, "I agree with Luang Mahasit. I'd like to add that many of us here know people in high circles who can talk to the Prime Minister and the Interior Minister on our behalf. We can write to those people asking for their sympathy and assistance. Some of us personally know the Prime Minister, maybe they should take a chance and write to him directly. It can't get any worse for us."

"That's a very good idea." Another former general got up to give his support. "I believe that if we all agree, we'll carry some weight. I was a classmate of the Commander-in-Chief of the Army at the military academy, I'll write to him. We won't ask for amnesty; that's too big an issue. We'll only ask to be imprisoned some place other than this malaria infested island. It would be too cruel to refuse our request and let us die here of malaria."

As the originator of this idea, and because of his gift for language, Luang Mahasit was unanimously approved by his colleagues to draft the petition to the Prime Minister and the Minister of Interior. Luang Mahasit immediately got down to work, while several of the prisoners wrote to the people whom they believed would listen to their plea and were in a position to help.

Khun Apipat looked up from his desk when a guard entered his office and informed him that a group of political prisoners was here to see him. Khun Apipat rose from his chair as Prince Sittiporn and Luang Mahasit, accompanied by four other senior political prisoners, walked into the room.

Prince Sittiporn stood before Khun Apipat's desk. "Khun Apipat, we have an urgent matter to discuss with you. It's so urgent that we felt we couldn't wait for you to come see us. So we asked permission from the warden at Taloh Udang Bay compound and walked here to have a talk with you. As you know, we've been here three and a half years, and this is the first time that we ever come to your office. This is a matter of life or death for us; otherwise, we wouldn't bother you."

Because Khun Apipat didn't receive many guests, and the people who came to see him were either his staff, guards, or prisoners, there was no need for them to sit down and have a lengthy conversation with him. So there were no other chairs in the room, except his, behind the big wooden desk. So, on this occasion, Khun Apipat stood while talking to the six political prisoners who would have outranked him, socially and officially, in any other setting.

"Pradit told me that you wanted to see me," Khun Apipat said greeting his unexpected guests. "I intended to go to Taloh Udang Bay tomorrow. What is it that you want to discuss with me?"

"As you're aware, there's a malaria epidemic on Tarutao. One of our colleagues has just died of malaria. Three more have been stricken and will die if they're not given quinine tablets in time," Prince Sittiporn said. He paused briefly to control his emotions, and continued, "We can't go on living like this, we'll all die. For three and a half years, we've endured the conditions here without any complaint, but this time we've lost the will and strength to confront this dreadful situation. So we've drawn up a petition to the Prime Minister and the Minister of Interior asking to be transferred to another prison, or anyplace where there isn't a malaria epidemic. We've come to ask a special favor of you. Please forward our petition to Bangkok and make certain that it reaches the Prime Minister and the Minister of Interior. We would all appreciate it very much." As he finished his speech, the Prince handed Khun Apipat several folded pieces of paper.

"Your Highness and gentlemen," Khun Apipat addressed Prince Sittiporn and the other five political prisoners, "I'm fully aware of the dire situation we face. I'll forward your petition to the people concerned and sincerely hope that the result will be a positive one. Frankly, without doctors or medical supplies, I can't contain the malaria outbreak. I hope your petition will help convince the authorities in Bangkok that the situation on Tarutao is very serious and that something must be done to help us. Although most of the people on this island are prisoners, they are still human beings and must be helped when they contract malaria."

Khun Apipat spoke with a sincerity and sympathy uncommon for a person with his position and reputation. However, when desperate men experience hardship or face a common enemy together, they tend to show sympathy and understanding for each other. And this was the most desperate time the people on Tarutao had ever faced.

Khun Apipat and the political prisoners realized they were confronting a common enemy, they knew they had only themselves to rely on. As the prisoners took their leave, Khun Apipat ordered two buffalo drawn carts to take them back to their compound.

In the three months after the six political prisoners visited Khun Apipat, the malaria epidemic worsened. As the death toll increased from two to five or six deaths a day, the most convenient way to dispose of the growing numbers of dead bodies was burial. Burying dead bodies became a routine activity on Tarutao, and a special team was created to handle this unpleasant task. As food supplies dwindled, strict food rationing was implemented. Desserts for the common prisoners, which had been cut to once a week, were reduced to once a month in February and March. Finally, in April, desserts were no longer served.

Meanwhile, the political prisoners waited anxiously for an answer to their petition. The three political prisoners stricken with malaria had recovered, they were saved by quinine tablets from the stock reserved for guards and TVTS staff. This was Khun Apipat's decision, somehow, he felt that he could not let these prisoners die.

In the early afternoon on April 20, 1943, the political prisoners received an answer to their petition. A TVTS staff member rushed into Khun Apipat's office with a telegram in his hand.

"Director, this telegram just came in from Bangkok this morning. Since it was marked 'most urgent', our man in Satun hired a boat and had a messenger hand-carry it here. He handed the director a telegram in a sealed envelope.

Tarutao was too remote to have a telegraph facility of its own, so the TVTS maintained a small room in the Satun Governor's office building and relied on the telegraph office there to communicate with the DOC in Bangkok. Khun Apipat read the telegram, and told the clerk to summon Pradit, his deputy, and then have a buffalo-drawn cart made ready for him. Five minutes later, Pradit walked into the room. Khun Apipat gave Pradit his instructions as the two of them left his office, and the director boarded the waiting cart. Khun Apipat then told the driver to head for Taloh Udang Bay.

It was almost four in the afternoon when Khun Apipat reached the political prisoner compound. The prisoners had just returned from their daily bath in the stream, and were sitting around waiting for dinner at four-thirty. When they saw Khun Apipat, they shouted for their colleagues in the bungalows.

By the time Khun Apipat reached the spot where the prisoners had gathered, everyone, even the nine foreigners, was present. The political prisoners knew Khun Apipat had news for them, otherwise, he would not have come all the way to Taloh Udang Bay. Their only concern was the result of their petition.

Khun Apipat looked around at the prisoners solemnly. When the anxious crowd quieted down, Khun Apipat spoke, "I have good news. As a result of your petition, the Ministry of Interior, under instructions from the Prime Minister, has decided to transfer all of the political prisoners to Ko Tao, an island in Surattani province in the Gulf of Thailand." Before Khun Apipat could continue, the prisoners burst into loud cheers and applause.

Khun Apipat waited for the cheers to subside, and then continued, "You will leave tomorrow at ten in the morning. Our two boats will take you to the port of Kantang in Trang province, from there you'll go to Surattani by truck. You'll stay overnight in Surattani, and the next morning you'll go by ferry to Ko Tao. I hope the conditions on Ko Tao will be better, it's closer to Bangkok than Tarutao and has no malaria epidemic."

Khun Apipat paused to clear his throat. He stood in silence for a few seconds, then he said, "I would like to thank all of you for cooperating with us during your stay here. I bid you farewell and wish you good luck. I hope that when we meet again, the circumstances will be better."

Before Khun Apipat could leave, Prince Sittiporn stepped forward to speak on behalf of the rest of the prisoners. "Khun Apipat, Tarutao has been our home for almost four years, and even though this is a prison, we've had a relatively good life here. And as for you, you've treated us very well, and we appreciate your help. We'll never forget your considerate treatment of us, you've saved the lives of three of our colleagues by giving them quinine tablets. These men owe you their lives." Prince Sittiporn pointed at three men sitting on the ground in front of the other prisoners. "We are indebted to you for sending our petition to the Prime Minister and the Interior Minister. Without your cooperation, our transfer to Ko Tao tomorrow wouldn't have happened. We'll never forget anything you've done to lessen our hardship."

Khun Apipat stood in silence. He was at a loss as to what to say. He had mixed feelings about what was happening. In a way he was relieved that the political prisoners would no longer be his responsibility after tomorrow. If they continued living on Tarutao, many of them would die of malaria. For reasons he didn't really understand, he would be sad if that were to happen. On the other hand, he would miss them. He'd had a good relationship with the political prisoners, they had respected his position and had complied with his rules and regulations. They had offered their ideas and resources for TVTS projects. Now, on the eve of their departure he began to realize what valuable assets they were.

In Taloh Wow Bay compound he was surrounded by

almost three thousand social rejects. It had not been pleasant to see, talk, and listen to thieves, bandits, and murderers everyday for the past four years, and he longed for someone who could hold an intelligent conversation. He missed the civilized world. So, whenever Taloh Wow Bay made him tense and weary, he would go inspect the political prisoner compound. It had become his oasis.

He enjoyed the intelligent conversations and pleasant times he'd had with many of the political prisoners. They were from the upper levels of society, and conducted themselves so much differently from the common prisoners. When they left tomorrow, Khun Apipat thought gloomily, they would take away with them the only culture and civilization on Tarutao.

Khun Apipat pulled himself together. As the director of the TVTS, he could not allow the prisoners to see his emotions and weaknesses. So he just turned around, walked back to his cart, and rode off without looking at the political prisoners.

The next morning two boats, the ADANG and the RAWI, arrived at Taloh Udang Bay a little before ten. Khun Apipat was aboard the ADANG. Four dinghies were dispatched to pick up the prisoners from the beach.

The prisoners had been ready and their personal belongings had been packed since the early hours of the morning. Although they were glad to leave Tarutao, they also felt that they would miss their life on this island. Some prisoners went to take a last look at the poultry that they had raised and cared for every day. Those who used to work in the vegetable plots went there one last time to water the vegetables that they had planted with their own hands. Other prisoners went to say goodbye to the guards with whom they had become friendly. But no one

was sadder to see the political prisoners leave than the nine
foreign prisoners-of-war and the dogs.

It was quite a blow to the prisoners-of-war when they
learned that the political prisoners were to be transferred
to another island on the other side of the Peninsula.
Although they understood the reasons and necessity for the
transfer, the departure of the political prisoners was going
to be hard on them, mentally and physically. Moreover,
they would certainly miss their companionship, all the
political prisoners had been friendly and kind to them.

Knox had enjoyed the exchange of views and experiences
with the former army officers. He was going to miss his
language sessions with Luang Mahasit, who, with Knox's
assistance, had made considerable progress in his work on
the dictionaries. He also regretted the end of the regular
Thai boxing workouts with the former sergeants.

Cunningham was furious at this sudden change. It
seemed that whenever he started to enjoy life and was
feeling optimistic about the future, something happened
to ruin it. He had stopped being obsessive about the land
on Langkawi, and had been making himself useful to
Prince Sittiporn. Not only did he enjoy exploring the
island, he had made valuable contributions to the agricultural
research. He could continue exploring, but he would miss
the Prince's valuable teaching and guidance.

All nine foreign prisoners had fitted comfortably into
the small society of Thai political prisoners. Their social
life would now be very limited, and they would miss
having people with similar interests to talk to. The political
prisoner area, normally lively with the sound of laughter
and talking, would be empty and quiet from tomorrow
onward.

They also realized that their living conditions would not

be the same as before. Without the political prisoners, there would not be enough manpower and expertise to look after the poultry and vegetables, and they would have to cook the food themselves if they didn't want to eat the same kind food the common prisoners ate.

"We can't live here just the nine of us. The worst thing is that we don't know how to cook," Cunningham said as they watched the political prisoners getting ready to leave.

"Why don't we ask Khun Apipat to transfer us to Ko Tao with the political prisoners?" Knox suggested.

"Kevin, that's a very good idea," Cunningham agreed. "Let's go talk to Khun Apipat. He's over there supervising the evacuation."

The director listened carefully to the foreigners' proposal.

"Gentlemen, although I sympathize with your situation, I'm afraid that I can't comply with your request," Khun Apipat replied. "You're not our political prisoners. You are prisoners-of-war sent to Tarutao by the order of General Yamashita, not the Thai Government."

"Can you ask Bangkok to approve our request?" Knox suggested.

Khun Apipat sighed before answering Knox's question. "I'm fully aware of the political situation in Bangkok. We are an ally of Japan, but in reality our country is being occupied by Japanese troops. Many of the policies and administration of the country are dictated by the occupying Japanese armed forces. I don't think the DOC, or even the Prime Minister himself, will want to rescind General Yamashita's order just to please a few prisoners-of-war. Please try to understand. If I send the request, I know I'll be reprimanded by my superiors. I'll be told to mind my own business."

"So there'll only be nine of us living in this large area.

What about our food?" Cunningham asked.

"I think you'll be more comfortable here than with the
common prisoners. There'll be several empty bungalows.
You can move into any of them. You might feel isolated
and lonely at the beginning, but you'll get used to it. As
for your food, I'll have it prepared specially for you."
Khun Apipat looked around, and said, "I have to go now.
The political prisoners are ready. I'll be back in a few
days." Khun Apipat turned around and walked to the
waiting dinghies.

The nine foreign prisoners followed Khun Apipat to the
four dinghies loaded with the last groups of prisoners.
They said a sad farewell to the political prisoners and
shook hands with them for the last time.

But it was the dogs that brought tears to the eyes of
some of the prisoners. Some prisoners had raised the
dogs as if they were children, and they worried that they
wouldn't be well treated and well fed. They knew that
the dogs would suffer after their departure, and they were
concerned about the dogs' welfare. Some prisoners held
the dogs in their arms for a long time, then pulled themselves
together, and walded away to the dinghies.

The dogs were intelligent enough to sense that their
beloved masters were leaving them forever. Some of the
dogs began to howl as the dinghies took their masters
away from the shore, some of them even swam after the
dinghies. The political prisoners had to ask the foreign
prisoners to take the dogs back and to hold them because
they were afraid that the dogs might drown if they tried
to follow the dinghies to the boats.

CHAPTER 9

"I can't eat this shit anymore!" Collin Cunningham exclaimed. He threw a tin bowl on the wooden table so hard that brown-colored liquid spilled out of the bowl. "We've been eating this garbage they call food twice a day for almost two weeks now. We have to do something about our food!"

Cunningham looked at the other eight men sitting around the table and saw similar feelings of frustration and anger reflected on their faces. The nine prisoners-of-war were huddled in a corner of the dining hall in the political prisoner compound. They chose a table at the far end of the room so the heavy rain of the season's first monsoon could not reach them.

It had been two months since the political prisoners' transfer. Khun Apipat sent a man to cook for them, but the food was the same as that of the common prisoners. They had been eating boiled rice with fish and vegetables for breakfast and dinner for the past two weeks.

After the political prisoners left, the nine foreigners had tried to look after the poultry and the vegetables by themselves, but they lacked experience and manpower, so the results were disastrous. Untended, the vegetables began to die, plot by plot. As they ran out of vegetables to feed the chickens, egg production declined. The situation worsened as the chickens disappeared nightly because there weren't enough men to watch over them. The foreigners presumed that either the guards or the malnourished common prisoners had taken them. Finally, when no chickens were left, the nine foreigners had to survive on the food provided by the TVTS.

"We all feel the same way, Collin," Knox commiserated. "But we have to accept the fact that the TVTS can't do better than this. Everyone on the island, even Khun Apipat and his staff, has been eating the same kind of food..."

"They must have become immune to food poisoning by now," interrupted Cunningham. "They're used to it, we're not. Besides, they were raised on rice, we weren't. If we continue eating this food, we'll all die of food poisoning or starve to death. Even if we survive on this swill, we'll be so weak and undernourished that malaria will finally kill us anyway."

"Then we'll just have to do something about it," Knox said. "Remember what Luang Mahasit told us. The political prisoners used their knowledge and talents to improve their living conditions. They had an expertise in agriculture that we don't have, but let's look at what we can do. We're professional soldiers who have been trained to use all kinds of weapons, to fight, and to kill. Collin used to be in the army. Surely he must know how to handle a rifle or a shotgun. Some of us here are also good marksmen."

"What are you getting at, Kevin? Are you suggesting we go out and rob for food?" Cunningham asked.

Knox couldn't help but laugh at the American's question. "Get serious, Collin," he said. "I'm suggesting that we ask Khun Apipat for a rifle and some ammunition. Tarutao is a jungle with wild animals. We can hunt and share our kills with him."

"Lieutenant, that's a very practical idea," Hawkins chimed in. "When we were exploring the island, we saw herds of wild boar roaming around everywhere. There are also plenty of crocodiles and small deer. I've heard that crocodile meat tastes good, like chicken."

"And as a last resort, there are also hundreds of monkeys," Brown added.

Everyone was excited by Knox's idea. The Indian sergeant, Rachan, joined in. "The way I feel now, I could eat anything, even snakes and lizards, except a human being. I'm sure all of us can handle a rifle. We can form hunting parties and take turns going out to shoot game."

"Let's go to see Khun Apipat then," said Cunningham with a smile.

"It would be hard to walk there right now in this heavy rain," Knox said. "Let's wait until the rain stops. It won't last long, I hope."

The monsoon rain lasted two days. The nine prisoners-of-war had no choice but to eat the only food available to them. When the rain finally stopped, Knox, Cunningham, and Brown told the guards that they were going to Taloh Wow Bay to see Khun Apipat. The guards didn't say anything, they just nodded their heads. While the three men headed for Taloh Wow Bay, the rest of the foreign prisoners divided themselves into teams to scout for wild animals.

"I don't know if it's a good idea to give you a rifle, even if it's just to hunt animals," Khun Apipat said. "It's against the rules to allow a prisoner to carry a weapon around, even if it is for the benefit of the prison community. How can I be sure that you won't escape and kill us, or use the rifle to harass Japanese troops? If that happened and you or the rifle were captured by the Japanese, it could be traced back here. Then I would be in a lot of trouble."

"Look, Khun Apipat," Cunningham said in growing frustration, "you said when we first arrived here a year ago that we shouldn't try to escape because there is no place to escape to. All the territories around here are under Japanese control, and there are Japanese troops everywhere."

Cunningham paused for a few seconds to get a grip on his emotions, then continued, "Right now we only care about the food we eat and our own survival on this island. We don't care about the war. If we're well off here, we don't have any reason to escape just to be shot or sent by the Japanese to some work camp worse than Tarutao. If the conditions on Tarutao become unbearable, that'll be the time to think about leaving. But during the year and three months we've been here, you and your staff have treated us well. You yourself have told us about the atrocities and hardship that you heard occur in other prisoner-of-war camps in Thailand and Singapore. We're not so stupid that we're willing to take a chance on being sent there. We're also not going to risk being shot on the spot by the Japanese if they find us wandering around with a rifle. No, sir, we want to survive and eat well, we don't want to get killed or be sentenced to hard labor."

"Allow me to make a suggestion, Khun Apipat," interrupted Knox. He was worried they were failing to convince the TVTS director to give this experiment a try. "As a guarantee that wc won't escape if you give us a rifle, I'm willing to place myself in your hands as insurance that the rifle will be used only for hunting and will be returned to you. You can lock me up until the rifle is returned. You can also give us a limited amount of bullets for each hunt. It would be madness to threaten the entire Japanese occupying force with four or five bullets and a rifle. I assure you that we aren't at all crazy. Very hungry, yes, but not crazy."

Knox paused to let Khun Apipat think about his idea. After a moment of silence, and with no response from the TVTS director, Knox continued, "Let's look at the positive side of our proposal, Khun Apipat. You'll be doing us a favor, which we'll never forget. I'm an officer of His Majesty's Army, and my word is my bond. I give you my word that we won't escape from Tarutao if you agree to our proposal. Besides, our plan will also benefit you personally, you'll have fresh meat for yourself and your staff."

Knox paused again and looked hard at Khun Apipat, sitting in deep, silent thought. His instincts told him to press further, that he was close to success.

"Khun Apipat, when we walked up here, we passed your guards and staff. Right now they look weak from malnutrition. If this continues, they won't be able to perform their duties properly, because they won't have the strength or the spirit to keep the prisoners under control. It's your responsibility to take care of your subordinates. No one will blame you if you authorize us to hunt to provide food for you and your staff. No one will blame you for taking this step under these circumstances."

Knox paused again to allow Khun Apipat to consider his logic. And again the TVTS director did not object. He remained silent. Knox knew that he almost had him now. Khun Apipat needed to be pushed just a little bit more.

"You can assign your guards to accompany us during the hunt," Knox continued. "I know you only have a limited supply of ammunition, so every shot has to count. You'll agree that, as professional soldiers, we can handle rifles more effectively than your guards. Khun Apipat, trust us and make use of us. We are trapped in this situation together, so we should cooperate and make the most of every resource available here."

After several minutes of serious thinking, Khun Apipat finally made the decision. He looked at the three prisoners-of-war and said, "All right, you've made a good case, you also have your consciences to uphold your honor, and the promise you made to me. It'll be for your own benefit, too. Let's see whether you are as good hunters as you are soldiers. I have rifles and shotguns. Which would you prefer?"

The three prisoners sighed in relief and smiled. "We'll take rifles," Knox said. "We're going to be hunting wild boar, and a rifle will be more effective than a shotgun because it has a longer range. So we don't have to get too close and risk scaring them away or exciting them into charging at us. What kind of rifles do you have here?"

"I have American-made Enfield rifles, M1917 bolt action using .30 in. caliber bullets," Khun Apipat replied.

"Good," Knox said eagerly. "The Enfield will do the job nicely. The .30 in. caliber is powerful enough to stop any charging wild boar, even crocodiles. I'll need eight rounds to start. Three will be used to adjust the sight for fifty yards range, and the other five to hunt. If you have the rifle and the bullets ready, we can start today. This is the beginning of the monsoon season, and the first rainfalls have come and gone. The wild boar will be coming out to eat the young bamboo shoots that are just starting to sprout. It'll be easy to locate them at this time of year."

Khun Apipat opened a locked wooden cabinet behind his desk. The cabinet contained two racks, the upper rack was lined with single and double-barreled shotguns, and the lower rack held several Enfield rifles. Khun Apipat selected a rifle and opened a drawer between the two racks. He picked eight bullets from a box in the drawer, and handed both the rifle and the bullets to Knox. Then, he opened another drawer which contained rifle cleaning kits and gave one to the British officer. He closed and locked the rifle cabinet, and returned to his chair.

"The rifle is quite new. It's an old model, but it's hardly been used," Khun Apipat said. "Please take good care of the rifle. I have to remind you that it's government property, and I'm responsible for its loss or damage. I'll assign two guards to accompany you to avoid any criticism. They'll be armed with shotguns, in case of emergency. You never know what to expect in the wilderness. Good luck, I'm looking forward to having a wild boar steak for dinner tomorrow night."

"If I'm right about their eating habits, you'll have it tonight," Knox said confidently.

The three prisoners got up. Knox put the bullets in his trousers pockets and let Brown carry the rifle and the cleaning kit. They thanked Khun Apipat and left the room.

As Knox, Cunningham, Brown, and two TVTS guards walked out of the prisoner compound into a clearing where the prisoners had planted rice and corn, Knox stopped, picked up a fallen coconut, and handed it to Brown. He took the rifle from Brown, and instructed him to place the coconut on a rock about fifty yards away.

Knox loaded three bullets into the rifle's magazine clip and set the sight for fifty yards. He took aim at the center of the coconut and fired.

The bullet hit the lower right part of the coconut causing it to spin and fall from the rock.

Knox adjusted the sight with a small screwdriver from the cleaning kit. He aimed the rifle at the coconut lying on the ground and fired. This time the bullet hit the coconut in the center and split it in half.

Knox told Brown to place another coconut on top of the same rock, and handed the rifle to Cunningham.

"Collin, give it a try to get the feel of it. Just one shot," Knox said.

Cunningham shook his head and said, "My past experience was in selling these rifles not shooting them. Don't let me waste a bullet. Better save it for a wild boar."

"All right, then, I'm ready. It's hunting time," Knox said. He loaded four more bullets into the magazine clip. With the rifle slung on his left shoulder, he continued on the road in high spirits, the others following him.

They didn't have to go very far. Shortly after they left the clearing, they encountered several brown creatures moving among a forest of bamboo on a slope not far from the road.

Knox signaled the others to be still and silent. He unslung the rifle from his shoulder, pulled the bolt back to load a bullet into the firing chamber, and held the rifle chest high.

Alone, he walked slowly to a distance about fifty yards from a herd of seven wild boars which were digging up and eating young bamboo shoots. Knox was close enough to clearly see their brown stocky bodies with short hard hairs and the distinctive long snouts. There were three full grown boars, each of which had two long pointed tusks curving upward from both sides of their mouths.

Knox singled out big boar standing sideways at its full height, he had a clear shot. He aimed at a spot a little higher than the front legs, and fired. As the noise thundered through the jungle, the marked boar slumped to the ground. The unfamiliar sound of gunfire frightened the rest of the herd and they stampeded into the dense forest. Knox could hear cheers behind him at the success of the first kill.

Knox told the two guards to cut down a bamboo stalk and tie the dead boar to it for easy carrying. He then told the guards to take the boar to Khun Apipat to have it dressed and prepared for dinner. He, Cunningham, and Brown, would continue to Taloh Udang Bay and hunt boar near there, so they wouldn't have to carry their kill very far. The guards smiled and waved to them as the three foreign prisoners continued on the road.

During the six months from June to November, the foreign prisoners hunted relentlessly for food, even during the heaviest monsoon rainstorms. During that time, they nearly exterminated the wild boar population along both sides of the five-mile road between Taloh Wow Bay and Taloh Udang Bay. Knox, Hawkins, Brown, and Rachan took turns leading hunting parties out almost everyday to hunt. They became experienced trackers and efficient hunters, and provided fresh meat daily for themselves and the TVTS.

Khun Apipat was so satisfied with their performance that he gave the prisoners-of-war another rifle to hunt. The once deteriorating food shortage situation temporarily improved, and the population of Tarutao was well fed with regular supplies of fresh meat. Surplus meat was salted, dried, and stored to be eaten with curry in future months. Wild boar curry became a standard dish on the TVTS menu.

In addition to wild boar, the hunters brought in other animals that could be eaten by humans. Small deer, crocodiles, pythons, and even monkeys frequently filled hungry stomachs on Tarutao.

The four corporals, one British and three Indians, turned

into expert animal skinners. Crocodile and python skins
from Tarutao became valuable and highly sought after
items among the occupying Japanese troops on the mainland.

"I can't cope with the problems facing us on Tarutao
anymore. My ideas and strength are all exhausted, I don't
know what to do anymore," Khun Apipat said.

Knox and Cunningham listened with concern. They
had come to the director's office one day in early December
to get more bullets for the rifles.

"What happened, Khun Apipat?" Cunningham asked.
"I thought the food problem was solved, at least
temporarily."

He had never seen the TVTS director so depressed, the
man had always seemed so confident and in control. It
was unlike Khun Apipat to sit slumped in his chair, looking
worn out.

"You're right, Collin. The problem is only temporarily
solved. We're fighting a losing battle. We'll never win
as long as Bangkok doesn't give us the assistance that we
need. You and your colleagues have done a lot to ease
the problem, but it's not enough."

Khun Apipat forced himself to sit up straight in his
chair and looked at the two foreigners. "There are two
problems that I can't solve without help from Bangkok.
First, the continuous shortage of rice. You know rice is
a staple in the Thai diet, the prisoners and guards can't
survive on meat alone. They need to eat rice with the
meat. But there isn't even enough meat to feed all of the
prisoners. This intense hunting has greatly reduced the
population of wild boar and other animals. So, we cook
the meat with rice and vegetables to increase the volume
and weight of the food to try and keep everyone's hungry
stomach filled."

Khun Apipat sighed and leaned back against the chair.

"I know you have too many mouths to feed, can't you transfer some of the prisoners to other prisons?" Knox asked.

"I've thought of that but the other prisons are also having similar problems," Khun Apipat replied.

"What is your second problem?" Cunningham asked.

"It's much worse than the first, it's the malaria epidemic. It's been of control for almost a year now. In the past eleven months, nine hundred prisoners have died of malaria, and the death toll increases every day. It's disheartening."

"Well, let's look at the bright side, Khun Apipat," Cunningham said. "At least the high death toll has reduced the number of mouths we have to feed. Otherwise, the food shortage would have been more severe."

"Yes, you could look at it that way. But the high death rate has created another big problem," Khun Apipat said. He felt better now that he was able to talk to someone about his problems.

"And what's that?" Knox asked.

"Burying the dead. There are so many corpses, the burying has been done hurriedly and carelessly."

"You're telling me, Khun Apipat!" Cunningham said. "We passed the graveyard on the way over here, and it was a ghastly sight! Decaying parts of corpses are sticking up out of the ground, and now the dogs are digging up bodies and eating them. It almost made me throw up!"

"And the smell! The whole area was covered with stench," Knox added. "We had to cover our noses while walking past it. Luckily we don't live in this compound. Why don't you cremate them?"

"We need to have a religious rite performed by Buddhist monks before the cremation," Khun Apipat replied. "It's inconvenient to bring the monks here from the mainland.

Therefore, I intend to have the religious rite and cremation for all of the dead at once."

"Meanwhile, we have no choice but to endure this dreadful condition," Cunningham said grimly.

Khun Apipat sighed. "And the people in Bangkok have no idea what we're going through. They pay no attention to my requests for assistance. I've written so many reports and memorandums to them, and I get nothing," he said.

Knox looked at him with sympathy and admiration. Khun Apipat was a good man, despite his appearance and reputation. He was a dedicated civil servant and a responsible administrator. The prisoners and his staff, including the guards, feared him, but they also liked him. He could have asked his superiors to transfer him to another post with fewer problems, or one closer to Bangkok. He had served on Tarutao for four years, so his request would have been justified. But it wasn't in his character to leave his staff, his guards, and the prisoners just when they needed a leader so desperately.

Suddenly, Knox had an idea. "Why don't you go to Bangkok in person and tell your superiors about the situation on Tarutao? Maybe they don't see the real picture or understand what's happening here. I think they need to hear it from you personally to be convinced. When was the last time you went to Bangkok and talked to your Director-General?"

"Frankly, I haven't been back to Bangkok since I came here," Khun Apipat replied.

"I don't believe it!" Cunningham exclaimed. Knox was speechless. "No wonder your superiors haven't taken your reports seriously. They hardly know you now. They probably think that you never go to Bangkok because you're enjoying yourself here so much. Kevin's right, it's about time you went to Bangkok and told the people there what is happening here."

Khun Apipat finally smiled. He looked at Knox and Cunningham with appreciation. "Thank you, my friends, for the advice. I'll go to Bangkok."

Winter in Thailand usually lasted from December to February, as cool air moved down from the north and blessed Bangkok and the central region with the most pleasant climate of the year. Bangkok in mid-December was especially delightful, the average daytime temperature was about seventy-five degrees Fahrenheit, and the normally high humidity was greatly lessened.

Sunshine brightened the corridor outside the office of the Director-General of the Department of Corrections. Khun Apipat sat alone impatiently on a wooden bench waiting to see his superior. His mind was so occupied with Tarutao's problems that he didn't even notice how pleasant the weather was outside.

The trip from Tarutao to Bangkok had been long and tiring. The ADANG took Khun Apipat from Tarutao to Satun, from there he traveled sixty miles on a bumpy road by bus to the Hat Yai train station. The train ride to Bangkok covered another six hundred miles.

Although he was exhausted from the trip, Khun Apipat welcomed the change from Tarutao's grim, punishing environment to civilized Bangkok. Even though it was wartime and Bangkok was experiencing occasional Allied air attack, it was still like going from hell to heaven.

Khun Apipat stayed at a hotel near the central train station, and that evening he had the best meal he had had in years. He slept soundly during the quiet night, undisturbed by the annoying buzzing of the mosquitoes which were common on Tarutao. The next morning, he felt fresh in his crisp neatly pressed khaki uniform. He took a tricycle rickshaw from the hotel to the DOC headquarters in the old part of the city. The DG-DOC was in a meeting, so he waited.

A young man in a khaki uniform poked his head out of the director's office. "The Director-General will see you now, Khun Apipat."

Khun Apipat stood and followed the clerk into the DG's office. During Khun Apipat's four years on Tarutao, the DOC had had two new DGs, and today he was meeting his present superior for the first time. This one was an army colonel transferred to the DOC last year.

"Khun Apipat, how are you and how was your trip? Please, sit down and tell me why you came all the way from Tarutao to see me." The DG greeted him courteously with a smile, and pointed to two chairs in front of his desk.

Khun Apipat took a seat and returned his superior's smile.

"Thank you for taking the time to see me," Khun Apipat said. The friendly greeting gave him confidence. "I wouldn't have come to Bangkok and called on you personally if the situation wasn't so serious. There were some problems before, but I managed to solve them myself without requesting assistance from the Department. But now, some of the problems have escalated beyond my ability to effectively handle them. The resources I have available on Tarutao are very limited and some are totally lacking."

Khun Apipat paused to clear his throat, and then continued, "You've probably read my periodic reports about the worsening situation on Tarutao. For almost the whole year now, we've been dealing with a constant rice shortage and lack of medicine and competent medical personnel to control an outbreak of malaria. To date, almost one thousand prisoners have died from malaria alone. If something isn't done soon, many more will surely die. So, I have come to request a regular supply of rice, a sufficient amount of quinine tablets, and a qualified medical team."

His smile disappeared and the DG's face turned serious as he spoke, "Khun Apipat, you should be aware that rice shortages and a lack of medical supplies are a problem everywhere in Thailand right now, even in Bangkok. Although I sympathize, I'm afraid that there's nothing I can do. We have a budget, but we can't spend it, because there's no rice or medicine available. And there aren't any doctors either. They've been sent to north Burma where our troops are fighting. Because supplies are limited, the Government has had no choice but to prioritize, and unfortunately, Tarutao is the lowest priority."

Stunned by the DG's bluntness, Khun Apipat remained silent for a few moments as he struggled to control his anger.

He then said bitterly, "What about myself, my staff and their families? We are government officials and employees. Are we also the lowest priority? I've worked with the guards and staff on Tarutao for four years. They've performed their duties well despite the hardships they've endured. They aren't much better off than the prisoners. You can't let them die of starvation and malaria. Please believe me, Director-General, Tarutao is the last place anyone would want his children to grow up. The guards and staff have sacrificed a lot working on that island in order to fulfill their sense of duty to the Government."

"Khun Apipat, you have to accept the realities of life. We didn't start this war, but we have to deal with it, anyway. War is cruel to everyone, not just to the soldiers who do the fighting, but to the innocent people as well."

"Sir, as the Director-General of this Department, you are responsible for the welfare of your subordinates. The problems on Tarutao are also your problems, and it is your duty to solve them," Khun Apipat said adamantly.

The DG pounded the desk with his right fist. "Look here, Khun Apipat," he said. "Don't tell me about my responsibilities and duties. I know them, and I also know my authority. Therefore, I authorize you to use your own resourcefulness to solve the problems on Tarutao. Do what you must, and don't ask me again for assistance. There won't be any. You are a senior official of this Department, if you don't possess the initiative to help yourself, no one can do it for you. Don't ask for pity from anyone, we ran out of pity a long time ago. This meeting is over. Go back to Tarutao, and solve your own problems." With these harsh words, the DG ended their meeting and rose from his chair.

Khun Apipat stood without saying a word and left the room. He was terribly upset and disappointed at the outcome of the meeting. The Director-General, the only person whom he thought would understand his situation and help him, had completely rejected him.

CHAPTER 10

A three-masted merchant vessel, her sails catching the easterly wind, moved slowly through the channel between the island of Langkawi and the Malay mainland. The cargo vessel was making its regular run between Penang and the port of Kantang in Trang province in southern Thailand, with an intermediate stop at the port of Kuah on Langkawi.

Although both Malaya and Thailand were under Japanese occupation, trading between Penang and Kantang continued. As the war went on, the demand for goods in both ports increased, resulting in growing merchant ship traffic. From Penang the boats brought canned food, clothing, medical supplies, and other industrial products which were badly needed in Thailand. On the return trip, the ships usually carried rice, vegetables, fruits, and live animals for Penang itself, and for transshipment to Singapore and the Malay mainland.

Although they could move faster in the open sea with its deeper waters and stronger winds, the merchant ships preferred to take the slower, but safer route closer to the mainland. Ever since the Allied forces had gone on the offensive in the fight for the control of the Pacific and Indian Oceans, their submarines had been harassing the retreating Japanese forces. Considerable damage had been inflicted on the Japanese Navy and convoys of cargo ships, and the captains of merchant ships from Penang were afraid that, on the open sea, they might be targeted by the Allied submarines.

The Chinese captain of the merchant vessel from Penang sat on the deck behind the ship's helm. He was enjoying the fine January weather as the ship passed the Malay boundary into Thai territorial waters. A crewman standing at the bow shouted at him and pointed ahead.

The captain stood up, looked beyond the bow, and saw a small boat, its sail down, floating directly ahead of them. He instructed the crew to slow the ship and get ready to lend a hand in case the boat was in distress and needed help.

As the merchant ship drew closer, the captain saw that there were five men in the small boat. They were dressed in what looked more like rags than clothes. They appeared to be haggard and weak, as though they had been floating at sea for weeks.

One of the crew threw a rope down to the small boat. A man picked it up and tied it to the bow of his boat. The captain told his crew to drop a rope ladder down to the small boat and tell the five men to come on board his ship.

"Who are you and why are you out here?" the captain asked. He spoke in Thai because the five men who had boarded his ship, and now sat on the floor in front of him, looked more Thai than Chinese or Malay. "Are you lost at sea? That hardly seems possible because land is so near, and with your sail you could reach it very easily."

One man, who acted as the group's leader, spoke, "We are from Tarutao, which as you probably know, is a prison.

I am Karn, a guard, and these four men are prisoners."
He was almost as shabby as the prisoners under his charge.
"The situation on Tarutao is dire. Food and medicine are
almost nonexistent, and people are dying of malaria every
day. I was sent out fishing with these prisoners, but we
lost our fishing net and can't catch any fish. We saw your
ship coming this way and decided to ask you for some
food."

"I'm sorry to hear of your misfortune. You're lucky
we passed by. I'll give you something to eat and also
some food to take back," the captain said. He then ordered
his crew to bring food for the hungry men from Tarutao.

"We are deeply in your debt, and as long as we live,
we will never forget your kindness," the guard said. He
and the four prisoners had finished eating a freshly prepared
meal. The captain had also given them some canned food
and quinine tablets to take back.

"Well, the way to a man's heart is through his stomach,"
the captain replied with a smile.

Karn delivered the food and medicine to Khun Apipat and
told him what had happened to him and the four prisoners.

"The way you all looked, you're lucky the captain even
allowed the five of you to board his ship, let alone that
he also fed you," Khun Apipat said.

"Khun Apipat, what happened to Karn today has just
given me an idea," Cunningham said. Cunningham had
just returned from exploring the land beyond Taloh
Wow Bay with Hawkins and Grant and dropped by Khun
Apipat's office to visit him.

"Karn may have discovered a new source of supplies
for us," Cunningham said. "We've all seen the merchant
ships that pass through this area. They must be fully

loaded with cargoes both ways. If we need something, we can send a boat out to intercept them, and ask for food and medicine."

"Collin, we are officials of the Thai Government," Khun Apipat replied. "Do you want us to become known as beggars of the sea? Besides, we can't beg every day, and we wouldn't obtain enough food for all the prisoners anyway."

"If you don't feel comfortable about begging, we can trade with them," Cunningham suggested. "We have plenty of hardwood trees here. We can offer them in exchange for food and medicine."

"I'd have to get approval from Bangkok to cut down wood and trade like that," Khun Apipat said. He was not enthusiastic about the American's suggestion.

"Cut out all this bureaucratic crap," Cunningham said shaking his head in annoyance. "You know it'll take forever to get approval from Bangkok. Your Director-General told you to use your own initiative, so use it."

Cunningham got up from his chair and walked over to Khun Apipat, who was sitting behind his desk. The American looked Khun Apipat directly in the eye and said, "Khun Apipat. I'm trying my best to help you. When you came back from Bangkok last month after seeing your Director-General, you told us yourself that you were very disappointed at the way he had treated you. I'm surprised that you've forgotten so quickly that he categorized you as the 'lowest priority on the list'. Our situation gets worse every day. No one else seems to care whether we live or die."

Cunningham paused and leaned in closer to Khun Apipat as if to emphasize his point. The American told him bluntly, "You have a choice of either being scorned as beggars of the sea and not starving to death or continuing to be the lowest priority on the list and dying of starvation anyway. It was your boss, wasn't it, who told you to use any available resources to help yourself. Looking at the people on Tarutao, I can say that all they are capable of is either begging or stealing. It's your decision, Khun Apipat."

Cunningham returned to his seat. He slumped down in the chair, in despair over the worsening situation.

"All right, Collin, I see your point," Khun Apipat agreed. "I'll have the guards take turns meeting the merchant ships and asking them nicely for food and medicine. We'll take whatever is offered to us."

"Captain, it's the people from Tarutao again. Are we going to stop and give them some food like last time?" asked one of the crewmen of the SEA DRAGON, a Penang registered merchant ship,.

The captain looked beyond the bow and saw a small sailboat floating ahead in the distance. "I've had enough of these beggars. If we keep giving them food for free, they'll never stop," he replied. "It's not our fault they're in prison and don't have enough food. It's their government's responsibility to take care of them. We've done our share by giving them food and medicine twice already. We gain nothing by stopping to help them, and we lose time and money if we don't get our cargo to the buyers on time. We're here to do business, not to give charity."

"They're directly in the middle of our course," a crewman shouted. "If they don't move, we'll run into them for sure."

"If they don't move, I'm going to ram them. It'll teach them not to bother us anymore," the captain said with a grim smile.

The heavily laden vessel continued on course, straight at the smaller fishing boat.

There was a loud crashing sound as the solid high bow of the SEA DRAGON crushed the fragile side of the small boat breaking it in half. Its four occupants jumped out of the boat just seconds before the impact. As the SEA DRAGON continued on its way, the survivors of the wrecked sailboat swam towards the floating wooden boards which had once been parts of the boat and held onto them to support themselves.

"I'll never forgive you for this, SEA DRAGON," one of the survivors shouted at the hit-and-run merchant ship.

Chim, the guard leading the unfortunate team that confronted the SEA DRAGON, reported the destruction of the fishing boat to Khun Apipat. "Director, we only have one fishing boat left, and we can't afford to lose it. We're going to need weapons to protect ourselves so that the next ship we meet doesn't ram us, too. It wasn't an accident. They definitely intended to ram us and thought that they could get away with it. They could have steered away from us but they didn't. If we don't teach them a lesson, no ship is going to stop to give us food anymore."

Pradit, Khun Apipat's deputy, spoke up, "Director, we are at war. There's fighting everywhere, and everyone has to look after himself. It doesn't matter who's right, it matters who wins. The SEA DRAGON has declared war on us. They struck first, believing that we were helpless and couldn't do anything to them. Those people on the SEA DRAGON didn't care at all whether our men were killed or not. Director, we have to think of ourselves first. If we don't do something about this, the guards and the prisoners will be reluctant to follow your next orders."

"You mentioned that the SEA DRAGON was heading

towards Kantang," Khun Apipat said to Chim. "She must pass this way again to return to Penang. Do you have any idea when she'll leave Kantang?"

"In a few days, I'd guess" Chim answered.

Khun Apipat sat silently thinking for a few moments. Then without saying another word, he opened the cabinet where he kept the guns. He handed Chim a rifle, a double-barreled shotgun, and two boxes of ammunition.

"Do what must be done to the SEA DRAGON," he said.

War had been declared.

"That's not the SEA DRAGON, but it looks like her from a distance. Let's approach and ask for food but be careful. Don't use the weapons unless it's absolutely necessary. These guns are only for getting even with the SEA DRAGON," Chim said. He sat with another guard and three prisoners in the last remaining fishing boat.

The merchant ship they'd been watching had come out of Kantang fully loaded with cargo. She moved slowly towards the smaller boat and stopped nearby.

A man appeared at the bow, and shouted down to Chim and his men. "What do you want? You're blocking our course."

"Can you spare some rice for us? We're from Tarutao and we need some rice badly," Chim shouted back.

"The rice shipment we're carrying has been ordered by a merchant in Penang. It's not our rice. If all the rice he ordered is not accounted for, we'll be penalized. Please understand," pleaded the captain of the merchant ship.

Chim hesitated a moment before responding, "All right. Continue your journey. But before you go, answer one question. Where is the SEA DRAGON, and when is she coming out this way?"

"Tomorrow morning. She's in Kantang now, loading cargo." The captain replied. He ordered his crew to hoist up the sails.

He waved farewell to Chim and his men as the sails caught the wind and the ship moved away.

The smaller, lighter sailboat, with its five occupants, was able to maintain speed, and ran parallel to the heavily laden SEA DRAGON. The sailboat had come out early that morning, waiting to intercept the merchant ship. The smaller vessel was close enough to see the name SEA DRAGON written clearly in English and Chinese on the merchant ship's bow. Chim, who could read Chinese, was certain this ship was their target.

The crew of the merchant ship stood on the starboard side, looking down at the smaller boat. "Slow down and stop the ship. We want to talk to you," Chim shouted.

Suddenly a shot blasted from a pistol in the hand of the captain of the SEA DRAGON. Chim felt the bullet whiz past, over his head. The captain's action clearly showed that the SEA DRAGON was not going to yield to Chim's instructions.

"Get ready," Chim grimly told his men. "I've done enough talking. If that's how they want it, we're going to teach them a hard lesson."

Chim stood up and steadied himself, holding the rifle in firing position. He aimed directly at the captain of the SEA DRAGON.

The captain stared in surprise when he saw the rifle in Chim's hands. As he stood there, undecided as what to do next, Chim fired.

A mere thirty yards separated the two vessels, and Chim was a good shot. The bullet hit its target, knocking the captain off his feet as it pierced his chest, killing him instantly.

The pistol fell to the floor. A crewman tried to pick it up, but had to lie down flat to dodge a hail of bullets as Chim and the other guard opened fire on him.

With their captain dead, the crew realized that it was useless to fight. Their lone pistol was no match against the combined firepower of a rifle and a shotgun. Deciding to surrender, they lowered the sails, and stopped the ship.

"Director, it was self-defense! I asked the captain of the SEA DRAGON to stop the ship and talk with us. He shot at me first, so I had to shoot back. Unfortunately, my first shot killed him on the spot," Chim reported. Khun Apipat was inspecting the merchant ship and her cargo, two hundred tons of rice packed in burlap bags and thirty suckling pigs.

"All right. What is done cannot be undone," Khun Apipat said. "My concern is how to feed everyone on this island. We have enough rice here to last us for a while. Get the prisoners to carry the rice to the storeroom and send the pigs to the kitchen."

"What about the ship and the crew?" Chim asked.

"Hide the ship in one of the other bays, but not in Taloh Wow Bay or Taloh Udang Bay. We might have some use for it later on," Khun Apipat ordered. "Confine the crew with the common prisoners. They'll be useful if we need a crew for the SEA DRAGON. If they try to escape or cause any trouble, kill them. Make sure they understand that!"

"Let's anchor here until the storm passes. We'll be well protected in this bay." The Chinese captain of the merchant ship, LUCKY LADY, was speaking to his sole passenger, a middle-aged Indian as the ship sailed slowly into a small bay on the eastern side of Tarutao.

The LUCKY LADY sailed from Penang heading for Kantang and then Krabi, another city further up the coast from Kantang. It was early May, and the ship had run into the first monsoon of the season after she had passed the northern end of Langkawi. The captain did not want to lose another hour of sailing time going back to Langkawi, so he decided to head for Tarutao, with its long shoreline and high mountains, to protect them from the raging monsoon.

The ship had just dropped anchor in the clear, calm water of the bay, when a crewman shouted, "Captain, there's a sailboat coming towards us!" He pointed beyond the bow of the LUCKY LADY.

The captain didn't pay much attention to the approaching sailboat. "It's probably just a fishing boat also seeking shelter from the monsoon," he commented.

"Captain, it's approaching our starboard side!" the crewman shouted. The crew hurriedly placed used automobile tires along the ship's starboard side to keep the two vessels from colliding and causing possible damage.

"We're from Tarutao Vocational Training Settlement on this island. May we come aboard and talk with you?" asked Nit, one of the guards assigned to lead teams to intercept passing merchant ships.

Khun Apipat's prediction that the monsoons might cause vessels to seek shelter on this side of the island was correct.

A ladder was lowered from the merchant ship. Nit and two prisoners climbed up the ladder, while another guard and a prisoner stayed behind on the sailboat. A crewman led them to the captain, who was having lunch with his Indian passenger on the bridge behind the helm.

"Sit down, please, join us for lunch," the captain said

courteously, gesturing at the empty benches around the table. Nit and the two prisoners looked presentable in their new trousers and shirts taken from the SEA DRAGON. Khun Apipat had ordered the teams to clean themselves up and dress in clothing taken from the captured vessel on the theory that a good appearance made a good impression. If his men dressed well and looked clean, the ships they met would not hesitate to welcome them on board.

"Thank you, but we won't bother you by staying long," Nit said. "I'm under instructions from my director to inquire about the possibility of bartering our hardwood logs and prisoner-made furniture for any food and medicine that you can spare. We have over two thousand mouths to feed everyday, and we don't receive sufficient assistance from Bangkok." Nit was a former thief who, having served his sentence, was released for good behavior and hired as a guard on Tarutao. He had become one of Khun Apipat's bodyguards and most trusted men.

"Captain, if we can spare some food and medicine, we should give them to these gentlemen, so they can be on their way," the Indian passenger said. He clutched nervously at a small wooden box on his lap.

The captain rose from his seat. "All right, I'll see what we have to spare. I'll inspect the logs and furniture later. I can sympathize with the people who are stuck on this island. The war has been hard on everyone," he said.

As he was moving away from the table, the captain accidentally knocked over a cup of tea, spilling its contents on the Indian, who reflexively dropped the box, and raised his hands to catch the cup. The wooden box slid from his lap, and fell on the floor. With a cracking sound, the lid of the box broke open, and four glittering gold bars tumbled from the box onto the floor.

"It's gold!" Nit exclaimed. He picked up the gold bar nearest to him and looked at it greedily.

"Give that back to me!" the Indian demanded. He looked at Nit with loathing. "It's part of the dowry for my daughter's marriage in Krabi."

It was customary for an Indian bride to present her groom with a dowry in gold, silver, or other valuable items during the marriage ceremony. The Indian merchant had converted his savings to gold bars, and he had no intention whatsoever of giving them up.

"Just one of these gold bars will buy us food for quite a while," Nit said. "I'll just take one gold bar. You'll still have three left for your daughter. I'm sure your daughter is so beautiful that there's no need to give all the gold bars to the already lucky groom." Nit put the gold bar in his pocket and laughed loudly.

"You're a thief! This is robbery! I won't let you take what is mine!" The Indian stood up and yelled at Nit as he walked away.

In an uncontrollable rage, the Indian grabbed a table knife and lunged at Nit, but before he could reach his target, one of the prisoners jumped on him from behind. The prisoner locked the Indian's neck with his right arm, and stabbed him in the back with a knife that he had hidden under his shirt. The knife cut the Indian's heart with one stroke. He was dead before his body hit the floor.

The sudden turn of events stunned the captain of the LUCKY LADY, and he angrily shouted commands at his crew to capture Nit and his two men. Pulling a revolver from his trouser pocket, the captain pointed it at Nit. He never had a chance.

A shotgun blast knocked him off his feet. He collapsed on the floor, blood oozing from his chest.

The guard who was left in the sailboat had killed the

captain. When he'd heard the argument on the LUCKY LADY, he'd climbed quietly up the ladder, and shot the captain to save Nit.

The three crewmen rushing to capture Nit stopped at once when they saw their captain killed.

Nit picked up the captain's revolver and pointed it at the three crewmen. The guard who had just killed the captain turned his double-barreled shotgun on the three crewmen and looked at Nit.

Nit smiled grimly and nodded. The deafening noise of gunfire and shotgun blasts filled the air, and the three crewmen fell to the floor dead.

"Kill them all! Leave no witnesses!" Nit yelled.

One crewman tried to flee to the bow of the ship. The two prisoners who'd come with Nit chased him with drawn long knives and finished him off. "You should have been satisfied with three gold bars. Look what your stinginess has cost you," Nit said to the lifeless body of the unlucky merchant. He picked up the other three gold bars from the floor and put them all, including the one from his pocket, back in the box.

"Let's have a look around the ship and see if she is carrying anything we can use," Nit said to his accomplices.

It was their first act of piracy.

Nit sent two men back to Taloh Wow Bay on the sailboat to in form Khun Apipat of the bloodshed. Khun Apipat came immediately aboard the ADANG.

"Director, I had no choice," Nit said to Khun Apipat when the director boarded the LUCKY LADY. He expected Khun Apipat to be furious at what he and his men had done.

Khun Apipat did not say a word. He stepped calmly over the dead bodies of the captain, the Indian passenger, and the crew, and went down into the cargo hold to inspect the goods.

"Director, these gold bars are for you," Nit said, opening the box and revealing its valuable contents to Khun Apipat.

Again Khun Apipat remained silent. He looked at the gold bars, nodded, but did not touch them. He appeared to be deep in thought.

Ever since the SEA DRAGON's plundering a few months earlier, Khun Apipat had been having conflicting thoughts. As an administrator and civil servant, he knew that what the guards and the prisoners had done was wrong. They should be punished for their crimes. As a leader and a man with a conscience, though, he could not blame everything on them. He had to take responsibility for allowing the plundering to occur.

On the other hand, he was also duty bound to see to the welfare of the staff, guards, and prisoners. Wartime difficulties and his superiors' neglect of Tarutao had forced Khun Apipat to use every available resource to solve their problems. It pleased him immensely to see smiles on the faces of the hungry guards and prisoners as they filled their stomachs with rice and pork taken from the SEA DRAGON.

Khun Apipat knew that if he kept sending his men out to ask for food from the merchant ships, the plundering would continue. It was inevitable, after all, most of his men were former criminals. Theft, robbery, and murder were their natural, instinctive responses to hunger and greed. He'd never dreamed he'd be in a situation that compelled him to make this kind of decision.

Suddenly, he heard the Director-General's voice and the words "lowest priority" echoed in his memory. That was it! He had to set his own priorities. Right now his first priority was to save his men, including the prisoners and himself, from hunger, sickness, and death. That done, he would cope with whatever happened in the future.

Khun Apipat had made his decision.

He discussed the cargo with Nit. "These chemicals are caustic sodas, we can sell them to some factories for a high price. The automobile and bicycle tires are also in demand all over the country, and people are willing to pay big for them. The money from selling these goods can buy a lot of food and medicine."

"Are we going to keep this ship?" Nit asked.

"No. We already have the SEA DRAGON. Load the cargo onto the ADANG, and burn this ship," Khun Apipat replied. Pausing for a moment, he then asked, "What about the dead bodies?"

"No problem, Director. I'll take care of them," Nit said. He told the prisoners to tie the corpses to the LUCKY LADY's two heavy anchors and throw them overboard.

Nit explained his plan to Khun Apipat, "If we burn the bodies with the ship, their remains will still float and become evidence. This way the weight of the anchors will keep the bodies at the bottom of the sea. They'll either decay or be eaten by fish. Either way, they'll be gone forever, and no one will ever know what happened to them."

Three men witnessed the aftermath of the bloody encounter. They'd hidden themselves in the dense forest of a hill overlooking the small bay where the LUCKY LADY, her passenger, and crew had met their violent end.

The three men were Knox, Cunningham, and Rachan. It was Knox's and Rachan's turn to go hunting. They'd decided to go to the eastern side of the island to look for fresh game. A year of continuous hunting by the prisoners-of-war had completely wiped out the population of wild animals in the areas near the road. Cunningham came along to explore the new area.

They were tracking a herd of wild boar near the eastern shoreline when they heard gunshots coming from the direction of the sea. Curious to see what was happening, they rushed to find a spot from which they could clearly see the bay, while remaining shielded from view by the thick undergrowth and tall tress.

The slaughter aboard the LUCKY LADY was over. The three men could see six corpses strewn about the ship, and figured out what had happened. They crouched patiently in the dense undergrowth to see what would happen next. At first they thought Nit and the four prisoners were acting on their own. After Khun Apipat arrived, they watched in disbelief as Khun Apipat supervised the transfer of the LUCKY LADY's cargo to the ADANG, the disposal of the dead bodies, and the destruction of the LUCKY LADY.

Know, Rachan, and Cunningham walked quietly back to their compound, all enthusiasm for hunting wild boars gone. They were thinking, each in his own way, about what they'd seen.

Knox was deeply disappointed in Khun Apipat. Although he knew that Khun Apipat was under extreme pressure to keep the prisoners fed, healthy, and under control, and he sympathized with the man as he struggled under the weight of these burdens, he'd never imagined Khun Apipat would sink so low. As a senior government official, he was obligated to set an example for his staff, guards, and prisoners. Maybe his disappointment in his superiors and long years of association with thieves and murderers had driven him mad. Perhaps the prison environment had corrupted him and turned him into the very thing he despised.

Two English proverbs came to Knox's mind. One was that "men are known by the company they keep." The second was that "he who kept company with the wolf would learn to howl."

Knox decided to avoid Khun Apipat lest he himself become unwittingly and unintentionally involved in the piracy. He knew that once he committed himself it would be too late to turn back. Knox had heard that the tide of war was turning in favor of the Allies. If the war ever came to an end, and the Allies emerged victorious, he intended to return to the British Army and pursue his military career.

Knox also believed the British would return after the war to continue their rule of Malaya and Singapore. As an ally of Japan, Thailand would be treated as a defeated nation. There would be a changes in the Thai government which would affect the TVTS, and, no doubt, pirating activities. Khun Apipat and his collaborators would be found out and punished. Therefore, it would be wise for him and his men to disassociate themselves from Khun Apipat and his accomplices.

Rachan was angry at the criminals aboard the LUCKY LADY. He was also angry with himself for not being able to prevent the cold-blooded murder of another Indian. He memorized the faces of all five accomplices and swore to himself that one day he would avenge the death of his countryman. He would tell the three Indian corporals what he had seen, certain that they would share his feeling.

Cunningham, on the other hand, was not at all surprised that Khun Apipat had finally succumbed to piracy. He had known all along that it would happen sooner or later. As a matter of fact, he had wanted the evil surrounding them to win over Khun Apipat, as it had won over him. Cunningham bitterly acknowledged that circumstances could indeed alter a man. From now on he would be able to talk to the TVTS director more openly. He would show Khun Apipat how to make fortune out of the war that had put both of them in so much misery.

The plundering of the LUCKY LADY had shown Cunningham how the war was going to pay back what it had taken from him. With his shrewdness and Khun Apipat's manpower, the war could make both of them very rich. And when the war ended, he would have enough money to buy the land on Langkawi and resume his plans to build his domain.

Cunningham had also followed the war's course. The Allies had already secured the sea route from Europe to Asia through the Indian Ocean. This meant that more freighters would be carrying vital cargo from Europe and India to Penang. Merchant ships from Penang would then carry the cargo to Burma and Thailand, unavoidably passing through the sea around Tarutao. The fear of submarine attacks, and the heavy monsoon rains from May to October, would force merchant ships to sail through the twelve-mile channel between Tarutao and the mainland. It would be so easy for the pirates from Tarutao to intercept them.

Cunningham felt no guilt about his plans. He had learned the hard way that all was fair in love and war, and that to the victor belonged the spoils. The war had convinced him that might did indeed make right.

The owners of the cargo on the merchant ships had been profiteering by selling goods at unconscionably high prices in both the open and black markets. They were indirectly, and in many cases directly, robbing innocent victims of the war. He had discovered that in any war innocent people were also killed, wounded, became homeless, and had their property and personal assets taken away from them. He felt he was an innocent victim of the war, and it would not be wrong for him to rob those selfish merchants before they could rob other people.

The next morning, Cunningham stopped by the TVTS director's office to offer his congratulations. "Khun Apipat, I must congratulate you for having made the right decision about the merchant ship yesterday."

"Collin, what are you talking about?" Khun Apipat looked at the American, feigning innocence.

"Oh, come on, Khun Apipat. I saw the whole thing. Do you want details on how many barrels of chemicals and tires you transferred from the merchant ship to the ADANG? What about the six dead bodies that you cleverly disposed of?"

When Cunningham saw that Khun Apipat remained silent and his face turned pale, he continued, "Don't worry. I agree with what you did. It was the right thing to do in that situation. The whole world is in a shambles, who's to say what's right and what's wrong?. We don't know what the outcome of the war will be, and it doesn't even matter who wins. We'll be both well-off after the war if you'll listen to me."

Cunningham paused to observe Khun Apipat's reaction. When he saw that the director was listening intently, he told him about his plan to make a fortune from the war for both of them.

"What about Knox and the other British soldiers? Do you think they'll join us?" Khun Apipat asked, apparently relieved after hearing what the American had to say.

"Frankly, I'm not so sure about Knox and his men," Cunningham replied. "Knox and Rachan were with me on the hill yesterday. I don't know what they're thinking because they've kept quiet ever since."

"They could be a problem for us."

"Don't worry about them. If they don't join us, they'll at least have enough sense not to go against us. Knox is a clever man. He's no threat to us now because we outnumber them and he can't leave the island."

"What about when the war is over?"

"If the Allies win, he can cause a lot of trouble if he wants to. However, if and when that moment comes, I'll handle the situation," Cunningham assured Khun Apipat.

"What about Hawkins and Grant? They aren't under Knox's command. Can we persuade them to join us?" Khun Apipat asked.

"I'm certain that those two will join us," Cunningham replied with confidence. "Didn't you know that Hawkins and Grant are fugitives running away from crimes they committed in Kota Baharu? Knox and his men were sent to capture them."

Cunningham smiled when he saw the surprised look on Khun Apipat's face.

"No, I wasn't aware of that. No one told me. Maybe that's why I've always felt uneasy about Hawkins and Grant. They acted very strangely when they first arrived."

"So, you see, Hawkins and Grant have no place to go and no one to turn to, except us. Knox once told me that when the war is over, if the British win, he will arrest them, and take them back with him."

"Do Hawkins and Grant know that Knox was after them?" Khun Apipat asked.

"No, they don't," Cunningham replied. "But once they know, believe me, Khun Apipat, they'll be furious and they'll keep a watchful eye on Knox and his men. They'll be useful to us. If we ever feel that Knox has become a threat to us, we look the other way, and let Hawkins and Grant take care of him."

"Collin, you're a clever man."

"I'm a survivor, Khun Apipat," the American said. "But back to Hawkins and Grant. Because of their military experience and background, they can teach your guards and selected prisoners to handle weapons effectively in combat. We have to be well prepared because some of the merchant ships might carry arms to protect themselves."

"You seem to have already thought of everything, Collin."

"I've made mistakes in the past, they were costly, but they taught me to be very thorough in my planning. There are a few more things we have to consider. We have to decide where to keep all the merchandise before it's sold. We can't store everything in this compound, there are too many people around here. The fewer people who know about our activities, the safer we'll be. And we'll have fewer people to share the spoils with." Khun Apipat was completely convinced, and together they spent many hours going over every aspect of their plan to make a fortune from the war.

Thus was born the pirates of Tarutao.

CHAPTER 11

"We don't have the men or arms to stop this piracy, but we do have the ability to warn merchant ships, and other ships, not to come near Tarutao or anchor here," Knox said to the five men on the balcony of his hut.

Outside, heavy rains fell and dark clouds dominated the sky. It was still the monsoon season and the six men spent most of their time holed up in their huts. In the month that had passed since the LUCKY LADY incident, the nine prisoners-of-war had divided into two opposing sides.

"I'm disappointed in Cunningham and Khun Apipat," Brown said. "I never would have thought they'd turn into pirates."

"So am I, although I did think something like this might happen," Knox said. "Ever since he lost his gold bars to the Japanese, Cunningham has been determined to make his fortune from the war. That loss, and his obsession with the land on Langkawi have influenced his thinking. He's always said that he wouldn't let the war beat him and that he'd be compensated for what he'd lost. This is just the kind of chance he's been waiting for."

"And that chance finally came when he saw Khun Apipat and his men plundering the merchant ship a month ago," Rachan added.

"I admit that Cunningham is quite shrewd," Brown commented. "He knew we'd been sent after Hawkins and Grant, and that's why he was friendly with them, he was hoping to recruit them to do his dirty work."

"I've never thought of Hawkins and Grant as being on our side," Knox said. "From the beginning, they've always been on the opposite side. They're the reason we ended up here. As far as I'm concerned, when the war's over, I'm taking them back to answer for what they've done."

"Lieutenant, if that's your intention, then we all have to be careful," Brown said. "The way things are now, I'm certain that Cunningham has told Hawkins and Grant about our real mission. Have you noticed that we haven't seen the three of them around for the past two weeks? They've intentionally avoided us."

"I heard from a guard that Khun Apipat has built new bungalows for them at Taloh Wow Bay," Rachan added.

"Then we have to be concerned about our own safety from now on. We can no longer trust anyone, except the six of us in this compound," Knox said.

"Lieutenant, what do you think they intend to do with us?" Brown asked.

Knox thought for a few moments and then replied, "I don't think Cunningham and Khun Apipat will move against us now. They're too busy right now plundering merchant ships and collecting the loot for themselves. They certainly don't want to have to deal with us now. They'll just have someone keep an eye on our activities."

"What about Hawkins and Grant?" Rachan asked.

"If they know we're after them, they have two choices: they can run away or try to eliminate us," Knox said slowly, after thinking it over for a few seconds. "They can't exactly leave the island right now, so they've chosen to stay away from us. But if we try to arrest them, they'll be ready to fight it out with us."

Knox paused, and looked outside. The heavy rains had subsided and turned into a drizzle. He returned to the conversation and said, "What we need now are weapons to defend ourselves, in case Hawkins and Grant decide to try and get rid of us now. It's also likely that Khun Apipat and Cunningham won't want us around as witnesses to their crimes. The rifle Khun Apipat lent me only has three bullets left. So far he hasn't asked me to give the rifle back, but he has avoided giving me any more bullets. We have to get us more weapons to defend ourselves."

"Sir, there is a lot of bamboo around here. We could build bamboo fences to form a defensive perimeter around our huts," Rachan suggested. "Our little fort will have one entrance. We can dig a pit at the entrance and boobytrap it with sharpened bamboo shafts pointing straight up. We then cover the pit with wooden planks. At night, before we go to sleep, we just pull the planks off."

"Very ingenious, Rachan," Knox answered with a smile. He looked at the others and asked, "Does anyone else have an idea? I'm open to suggestions."

"We can tie groups of used tin cans to strings or vines and set them up in a ring around our compound as a warning system," Brown advised. "During the day we can lower them on the ground to avoid arousing suspicion. At night we can string them up about knee-high. If any comes by unannounced, the rattling sound of the cans will warn us."

"What about dogs that might wander in here and run into those cans?" Chai, one of the Indian corporals, asked.

"What dogs?" Brown said. "Haven't you noticed that there hasn't been a single dog around here for the last two weeks? All the dogs in this compound, and at Taloh Wow Bay, have been eaten by the guards and prisoners. The people on this island have been so underfed that they decided to include dog meat in their menu."

The group fell silent. In the year since the political prisoners had left, the dogs had been their companions. Brown's remarks came as unpleasant news.

Knox then said, "We have to make bows, arrows, and spears from bamboo and practice using them until we can handle them expertly. They might come in handy one day. We have no other choices for weapons."

"I can see you in your new position when we return to the Army: Lieutenant Knox of the Bow and Arrow platoon, the silent raiders," Brown joked.

"Don't knock it, Brown. Our forefathers defended England with bows and arrows, and Genghis Khan conquered China with bows and arrows." Knox said, while Brown smiled sheepishly.

"How are we going to warn the merchant ships?" Rachan asked Knox.

"Oh, yes. We have to set up two lookouts on high ground, one each on the eastern and western sides. We'll have to keep the paths between them clear, so we can go back and forth easily. If and when we see a ship coming, or anchoring near the shore, we have to get as close to them as possible, and warn them about the pirates. We must try to convince the captain of the ship to leave at once. Right now, there's no need to have a lookout on the western side, because we're in the southwest monsoon season, and ships will only seek shelter on the eastern side. When the rains stop, we'll go to work."

One mild July afternoon after the monsoon had subsided and the rains had stopped, Knox was supervising the fixing of boobytraps at the entrance to their small walled compound when Prem, one of the Indian corporals, who was posted at the eastern lookout, came running to report to him.

"Sir, a sailboat is coming from Langkawi, heading in the direction of Taloh Udang Bay. But, it's too small to be a merchant ship, it only has one mast, and I don't think it belongs to the TVTS. It doesn't look familiar." He paused, and then asked, "Do you want me to go down there and have a look, sir?"

Knox thought for a few seconds, and answered, "No, you go back to the lookout. I'll go down there myself." He turned to Brown and said, "You'll come with me, Brown, and bring the rifle."

Knox led the way, holding a machete in his right hand. Brown followed behind him with the rifle, loaded with the three remaining bullets. They headed towards the left end of the bay, following a path along the bamboo pipes installed by the political prisoners years ago. The pipes carried water from a waterfall to their compound. Knox and his men had traversed this trail several times before to the waterfall in order to repair broken pipes and the poles that supported them.

The waterfall, twenty-five feet wide and five feet high, was a continuous flow from a stream which cascaded down to a pond surrounded by rocks. Overflow from the pond exited through two outlets, one became the stream that flowed near the prisoner compound. The other became a stream that led out to the sea about half a mile away.

Knox and Brown waded across the knee-deep pond to the other side of the waterfall. They climbed atop a few large rocks leading to a trail covered with tall grass and bushes. Knox had to clear some spots on the trail with the machete he carried.

After walking a hundred feet, they came to a clearing, and saw the broken down roof of a hut. The hut itself was concealed by tall grass and dense bushes. Knox recalled that Luang Mahasit had told him that Mee, the fisherman who'd helped the five political prisoners escape five years ago, used to live in a hut beyond the waterfall. This must be Mee's hut, thought Knox.

Suddenly they heard voices, one of them female, crying out for help amid sounds of a struggle.

Knox exchanged astonished looks with Brown, who instinctively tightened his grip on the rifle. Knox rushed in the direction of the cries, with Brown hot on his heels. When they reached the remains of the old hut, they stood for a moment, startled by the scene before them.

Hawkins and Grant were struggling with a woman in a colorful sarong and a white blouse. They were trying to force her to the ground, but the woman fought them, realizing what they intended to do to her. Not too far away, an old man lay unconscious, apparently the victim of the two men.

Hawkins and Grant were too busy with the woman to notice Knox and Brown, who approached them in silence.

Brown struck Grant on the back of the head with the rifle butt, knocking him unconscious. As Grant slumped to the ground, Hawkins looked up in surprise and anger at Knox. Before the big sergeant could move, Knox kicked Hawkins hard with his right shin, aiming for the stomach. The forceful kick sent Hawkins sprawling on the ground away from the woman. Knox caught only a brief glimpse of the woman's face, but he noticed her brown complexion, long black hair, and wide, dark eyes.

Hawkins, who recovered quickly from the unexpected kick, lunged at Knox, knocking him down to the ground. The machete fell out of Knox's hand. Hawkins then jumped on top of Knox, who reflexively raised both his feet up and pushed them with full force against Hawkins's chest.

Knox's tactic effectively stopped Hawkins, and the big man fell down again.

Both men got to their feet staring defiantly at each other.

"You! I knew we'd meet someday, but this is sooner than I expected," Hawkins said. "I know why you and your men came from Kota Baharu. Cunningham told me they sent you after me. And now you're interrupting my pleasure."

Hawkins swung abruptly at Knox's face with his right fist, hoping to catch Knox off guard. But Knox had anticipated the move and dodged to his left. As Hawkins's fist went flying through empty air, Knox stepped back a few paces and kicked Hawkins in the neck with his right foot, even though Hawkins was the taller man by four inches. The kick stunned Hawkins. Knox followed up with a left kick to Hawkins's right cheek, dropping the big man to his knees. Red bruise marks appeared on Hawkins's face within seconds.

Hawkins told himself to be more alert as he got up and carefully guarded his face with both arms. Knox observed Hawkins's movements. When the big man came within kicking distance, Knox quickly released his right foot, aiming it at Hawkins's left thigh. Knox's boot hit hard against Hawkins's thigh with a loud slapping sound. Hawkins staggered to the left, and Knox followed up with a left kick to Hawkins's right thigh. Hawkins began to limp as pain shot through his thighs.

Hawkins had learned his lesson, he stepped out of kicking distance. He paused for a moment, trying to think of a way to break Knox's defense. He knew he wouldn't have a chance to hit Knox with his fists if he stayed too far away. But if he came any closer to Knox, he would be kicked until he could no longer stand on his feet.

So he decided to change his tactics.

Hawkins dashed in fast. His plan was to tackle Knox and knock him off his feet. He hoped to use his bigger, heavier body to wrestle Knox to the ground and then use his powerful fists to hit Knox in the face.

Hawkins discovered the hard way just how dangerous Thai boxing was, as Knox raised his right knee up to block Hawkins's tackle. Knox's bony knee collided with Hawkins's unguarded chin, knocking the big sergeant out cold.

Knox motioned Brown to look after the old man as he walked over to the woman, who was tidying up her dress. The woman stood up. Knox noticed that although she was taller than the average Asian woman, she was still three to four inches shorter than he was. Knox guessed she was just out of her teens. Her features looked like a mixture of Thai and Malay. She was beautiful, thought Knox. The sarong, tightly wrapped around her curvaceous body, made her slim waist and firm hips even more striking. Knox was captivated by her exotic beauty.

"Thank you very much for saving me from these two men. They attacked us unexpectedly as we got off our boat." To Knox's astonishment, the woman spoke in English with a British accent.

"Who are you? What are you doing here?" Knox asked. Worried that his questions might sound harsh, he smiled warmly at the woman and explained, "This island is a prison and, as you just learned, certainly not a safe place for a beautiful lady like yourself to visit." He paused then asked, "Where did you learn to speak English so well?"

"My name is Malatee, but everybody calls me by my nickname, Noi. That's my father over there." The woman introduced herself and pointed to the old man, who had regained consciousness and was now sitting up with

Brown's help. "My father and I used to live in this hut
many years ago. We're now living on Langkawi. I have
an older sister who is married to a guard at Taloh Wow
Bay. We came here to visit her, and I brought her some
gifts from Penang."

"Wait a minute!" interrupted Knox. "You said you
used to live here, but now you live on Langkawi?" In his
excitement, Knox repeated her words. Malatee nodded,
puzzled at Knox's reaction.

Knox's mind flashed back to the story Luang Mahasit
told him sometime ago. "Now I remember!" he exclaimed.
"Your father must be the fisherman who helped five political
prisoners escape to Langkawi in 1939!"

"Yes, he was. How did you know?" It was Malatee's
turn to be surprised.

"Someone told me the story. Your father was greatly
admired for his daring," Knox said.

"That was five years ago. I was a young girl then,"
Malatee said. "The five political prisoners took care of
my family just as they promised. They bought us a cottage
in Langkawi, and sent me to a convent school in Penang
where I learned English."

Malatee paused to look at her father. She smiled in
relief when she saw that he was alert and waving at her.
"I recently finished my last year of school in Penang, and
returned to Langkawi to live with my father and an older
brother. Who are you? You look and talk like an
Englishman but you fight like a Thai boxer."

Knox did not answer her question immediately. The
two of them walked over to where Brown and Mee, the
old fisherman, were sitting. He introduced himself and
Brown and told them, in Thai, for the benefit of Mee
who did not understand English, how they came to be on
Tarutao.

As Knox finished the tale, and sat chatting with Mee and Malatee, Hawkins and Grant slowly sat up. Brown raised the rifle and pointed at them. The two men got up on their feet and looked at them with hostility. Without saying a word, they turned and walked away, disappearing from sight. "We can't stay here now," Malatee said with concern. "Those two men might tell Khun Apipat that we are here. After we helped the political prisoners escape, Khun Apipat sent word to us not to come here anymore. He'll imprison us if he finds out that we've defied his order by coming here."

"Give me the gifts for your sister. I'll deliver them to her for you," Knox offered. He felt himself beginning to care for the woman whom he had just met.

"Thank you. You are very kind," Malatee said. She gave Knox a sweet smile, and his heart leapt. "But I would like to see her in person. It's been a few years since we've seen each other. What you can do for me is deliver a message to my sister that my father and I will be at the south end of Pine Bay on the western side of the island for the next few days. She can meet us there."

"Does she know how to get there?" Knox asked.

"Yes, she does. There's a trail along the mountain ridges from Taloh Udang Bay to Pine Bay. When we were children, we used to walk this trail all the time."

"Can I visit you there? I'm concerned about your safety," Knox asked.

"Yes, you can." She smiled again at Knox, and again his heart skipped a beat. "You can come with my sister. We have to leave now before the tide turns, or else we'll be stuck here."

Malatee got up and walked with her father to the sailboat. They paddled the boat a short distance from shore, and then hoisted the sail. Knox and Brown waved

goodbye and stood watching until the sailboat had
disappeared around the bend at the end of the island.

Rachan had become acquainted with a guard who was
partly Indian. Under Knox's instruction, Rachan asked the
guard to go to Taloh Wow Bay, find Yai, Malatee's sister,
and discreetly deliver the message to her.

The next morning Yai appeared at Knox's hut with her
husband, Tam. Yai was in her mid-twenties and as tall
as Malatee. She bore some resemblance to her younger
sister, but was not as strikingly beautiful. However, she
was good natured and smiled often while talking. Tam
was a Thai in his early thirties with an honest face and
a reserved manner. Knox liked them both immediately.

When they were ready, they left Taloh Udang Bay for
Pine Bay. Yai and Tam led the way, Knox and Brown
brought up the rear. Knox carried a machete in his right
hand, and Brown carried the rifle slung over his left
shoulder.

It took three hours to cross to the western side of the island
on the trail, which wound over several mountain ridges.
The trail on both sides was covered with jungle so dense
that most of the time they could not see the sky clearly.
Some parts of the trail were blocked by bushes so thick
that the three men had to take turns clearing the trail with
the machete.

As they came over the last ridge, they found themselves
in a clearing. Above, they could see the blue sky; below,
they could see the sea in the distance. Stretched before
them from the foot of the mountain to the beach, was a
vast flat land, no dense jungle, only bushes of sea lettuce
and mangrove forests.

Tam told Knox and Brown that this bay had a beach

two miles long, which was no doubt the most beautiful beach on Tarutao. From their vantage point they saw a strip of pine trees lining the whole length of the beach. The long rows of pine trees served as effective windbreaks during the monsoon season. They walked down to the beach along a stream that flowed from the mountain towards the sea at the south end of the long bay.

As they neared the sea, they discovered that they were in the middle of a mangrove forest. Mangrove forests grew in areas where fresh water and sea water came together. The tide was low, and they could see the trees' long, strange roots, extending downward from the trunks, forming dense thickets. Tam told them that he had learned from Mee that mangrove forests were very useful. Many kinds of fish used the roots as their nesting places and sources of food. As the fish grew big enough to brave the sea, they followed the stream out to the sea at high tide. The spot where the stream flowed into the sea was deep enough for Mee to bring his sailboat in and moor it safely.

Mee and Malatee had set up camp on the left bank of the stream. They were well protected from the wind by a high sand dune, which also concealed them from passing ships.

Mee and Malatee were cooking food on a fire of dried mangrove roots when they saw Yai and the three men approaching. They greeted their visitors, and Malatee and Yai embraced. Malatee then shook hands with Knox and Brown and asked them to stay for lunch.

After lunch, Knox and Brown felt that they should allow Mee and his family the courtesy of a family reunion in privacy. They excused themselves and walked away to look at the beach. Tam was right when he'd claimed that the beach at Pine Bay was the most beautiful on Tarutao.

The wide expanse of fine white sand extended straight out, ending at the foot of a distant mountain. No other humans were in sight, but there were numerous other living creatures on the beach. Crabs of different sizes scuttled into their holes, and hermit crabs took refuge in their shells when their keen senses detected Knox's and Brown's approaching footsteps.

A female voice behind them halted Knox and Brown. They turned around and saw Malatee walking towards them.

"Thank you for delivering the message to my sister," Malatee said to Knox. She smiled sweetly at him.

Brown had enough sense to know that Malatee and Knox wanted to be alone. He excused himself, saying, "I'm tired from walking all day. I hope you don't mind if I leave the two of you alone together. I'm going to find myself a nice place in the shade and lie down."

Brown left Knox and Malatee and headed for the pine trees.

"That sergeant is a nice man and always in a good humor. He seems to be very fond of you," Malatee said as they continued walking along the beach.

"Yes, we're very close. We've been together for several years now. He has become like a younger brother to me." Knox paused, then asked, "You have an older brother, haven't you? Where is he now?"

"He didn't come with us because he has a bad cold. He is at home on Langkawi," Malatee replied.

"Your name, Malatee. It sounds exotic. Does it have a meaning?"

"Yes, it means jasmine, a flower with a nice fragrance."

"Well, the name and the scent fit you perfectly," Knox said, and both of them laughed. Knox continued, "I prefer the name Malatee to your nickname, Noi. To me it sounds more appealing. Is it all right if I call you Malatee?"

Malatee laughed softly before replying, "Yes, you may. And what may I call you, Lieutenant?"

"Please call me Kevin."

There was a pause. Knox looked westward and pointed out to the sea. He asked, "What is the name of that big island in the distance?"

"That's Adang island," Malatee replied. "Actually, it's a group of four sizable islands, Adang is the largest. The other three islands are Rawi, Butang, and Lipe, the smallest. They're all near one another. There are villages of Sea Gypsies on Lipe and Adang. My mother came from there, so I am half Thai and half Sea Gypsy. One day, we'll visit those islands. They are pristine and beautiful, the water is clear and there is plenty of coral. Together the four islands have more than fifty beaches."

"Well, I'll have to ask Khun Apipat for holiday leave to visit those islands. I haven't taken a holiday in years, so it's about time," Knox said lightheartedly. Both of them laughed.

"Let's sit down and watch the sunset behind Adang, it's a beautiful sight. We're lucky that the weather today is sunny and clear," Malatee said. She sat down on the white sandy beach, and Knox sat beside her.

Malatee was right about the sunset. It was one of the most breathtaking sights Knox had ever seen. He admitted that he hadn't really had the chance to watch a sunset in many years. When he was in Kota Baharu, the city was on the eastern side of the Malay Peninsula, therefore, he only saw sunrises. On Tarutao, Taloh Udang Bay, where he lived, faced southward, and both sides of the bay were lined with high mountain ranges which blocked the view of both sunrise and sunset.

Today fate had been especially kind to him. Just when he'd least expected it, he found himself sitting next to a beautiful woman watching a spectacular sunset on an unspoiled beach on Tarutao.

It was so romantic. Unfortunately, there was a war on, he was still confined on this island, and this pleasant moment would soon be over. However, as Knox watched the sun slowly disappear beyond the horizon, for the first time since he'd set foot on the island he was thankful that fate had brought him to Tarutao to enjoy this moment.

After the sun had completely set, the two of them walked back to the camp in the approaching darkness.

"Malatee, tell me what is happening with the war," Knox said. "The news we receive here about the war is old and inaccurate."

"Well, from the newspapers and radio reports in Penang, it looks like the Allied forces are on the offensive in both Europe and the Pacific," Malatee said. "They have successfully driven back the Germans and the Japanese, who have been retreating after almost every battle. The Germans have been defeated in North Africa. The Allies have landed in France and Italy, and are advancing into Germany. In the Pacific, the Japanese forces have been defeated in battle after battle. Fortunately, this area is no longer a combat zone, so the people around here are not suffering from the ravages of war."

"Malatee, there is a different kind of problem here," Knox said, his face and voice suddenly serious. "Many people have been suffering from the plundering by the pirates in this area. Quite a few of them have already lost their lives. Several merchant ships from Penang have been attacked, plundered, and destroyed by pirates from Tarutao."

"Pirates from Tarutao!" Malatee exclaimed incredulously.

"You mean there are pirates on this island? That's unbelievable! This is supposed to be a penal colony."

"Believe me, Malatee. I saw one incident with my own eyes. Everyone on board, including the crew of the merchant ship, were killed by pirates."

"Who are the pirates?" Malatee asked.

"Khun Apipat and some of the guards and prisoners." Knox's reply visibly startled Malatee, who remained silent. "The two men who attacked you and your father yesterday are former British soldiers whom I believe are also involved in the piracy."

Knox paused, then spoke again, "Malatee, you and your father have to be very careful about coming here again in the future. The people on Tarutao have changed for the worse since the time that you were here years ago. Their own deteriorating condition caused by the war has made them desperate. They're willing to kill for food, it's every man for himself on this island. The piracy began with the objective of obtaining food and medicine, but now they take anything that they can sell."

"That's terrible!" Malatee said. "I take it you disagree with Khun Apipat and the pirates." She paused and continued when Knox nodded in agreement, "Will they do you any harm?"

Knox was touched by her concern. "So far they've left us alone because we haven't interfered with their operation," he replied. "Malatee, you must go to Penang and inform the authorities there about the pirates. Also tell the merchant ships not to come near Tarutao, or seek shelter here during the monsoon. The pirates will be waiting for them."

"Kevin, there hasn't been a responsible authority in Penang since the British administration ceased to function after the Japanese invasion," Malatee said. "The Japanese occupying force has contributed nothing to the welfare of the people there."

Malatee paused to cross over a log half buried in the sand, and then continued talking, "Most of the ships belong to the Chinese. They have to take care of this matter themselves. The Japanese are not going to help them, especially considering the fact that Japan is also at war with China. Besides, the Japanese suspect that many Chinese businessmen in Penang have been supporting the resistance movement against the Japanese occupation. So you see, Kevin, there is no governing authority in Penang that they can turn to for help. There, too, it's every man for himself."

The next morning they departed. Malatee and her father sailed back to Langkawi. She told Knox that she would be back to meet him at this spot in the first week of September. She would bring food and medicine for him and his men. Knox told her that he would be watching for her boat from the lookout at that time.

As Mee's small sailboat disappeared from sight, Knox, Brown, Yai, and Tam left the camp and began their long walk back to Taloh Udang Bay.

The unexpected meeting with Malatee brought Knox new pleasure in life. Before the war, Knox had dedicated himself completely to the British Army. Being a good professional soldier was the heart and soul of his life, he'd paid little or no attention to romance. On the other hand, he admitted to himself, no other woman had ever made the impression on him that exotic and beautiful Malatee had. From now on he would be counting the days until the small boat sailed across the channel from Langkawi, bringing with it the woman who had given his life new meaning and joy.

CHAPTER 12

"Collin, it works! Your idea works!" Khun Apipat sauntered into the living room of Cunningham's bungalow in Taloh Wow Bay one afternoon in early August.

Khun Apipat had had a bungalow built for the American, and another one for Hawkins and Grant, near his house so that they could easily communicate with one another.

"Khun Apipat, what happened? It must be a good news judging from the smile on your face." Cunningham had been resting, stretched out on a wooden bench, all afternoon, but he sat up when he saw the excited look on the TVTS director's face.

"It is indeed good news, Collin," Khun Apipat said as he sat down in a rattan chair. "Two months ago, you suggested that we try and recruit the clerks in the Kantang and Satun telegraph offices to work for us. You wanted them to provide us with information on movement of the merchant ships mentioned in the telegrams."

"And you're telling me you've done it?"

"Yes, Collin, we've done it!" Khun Apipat said proudly. "My son has recruited a clerk in Kantang telegraph office. And this is what we got from him."

Khun Apipat handed Cunningham a folder. The American opened it and took out several sheets of paper.

He scanned the contents quickly, and looked up at Khun Apipat with a smile.

"Can you read my son's handwriting?" Khun Apipat asked. "The clerk wouldn't give the telegrams to my son, but he allowed him to copy them."

"Your son has done a good job, Khun Apipat," Cunningham said. "My congratulations. This is exactly what we need, and it'll make our operation a lot easier and less risky. Now that we have the merchant ships' sailing dates in our hands, we'll know when to send our teams out to intercept them."

Cunningham picked out a few sheets to show Khun Apipat. "There'll be seven merchant ships sailing from Penang to Kantang in the next two weeks. We don't have to attack them all, we can select the ones that are carrying cargo we need, such as medicine, canned food, and goods that can be sold on the black market. These telegrams confirm the shipments of cargo that the merchants in Kantang have ordered. They also give details about the cargo."

Cunningham paused, then continued when he saw that Khun Apipat was listening attentively. "We also need food, especially rice, for our people here. We know that on their return trips to Penang the merchant ships usually carry rice, vegetables, and live animals. Your son can have some men observe the loading at the port in Kantang. That way we'll know exactly what they're carrying and when they're leaving. Therefore, we should allow some ships to go to Kantang peacefully, and then attack them as they return to Penang fully loaded with the food."

"Collin, your planning is ingenious!"

"As I've said before, Khun Apipat, we make a good team. My planning, your raiding teams, and the training provided by Hawkins and Grant." Cunningham grinned at the director and asked, "Now, what about the telegraph office in Satun? Any success?"

"My son is working on that now," Khun Apipat replied. "He concentrated first on Kantang because there have been more cargo movements there than in Satun."

"Ask your son to find out whether any of the ships from Penang or Kantang carries arms for self defense. I don't want any casualties on our side."

Khun Apipat laughed, "Collin, don't worry about that. The Japanese have issued a strict order that none of the ships sailing in this area, including fishing boats and merchant ships, are to carry any arms. They're concerned about the resistance movement against them. That order has effectively disarmed all the ships passing through Thai and Malay waters."

"Good. Then that's one thing I don't have to worry about just yet. Now, let's plan how to intercept these seven ships."

Cunningham and Khun Apipat spent the next hour going over their plans. When they finished, as Khun Apipat prepared to leave the room, Cunningham reminded him, "Please make sure that your men strictly follow the plans and instructions."

"Don't worry, Collin," Khun Apipat assured the American. "My standing orders are to leave no witnesses, and burn all the merchant ships. My men know that any disobedience will lead to death.

Two large merchant ships from Penang were sailing about two hundred feet apart in the twelve-mile channel between the Thai mainland and Tarutao. Wind conditions were favorable, so the captains of both ships, which belonged to the same shipping company, expected an on-time arrival in Kantang. Both ships carried medical supplies, chemicals, machine tools, and bicycle tires ordered by merchants in Songkla and Bangkok.

"Two sailboats on the port side," shouted a crewman standing at the bow of the ship sailing closer to Tarutao.

"Yes, I see them," the captain said to the crewman manning the helm. "It looks like they've come out from Tarutao and are heading in the same direction as us. Probably local fishermen."

Half an hour passed. The same crewman on the first ship shouted again, "Captain, the sailboats have changed their course. They're coming directly across our path."

"Let's see who they are," the captain said to the helmsman. He raised a pair of binoculars to look at the two sailboats and exclaimed in surprise, "They're policemen! They must be Thai policemen!"

"What are they doing out here?" the helmsman asked.

"I have no idea, but I can see their uniforms clearly," the captain replied, still looking through the binoculars. "They are signaling us to slow down. I wonder what they want."

The two sailboats were now directly in the course of the two merchant ships. The captain of the first merchant ship had to make a decision.

"I don't want any trouble with the Thai police. Since we are in their territory, we should cooperate," he said to the helmsman. "Slow down the ship and prepare to stop." The crew began to lower the sails, and the second merchant ship followed suit.

The two sailboats, each with five uniformed policemen, moved in closer to the two merchant ships. They then separated, one boat came straight toward the first ship and the other boat headed for the second ship.

"Lower the ladder! We want to board the ship!" A police sergeant standing on the bow of the boat shouted to the crew of the first ship. He was armed with a rifle and two other policemen had shotguns with them. The other two were unarmed. They were probably the crew of the boat.

"Is there anything wrong?" the captain of the first ship asked as the police sergeant and two policemen came on board.

"We've been instructed by the Japanese occupying force to search every merchant ship for arms," the sergeant said. "There have been reports of gun running in support of the resistance movement on the mainland."

"I can assure you that we are unarmed," the captain replied. "The Japanese troops in Penang searched us before we left."

"I have to follow my orders," the sergeant said sternly. He then asked, "How many in your crew?"

"Five. Six including myself," the captain answered. He was starting to feel uneasy about this encounter.

"Have them all line up here," the sergeant instructed. "I want to take a look at them."

All right. Let's do what he says, the captain thought. It shouldn't take long. We haven't done anything wrong, and we don't carry any arms. He ordered the crew to come up and line up facing the policemen.

Acting on their captain's order, the five crewmen stood in front of the three policemen. The captain stood next to the police sergeant who was holding the rifle in his right hand. Suddenly, using his free hand, the sergeant pushed the captain in the direction of the five crewmen. Before the surprised and angry crewmen could react, the three policemen pointed their weapons at them.

"We are taking over the ship, if you want to live, you won't resist," Nit said. He was the one dressed in the sergeant's uniform.

"You are policemen. You can't do this!" the captain protested.

"Yes, we can, because we're not policemen," Nit said. "Anyone can have these uniforms made and wear them." He laughed, it had almost been too easy to take control of this ship.

"What are you going to do to us?" the captain asked nervously realizing that he had been fooled by the pirates.

"Take this ship to Tarutao."

The captain looked at the second ship, it was so close he could see her captain and crew standing helplessly with their hands above their heads. The second ship had also been seized. He had no choice but to do as he was told.

The two merchant ships moved slowly into a bay north of Taloh Wow Bay, towing the two small sailboats behind them. Nit ordered the captain to stop the ship and lower the anchor. The second ship, under the control of Chim, who was also dressed in a police sergeant's uniform, did the same.

The two captains and their crews were forced at gunpoint to unload the cargo and transfer it to shore aboard the sailboats. After all the cargo had been unloaded, the captains and crews were ordered to return to their own ships.

As the captain and crew of the first ship were about to sit down and rest, the sound of repeated gunfire from the second ship stunned them. They looked on in horror as the dead bodies of their colleagues sprawled on the deck of the second ship.

The captain of the first ship turned to Nit and shouted angrily at him, "You said that you wouldn't harm us if we cooperated. You are a liar and a murderer!"

With uncontrolled rage, the captain sprang at Nit, who alertly stepped aside. As the momentum carried the captain forward, Nit struck him forcefully on the chin with the rifle butt. The captain dropped unconscious to the deck of his ship.

A crewman rushed forward to help his captain, but before he could do anything, he was hit hard in the stomach with a shotgun butt by another pirate. He writhed on the deck, clutching his stomach. The guard followed up, with a knock out blow to the chin from the shotgun butt. The other crewmen were held back by a shotgun-wielding pirate in police uniform.

Nit smiled grimly and spoke to the unconscious captain, "It was your own fault, you believed the word of a pirate." He looked across at the second ship and shook his head as he talked to his men. "I don't know why Chim wasted bullets on them. He should have done it my way. The result is the same."

Nit paused for a few seconds and then ordered his men, "Tie them up in pairs. Hurry! Tie the captain with him." He pointed to the unconscious crewman. Then he gave another order which shocked the crew of the first ship, "Tie the ship's anchor to the captain's body and throw them all overboard."

The crew pleaded and cursed as they realized what their fate was to be. Nit and his men paid no attention to them as they chained the victims together. They then threw the captain and crewman, both tied to the ship's extra anchor, into the sea. The combined weight of the two men and the anchor pulled the other four men, who were tied in pairs, down with them. The four unfortunate men gave their last cries as their bodies rapidly descended to the bottom of the bay.

Nit looked at the spot where the bodies went down until

he was satisfied that they were all dead. Then he turned
to his men and gave a last order: "Burn the ship!"

"Khun Apipat, let's celebrate, we've done well in the
last five months," Cunningham said. He handed the TVTS
director a glass of whiskey taken from one of the ships
that they had plundered.

"Yes, and the most important thing is that we haven't
suffered any casualties," Khun Apipat said. "And we
didn't leave any witnesses or evidence. Every ship we
attacked was burned to ashes."

"Are you certain about the witnesses?" Cunningham
asked.

"Very certain," Khun Apipat replied. "The men were
thrown into the sea with the ship's anchor tied to them.
They all drowned and were eventually eaten by sharks.
There are enormous numbers of sharks around Tarutao.
It's the most efficient way to get rid of witnesses."

Khun Apipat paused to sip his whiskey, and continued,
"Don't worry,Collin, everything has gone according to
plan. We owe it all to your clever and careful planning.
It was ingenious of you to have our men dress up in police
uniforms. That was very shrewd. Otherwise, I don't know
what else could have made all the merchant ships stop and
allow our men to board them so easily."

"We couldn't have done it without your permission to
spend money on improving the efficiency of our operation,"
Cunningham said. "The purchase of another sailboat and
some police uniforms were well worth it. Although,
truthfully, I would have preferred a motor boat to a sailboat."

"But the motor boat is much more expensive, Collin,"
Khun Apipat said. "We should wait until next year, when
we have more money." Khun Apipat paused to sip the
whiskey again, and then asked, "How many ships have we

attacked so far?"

"From the middle of August to the middle of December, twenty-one ships. I expect we'll have to attack more next year when the Allies control the sea routes in the Atlantic, Pacific, and Indian Oceans. More goods will be arriving from Europe and the United States."

Cunningham refilled his glass and Khun Apipat's. He looked out the window towards the prisoner compound and asked, "How is our food holding out? Have we got the malaria under control?"

"Things are much better now, Collin, thanks to our clever planning," Khun Apipat said. "We've ended the food shortages, and we have two months rice in stock. The medical supplies, especially the quinine tablets which we now have in abundance, have enabled us to contain the malaria epidemic. The death toll has been gradually reduced over the past two months."

"Your Director-General would be proud of you," Cunningham said with a smile. "You've done exactly what he told you to do. Use any resource available. Use your own initiatives. You've done both." They laughed loudly at their deviousness.

"Collin, I don't think he'd approve of our methods."

"Well, Khun Apipat, you can't win them all, but at least we're still alive and well. We can repent our sins later, first we have to survive. If the Director-General had had to face the same situation we did, he probably would have done the same things we did."

Cunningham took another sip then asked, "By the way, how is your son doing? He is quite important to our operation."

"He's well and very cautious just as you've warned him to be," Khun Apipat replied. "I've told him to be alert for any police investigations. Losing so many ships and

so much cargo must have alarmed a lot people, especially
the ship owners and their customers."

"It pays to be careful, Khun Apipat. Better safe than
sorry. Tell that to your son, and tell him never to forget
it."

CHAPTER 13

The city of Songkla in southern Thailand was enjoying a fine January morning. Colonel Banchongsak, commandant of Thai Provincial Police Zone 9, which covered the five southern provinces of Songkla, Pattani, Yala, Naratiwat, and Satun, heard a knock at his office door, and looked up from the documents he was reading. A police sergeant came in and informed him that two businessmen had arrived to see him. The Colonel nodded his permission for them to enter.

The two men walked into the room, one of them was Charn, a well-known merchant in Songkla and a long-time acquaintance of the Colonel. The Colonel did not know or recognize the other visitor.

"Colonel, this is Suchart, a friend of mine, he is a merchant in Satun. We have a problem we would like to discuss with you." Charn and his friend sat down opposite the police chief.

"Charn, Suchart, how are you? What's the problem?" the Colonel asked.

"Suchart and I ordered goods from Penang several months ago but we never received them," Charn explained. "We sent people down to Penang to find out what happened. The goods left for Kantang months ago on merchant vessels, but when we checked with the port of Kantang, we learned that the ships had never arrived there. Presumably they were lost at sea en route."

"Could they have been destroyed by the monsoons?" the police chief interrupted.

"That's unlikely, Colonel," Charn replied. "The captains and crews of those ships were experienced seamen. They knew what to do if the ships ran into monsoons. Even if they capsized because of the storms, there would probably still be survivors, debris from the ships, and even cargo washed ashore, because they were not sailing that far from the mainland. But there was nothing. The ships, the crew, and the cargo just disappeared. I've asked around and found out that not only has our cargo been missing, but other merchants are also missing shipments."

Charn paused to clear his throat before continuing, "We believe that those ships were attacked by pirates who took the cargo and sank the ships."

"And the crews must have all been killed," Suchart added.

"I've been receiving reports of ships lost at sea, but none have mentioned pirates," the Colonel said.

"Other strange things have happened, Colonel," Charn said. "Although the merchants who ordered goods and materials from Penang have never received their goods, and only a few ships have come in from Penang during the past six months, goods from Penang have been sold in the markets in Satun, Kantang, Hat Yai, and even Songkla. How did they get there?"

"Charn, if there are pirates, where did they come from?" the police chief asked. "They must have bases, or at least one base, where they keep their ships, their men, and the stolen goods."

Suchart voiced his opinion, "There are many islands

between Kantang and Penang, it could be one of them."

Colonel Banchongsak thought for a few seconds, and then said, "We've been keeping track of all the ships in this area. The Government in Bangkok, which received the request from the Japanese, has instructed us to inspect all ships entering and leaving the ports on both sides of the Peninsula. They're concerned that the Allies might run arms and supplies to resistance movements in Malaya and Thailand. We've also inspected all the islands we thought might harbor ships and provide hideouts for men and arms. But we've found nothing."

"In that case, Colonel, we believe that the pirates must have come from Tarutao," Charn said. "As you know, Tarutao is a prison with over two thousand inmates, criminals of all kinds. They must have done it with or without the knowledge of the prison's director and guards."

"That is a strong accusation, Charn," the Colonel retorted. "For something that serious we'd need hard evidence. But I agree that you may be right about the cause of the missing ships, crews, and shipments. I'll look into the matter immediately."

One week later, a police lieutenant reported to Colonel Banchongsak. "Colonel, as you ordered, I checked with the Satun police chief about the possibility of pirates on Tarutao. He didn't believe it. He said that a man like Khun Apipat would never allow it to happen. He has known Khun Apipat for many years, he was stationed in Chiangrai when Khun Apipat was the warden of the prison there. He assured me that Khun Apipat would never become involved in piracy."

"Then we'll have to take the Satun police chief's word for it," the Colonel said. "Charn could be wrong about this."

"He is not totally wrong, Colonel."

"What do you mean?"

"Well, frankly, I didn't completely believe the Satun police chief," the lieutenant replied. "Something tells me he could be covering up for Khun Apipat. After all, they've been friends for years. So I decided that I should talk to someone else."

"Any better results?"

"Yes, Colonel."

The Colonel became immediately interested, and he listened attentively as the lieutenant continued, "I talked to a police sergeant in Satun whom I've known for a long time and think can be trusted. He confirmed what Charn told you about the goods being sold in this area. He said you can find large quantities of canned food, medicine, bicycle tires, spare parts, and even some chemicals on the black market throughout the South."

"That's interesting. I take back what I said about Charn."

"I've asked the sergeant to find out who has been selling these goods and where they were obtained."

"That's a good start, Lieutenant. We'll have to set up a special investigations unit to probe deeper into this piracy issue. Judging from what you told me, if we rely on cooperation from the Satun police chief, it may jeopardize our investigation."

"Sir, I absolutely agree, in fact, I think we should bypass the whole Satun police force, and do it on our own."

"I'll ask Charn to send some of his people to the black market to buy some of the goods. It's natural for a merchant like him to do that. I want to know the distribution channels and supply sources of those goods."

"Colonel, I've also learned from a few ship owners in Kantang that some of their ships carrying foodstuffs to

Penang never returned. They checked with Penang, and were shocked to find out that their ships had never even arrived in Penang. If these incidents continue, it won't be long before they come to see you with complaints."

"Did they also believe that their ships were attacked by pirates?"

"They certainly did. But they believe that the pirates come out of Langkawi rather than Tarutao. Langkawi is more isolated and has several bays and coves ideal for pirate hideouts."

The Colonel sat in silence for a moment before speaking, "This is getting more complicated. We can't just limit our search for pirates to Tarutao. They could be Malay pirates from Langkawi. In the old days, before the British took over Malaya, Langkawi was known as a safe-haven for pirates in the Andaman Sea. Maybe because there is no authority to enforce the law at the moment, piracy has returned."

One week later, Charn hurried into Colonel Banchongsak's office exclaiming, "Colonel, it's finally happened! Your plan has worked!"

"Tell me what happened, Charn," the Colonel responded.

Charn took a seat in front of the Colonel's desk. "Two days ago my men made contact with a merchant in Satun who had chemicals and other goods to sell," he reported. "Several months ago I'd ordered five barrels of caustic soda from Penang for a factory in Songkla. But, the caustic soda never arrived. So I checked with my supplier in Penang who told me that they had loaded five barrels of caustic soda on a merchant ship called the LUCKY LADY which left Penang in June of last year. That ship never reached Kantang and no one knows what happened to her. She just disappeared at sea without a trace."

Charn cleared his throat, then continued, "The shipping agent inquired further and confirmed that the LUCKY LADY had passed Langkawi, and was headed into Thai water. Therefore, she must have disappeared somewhere between Satun and Kantang."

"Any chance she was destroyed by a storm?" the Colonel asked.

"No, Colonel, I have proof that the ship must have been plundered and the cargo taken from her," Charn said seriously.

"Go ahead, I'm listening." The Colonel became enthusiastic.

"The five barrels of caustic soda had serial numbers written on each of them," Charn disclosed, pleased that he finally had the proof to convince the police chief of the piracy. "I had the supplier in Penang telegraph the numbers to me. When my men asked the Satun merchant if they could see the merchandise, they were shown five barrels which contained caustic soda. They discreetly checked the serial numbers on the five barrels. And guess what, Colonel? The numbers on the barrels matched the ones in this telegram."

Charn handed the telegram to Colonel Banchongsak, who looked at it with interest. "Colonel, this telegram is the evidence that those particular barrels of caustic soda were shipped to me. However, I don't know how those barrels of caustic soda happened to leave the LUCKY LADY and end up in this merchant's warehouse in Satun. It's strange considering that the LUCKY LADY herself never reached Kantang or Satun."

"What's the name of the merchant who has your caustic sodas?"the Colonel asked.

"His name is Tamrong. Do you know him, Colonel?" Charn replied. A smile had appeared on the Colonel's face.

"Charn, if this merchant, Tamrong, is the same man whom I know, then we should get something out of him. He owes me a favor."

"Good, because I've already asked Tamrong to come here," Charn said, satisfied now that the Colonel believed him. "I sent a message to him that I wanted to negotiate the purchase of the caustic sodas, but that I didn't feel well. I asked him to come to Songkla and meet me if he wanted to sell his merchandise. He agreed to come here tomorrow morning. Colonel, please talk to him and find out where he got my caustic sodas."

"All right, I'll talk to him," the police chief said. "I want to know who supplied him with the caustic soda too. That person must be the pirates' accomplice."

"It's a trap! I shouldn't have come here!" Tamrong exclaimed when he saw Colonel Banchongsak who, out of uniform and in casual dress, walked into his hotel room in Songkla with Charn.

"Tamrong, it's all right. I just want to talk to you and ask you some questions." The Colonel tried to calm the nervous merchant down.

"Charn here told me that the caustic soda you've offered to sell to him was actually ordered by him from Penang several months ago. He has the evidence to prove it." Colonel Banchongsak went straight to the point. "You can trust me. I've gotten you out of trouble like this before. Do you remember?"

The Colonel paused as Tamrong solemnly nodded in submissive affirmation. He then continued, "I want to know where and from whom you got the caustic soda. Tamrong, believe me, this case is far more serious than the one that you were involved in before. You could be

in a lot of trouble if you don't cooperate. Now tell me
who sold you the caustic soda."

Tamrong looked at the Colonel with pleading eyes. He
appeared worried as he nervously said, "Colonel, you have
to protect me if I cooperate because the people involved
are very mean and quite influential. They can easily have
me killed."

"All right, we'll protect you. Now tell me," the Colonel
said firmly.

Tamrong hesitated for a few moments, then said, "I
bought the caustic soda from the son of Khun Apipat, the
director of Tarutao prison." Colonel Banchongsak and
Charn smiled triumphantly as Tamrong continued, "But he
didn't tell me where or how he obtained the caustic soda,
and I dared not ask. He also has a lot of automobile and
bicycle tires for sale."

"Very good, Tamrong. That's just the information we
need," the Colonel said with satisfaction. "Now, Tamrong,
listen to me. For your own safety, and to keep Khun
Apipat's son satisfied, you must sell the caustic soda to
Charn. But don't make too much profit out of it because
those goods originally belonged to him."

Tamrong nodded and remained silent. The Colonel
continued, "I want you to continue contacting Khun Apipat's
son. Show an interest in doing more business with him.
Tell him that you'll find buyers for any goods that he may
have in stock. If he's willing, get him to take you to see
where he keeps his merchandise."

There was a pause. Colonel Banchongsak continued
when he saw a worried look on Tamrong's face. "Don't
worry, Tamrong. You'll be all right, if you do what I've
said. Right now I just want information. We won't rush
to arrest him anytime soon. I want to have enough evidence
so that we can arrest all the pirates at the same time once

and for all, including Khun Apipat if it can be proven that he is really involved."

"Colonel, please handle the whole thing carefully. I have to live in Satun, and Khun Apipat is very influential there, even though he himself is on Tarutao. Whatever your plan is, don't involve the Satun police force. And another thing, please keep our meeting a secret."

"Don't worry so much, Tamrong," the Colonel said soothingly. "Only Charn and I will ever know of this meeting. You just act naturally and continue doing what you normally do. You'll be fine."

Satisfied with the meeting with Tamrong, Colonel Banchongsak and Charn left the room together. As they walked down to the lobby of the hotel and headed for the front door, they passed a group of men leisurely reading newspapers on the lobby's sofas. A man in a flowered shirt lowered his newspaper and looked suspiciously at Colonel Banchongsak. He obviously recognized the police chief, and was surprised to see the Colonel out of uniform and in this hotel. It was his duty to be alert. He was a former policeman, recently discharged from the Satun police force. In his new job, he had been assigned by Khun Apipat's son to keep an eye on Tamrong.

"I've managed to sell the caustic soda I bought from you to a merchant in Songkla," Tamrong told Sanoh, Khun Apipat's son. It had been two days since he returned to Satun from Songkla.

"Good. I hope you've made some profit," Sanoh said. He was in his late twenties, and resembled Khun Apipat, but with darker, curlier hair.

"I have a buyer who is interested in automobile and bicycle tires. You once mentioned that you have plenty of those in stock," Tamrong said.

"Yes, I still do."

"Would it be possible for me to inspect them before deciding whether to buy them?" Tamrong asked.

"Certainly. They are kept on an island," Sanoh replied with a friendly smile. "We have to go there by boat. It's not that far from Satun. If you want, we can go there tomorrow morning. The sea is usually very calm in early February, so don't worry." Sanoh emphasized the last sentences when he noticed a concerned look in Tamrong's eyes.

A thirty-five foot motor boat with a single inboard engine left its berth on a canal at the outskirts of Satun. It followed the wide canal out into the Andaman Sea. Once on the sea, its captain increased the speed, heading in the direction of Tarutao. There were six men on board, Tamrong, Sanoh and his two men, the captain and a crewman.

The sea was as calm as Sanoh had promised Tamrong it would be. A light breeze invigorated Tamrong and Sanoh as they stood at the bow of the boat. Despite the increasing heat from the late morning sun, they enjoyed the fresh sea air.

Tamrong was engrossed in the scenic views of Langkawi to his left, and Tarutao directly in front of him in the distance. He did not notice Sanoh's men sneaking up behind him. One of the men had on a flowered shirt. The other man, large and muscular, picked up the anchor rope with both hands. He put the rope around Tamrong's neck, tightened it, and brought the merchant to his knees.

Caught by surprise, Tamrong thought he was suffocating. He tried in vain to unwrap the rope from his neck. As his sight blurred, he could see Sanoh nodding his head. The man holding the rope loosened it just enough to let

Tamrong breathe in small sips of air. Tamrong coughed and gasped for air.

"Tell me what you told Colonel Banchongsak in Songkla three days ago. I know that you saw him, don't deny it," demanded Sanoh, no longer smiling, and far from being friendly.

"I didn't say anything about our association. I've known the Colonel for many years. When he heard that I was in town, he came to see me, to talk about old times," Tamrong replied, hoping his answer would convince Sanoh.

But Sanoh was not satisfied with the reply. He gave another nod, this time with a grimmer face. The man with the muscles not only tightened the rope to choke Tamrong, but also tied the rest of the rope twice around Tamrong's body, pinning his arms to his sides. The man in the flowered shirt helped throw Tamrong's body over the railing into the sea with the anchor.

The captain slowed down the boat until it finally stopped. They waited until the rope, which shook for about half a minute, became completely still, indicating that Tamrong's struggling had ended. The man with the flowered shirt then cut the rope tied to the anchor.

"Well, I needed a new anchor anyway," Sanoh said with a soft laugh. He then shouted to the captain, "Let's go to Tarutao."

Sanoh told Khun Apipat what he had done, explaining, "Father, I had to make a decision. You've always told me we're better safe than sorry."

"From now on, we have to be more careful where and to whom we distribute our goods. With Tamrong missing, the police will be more discreet in their investigation. I don't think they'll give up just because they lost one informant," Cunningham said to the group in Khun Apipat's office.

Khun Apipat had summoned Cunningham, Hawkins, and Grant to meet with him and his son and told them what had happened.

Cunningham continued, "I knew that sooner or later the police would be brought in to investigate the missing merchant ships. Khun Apipat, I think you should establish some contacts in Bangkok to sell the merchandise there. From Bangkok, it'll be difficult to trace where the goods came from. I'm not concerned about the Satun police, I know you can handle them. But the Zone 9 police based in Songkla also have jurisdiction over this area, and Satun is too close to Tarutao."

"Maybe we should try to divert their attention somewhere else," Hawkins suggested.

"The Hawk is right," Cunningham said. He had taken to calling Hawkins "the Hawk," which he said was an appropriate name for a leader of pirates. "So far the police have no proof or evidence to connect the goods sold on the mainland to us. The piracy story is just another rumor. However, I think the police will continue the investigation, because this many missing merchant ships can't go unaccounted for forever. Sooner or later, the ship and cargo owners will complain to the authorities. Therefore, as the Hawk has suggested, we have to divert the police's attention from Tarutao."

"Does anyone have any suggestions?" Khun Apipat asked.

"What about Langkawi?" Cunningham said. "I believe it's the most appropriate place, considering the fact there are about one hundred islands around Langkawi. All of you must know that the Japanese returned the administration of the four northern Malay states, including Langkawi, to Thailand in 1943. However, the Thai authorities have yet to refamiliarize themselves with Langkawi and its surrounding islands."

Seeing that every one was listening attentively, the American continued, "We have to focus attention on Langkawi by having our ships sail there occasionally. We'll find an island or a cove there to set up a decoy base. We can even send some people to stay there temporarily and build some huts. And we can store some of the less valuable items there to satisfy the police in case they decide to raid the place."

"That's very clever, Collin. I like that idea," Khun Apipat said.

"That's not all I have in mind, Khun Apipat. There's one more thing we have to consider," Cunningham said. "We have to find a new place to store our goods. We can no longer store them in the warehouse in the TVTS compound because the police may decide to drop by one day to have a look. We have to find some caves on Tarutao to hide the goods. And again, I still believe that the fewer people who know about this the better. So, you should assign your most trusted men to look for a new storage site, and move the goods there as soon as possible. Hawkins, Grant, and I will also look around."

"Collin, there is another factor that we should consider," Hawkins added. "As you know, the southwest monsoon season has been over for a few months, and the Andaman Sea will be calm from now until May. Although we believe the Thai authorities still don't take the story of piracy very seriously, I think people in the shipping business know what really happened. Therefore, they'll try to avoid sailing close to Tarutao and the mainland because there is no need to seek shelter from the monsoon until May. I've noticed lately that only a few small ships still sail in the channel between the mainland and Tarutao. The larger ships, on the other hand, have been using the route further out, thinking that it's safer out in the open, deeper sea."

"What are you driving at, Hawk?" Cunningham asked.

"I'm getting there, Collin. I think we should set up another base some place other than Tarutao, and I don't mean Langkawi."

"Where do you suggest that someplace else be?" Khun Apipat asked.

"Adang island, or one of the other islands near it," Hawkins replied. "The Adang group of islands are strategically located for our purposes. They're on the route that the big merchant ships are now taking. Only harmless Sea Gypsies have set up villages there, so the merchant ships believe that they'll be safer seeking shelter there, rather than Tarutao."

"You've been doing your homework, Hawk," Cunningham complimented.

"I picked up this information talking to the guards and prisoners who are familiar with this area," Hawkins said. "If you'll permit us, Khun Apipat, I would like to take some men to explore Adang and the nearby islands to find a suitable place to set up a base there."

"Well, I agree with the Hawk," Cunningham said. "It'll make our operation more effective because we'll control the sea on both sides of Tarutao, and even beyond Adang. We have enough men to set up another base on Adang. What we need are more ships to facilitate our own communications, and use in our operation, which will certainly increase in the future. So from now on, we shouldn't immediately destroy any captured ship. If we think that a certain ship is useful to us, we should keep her."

"Collin, I'm impressed by your ambitious mind and

daring plan. You always think big and are willing to accept any consequences that may occur," Khun Apipat said, smiling with admiration at the American.

"I believe in the old saying : 'fortune favors the bold.' Those who were daring made history. And now I that have every opportunity in the world to make my dreams come true, I will not fail." Cunningham had quietly drawn up a plan of his own to expand his domain from the single plot of land that he had discovered on Langkawi, to include the three groups of islands belonging to Langkawi, Tarutao, and Adang.

CHAPTER 14

The three-masted SEA DRAGON, her sails full of easterly wind, moved sped westward toward the island of Adang. She had been idle in the year since she and her crew were captured and held captive on Tarutao. Her teak hull danced against the waves, full of life and spirit, her sails, still in good condition, welcomed the feeling of the wind. She was testing the strength of her hull and sails in preparation for the task that her new master had in mind. She was to become the flagship of the pirates of Tarutao.

"I'm so glad to be out of there. We've been on Tarutao for almost three years, and I'm so sick and tired of it," Hawkins said to Grant. They were standing on the deck of the SEA DRAGON, behind the helm station.

Hawkins had convinced Khun Apipat to allow him to sail the SEA DRAGON to Adang. Khun Apipat, who liked Hawkins's plan, could not refuse because she was the only available ship.

Hawkins had been doing some planning of his own, and he needed command of a ship capable of sailing on a long voyage. He had had his eyes on the SEA DRAGON for some time, and had been looking for an opportunity to test her on the sea. He had recruited the SEA DRAGON's four original crewmen, and convinced Khun Apipat to release them from confinement long enough to be his crew on this trip to Adang.

"I have to hand it to you, Hawk, I don't know how you were able to convince Khun Apipat to allow us to leave Tarutao," Grant said. He took a deep breath of fresh sea air. "It was clever of you to think of using Adang as another base for our operation."

"Well, I've given Khun Apipat good reasons why we have to explore Adang, and if we wait too long to make a decision, it'll be too late to do anything. It'll take a month or more to explore Adang and the nearby islands. If we happen to find the right site to set up a base, then we'll have to spend more time clearing the land and building living quarters. By the time we finish, it'll be almost monsoon season again. We have to get everything ready before the monsoons come. So, Khun Apipat agreed, and here we are, out of Tarutao, and away from that clever Cunningham."

"I thought you liked Cunningham. You get along well with him," Grant said, astonished by Hawkins's remark about the American.

"Like him? Do you think he likes us? No, sir, definitely not. He's been using everyone, including Khun Apipat, to make himself rich. When the time comes, I'll bet anything that he'll walk away, or rather sail away, alone with all the money. I can read him like a book. No, Cunningham thinks that we're just his stupid goons, but I've been doing some planning of my own. Let him think that way for now. In the end, we'll see who'll have the last laugh."

"So, are you going to tell me about your plan, Hawk?" Grant asked.

"Yes, you're the only person I can trust," the Hawk replied. "While Cunningham has his eyes on Langkawi and Tarutao for this empire he's been dreaming about, we've got to find a place of our own. I've found that place, Grant. It's Adang. Its location is perfect for us because it's far from the mainland. I don't think the British authorities will find us there."

"What about Knox and his men?" Grant interrupted. "They'll know where to find us, or they'll figure out where we are."

"I don't intend to let them leave Tarutao alive!" Hawkins said grimly, his voice serious at the mention of Knox's name.

"Tell me why you've chosen Adang to be our hideaway," Grant asked, bringing Hawkins back to his plan.

"From Adang it's an easy sail to Burma, Thailand, Malaya, Sumatra, even all the way to India," the Hawk explained. "Adang's high mountain is a perfect vantage point, we'll be able to see for miles. We'll be able to spot arriving ships from any distance, and decide whether to stand and fight, or leave the island. I plan to have a ship standing by, loaded with provisions for a long sea journey."

"I thought you liked fighting," Grant commented.

"Only if I have a chance of winning. I certainly won't fight to my death. I'm still too young to think of dying. That was why we broke out of the Kota Baharu stockade in the first place, remember? I believe in the saying that "he who fights and runs away may live to fight another day'."

"Nothing's wrong with that," Grant agreed. "Life is full of opportunities. Look at us, here we are out of Tarutao while Cunningham, Knox, and his men are still there."

"I've been following the development of the wars in both Europe and Asia," Hawkins said. "It's only a matter of months before the Germans decide to surrender. When that happens, the Allies will concentrate their efforts on Japan, which won't last long either. As a victor in the war, the British will certainly return to rule Burma, Malaya, and Singapore. She may even consider planting the Union Jack also on Thailand."

Hawkins looked beyond the bow of the SEA DRAGON. The island of Adang appeared before them, shaped like a monstrous crocodile stretched across the horizon. From the distance it seemed like it was about to devour its prey, the small island of Lipe lying to the south of Adang. Behind Adang, blocked from view by a high mountain, sat the islands of Rawi and Butang.

"So from now, until the war ends, we have to think only of ourselves," Hawkins continued, revealing his plan to Grant. "We'll collect as much loot as we can for ourselves from passing merchant ships. When the war finally ends, we'll be well-off enough to settle down somewhere safe from the British authorities. What do you think of it?"

"And I've always thought Cunningham was the clever one. You certainly have one up on him, Hawk," Grant said in admiration of his fellow fugitive.

Hawkins gave a satisfied laugh at Grant's remark. He continued, "Cunningham will be fighting with Khun Apipat over the fortune they've hoarded on Tarutao. I'm willing to bet anything that right now, Cunningham is scheming to confiscate most, if not all, the fortune from Khun Apipat, who I don't think is that stupid. As a matter of fact, I think Khun Apipat is a good match for Cunningham. He's clever and ruthless. And his son is a cold-blooded murderer and the greediest person I've ever seen. Cunningham won't have an easy time."

He looked at Grant and continued, "That's why we're not touching any of the fortune on Tarutao. There's plenty of wealth out here for us to take for ourselves. When the war ends, there will be even more goods flowing into this area, the kinds of things people really need and are willing to pay high prices for. And, my friend, we'll be ready to intercept them."

"What about the guards and prisoners Khun Apipat has assigned to watch us?" Grant asked with concern. "They'll report our activities Khun Apipat."

"Don't worry, Grant, these men are robbers and thieves. They're not loyal to anyone, not to Khun Apipat, not to us. They're greedy. So, we'll satisfy their greed and convince them that they'll gain more by working with us than by risking their lives for Khun Apipat and getting little, or maybe nothing at all, in return. They're not that difficult to handle."

As the SEA DRAGON was approaching the mile-wide channel that ran between Adang and Lipe, Hawkins shouted in Thai for the helmsman to take the ship into the channel and head for Lipe.

"I want to take a look at Lipe first. It's the smallest of the four islands, so it won't take long to explore. Besides, I was told that the Sea Gypsy village on Lipe is bigger than the one on Adang," Hawkins said.

"And the bigger the village is, the more women there are, right? I know what you are after, Hawk. It's not just the wealth," Grant interrupted with a knowing grin.

"You're right, Grant. All the wealth in the world would be worthless if there were no women. I still can't get over the opportunity we missed with that pretty Sea Gypsy girl on Tarutao. If that damned Knox hadn't spoiled it for us, we could have enjoyed her again and again. If I find her on Adang or Lipe, Grant, nothing is going to stop me from having her," Hawkins said.

The SEA DRAGON dropped anchor in the channel about three hundred feet from Lipe.

Lipe was small, only a mile and a half long, and less than a mile wide. There were no high mountains on Lipe, like on Adang and Rawi, only small hills, which dotted the length of the island. Overall, compared to the other islands, Lipe was fairly flat. There was ample land for a few hundred Sea Gypsies to build their huts.

Half the island was surrounded by sandy beaches lined with rows of tall coconut trees that served as protective windbreaks for the villages further inland. To Hawkins and the men on the SEA DRAGON, this picturesque little island was a sharp contrast from the grim environment on Tarutao.

Hawkins, Grant, four prisoners and Chim, the guard who captured the SEA DRAGON a year earlier, boarded a dinghy. With two prisoners rowing, the dinghy headed for Lipe, the largest Sea Gypsy community in the southern Andaman Sea.

"Sea Gypsies" was the English name for the nomads who traveled in small wooden canoes from island to island in the Andaman Sea. They ranged from Indonesia to Burma, and were known by different names in several languages. They were called "Selang" by the Burmese, "Orang Laut" or "Orang Selat" by the Malays, "Badjo," "Barak," or "Rayat" by the Indonesians, and "Rayat" or "Kuala" in Eastern Sumatra. The Thais called them "Chao Lay" meaning sea people. All these names mentioned the association of these people with the sea.

There were three groups of Sea Gypsies in the Andaman Sea. The southern group was called the Urak Lawoi, and they lived on Lipe and Adang. The other two groups, the Moken and the Moklen, were found mostly on the island of Phuket and the two Surin islands in the northern Andaman Sea near Burma.

In 1909, as the colonial powers expanded their quest for territories in Southeast Asia, Thailand, which was still called Siam at the time, surrendered her territorial rights over the four northern Malay states of Kelantan, Kedah, Perlis, and Terengganu to Great Britain. This was in exchange for a loan of four million pounds sterling at four percent interest and Great Britain's surrender of extraterritorial rights over her subjects in Thailand. But Thailand remained concerned that her possession of Adang, Lipe, Rawi, and Butang, in the Andaman Sea, would be threatened by the British rule of the four northern Malay states.

As a preventive measure, in 1909, King Rama V instructed the governor of Satun province to persuade the Sea Gypsies of the Urak Lawoi group, who were scattered over several islands in the southern Andaman Sea, to settle on the islands of Adang and Lipe. Once the large community of Sea Gypsies, who were Thai nationals, settled on Adang and Lipe, Thailand could rightly claim control over the two islands, and the nearby islands. Faced with this move, the British agreed to recognize Thailand's rights over Adang, Lipe, Rawi, and Butang, which were thirty nautical miles away from Langkawi.

The dinghy landed on a white, sandy beach on the north side of the island.

"Better leave our weapons in the dinghy," Chim, who'd visited Lipe a few times before, said, "The Sea Gypsies are peaceful and friendly, and I don't want to antagonize them by carrying weapons around."

Hawkins nodded in agreement as he took the pistol from his belt and laid it on the floor of the dinghy. Grant and the others followed suit with their rifles and shotguns.

As they walked up the beach, a dozen small, brown-skinned, naked children ran from the village to greet them. Their features resembled the Malayans but they had curly dark brown hair. The children were cheerful and excited to have visitors. Hawkins felt relaxed and playful. He ran his hands through the curly hair of a few boys as they thronged around him.

"The man standing in front of the others is the village chief," Chim said as they walked up to the waiting crowd.

Hawkins saw an elderly man standing a few paces in front of a group of men and women. All the men, including the village chief, were naked from the waist up. Most of them wore dark colored calf-length trousers, and some wore sarongs. All the women were wrapped in sarongs from the waist down. Most of the women were bare-breasted, but a few of the younger women wore white blouses.

"Grant, this is paradise! Look at those breasts!" Hawkins said as he kept staring at the women.

"Take it easy, Hawk, we just got here. Let's find some food first, I'm hungry," Grant said.

Chim came closer to Hawkins and Grant and whispered to them, "Don't pay attention to the bare-breasted ones. They are already married, despite their youth. Sea Gypsy girls are usually married at the age of sixteen or seventeen. It's traditional for the married ones to be bare-breasted. Only the unmarried girls still wear blouses."

Hawkins looked at the women and sighed. He whispered back to Chim, "I like them when they are young and experienced. Besides, the ones with blouses on are either homely or still too young and not even ripe for plucking. Better find me a widow, but not one too old or ugly."

As they approached the Sea Gypsies, Hawkins glanced around to see if he could spot the woman that he'd met on Tarutao. But to his disappointment, she was not there.

Hawkins asked himself, "Who was she, and where did she come from?"

He also did not see the old man who was with her on Tarutao. Maybe they were somewhere in the village, or even on Adang, he'd try to find out later on.

The Sea Gypsy chief and villagers welcomed the men from Tarutao, inviting them to sit on rattan mats under the shade of a group of tall coconut trees. The Sea Gypsies served them sweet, refreshing coconut juice, and fed them freshly caught spiny lobsters and fish. They sat surrounding the men from Tarutao and smiled as their visitors devoured the meal that they'd prepared.

With his hunger sated, Hawkins began eyeing a few of the good looking girls with slender bodies and firm breasts. Grant, noticing Hawk's stares, spoke to the big man in English.

"We've all finished eating, now let's have a look around. Don't spoil everything on our first visit, Hawk. We need to stay friendly with these people. We still have plenty of time."

"All right, Grant. Let's go then, if I continue looking at these women for five more minutes, something is going to happen. Don't forget, Grant, I haven't been with a woman in years."

Hawkins forced himself to get up. The others followed. Thanking the village chief and the other Sea Gypsies for the food, they walked towards the dinghy.

CHAPTER 15

The series of screams that echoed through the darkness of the cave stopped Cunningham and his small expedition party in their tracks. They raised their torches, trying in vain to see the source of the screams, worried that they might be coming from the two prisoners who went into the cave ahead of them.

After Hawkins and his team left to explore the Adang group of islands, Cunningham, with Khun Apipat's permission, left the TVTS compound with two guards and four prisoners. They were going to search for a suitable place on Tarutao to hide the loot that they had stolen. From Taloh Wow Bay, they walked north along mountain ridges for about four miles, when they spotted a large opening at the base of a mountain. They decided to go in and have a look.

Cunningham sent two prisoners with torches into the cave as advance scouts while he and the rest of the party followed at some distance behind them. As they went deeper, the cave became wider, its floor, walls and ceiling covered with limestone. Limestone stalactites of various shapes and sizes hung from the ceiling, some of them almost touched the floor. From the floor, columns of limestone stalagmites rose upward, some of them joining the stalactites. As they stood admiring the cave's natural wonders, they heard the screams.

They rushed in the direction of the terrifying sounds, shotguns and knives at the ready, but were shocked by the gruesome sight that met their eyes.

Fifteen paces from where they stood, the floor of the cave ended in a stream. There, in a pool of blood, two adult crocodiles were having a tug-of-war with the apparently lifeless body of one of the prisoners. One crocodile had its strong jaws on the unfortunate prisoner's neck, while the other one had clamped its jaws onto one of his legs. Slowly both crocodiles dragged the body along the floor of the cave, and into the stream, where they finally disappeared. Nearby another group of young crocodiles tore apart the blood covered body of another prisoner.

The whole ghastly scene lasted less than a minute. As the stunned group watched, the crocodiles, and the bodies of their two victims, disappeared into the deep stream.

Cunningham and his remaining men stood motionless, looking at the horrifying scene and then at one another.

"What are we going to do now?" Karn asked in a shaky voice. "We can't continue this way, this stream is infested with maneating crocodiles."

"Actually, this place is the most suitable spot to hide our loot," Cunningham replied, looking around the cave with approval. He recovered from the shock quickly, and his mind had already started thinking of ways to turn this horror to his advantage.

"It has plenty of space to keep all the goods, and we'll have the best guards: crocodiles. They don't move very fast on land, so as long as we see them first, there's no reason to be afraid. Well, at least they've left us alone. Apparently they're satisfied with our two unfortunate friends," he joked.

Suddenly, Cunningham looked around at the cave and stared at the stream. Then he stared at the torches intently. He said, "I think this stream leads out to an opening at the other end. There's a breeze blowing this way. Look at the torches!"

He pointed at the flames of the torches that the men in front of him were holding. The flames were blowing towards him.

After returning to Taloh Wow Bay, Cunningham reported his discovery and the deaths of the prisoners to Khun Apipat. On a hunch, he was examining a map of Tarutao, when he suddenly found what he'd been looking for.

"I'm right, Khun Apipat!" he said excitedly. "The other end of the stream in this cave must join up with this river which flows out to Pante Bay on the western side of the island."

The map of Tarutao they were looking at was made by an expedition team of the Department of Corrections when they explored the island in 1937.

"Collin, this is very interesting. You've made quite a discovery," Khun Apipat said. He pointed at the map, his voice was as excited as the American's. "But we have to make sure that the stream in that cave really meets up with this river. The only way to find out is to sail around to the other side, follow the river in, and then watch for any stream that comes out from the mountain."

Cunningham studied the map for the moment, then said, "I hope we're right. If we are, then this cave will be the perfect place to store our goods. Look at the map, Khun Apipat. At the eastern side lies a bay which is not too far from the cave. The map shows that the shape of the bay with an island in front of it will provide good shelter for the ships that we bring in to unload the cargo. From there it will be easy to transport them overland to the cave."

Cunningham studied the map again, thinking carefully. Thinking aloud, he said, "If the stream really does meet up with this river, then it will be our escape route in an emergency. We'll have to have a ship standing by in the river at all times. And there's another thing, we have to make sure the river and the bay on the eastern side are deep enough for a good-sized boat to get in and out fully loaded, even at low tide. After all, the tide difference around here is about seven feet."

"Let's go take a look at them to see whether we're right," Khun Apipat said.

The next morning Cunningham, Khun Apipat, and two of his trusted guards, Nit and Karn, left Taloh Wow Bay on board the ADANG. They cruised north along the eastern shore, heading for the bay they'd discovered on the map. Thirty minutes later, they reached the bay they were interested in. To their relief the bay measured at least thirty feet deep.

Khun Apipat and Cunningham liked what they had found. A sizable island at the entrance to the bay protected it year round from the wind and waves. That island would also conceal the activity in the bay from any passing ships. And, best of all, even at low tide, the bay was deep enough to accommodate a big merchant ship, fully loaded with cargo.

Cunningham measured the map with a ruler, and calculated that the distance from the shoreline to the cave was only about half a mile. Pleased with the success of their discovery on the eastern side of the island, they continued their trip to the western side and cruised around the northern tip of Tarutao.

When they reached Pante bay, with its long white beach, they saw a wide river flowing from the interior of the island, and Khun Apipat ordered the captain of the ADANG to follow the river in. Again, luck was with them. The river was deep enough for the ADANG to cruise comfortably between the dense mangrove forests that populated both sides of the river.

The crew of the ADANG measured the river's depth with a rope tied to a small anchor, and her captain relaxed when they learned the river bottom was just a mixture of sand and mud, no rocks.

They cruised slowly along the narrowing river. After a mile the river became too narrow for the ADANG to travel any further. Khun Apipat ordered the ADANG stopped and dinghy lowered into the river. Khun Apipat, Cunningham, Nit, and Karn continued the trip with two crewmen rowing the dinghy, as the river slowly narrowed to a stream.

Suddenly, a visibly excited Cunningham pointed ahead and said, "That's the cave!"

A large opening in the limestone wall of the mountain appeared before them. As they drew closer, they were unnerved by the sight of at least twenty crocodiles of various sizes lying on both sides of the muddy banks of the stream flowing from the cave. Khun Apipat brought the boat to a stop at the mouth of the cave, and looked around with a smile.

"Collin, this is perfect. I'm certain that this is the same stream that you've discovered inside the cave at the other end."

"Khun Apipat, I have physical evidence that proves it's the same stream," Cunningham said, pointing at an object on the bank. It was unmistakably a human head half buried in the muddy bank. Nearby on the same bank, a family of full grown crocodiles was basking, unperturbed by the intrusion of the small boat with six men.

Cunningham continued, "I believe that belonged to one of the prisoners, although it's hard to tell from here."

"We're not prepared to go into the cave today," Khun Apipat said. "Next time we'll bring enough lamps, torches, and weapons to explore the cave. So far, I'm satisfied with what we've found today. I don't think anybody knows about this cave. You're right, Collin, the cave at the other end will be the safest place to store our goods, and this stream will be a perfect escape route in emergencies. For the sake of our own security, we must keep this discovery to ourselves and trusted members of our group." He looked knowingly at the five men in the boat.

Knox abruptly pulled Malatee down behind a large fallen tree as he dropped to his knees. He motioned with his hand telling her to be silent. As they crouched behind the tree, Malatee followed Knox's stare and watched the ADANG cruise slowly past the river's mouth and out to the sea.

Since their first meeting in July of the previous year, Knox and Malatee had been meeting every two months. Their rendezvous had always been at the south end of Pine bay, and Malatee always came with her father and Lek, her older brother. On every trip she brought food and medicine for Knox and his men and news about the war. She stayed for a few days, but before parting, they would set an approximate date for Malatee's next trip.

Knox and his men would take turns at the lookout waiting to spot Malatee's sailboat. When he was sure it was Malatee's boat, Knox would rush with Brown to Pine Bay to be certain that Malatee and her family had arrived safely, and that there was no one waiting to attack them when they landed.

Knox's concern for Malatee's safety had grown into a deep feeling of tenderness. It was a feeling Knox had never had before for a woman. Knox wondered whether he really wanted the war to be over so soon. One part of him did not want the war to end. He wanted to continue to enjoy the excitement of spotting Malatee's sailboat crossing the channel from Langkawi, the joy of seeing Malatee's beautiful face, and the pleasure of her companionship as they strolled together, having the whole deserted beach of Pine Bay to themselves.

Even the sadness he felt every time Malatee had to return to Langkawi became meaningful to him. It was the driving force that kept Knox looking forward to their next meeting. Knox was afraid that when the war was over he would have to go back to the British Army. He might then be transferred back to England or to some other place far away from Malatee, the only woman he had ever fallen in love with.

At their prior meeting in March, they decided to venture north beyond Pine Bay. While Mee remained at the camp, Knox, Malatee, Brown, and Lek took the boat up the western coast. They anchored at a cove at the south end of Pante Bay. Brown and Lek watched over the boat while Knox and Malatee went for a walk towards the river.

As they approached the mouth of the river, Knox was not certain whether his sense of hearing was functioning properly, or it was really the sound of a motorboat that he heard coming downstream towards them. A sense of danger prompted Knox to lead Malatee into the woods and take cover behind a fallen tree.

Cautiously, Knox raised his head up from behind the log just high enough to see Khun Apipat, Cunningham, and the two guards standing on the bridge of the ADANG, talking and looking out at the sea.

"What are those two doing here in this river?" Knox asked Malatee in a low voice.

"I have no idea. There's nothing in that river except mangrove forests and crocodiles," Malatee replied. "There's a cave full of crocodiles at the end of the river, but that part of the river is too narrow for that big motorboat to go in."

"I don't think they went in there crocodile hunting," Knox said. "I didn't see any dead crocodiles on their boat. They must be up to something, because Khun Apipat is not the kind of man who takes pleasure in cruising just for fun, especially in a river full of mangrove forests and crocodiles. The fact that Cunningham is with him means that this trip is a serious one. They were either looking for something or they came to leave something somewhere up the river."

"Do you think they might have killed someone and brought the body up the river to dispose of it?" Malatee asked.

"I don't think so. If that were the case, Khun Apipat himself wouldn't be here. Any of his men could have done that very easily."

"What about the loot they've plundered from the merchant ships? They might be keeping it somewhere in there."

"You might be right on that, Malatee," Knox said. "It has to be something that important in order to bring Khun Apipat himself all the way here."

"Do you want to go up the river to find the place where they might be keeping the loot?"

"No, we better not, it could be dangerous. We don't know whether Khun Apipat has left men there or not. If they see us snooping around their treasure trove, they'll never let us come out alive. It's not worth risking our lives, especially yours, Malatee. Besides, I'm not interested in their treasures."

After the ADANG had disappeared from sight, Knox and Malatee left the woods, and began walking back to the cove where they had moored the boat.

"Anyway, it's lucky for us that they turned right after leaving the river. Apparently they were heading back to Taloh Wow Bay," Knox said relieved. "If they'd turned left and cruised along this side of the island, they might have spotted your sailboat. Then it would have been extremely dangerous for all of us. If Khun Apipat's trip really involved their treasures as we suspect, I'm certain that he won't let us live to be witnesses against him."

Knox was right about their luck. Khun Apipat had originally intended to sail back to Taloh Wow Bay the long way, by cruising along the whole length of the western side and around the south end of the island to the other side. But in the excitement of their discovery, Khun Apipat forgot to tell the captain of the ADANG of his plans for the return trip. He and Cunningham were concentrating on their plans to transport stolen goods to the cave and prepare an escape route via the river. As a result, the captain, who naturally wanted to take the shortest route back to Taloh Wow Bay, made a right turn, and headed for the northern tip of the island.

CHAPTER 16

When Colonel Banchongsak stepped out of a police patrol boat onto the pier at Taloh Wow Bay one sunny afternoon in early April 1945, Khun Apipat was there to greet him, a thin smile pasted on his face.

"Colonel Banchongsak, welcome to Tarutao. What a pleasant surprise, how nice of you to come visit us."

"Khun Apipat, how are you? We've been patrolling this area because there've been reports of gun running in the Andaman Sea to support the resistance in Malaya. Since I was passing by, I thought I would pay you a visit and see how you're doing. How is the malaria situation here?"

"Much better. Last year we lost almost one thousand people from malaria alone, but the shipments of medicine we've received have really helped us put a stop to the malaria outbreak," Khun Apipat lied. In reality, the medicine he'd used to cure the malaria victims and contain the epidemic came from cargo vessels they'd pirated.

"We've also received reports that several merchant ships from Penang and some of our own ships from Kantang have been lost at sea. Rumors have been going around that they were attacked by pirates," Banchongsak said. He scrutinized Khun Apipat, hoping to detect any sign of guilt, but he found none.

"Pirates in this area!" Khun Apipat exclaimed. "Colonel, if there were pirates operating around Tarutao, I would have heard. Maybe they are from Langkawi, in the old days that island was a known safe-haven for pirates. Maybe you should explore Langkawi and the surrounding islands. You might find something there. I understand they're now under the administration of the Thai Government, so it shouldn't be a problem for you to go there." Khun Apipat's voice was convincing and sincere, to all appearances he was just a concerned prison official doing his best to help out a brother officer.

"What chance is there that some of the prisoners here might be sneaking out and plundering merchant ships on their own?" the Colonel asked.

Khun Apipat shook his head. "That's impossible, Colonel. First of all, they don't have a boat big enough to overtake the big merchant ships. Secondly, they are all too weak from illness and malnutrition caused by the shortage of food and medicine. They wouldn't have the strength to compel anyone, much less seize a ship. And they don't have any weapons. Finally, as long as I am in charge here, no one can leave this island without my knowledge," he said. He tried to sound hurt that the Colonel would doubt his administrative ability.

"It was just a thought, Khun Apipat, think nothing of it. But thank you for your suggestion about Langkawi, I hadn't thought of it, and I think you may have a point there. I'll certainly look into that area."

They were strolling around the grounds, looking at the facilities, Banchongsak trying to look casual, while keeping a sharp eye out for anything unusual. Suddenly he pointed to a building and asked, "What is that large building?"

"It's our warehouse. You can have a look if you want to, but it's almost empty because the shipments haven't come as frequently as they did before the war."

"That's all right, Khun Apipat, I've taken enough of
your time. Besides, I have to continue my patrol. But if
you hear any information about pirates in this area, please
contact me as soon as possible."

Khun Apipat accompanied the Colonel back to his
patrol boat and as the boat sailed away, he waved farewell
to his visitor.

The timing couldn't have been better, he thought.
Cunningham was right when he suggested that we move
all the captured goods to the cave. Now that stupid Colonel
will be off, chasing his tail on Langkawi. When the boat
was safely out of earshot, Khun Apipat laughed out loud,
satisfied that he had completely fooled Colonel Banchongsak.

Khun Apipat had made a mistake in underestimating
Banchongsak, who was neither stupid nor fooled by the
performance. His instincts, developed from long years of
police work, told him that something was not right with
Khun Apipat and the TVTS. He didn't bother to look at
the warehouse because he did not expect Khun Apipat to
keep pirated goods in the TVTS compound.

Banchongsak was furious when Tamrong disappeared
without a trace over a month ago. He became convinced
that the story about piracy in the Andaman Sea was no
mere rumor, and that Khun Apipat and his son were indeed
behind it.

But his major problem was finding enough evidence to
connect Khun Apipat and his son with the piracy. So far,
he had made no progress in his investigation and now,
Tamrong, his only lead on the piracy network, was probably
dead.

He had to find a way to penetrate the pirate organization,

and he had to be more careful. Tamrong's disappearance proved that the pirates of Tarutao were efficient and ruthless. He decided to pay Khun Apipat a visit on Tarutao and look over the situation himself. After talking to Khun Apipat and briefly looking around Tarutao, Banchongsak believed he had found a way.

Two weeks later, he was in the office of the Director-General of the Department of Corrections in Bangkok.

"Colonel, how are you? It has been a long time since we last met." The DG-DOC rose from his chair to greet his guest. "You said on the phone that you have something very urgent to discuss with me. What can I do for you?"

"Director-General, it's good to see you again," the Colonel returned the greeting. His voice became grave, "I have come to ask for your cooperation in an investigation. I have written authorization from the Minister of Interior."

The Colonel handed the DG a sealed envelope marked TOP SECRET, then sat silently as the DG opened the envelope and took out a single sheet of paper, also stamped TOP SECRET.

Slowly, the DG read the missive, his face growing more somber with each sentence. He looked across his desk at Banchongsak, and asked, "How serious is the problem with the pirates on Tarutao?"

"Very, people are dying and ships are vanishing. That's why I urgently need your cooperation."

"What do you want me to do?"

The Colonel took a folded piece of paper from his shirt pocket and handed it to the DG.

"The first two names on the list, please send them to Tarutao as guards."

The DG unfolded the paper and scrutinized the typed list of names on the paper. He then asked, "What about the other three names?"

"They are now in the prison in Songkla. Please have
them transferred to Tarutao."

"When do you want it done?

"As soon as possible. Please be discreet about the
whole operation."

"I know what TOP SECRET means, Colonel," the DG
said acidly. The DG did not welcome at all a police
investigation of one of his prisons and the officials under
his command. However, there was nothing he could do
but comply with Colonel Banchongsak's request, or rather,
demand. The Minister of Interior had specifically ordered
him to cooperate fully with the police chief from Songkla.

"Now that you know what to do, I will leave. Thank
you for your understanding and cooperation." Colonel
Banchongsak got up from his chair, smiled at the director,
and left the room.

The network of informants necessary to penetrate the
secrecy of the pirates of Tarutao had been established.

"Khun Apipat, have you heard the news? The Germans
have surrendered!" Cunningham said. He was excited as
he walked into Khun Apipat's office on the afternoon of
May 10, 1945. Hawkins, Grant, and Sanoh were already
there.

"Yes, Collin, I have," the TVTS director said. "The
Governor of Satun sent me a telegram he received from
Bangkok about the surrender, and the courier hand-delivered
it this morning. It says that Germany surrendered on May
7, but the war in Europe wasn't officially over until
yesterday."

"Any news about Japan and the war in the Pacific?"
the American asked.

"Well, with the surrender of Germany, the Allies can now concentrate all their efforts on Japan," Khun Apipat replied. "I don't think Japan can hold out very long."

"This is the moment that we've been waiting for," Cunningham said eagerly, looking at everyone in the room. "It's harvest time. With Germany defeated, the Allies now completely control the sea routes in the Atlantic, the Mediterranean, and the Indian Ocean. That means that there'll be more goods transported by sea to Asia. Most of the factories in the United States, Britain, and Europe will soon be returning to the production of consumer and industrial goods rather than armanents and military supplies."

"What is your plan, Collin?" Khun Apipat asked.

"And it's monsoon season again," the American replied. "The smaller merchant ships from Penang will have to risk sailing through the channel between the mainland and Tarutao. The bigger ones will still be able to avoid this route, however, and they'll be sailing the deeper waters between Tarutao and Adang, or even beyond Adang, thinking that they'll be safe from us. So, now's the time to divide our operation into two groups. While we on Tarutao hit the ships that pass between here and the mainland, Hawkins and the team on will take care of the ships on the open sea."

"You've thought of everything, Collin," the TVTS director said.

"Well, Khun Apipat, when the war in Asia is over, and you said that'll be soon, the British will be back in Malaya and Singapore," Cunningham said. "When that time comes, it'll be difficult for us to operate. So, we have to act while we can, while there's no one around to uphold the law in this area. What do you think, men?"

"I agree with Collin," the Hawk said. "Grant and I have already set up our base on Adang. We're ready for action."

"We need more ships, so from now on don't burn all the ships," Cunningham suggested.

"Why do we need more ships?" Sanoh asked. "They'll only become evidence against us later on."

"Because after several merchant ships have been attacked and word gets around, they'll no longer sail alone," Cunningham explained. "They'll either sail in pairs or in a convoy and might even be armed. Therefore, we'll have to be ready in case they do as I've predicted. We may have to attack two or three ships at the same time. We have enough men, but we lack the ships. We'll only keep the ships that we can use, and we'll destroy the rest."

"Collin's reasoning is sound," Khun Apipat agreed. "I want to emphasize that it's important not to use the ships that are used at Taloh Wow Bay."

"I'll use the SEA DRAGON at Adang, and I'll try to capture another ship as a backup in case Collin is right," Hawkins added.

"And there's another important thing, Sanoh, you are our man on the mainland," Cunningham said, looking at Khun Apipat's son. "You must keep in constant contact with your sources in the telegraph offices in Satun and Kantang. We need all the information we can get on the merchant ships sailing from Penang, and those two Thai ports. We want to know all the details, what cargo they'll be carrying, estimated arrival and departure dates, and if they're armed, what weapons they have."

"I'll do my best to get you that information," Sanoh said, smiling confidently.

"What about Knox and his men?" Hawkins asked. Of the men in that room, he had the most reason to be concerned about the six British soldiers.

"Khun Apipat says they've been inactive and have kept very much to themselves," Cunningham replied. "So far they haven't done anything to bother us. We know Knox is your problem, Hawk. That's why we think it's better for you and Grant to be on Adang away from him."

"Khun Apipat, Collin, listen to me," Hawkins said. "You have to think ahead to when the war is over. Knox and his men will then be free, and they know what's going on around here. If we let them leave Tarutao alive, our operation will be blown. And if the British return to Malaya to resume their rule there, then they won't let us or anyone else obstruct the trade between Penang and the ports around here. Collin, you're aware of this possibility. You said so earlier yourself."

Seeing that he had everyone's attention, Hawkins cleared his throat, and continued, "If Knox returns to the British Army, I'm certain that he'll tell them about our activities. He'll definitely report about Grant and me. The British will send either Knox and his men or someone else to come after Grant and me, which will affect our operation one way or the other. Believe me, Knox is not just a problem for Grant and me, he's a threat to everyone involved in our operation."

"I see your point, Hawkins," Khun Apipat said. "When the time comes, I'll take care of Knox and his men. But for now, let's concentrate on our operation."

Khun Apipat waited for a reaction from Hawkins and Grant, but there was none, so he continued, "Hawkins and Grant will be in charge of the base on Adang, and the SEA DRAGON will be their ship. "The rest of us will supervise the operation from Tarutao, except for Sanoh, who will get Collin information on the merchant ships. If no one has anything else to add, let's get to work."

Khun Apipat's transformation was complete. No shred remained of the responsible, moral director of the TVTS, he was wholly the venal leader of the pirates of Tarutao.

"Loh pang! Loh pang (lower the sails)!" Karn, the leader of a raiding party of the pirates of Tarutao, shouted in the Chinese dialect of Hokkien.

The Chinese in Penang and in Malaya were mostly Hokkien from the province of Fukien in the southeastern part of China. They had migrated to the Malay Peninsula over a period of some three hundred years.

Believing it would be better to do as the five armed men told him, than to resist and be killed, the Chinese captain ordered his four man crew to lower the sails of the merchant ship from Penang. The heavy, three masted ship slowed down, coming to a complete stop near the small sailboat from which one of the men shouted at them.

"Loh ting! Loh ting (drop the anchor)!" Karn shouted again in Hokkien. The merchant ship once again obeyed the command.

A rope ladder was lowered to the sailboat. Karn and three of his men climbed up the ladder to the merchant ship and faced the captain of the merchant ship.

"You look familiar! I've seen you before somewhere!" the captain exclaimed in Thai as he stared at Karn. "Now I remember! You were the man from Tarutao who asked us for food last year. You look much better than before."

"Yes, I remember our meeting, too. You were kind to us then, but now, we need your cargo, all of it," Karn demanded. His stomach tightened as he realized that he now faced a difficult decision.

Khun Apipat had given strict orders not to leave any witnesses. Although Karn was a former bandit and murderer, and now a pirate, he still retained some decency and acknowledged his debt of gratitude to the captain.

Now fate, by bringing him face to face with this captain again, seemed to demand that Karn repay that debt. Karn, like most Thais, believed in destiny and karma, so he made his decision accordingly.

"I have to take the ship and the cargo, but I'll let you and your crew live," Karn said. "I'm still grateful to you for what you did for me once, and I'll show my gratitude by dropping you and the crew off at an island. You have to fend for yourself from there, but don't go to Tarutao or Adang. You will be killed if you are caught there."

The merchant ship, towing the pirates's sailboat behind her, sailed towards an uninhabited island located midway between Tarutao and Adang.

After leaving the lucky captain and his crew on the island, Karn directed the captured merchant ship to Adang where Khun Apipat assigned him to work with Hawkins and Grant.

"Loh pang! Loh pang!" Nit, the leader of another raiding team, shouted at a merchant ship his team had intercepted.

"Loh ting! Loh ting!" Nit shouted again. The bigger, slower merchant ship had no choice but to obey the command from the heavily armed occupants of the smaller, faster sailboat. Nit, who had plundered the LUCKY LADY a year ago, boarded the ship with three members of his team, leaving one man to guard the sailboat.

"Tie the crew up and take them to the bow of the ship," Nit ordered as the captain and his four crewmen raised their hands to surrender peacefully.

The five victims were herded towards the bow. They were tied, as a group, to the ship's spare anchor, and stood there shaking, waiting for Nit to decide their fates. The captain and the crew were all Chinese and spoke no Thai. They sensed, however, what was about to happen to them and started to plead with Nit in Hokkien Chinese.

"I don't understand a word you're saying. Even if I did, I couldn't let you live anyway," Nit said grinning grimly.

Suddenly, he stopped grinning and pushed hard at the captain's chest with both hands, sending the helpless man and the anchor into the sea. The combined weight of the captain and the anchor pulled the crew, one by one, screaming into the sea. Nit waited until all of them had disappeared into the deep water of the channel. When the rope that had tied his victims together became still, Nit nodded at one of his men to cut the rope loose, and then ordered his team to take the merchant ship to Tarutao.

"Lieutenant, a big merchant ship is coming into the bay, it looks like they intend to take shelter from an approaching monsoon," Visnu said. The Indian corporal had run down from the lookout, and stood panting as he made his report to Knox.

"I'll go down there to warn them," Knox said, as he rose from a bench in front of his hut.

He looked up at the sky which was turning dark gray as rain clouds began to cover the skies over Tarutao. The wind was blowing with increasing force, growing louder as it beat up against the leaves of the tall coconut trees which lined the shore of Taloh Udang Bay. It was a typical July weather on Tarutao.

Knox, followed by Brown and Visnu, left the fenced-in compound and headed for the bay on the eastern side. It was the same bay where the LUCKY LADY had met her fate a year ago.

Twenty minutes later they reached the lookout, and saw a three masted vessel slowly approaching the bay. Following a trail along a mountain ridge, they walked down to the bay, and out onto the beach as a high tide brought the ship closer to shore.

"Hello! Can you hear me?" Knox shouted at the top

of his lungs. "Beware of the pirates! They are around here! You better get out of here now!"

Knox shouted repeatedly, alternating between English and Thai, hoping that the crew of the merchant ship would understand at least one language. The Chinese captain could understand English. He walked to the bow of the ship and looked in astonishment at the two Englishmen and an Indian shouting at him from the beach.

"Who are you? What are you doing here?" the captain shouted back in English. "How do you know that there are pirates around here?"

He was concerned about the pirates because many of his colleagues had never returned from trips to Kantang, and he'd heard rumors that they had been attacked and killed by pirates.

"We are British prisoners-of-war sent here by the Japanese," Knox shouted, happy that the captain could speak and understand English. "The pirates are the guards and prisoners here on Tarutao. They are a ruthless bunch who leave no witnesses. You'll all be killed whether you put up a fight or surrender. You'll be better off dealing with the storm by going back to Langkawi than staying here and being slaughtered by the pirates."

"When we came in I saw no ship," the captain said, still uncertain whether he should believe Knox.

"Please believe me," Knox pleaded, trying to convince the captain. "Last year when a ship called the LUCKY LADY anchored here, all her crew were murdered by the pirates. I saw it with my own eyes."

"The LUCKY LADY! My friend was the captain of that ship," the captain exclaimed. "He never returned to Penang. He, the ship, and the whole crew just disappeared. No one has heard from them or about them since that time. We'll leave right away and head for shelter at Langkawi.

Thank you for the warning."

The captain then ordered his crew to pull up the anchor and get ready to leave the bay.

Knox and his men walked back up to the lookout, pleased that they had saved some lives from the merciless pirates of Tarutao. From the lookout they saw the merchant ship braving the turbulent sea heading for Langkawi.

"Lieutenant, look!" Visnu shouted excitedly as he glanced and pointed to his left.

Knox and Brown followed the Indian's gestures. They saw a small sailboat coming from the direction of Taloh Wow Bay heading after the merchant ship.

"It must be the pirates! But they are too late!" Knox exclaimed in relief.

"They're not giving up so easily," Brown said. "They're chasing after that ship."

"They'll never make it," Knox replied. "The storm is getting stronger now."

Nit and his team had hoped to prey on a ship forced to seek shelter at Tarutao by the monsoon. They saw the merchant ship leaving the bay, heading the other way, and decided to try capture it.

However, the farther the small sailboat traveled from Tarutao, the higher the waves became. She rolled up and down violently under the full force of the storm, too far out for the high mountains on Tarutao to shield her from the storm.

Nit felt that it was useless and dangerous to continue chasing the speeding merchant ship, a strong wind filling her sails. Finally, he decided to give up the chase and turned the sailboat back to Taloh Wow Bay.

"Director, that English officer and two of his men went

down to the bay and talked to the captain of that merchant ship," reported a guard. Khun Apipat had ordered him to watch the activities of Knox and his men at Taloh Udang Bay. "They spoke in a language I didn't understand, but they must have warned the crew about us. After they finished talking, the merchant ship, which had already lowered her anchor, pulled the anchor up and left immediately. They would have stayed in that bay if the Englishman hadn't talked to them."

"What do you think, Collin?" Khun Apipat asked.

"I think the guard is right, Khun Apipat. Knox must have warned them. Otherwise they had no reason to leave the bay so abruptly. Remember the storm was blowing hard at that time."

"What do you think we should do with them?" Khun Apipat asked. "After all, this might not be the first time they warned a ship. They may have done it several times before without our knowledge."

"And they will do it again," Cunningham agreed. "Hawkins was right about Knox. He has become a problem. Knox must have been plotting against us and waiting for an opportunity to spoil our operation. So, now, we have to do something about him."

Khun Apipat thought for a few moments, then decided, "Send for Hawkins and Grant. Tell them to take care of Knox and his men. We all know that they have a very good reason to see that Knox and his men never leave this island alive."

CHAPTER 17

It was a moonless night in mid-August. Darkness blanketed Taloh Udang Bay so thoroughly that only shadows were visible as the men moved from tree to tree until they reached the outer perimeter of the compound where Knox and his men lived.

The inner compound was surrounded by bamboo walls protecting the living quarters of Knox and his five men. Knox lived alone in one hut. Brown and Rachan shared a second hut, and the three corporals occupied the remaining hut.

One of the intruders moved forward towards the entrance of the walled compound. In the dark, he tripped over a vine tied to some used tin cans and empty bottles. As the cans and bottles rattled loudly in the still night, the intruders dropped quickly to the ground and lay still, straining to hear if there was any activity inside the compound. They neither saw nor heard any movement. All the occupants of the huts seemed to be sleeping soundly. It was two in the morning.

The intruders waited, making certain that the rattling noise had not alerted anyone in the compound. Then eight of the intruders rushed into the compound's open entrance.

Suddenly, the two men leading the assault fell down,

screaming as sharpened bamboo sticks penetrated various parts of their bodies. A second pair following closely behind them could not stop in time and fell on top of the first two intruders. As they felt the sharp bamboo sticks that protruded from the bodies of their colleagues piercing their own flesh, they also shrieked in pain.

The third and fourth pairs saw and heard what happened, and stopped themselves just in time. One of them lit a torch to see what was happening. In the torchlight, they saw the blood-covered bodies of the first pair, seemingly dead. The second pair struggled in vain to pull themselves free from the bamboo stakes. Their bodies were soaked with blood.

The other three men lit their torches and threw them onto the dried rattan leaf roofs of the three huts. The roofs immediately caught fire. The four men then raised their shotguns, ready to shoot anyone coming out of the burning huts.

To their astonishment and disappointment, no one came out of the huts. They waited until all the three huts were completely burned down, then started searching in vain for the bodies of the occupants, who had been seen entering the huts at nine that night. None of them had been spotted leaving the huts or the compound after that.

It was Yai, Malatee's sister, who saved the lives of Knox and his men.

She overheard the wife of one of the guards casually mention that her husband, who had gone to Adang with Hawkins and Grant, had had to come back earlier than expected. The wife boasted that her man had a very important job to do in a few days. Yai acted as if she did not believe the wife, who then tried to impress her by stating that her husband was an important, trusted member of Khun Apipat's inner circle. She bragged that although Knox was a lieutenant in the British Army, he would not leave Tarutao alive because of her husband's work.

Yai was aware of her sister's friendship with Knox and became concerned for Knox's welfare. She asked her husband, one of the few guards not involved in the piracy, to discreetly warn Knox and his men of the danger.

Tam had become acquainted with Knox over the past year, and had grown to like and respect the Englishman. He decided to go to Taloh Udang Bay early the next morning. He carried along a bucket and told the guards at Taloh Udang Bay that he was going to go clamdigging.

When the normally friendly Tam walked past the British soldiers' compound without stopping to greet them or even looking at them, Knox sensed that something must be wrong. He sent Rachan and Prem down to the beach to collect clams near Tam. After a while, Rachan returned and told Knox what he had learned.

Knox had expected that sooner or later Hawkins would convince Khun Apipat to kill him and his men. They knew too much about the piracy to be allowed to leave Tarutao alive. Therefore, he had drawn up a self-defense plan, and it was this well-prepared plan that caught the intruders by surprise and fatally injured half the assailants.

Their home-made alarm system had worked effectively. When they heard the rattling noise at the outside perimeter, Knox and his men quietly lifted up their wooden floorboards and quietly dropped through the openings to the ground underneath the huts. They then crawled away from the entrance, to the far end of the walled compound.

At the base of the wall lay a wooden board, its top camouflaged with coconut leaves. They lifted up the board, which concealed a large exit hole.

The hole led to the other side of the wall, which was also covered with another camouflaged board. They climbed up quietly one by one and lay down flat on the ground. Slowly, they crawled silently on their bellies away from the compound until they reached the wooded area.

Knox had drilled himself and his men in these defense and escape maneuvers until they could all do it quickly and quietly.

Once in the woods, they headed for a large tree where they had hidden their home-made bamboo spears, bows and arrows. There were also three machetes, which Knox and his men had picked up from guards and prisoners who'd left them unattended while clearing land.

Knox and his men had often discreetly practiced archery in the woods, and after constant practice had become adept at handling their makeshift weapons, which were now their only means of self defense. Khun Apipat not only refused to give him more bullets, he took the rifle back.

Knox had planned their escape carefully. They would follow the trail to Pine Bay where they could hide until Malatee came for her next rendezvous with Knox. They would then sail with her back to Langkawi and stay there until the war ended.

Hawkins was furious at the failure of the assault. He believed he had planned the attack well and that Knox and his men would not survive it.

Four days earlier, Khun Apipat had sent a messenger to Adang to tell him and Grant to return to Tarutao at once. After Khun Apipat and Cunningham told him about Knox's interference with their operation, Hawkins eagerly volunteered to personally take care of Knox. He asked Khun Apipat to provide him with enough men to do the job. Khun Apipat gave him four guards and ten prisoners, former bandits and murderers.

Hawkins was confident of his plan and had looked forward to getting rid of Knox and his men once and for all. They had been a thorn in his side far too long. He did not know why the plan had gone wrong and blamed himself, admitting that he had underestimated Knox, who certainly had outsmarted him.

He himself watched Knox and his men go into their huts at nine and had waited to make sure that no one came out of the huts later. He cursed himself for waiting until two in the morning, instead of striking earlier. He wanted to make sure that they were sleeping soundly when his men attacked the three huts, simultaneously finishing off the six British soldiers. He had not expected any serious resistance because he knew that Knox and his men did not have any weapons that could match the shotguns his men were using.

But something did go wrong, not because Knox and his men fought back, but because they simply vanished from the compound.

Hawkins waited until the fire burned itself out before entering the compound with Grant and his remaining men to inspect the damage.

The first thing they encountered was the gruesome sight of four corpses in the rectangular pit at the entrance. Several long bamboo stakes protruded through their bodies. Hawkins ordered the remaining six prisoners to get the bodies out of the pit.

Hawkins told Grant and the four guards to spread out and search among the remains of the huts for the charred bodies of his hated enemies. But not a single corpse was discovered. Hawkins could only conclude that Knox and his men had somehow slipped out of the huts and the compound.

They searched along the bamboo wall and found the escape tunnel under the wall. Hawkins directed his men to look for the tracks of the six British soldiers in order to determine which direction they took. They discovered tracks leading north towards the ridge between the western and eastern mountain ranges.

"It's two hours till sunrise, so let's wait until dawn to go after them. We can't afford to underestimate that damned Knox anymore," Hawkins said, realizing that Knox was not a man to be taken lightly. "He's crafty and may set up booby traps for us in the dark. He had to know that sooner or later we would find their tracks and go after them. So it's better to rest now and follow their tracks when there's light again. Knox and his men won't leave this island anytime soon. As far as we know, they don't have a boat, so if they're still on the island, we'll find them sooner or later."

"Lieutenant, there's a fire in the compound!" Brown said to Knox. In the inky darkness, they were following a trail that would lead them to Pine Bay six miles away.

"They're burning our huts down, thinking we're trapped inside," Knox said as he led his men on the trail. He had walked this trail several times before to his rendezvous site with Malatee. "We have a good head start. Hawkins'll have to wait until the fire burns out to discover that we escaped. When he realizes that we're still alive, he'll come after us in a fury, which will make him careless."

Knox stopped walking, looked around, and said to Rachan. "This is a good place to set up the booby traps. Go ahead, Rachan."

As Rachan and Chai went to work, Knox spoke to the rest of his men. "The booby traps might take some of the careless ones out of action and slow the rest of them down. We don't know how long we'll have to wait until Malatee comes. It could be any day now. Anyway we have enough provisions to last us three days in this wilderness. After that, let's hope we can get a deer or wild boar."

When the booby traps had been set, Knox and his men continued along the trail.

At daybreak, the tracks could be seen clearly, and Hawkins led Grant, the four guards, and the six remaining prisoners in pursuit of the six British soldiers. Once they got into the jungle, Hawkins assigned two prisoners to scout ahead of the party.

The deaths of the four prisoners had taught them the hard way to proceed slowly and cautiously. The trail was quite narrow and most of the time they had to walk single file. For a long time, they followed the tracks without incident, alert to their surroundings, looking for any sign that might indicate the presence of a booby trap.

When the two scouts saw a fallen tree blocking their path they thought perhaps it was intended to divert them from the trail, into the bushes in which booby traps were set up waiting for them. So they decided that it would be safest to remove the fallen tree and continue straight on the trail.

They looked carefully around the tree, trying to see if it was booby trapped. The tree had fallen in such a way that it lay diagonally, one end touching the ground. The other end rested on a broken trunk about one meter off the ground. One of the scouts bent down to lift the fallen tree out of the way, while the other stood guard watching for any unusual signs.

Hawkins, following about thirty paces behind, saw what

the two scouts were doing and his sixth sense told him that something was wrong. "Don't touch it!" he yelled.

His words of warning came too late. As the scout lifted up the tree, he unintentionally released the top end of a long bamboo stem pinned to the ground by the weight of the tree. With no weight to hold it down, the bamboo stem, which had been bent down like an arch, suddenly sprang up into the air. Its top end gave a tremendous pull to a vine tied at the other end to a cage-like square block made of bamboo. Each corner of the block had a sharpened bamboo stick extending out about a foot and a half.

The whole horrifying scene took three seconds. The two scouts never had a chance to dodge the terrifying object that swung at them. The prisoner standing guard was the unlucky one. He stood right in the path of the flying object. A loud thudding sound, followed by a painful scream echoed through the still jungle as a sharpened bamboo spear buried itself in the prisoner's chest. His dead body landed on top of his colleague.

Hawkins and the rest of the men stood frozen in their tracks. They dared not rush to help, they were afraid that they might accidentally activate another booby trap.

After a brief check of the area to be sure that there were no other booby traps, Hawkins told the guards to take the booby trap out of the body of the dead prisoner and lift the other shaky, but fortunate, scout to his feet.

"That damned Knox and his damned booby traps!" Hawkins said to Grant as the two of them stood looking in dismay at the terrifying scene. "We've already lost five men, and we haven't even had a glimpse of any of them. I'm telling you, it'll be a pleasure to kill them with my own hands."

"Yes, but we have to find them first," Grant said worriedly. "If things go on like this we won't have a man left by the time we catch up with them."

"We'll find them," Hawkins said grimly. "A guard told me that this trail leads to Pine Bay, which is surrounded on one side by mountains and the other side by the sea. It's a dead end, they won't have anyplace to go. We have no choice but to continue on this trail. We'll just have to be more careful. Grant, you and I will lead the way from now on. We'll show these men that we're not afraid and that we really mean to get those bastards."

Knox and his men arrived at Pine Bay just before noon. They went straight to the south end of the bay, where Malatee usually camped whenever she came to Tarutao. But this time when they reached the campsite, the sailboat was nowhere in sight. They hoped Malatee and the boat would show up very soon. They knew they were outnumbered by Hawkins and his men, and with nothing but crude, homemade weapons, would not survive a direct confrontation with their pursuers.

"Lieutenant," Brown suggested, "Since we don't know how long we'll have to wait here, I suggest that you assign some of us to protect our rear. We might be able to delay them by leading them the other way. When Malatee comes, the rest of us here will have time to board the boat. If it's low tide when she comes, the boat won't be able to come close to the shore. Then we would have to walk quite a way to the boat, which makes us open targets."

After thinking it over for a few moments, Knox agreed, "Yes, either you or Rachan, accompanied by one of the corporals, should go back on the trail about one or two miles. If Hawkins and his men show up, try to hit some of them with your arrows, then lead them around in circle up the mountain behind the camp here."

Knox stood and pointed to the mountain nearest the sea.

"That mountain ends in a cliff which drops straight down to the sea. The water around there is quite deep, even at low tide. When Malatee arrives, I'll light a fire on the beach. When you see the smoke, it's time to move towards the sea and the cliff. When you reach the cliff, jump into the sea. We'll be waiting for you there with the boat."

"What do we do if it gets dark and Malatee still hasn't come?" Rachan asked.

"Good point, Rachan. You come back to the camp because you can't see the smoke at night, anyway. My concern is that the two men who'll handle this assignment be good swimmers."

"In that case you lose, Rachan," Brown said with a smile. "You have to admit that I'm a better swimmer than you, a true landlubber. Besides, I'm also handier with a bow and arrows. Don't forget that Robin Hood was an Englishman."

"All right, you win, Brown," Rachan agreed, pointing to an Indian corporal. "Take Prem with you. He's a good swimmer."

"All right, then. Brown and Prem will protect our rear and buy us time," Knox said. "But remember, don't try to be heroes. Look for a chance to ambush them, then retreat. Keep on doing that, but be careful not to get yourself trapped in an area where you can't escape. You wouldn't have a chance because they outnumber and outgun you."

Knox paused, and then reemphasized his point, "Remember, your objective is to delay them, not to engage them in combat. The most important thing is to get yourself to the boat alive and well. That's an order!"

As Brown and Prem were getting ready to move out, Knox turned to the two remaining corporals and gave them an order, "Visnu, Chai, start collecting dry mangrove roots and any other wood you can find. Make sure that they are all dry. Then build a bonfire with it. Make it a big one that gives out a lot of smoke."

Knox paused, then asked, "You have flints, don't you?"

"Yes, I do," Visnu replied.

"Light the fire as soon as you see Malatee's boat coming in."

At the end of the last mountain, Hawkins stopped at a small clearing. He could see picturesque Pine Bay in the distance and stood enjoying the beautiful scenery as Grant and the rest of the party joined him. Nine men were left from the fourteen that he had started with.

As Hawkins bent down to tie a loose bootlace, an arrow whizzed past his head and pierced the neck of a guard who was standing right behind him. Instinctively, everyone dropped to the ground and looked around to see where the arrow came from. But, they saw no one.

Hawkins and his men remained on the ground for a while, then slowly stood up. This time two arrows flew past their heads and lodged in the trees behind them. Hawkins glimpsed the movement of bodies in the undergrowth ahead. He raised his rifle hoping to find a target, but didn't have a clear field of fire.

"Just one clear shot. Two seconds is all I need," Hawkins said to himself. Constantly hunting wild game for the TVTS had made Hawkins an expert marksman.

Hawkins's confidence returned when he realized that his opponents probably only had bows and arrows as their weapons. They didn't seem to possess a rifle, a shotgun, or even a pistol.

He crouched behind the brush, preparing to go after his unseen enemy. He signaled with his hand for Grant and the rest of the men to follow him. When they reached the spot where they'd seen somebody moving, they found human tracks heading up the mountain to the left of Pine Bay.

The tracks led them away from Pine Bay, towards the trail they'd just been on, and the tracks were fresh. So, the men who made the tracks could not be far away.

Hawkins smiled grimly in anticipation of the coming confrontation with his hated foes. Believing Knox and his men to be just ahead, Hawkins led his men in a relentless pursuit through the forest.

"Lieutenant! The sailboat is here! Malatee is here!" Visnu came running to the campsite to tell Knox the good news.

Knox rose from his seat on the ground. He looked out at the sea and saw a small sailboat with two passengers slowly approaching Pine Bay. It was a welcome sight.

"Chai, light the bonfire now. Build up a lot of smoke so that Brown and Prem can see. Visnu, you better give Chai a hand," Knox ordered in an excited voice.

He turned to Rachan and said, "Let's take all our provisions and weapons to the boat now. We have to tell Malatee to turn the boat around and get ready to go out."

As Visnu and Chai went to do as they were told, Knox and Rachan collected their belongings and ran to the approaching sailboat.

The passengers were Malatee and Lek. She watched in astonishment as Knox and a big man, whom she believed to be one of Knox's men, ran from the beach towards the boat.

Malatee jumped from the boat into the waist-deep water. She waded towards the two men, sensing that something must be wrong. She had never before seen Knox in so excited and in such a hurry.

Knox reached the boat and tossed in the bows, arrows, and spears. He turned around to face Malatee. Overcome by the joy of her arrival, he embraced her passionately. Malatee blushed slightly because Knox had never held her like this before.

"Malatee, I'm so glad to see you," Knox said exuberantly. "Actually, I hadn't expected you to be here for a few days. But we're lucky you decided to come early."

Knox then told Malatee what had happened. He introduced her to Rachan as the Indian reached the boat and loaded the rest of their belongings into it.

"I've decided to come now because I have a good news to tell you. The Americans dropped two atomic bombs on Japan last week, and it's now certain that Japan is defeated," Malatee said with great excitement. "It's expected that Japan will surrender very soon. I've come to ask you and your men to return with me to Langkawi on this trip. My father stayed behind, so that the boat wouldn't be overloaded with you and your men on board."

As Knox, Malatee, and Rachan were climbing into the boat, Visnu and Chai came running down from the beach. They had lit the bonfire and made sure that columns of black smoke billowed high into the sky.

After Visnu and Chai had climbed aboard the boat, Lek put the sail up and turned the boat towards the cliff ahead to wait for Brown and Prem.

Brown swore at himself when his arrow narrowly missed Hawkins. He waited until Hawkins and his men began to raise their bodies up from the ground. He and Prem released the arrows from their bows at the same time and were disappointed when the arrows missed their targets. However, they had successfully misled Hawkins and his men. By revealing themselves, they had lured Hawkins into following them.

Brown and Prem slowly retreated towards the mountain, drawing Hawkins and his men away from Pine Bay. Occasionally they looked in the direction of Pine Bay, hoping to see black smoke rising into the sky. They had been engaging Hawkins and his men in a game of hide and seek for almost three hours when, suddenly, columns of black smoke rose above the trees in front of them.

"Prem, that's the prettiest sight I've ever seen," Brown exclaimed joyfully. "It means Malatee is here! Let's get out of here. It's about time we went swimming."

Hawkins also saw the columns of black smoke rising in the direction of Pine Bay. Curious to find out what could have caused the fire, he had one of the prisoners to climb a tall tree to report what was happening.

"The smoke is coming from a bonfire on the beach. There's a sailboat near the shore." The prisoner shouted his report from the top of the tree, where he had a clear view of Pine Bay.

Hawkins shouted questions at the prisoner. "What's the sailboat doing there? Are there people on board? How many?"

"The sailboat is moving out to the sea. There are about five or six persons on it."

"Can you identify the people in the boat?"

"It's too far to see their faces," the prisoner replied.

"That boat must have come to pick Knox and his men up. That Knox is really clever. I wonder whose boat it is," Hawkins said to Grant, chagrined that Knox had fooled them again.

"If Knox and his men are now on that sailboat, then whom have we been chasing?" Grant asked.

"It's a decoy. Knox must have one or two of his men

lead us away from the beach so that he and the rest of his men could safely board the boat."

Hawkins then shouted at the prisoner who was still on the tree. "Which way is that sailboat heading?"

"It seems to be going south."

"They're going to Langkawi. It's the nearest, safest place for them," Hawkins decided, then he smiled. "That means they'll have to stop somewhere to pick up their colleagues. So, let's follow them. I might be able to take a shot at them. If luck is on my side, I might even have a shot at Knox himself."

"There they are!" Knox shouted as he saw a movement high up on the cliff among a group of trees.

"Yes, I can see them now," Lek said, directing the boat towards the cliff. "Someone is waving something to catch our attention."

It was Brown, he'd taken off his dirty white shirt and was waving it at the sailboat. As the boat approached the hundred-foot-tall cliff, Brown and Prem jumped feet first into the calm sea. They were very lucky that the sea that day was unusually calm for August, a monsoon month. Otherwise, the normally raging waves would have smashed them against the solid wall of the cliff. Brown and Prem sank beneath the waters for a few seconds, then bobbed back to the surface.

"Hey, Prem, how are you feeling? It's so refreshing to have a swim after all that walking and running," Brown shouted cheerfully. The two of them then swam towards the sailboat which was approaching them.

"Say, is this boat going to Langkawi by any chance? Please arrange two first class seats for us," Brown shouted joyfully at the smiling faces on the boat. Several hands helped pull Brown and Prem up on the boat.

"That was a beautiful dive, Brown," Rachan said with a smile as Brown leaned against the sailboat's single mast.

Knox told Lek to head for Langkawi, as Brown and Prem exchanged greetings with Malatee and Lek.

As the sailboat moved past the cliff, Brown, who was still leaning against the mast facing the stern, happened to glance up at the top of the cliff. He blinked his eyes a few times to see the object that he had spotted above the cliff more clearly, but he knew what it was as soon as he saw the sunlight reflected on a metal object. It was the barrel of the rifle that Hawkins was aiming at Knox, who was sitting high up on a pile of ropes and provisions looking out at the sea.

Knox was feeling relieved that he and all his men had managed to evade Hawkins and the pirates of Tarutao. None of his men was hurt. It was lucky that Malatee came to Tarutao at the right moment.

Knox was smiling lovingly at Malatee when, suddenly, Brown sprang up from his seat and yelled, "Lieutenant, look out!"

As Brown threw himself on top of Knox, the loud report of a rifle echoed between the cliff and the sea. Brown slumped over Knox, blood flowing from his neck. Everyone lay on the crowded floor of the sailboat which was speeding away from the cliff.

"It's Hawkins!" Rachan said, looking up from behind the mast where he was seeking cover as another bullet whizzed past the boat.

"Damn! I missed him again! Brown spotted me and saved Knox's life," Hawkins said.

Knox was in shock, unable to utter a single word as he realized that Brown had saved his life by sacrificing his own.

Knox held the lifeless body of Brown firmly against

his chest, unperturbed by the blood that dripped all over his lap. Tears ran down his cheeks, but he made no effort to stop them. It was the first time that Knox had ever shed tears.

Knox's physical and mental endurance had passed its limit. This sudden turn of events, coming so soon after their hair's breadth escape, was too horrifying for him to accept emotionally. One moment he was elated by their successful escape, with everyone safe and sound, and was anticipating a good life now that the war would end very soon.

Then a second later, he was mourning the loss of a man who had been devoted to him for years and whom he had regarded as his younger brother. He couldn't believe that the man he'd been talking to and laughing with a minute ago was now lying lifeless in his lap.

Knox sat stunned by the terrible blow cruel fate had dealt him as the sailboat headed for Langkawi and freedom.

CHAPTER 18

The large crowd that had gathered around the entrance to the Municipal Building in Singapore abruptly quieted as a four-car motorcade came to a stop in front of the building. Seven Japanese in military uniforms stepped out of the two middle cars. Several armed British soldiers emerged from the other two cars and surrounded the Japanese. Together they walked up the wide steps lined on both sides with armed Royal Marines.

The Japanese delegation, led by General Seishiro Itagaki, entered the Council chamber, which had been prepared for this historic event, the surrender of the Japanese armed forces in Southeast Asia to the Allies on September 12, 1945.

Admiral Louis Mountbatten, who had been the Supreme Allied Commander of Southeast Asia (SAC-SEA) since 1943, came out of the chamber looking distinguished in his white Royal Navy uniform. He had presided over the signing ceremony, which had taken nine minutes. The Japanese delegation had left, escorted back to their place of confinement. Mountbatten walked down to the parade ground in front of the building, followed by several high ranking officers. Among them was Brigadier L.E.C.M.

Perowne, the Commander of the 74th Indian Infantry Brigade, Knox's new commanding officer.

Knox and his men escaped from Tarutao on August 15, 1945, the same day that the Japanese decided to surrender. At first they stayed with Malatee and her family in Langkawi for a week. In the meantime, they learned that the war had indeed ended, and the official surrender ceremony was scheduled for September 2, 1945 on board the USS MISSOURI in Tokyo Bay.

Knox and his men then left Langkawi for Singapore, which had become Allied headquarters in Southeast Asia. They reported to the British Army garrison there and were assigned to the 74th Indian Infantry Brigade, responsible for the security of northern Malaya.

"Admiral, that's the lieutenant whom I had told you about, the one who was confined on Tarutao with his men," Brigadier Perowne told Mountbatten as he spotted Knox standing among the crowd. "I would like you to meet him. He has a few interesting stories to tell. May I call him over?"

"As you wish, Brigadier," the Admiral said. He was in a cheerful mood after the signing ceremony.

His commanding officer signaled for Knox to come over. As Knox stood at attention before them, Perowne introduced him to the Admiral.

"I've been told about your time on Tarutao, Lieutenant," the Admiral said. "I understand you had some problems with pirates. It sounded terrible. Tell me more about it."

Swiftly and succinctly, Knox told the Admiral about the pirates on Tarutao and their threat to the trade between Penang and Thailand and Burma. He also informed him of the presence of Hawkins and Grant, fugitives from the British Army, whom Knox and his men had been sent to capture.

"We can't do anything directly to the pirates because they only operate in Thai waters," the Admiral said after hearing Knox's tale. "They are the Thai government's problem. I have to refer the matter to our embassy in Bangkok and let them raise the issue with the Thai authorities."

"Sir, what about Hawkins and Grant?" Knox asked.

"I believe we have an agreement on the extradition of prisoners and criminals with Thailand," the Admiral replied. "I'll ask our embassy in Bangkok to proceed with this matter."

"Sir, if we're to take any direct action against Hawkins and Grant, I would like to volunteer," Knox said.

"Lieutenant, I'll let you know if I require your service," the Admiral replied.

A British Army captain approached Mountbatten and saluted him. "Admiral, the parade is ready to commence."

Perowne looked at Knox and said, "That's all, Knox. The Admiral has a parade to review."

Knox saluted both of them, turned around, and returned to the crowd.

Three days later Knox, who had been assigned a platoon at the army garrison in Butterworth, was instructed to meet Perowne at the headquarters of the 74th Indian Infantry Brigade in Penang.

"Congratulations, Knox. You've been promoted to captain."

"Thank you, sir."

Perowne got straight to the point. "I have a special mission for you. The Army has not forgotten the crimes Hawkins and Grant committed in Kota Baharu four years ago."

"Sir, Hawkins has recently committed another murder. He killed Sergeant Brown."

The Brigadier looked directly into Knox's eyes, and continued, "I haven't forgotten that, either. We want them to receive the punishment they deserve. But frankly, I don't think the extradition procedure will work with Hawkins and Grant. You told me that they've participated in the piracy together with the prison director on Tarutao."

"Yes, sir. They have."

"Therefore, I don't believe that the director of the prison,...what's his name?"

"Khun Apipat, sir."

"Yes, I don't believe that Khun Apipat will hand them over to the Thai Government so that they will be extradited to us. On the contrary, I think Khun Apipat might even help Hawkins and Grant escape from Thailand. He has a good reason to do so. If we can capture Hawkins and Grant, we might be able to make them testify against him and the pirates. I'm sure that Khun Apipat won't want that to happen. Therefore, it'll be safer for him if Hawkins and Grant leave Thailand. If that's the case, then we'll lose track of them."

"I agree with your assessment, sir. Does the special mission you mentioned earlier have anything to do with Hawkins and Grant?"

"Yes, it does," the Brigadier replied with a smile. "I want you to find a way to discreetly obtain information on the whereabouts and activities of Hawkins and Grant. If I'm right, and they decide to leave Thailand, we'll be ready for them if they set foot in any British territory."

"Sir, I assure you that you'll be kept informed of Hawkins's and Grant's movements," Knox said with confidence. He already had a man in mind for the job.

One afternoon in early November, a small boat with single sail glided onto the beach at Lipe. Its only occupant had braved the sea, sailing alone for six hours from Langkawi. The man was half Thai and half Sea Gypsy. He was in his mid-twenties and had lived with the sea since the day he was born. His only clothing was a pair of dark colored shorts, and his skin was as dark as burned toast. His unruly dark hair had streaks of light brown, the result of constant exposure to the sun. A smile lit his rugged face as he saw a stocky man about four or five years younger than himself walking towards him from the shore.

The man called out to the sailor and greeted him in the Sea Gypsies' language, "Bahasa Pulau" (the island language). Many words however had cognates in the Malay and Indonesian languages.

"Lek! It's you! I'm glad to see you!"

"Teca! Good to see you again," Lek said to the younger man as they embraced. "It's been a few years. You're a grown man now."

"How come you're here by yourself?" Teca asked. "Where are Mee and Malatee?"

"My father doesn't feel well. Malatee is taking care of him. I've come to attend the Plahu Placak Festival."

"I see that you still remember our tradition," Teca said with a smile. "The festival lasts three days, I hope you haven't forgotten about that. So that means you have to stay at least three days."

"I remember. I also know that the first day of the festival is tomorrow. So that's why I came today. I'll stay for some time, Teca. Since I have Malatee to look after father, I now have time to visit my friends and relatives on my mother's side."

"Good. Then you have to stay until my wedding. It's one week after the festival."

"Teca, you are a lucky man! Is she pretty?"

"You'll meet her soon. Come to my hut. You have
to stay with us. My father and sister will also be glad
to see you," Teca said. Lek had secured his boat to a
fallen coconut tree buried deep in the sand, and the two
of them were walking up the beach together, headed for
Teca's hut.

In general, the Sea Gypsies were animists. They worshiped
the souls of their ancestors, believed in superstition, and
had their own ancient traditions. The Plahu Placak Festival
was a traditional event taking place twice a year during
the full moon in June and November. The event began
two days before the full moon.

In the afternoon of the first day, all the Sea Gypsies
in the village gathered on open ground to pay respect to
their ancestors. A wooden carving of the face of the first
Tuhat (ancestor) who settled down on Lipe was erected
in a shrine in the center of the ground. Prayers were said
to the souls of their ancestors asking for good lives and
protection against evil. After the prayers, everyone danced
around the shrine until six in the evening.

In the morning of the second day, a group of male and
female Sea Gypsies went into the jungle to find wood to
make a Plahu (boat) and name it, Placak. Together they
built the Plahu Placak. It was six feet wide and ten feet
long, complete with a sail and paddles. It was in fact
another small sailboat. All work on the Plahu had to be
finished by midnight.

All the Sea Gypsies then placed parts of their hair and
fingernails wrapped in pieces of cloth inside the Plahu.
The belief was that bad luck, which was contained in those
parts of their bodies, would float away with the Plahu.
Some even put food and coins into the Plahu to be used

in their afterlife.

"Lek, did you make a wish?" Teca asked as he saw Lek throw coins into the Plahu.

"Teca, I wished for a fiancée as pretty as your Buruk," Lek replied with a smile. Buruk, a pretty girl in her late teens, stood next to Teca, smiling at Lek's kind words.

"You should spend more time around here, Lek," Buruk said. "You'll have no problem finding yourself a wife."

"I heard that there'll be several weddings next week, Teca. Lema, your sister, is also getting married. The way you kids are carrying on the tradition of marrying young, all the pretty ones will be married soon. There is no one old enough left for me," Lek said laughing.

"Yes, well, Lek, there is a problem here that has prompted many young girls, especially good looking ones, to be married soon," Teca said, his voice suddenly turning serious.

"What's happening, Teca?" Lek was curious.

"Five months ago, a group of about fifteen men came from Tarutao to live on Adang. They are guards and prisoners and they're led by two foreigners."

"The foreigners. What do they look like?" Lek asked excitedly.

"One big man with dark hair, light brown skin, and pointed nose," Teca replied. "The other one is smaller with whiter skin, brown hair, and a pointed nose. At first, we thought that they were good people, but later on we learned that they robbed ships and killed their crews. We don't welcome them to our island anymore."

"Have they harmed your people?" Lek asked.

"So far they haven't caused any problem for us but we didn't like the way they looked at our women. Some of them came to talk to our girls. The women and the young girls are afraid of them. That's why many of them want to get married. They want husbands to protect them."

"Teca, the music has started. Let's dance." Buruk said. The sound of drumbeats had brought her over to Teca and Lek.

Several men and women, old and young, got up and danced. Each couple stood firmly in one place, facing each other. They shifted their legs back and forth, moving their hips to the rhythm of the music, gesturing with their hands in an up-and-down motion, and singing.

They danced this way until the early hours of the morning, and then rested, waiting for high tide.

"It's high tide! Let's carry the Plahu into the sea. Come on, everyone!" Teca said.

Lek, Buruk, Teca's sister Lema, and Duwa, Lema's fiancé, got up from where they'd been sitting and walked with the other Sea Gypsies towards the Plahu. They carried it into the sea until the water almost came up to their shoulders.

"This should be far enough," one of the men said. "Let the wind and the current carry it away."

"We have to make sure that the Plahu doesn't return," another man said. "It will be bad luck if it does."

"What happen if it comes back?" Lema asked.

"We just have to keep pushing it out until it heads out to sea," Lek replied.

To their dismay the Plahu floated back towards the shore four times. Several people looked worried.

"What should we do? The bad luck won't go away!" Teca exclaimed.

"We are men of the sea, we can find a way to overcome this problem. I have an idea," Lek shouted, his words catching the attention of the others.

"What's your idea, Lek?" Teca asked.

"The Plahu has a sail," Lek replied. "Let's put it up. That's how we normally do it with a real boat."

"We've never done that!" a man exclaimed. "There was never any need to before."

"Maybe there is more bad luck this time," Lek said. "Let's do it now. The wind is picking up."

Lek was right. With the sail catching the wind, and the tiller fixed to guide the Plahu into the open sea, the Plahu Placak sailed away amid the cheers and to the relief of the gathering of Sea Gypsies.

However, the ceremony was not over yet. The men went into the jungle again and brought out stacks of wood. They built seven crosses, each as tall as a man, to represent the seven days in a week. The Sea Gypsy elders prayed to the crosses, and later placed them on the beach to chase away any new bad luck that might come their way.

The women were also busy. They carried fresh water from the village wells and poured it into several containers on the ceremonial ground. The elders said another prayer in front of these containers. The following day every Sea Gypsy would wash their faces and sprinkle their huts with this water for good luck. That night, they celebrated the ending of the Plahu Placak Festival by dancing again to the sound of the drums, called "rummanas" in their language.

"Teca, look!" Buruk said with alarm. She stopped dancing. A few couples nearby had also stopped, and stood staring with a startled look on their faces. Soon everyone had stopped dancing and stared at the entrance to the dance ground. The music died down.

The torches surrounding the area and lining the entrance shone on a group of seven men who stood looking at them with smiling faces. Two men stood a few steps in front of the group. They were Hawkins and Grant.

"What are they doing here? They are bad luck!" Teca said. The village chief and a few elders went over to Hawkins and his men and courteously invited them to sit down and join the celebration.

Hawkins and Grant had returned from one of their raids, arriving after the sun had already set. Hawkins was inspecting their loot on the deck of the SEA DRAGON when he heard the sound of music and singing carried by the wind from Lipe.

"Chim, what is happening on Lipe?" Hawkins asked the guard standing next to him. "It sounds like the Sea Gypsies are having a party."

"They are celebrating the Plahu Placak or boat floating festival," Chim replied.

"Oh, really? Sounds interesting," Hawkins said. "Let's go have a look, Grant."

"Why not? We've worked hard. We deserve some relaxation." Grant answered.

"All the Sea Gypsies on these two islands must have come to this festival. Maybe that woman is there, too," said Hawkins, who was still looking for Malatee.

"Hawk, I don't see that woman you've been crazy about anywhere here," Grant said. He'd looked around the dance ground in the minutes since their arrival, but didn't see her. The music started again, and the Sea Gypsies resumed dancing.

"Maybe she is not from Lipe or Adang. That's all right, Grant. I've just found a substitute." Hawkins looked beyond the other dancers at a girl sensuously moving her curvaceous body to the rhythm of the music.

Buruk had caught the Hawk's eyes.

"She is beautiful, Hawk. But be gracious. Remember that we're outnumbered here. Better find out first from Chim who she is."

Ten minutes later Chim returned to where they were sitting and told Hawkins what he had learned about the girl. "She is a niece of the village chief engaged to be married next week to the man she is dancing with."

"I'll find a way to have her," Hawkins said confidently.

"Hawk, she's leaving the dance with another girl," Grant said.

"They're heading towards the beach. Just the two of them. The other girl is nice looking. She's yours, Grant." Hawkins's gaze followed Buruk and Lema as they disappeared into the dark.

"Let's get them now, Grant. This is the right time. We'll take them to Adang. The Sea Gypsies wouldn't dare go after them there. Let's move."

Hawkins, Grant, and the other men left the dance ground and headed towards their dinghy. They saw two shadowy figures standing on the beach further to the left. Hawkins told the others to wait at the dinghy. He and Grant then rushed towards the two figures.

Buruk and Lema were walking back to the dance ground when the two men surprised them.

Hawkins swept Buruk off the ground with both hands, pinning her arms and body to his chest to keep her from struggling. Grant did the same with Lema. The two girls fought in vain; but they were overpowered by the two men.

"Let's get back to the dinghy, Grant. Hurry!" Hawkins said.

Suddenly a figure jumped Hawkins from behind, forcing both the big man and Buruk into the sand.

It was Teca. He picked up a stick and moved towards Hawkins, saying something in a language Hawkins couldn't understand.

Teca was in a blind rage. Intent on punishing Hawkins for what the big man was doing to his fiancée, he didn't notice a figure leaping out of the dark at him. He even ignored Buruk who yelled a warning.

The attacking figure was Chim, holding one of the seven wooden crosses firmly in both hands.

Teca felt like his head had exploded as Chim bashed his right temple with the heavy cross. The blow knocked him down on the beach. The last thing Teca heard before he lost consciousness was Buruk screaming.

CHAPTER 19

"Knox, I have an urgent assignment for you, one I think you'll like," Perowne said as Knox came into his office.

"Does it have anything to do with Hawkins and Grant, sir?" Knox asked.

"It might, but we're not certain," the Brigadier replied. "The Governor of Penang has received a long list of complaints from the ACMP, the Association of Chinese Merchants of Penang. During the past two years, their members have suffered the loss of about eighty vessels and millions of pounds worth of merchandise. They claim their losses are being caused by pirates from Tarutao and Langkawi."

"Langkawi? I haven't been aware of any pirates there."

"That's what we intend to find out. The ACMP has asked the Governor if the British Army can provide armed escorts for their vessels. The Governor has passed the matter on to me, and I believe we have the capability to do it. Knox, I want you to organize armed escorts for the ACMP."

"When do you want us to begin, sir?"

"The first of December, five days from now. I want you to call on the chairman of the ACMP to work out the details with him. I leave everything to your discretion."

"Thank you for having confidence in me, sir."

"By the way, Knox, any information on Hawkins and Grant?"

"I sent a man to Tarutao three weeks ago to find out about Hawkins and Grant, but I haven't heard from him since."

"Who is this man? Is he reliable?"

"He is half Thai and half Sea Gypsy. He lives on Langkawi now, but he used to live on Tarutao before it became a prison. I have complete confidence in him, sir, and I'm sure I'll hear from him soon."

"Very well. Then let's just concentrate on this matter of armed escorts."

"Loh pang! Loh pang!" Nit, the most ruthless pirate on Tarutao, shouted as his small sailboat approached a large merchant vessel.

He'd been waiting for this particular vessel from Penang. Sanoh's information on the merchant vessels that sailed between Penang and Kantang was invaluable. The information on this vessel came in two days ago, and she was a treasure trove. In her hold, she carried chemicals, automobile spare parts, and machine tools, commodities which had been in high demand since the war ended.

The merchant ship was slowly sailing northward, passing Tarutao as if she were out for a pleasure cruise in the warm December sunshine. The sea was calm, the voyage uneventful, and the crew expected to arrive on-schedule in Kantang.

Suddenly, into this peace barged a sailboat from Tarutao with a crew of five. They intercepted the merchant ship, demanding that she lower her sails. The crew complied, lowering the three sails, and bringing the vessel to a halt not far from the sailboat.

"Loh ting! Loh ting!" Nit shouted again, ordering the merchant ship to lower its anchor.

Again his command was obeyed. Nit smiled and his eyes shone at the thought of another quick and easy raid.

As Nit and three other men stood on the sailboat pointing their weapons at the merchant ship, a fifth member of his team threw a rope up to a crewman, ordering him to tie it to her bow. Nit shouted another command and the crew lowered a rope ladder from the merchant ship. Nit smiled, this routine was becoming very familiar to him.

Nit climbed up the ladder, followed by three of his men. One man remained behind on the sailboat, standing guard with a shotgun trained on the merchant ship in case there was resistance.

Nit's head popped up on the port side of the merchant ship and as he prepared to step on board, a strong hand shot up from the deck of the ship and grabbed the rifle in Nit's right hand. Pulling with great strength, it forced the pirate off balance and sent him sprawling on the deck of the ship.

A big man rose to his full height with Nit's rifle in his hands. He rushed at Nit and hit him on the chin with the rifle butt, knocking the pirate out with one blow. The he shouted an order that completely stunned the three men climbing up the rope ladder behind Nit.

"No prisoners! Kill them all!"

It was Rachan who gave the command.

Rachan raised the rifle at the first man about to cross over the railing of the merchant ship, and shot him in the chest.

Prem and Chai, the two Indian corporals, emerged from their hiding places at the stern of the ship. Both of them carried Sten MK5 submachine guns which they fired repeatedly at the other two men on the rope ladder.

The three pirates fell from the ladder, their lifeless bodies thudding to the deck of the sailboat below.

From the bow of the ship, Visnu, another Indian corporal, cut down the stunned guard in the sailboat.

The whole scene lasted less than ten seconds.

"Set the tiller in the direction of Taloh Wow Bay and secure it," Rachan told his three corporals. "Put up the sail, and let it go. Leave the bodies the way they are. Confiscate the guns."

Knox had chosen Rachan and the three Indian corporals to be the first team of armed escorts. Knox's orders were to take no prisoners. He wanted the bullet-ridden pirate corpses to serve as a message to the other pirates that from now on the merchant ships would be well protected. He hoped the sight would discourage the pirates from further raids.

A crewman from the merchant ship cut the rope that tied the sailboat to the ship. With the sail up and nothing to hold it, the small sailboat headed towards Taloh Wow Bay.

As Nit began to regain consciousness he realized that his hands and feet were securely tied. He looked at Rachan and recognized the big Indian immediately, they had met several times before on Tarutao. He knew that Knox and his men had eluded Hawkins's hunting party and escaped from Tarutao, but he'd never expected to see the four former Indian prisoners-of-war serving as security guards of the merchant ship.

Nit looked around for his men but saw no one. He presumed that they were either captured and confined, or dead.

"Are you looking for your men?" Rachan asked as he watched Nit. "They're all dead. We sent them back to

Tarutao on the sailboat to convey our greetings to Khun Apipat."

The reply stunned Nit, and he remained silent.

Grim-faced, Rachan said bluntly, "It's about time you paid for all the crimes and sins you've committed. It's your own karma that's sent me to do to you what you've done to the others."

"What are you going to do to me?" Nit asked. Then, arrogantly he added, "You have no authority to arrest me in Thai waters. If you do anything to me, Khun Apipat will never forgive you. I'm a TVTS guard, an employee of the Thai Government. You have to let me go."

"Khun Apipat's time to pay for his own karma will come sooner or later," Rachan said fiercely. "And as for my authority to deal with you, well, I've got the same authority you had to plunder merchant ships and murder their crews and passengers."

Rachan paused to control his rising anger. "Do you still remember what you did to a ship called the LUCKY LADY a year and a half ago? I saw what you did with my own eyes. You brutally murdered everyone on board, including an Indian passenger, and disposed of all the bodies by tying them to the anchor and throwing them into the sea. I've heard that since then, you've gone on to throw your victims overboard alive and tied to an anchor. You enjoyed hearing your victims scream while sinking. Now, I'll give you the opportunity to experience it yourself. As I've said, it's your own karma."

Nit listened in silence. He became pale when he learned what Rachan had in store for him and discovered that his ankles were tied to a heavy anchor.

Nit's heart sank as he listened to Rachan's orders to Prem and Visnu, "Throw him into the sea!"

Nit screamed and cursed as his body and the anchor

hit the water, sinking rapidly to the bottom of the Andaman Sea. The most ruthless and fearsome pirate of Tarutao had met his fate.

"Lek, you're back! I'm so glad to see you!" Knox said, feeling relieved when Lek and two Sea Gypsy men were shown into his quarters in Butterworth. "It's been almost a month, and I was beginning to worry about you."

"It's taken longer than I expected," Lek said. "After I left Langkawi, I went to Tarutao first to find out where Hawkins and Grant were. I learned that they'd gone to Adang to set up a base there. So I went to Lipe to ask my friends there about Hawkins and Grant. I can confirm that they're still on Adang, I saw them both with my own eyes.

He paused for a moment, and looked at his companions before continuing, "Something bad happened on Lipe. Hawkins and Grant were involved, and the Sea Gypsies have asked me if I can do anything to help them. So I decided to bring my two friends. They represent the Sea Gypsies on Lipe and Adang, and have personally been made to suffer."

Lek paused to introduce the two Sea Gypsies to Knox. "This is Teca." Lek pointed to a man with a fresh scar on his right temple and then at the other man who was younger, "And this is Duwa."

"What happened to them, Lek?" Knox asked. "You said Hawkins and Grant were involved!"

"Teca is a close friend of mine, he is engaged to a niece of the village chief. Duwa is engaged to Lema, Teca's sister. Both girls were abducted by Hawkins and Grant and are still being held captive on Adang."

Knox was furious, but he managed to look at Teca and Duwa with sympathy on his face, rather than fury.

Lek continued, "The Sea Gypsies didn't know what to do about them. Hawkins and Grant have about fifteen men with them. They are guards and prisoners from Tarutao, and they are all armed. The Sea Gypsies have no chance against them because they have no weapons and haven't been trained to fight."

Lek paused then asked Knox, "Is there any way you can help them? If nothing is done about Hawkins and his men, all the Sea Gypsies will have to leave Lipe and Adang and settle somewhere else."

"Lek, I want to personally take some men to Adang and eliminate Hawkins and Grant once and for all," Knox said. "But I have to get permission from my superior officer. And, Adang is in Thai territory. The British just can't send troops there, not even to capture our own fugitives. We need permission from the Thai Government."

Knox paused to let Lek translate his words for the two men. He saw disappointment in their faces as they listened to him. When Lek finished, he gave Knox a disheartened look.

Knox sat solemnly for a few moments, then said, "All right, Lek. I'll discuss the Sea Gypsies' problem with my commander to see whether he knows a way to solve this problem. I have to leave tomorrow to escort a convoy of merchant ships to Kantang, but I'll be back in one week. You can either wait for me here, or return to Langkawi and come back in a week."

"Father, I have big news for all of us," Sanoh said rushing into Khun Apipat's office. Cunningham was also in the room.

"I hope it's good news," Khun Apipat responded.

Khun Apipat had been in a foul mood in two weeks since the small sailboat had returned with its dead passengers. What concerned Khun Apipat most was that Nit, a trusted guard, had vanished without a trace. If he'd been arrested by the Thai police, Nit might be forced to become a witness against him.

Cunningham, on the other hand, believed that the merchant ship had hired armed guards and that Nit had been killed in the attempt to seize the ship. The bullet wounds on the four dead bodies were caused by submachine guns, which were used by military services and professional armed guards.

"A telegram to a group of merchants in Kantang came in from Penang yesterday afternoon. The telegram notified the merchants that the goods they ordered would be carried by a convoy of five ships leaving Penang four days from today," Sanoh said excitedly.

"That is indeed good news, Sanoh," Cunningham said. "I've been saying that there are too many merchant ships in Penang for armed guards to travel with every ship. Sooner or later they'll have to form a convoy and sail together with one ship acting as escort."

"Collin, the telegram didn't mention an armed escort," Sanoh replied. "Maybe they just feel safer sailing together."

"We still have to be careful," Cunningham cautioned. "Don't forget what happened to Nit and his men."

"Do you think we should attack those five ships?" Khun Apipat asked.

"Certainly, Khun Apipat," Cunningham replied with confidence. "We'll take them, whether they have armed escorts or not. We have enough ships, men, and firepower to do it, it's just a matter of good planning. And, if we capture those five ships, think of all the merchandise we'll have in stock. We'll even be able to stop raiding for a while and concentrate on selling the merchandise."

"That's a good point, Collin," Khun Apipat added.

"But I think we need Hawkins and his men on Adang in on this raid."

"Yes, we can use them," Cunningham said. "Their big ship will be useful. You better send for them now."

"I'll do that right away," Khun Apipat agreed.

As the convoy of five merchant ships passed the western shoreline of Tarutao, heading north for the port of Kantang, several sailboats and the three-masted SEA DRAGON sailed out from Pante Bay to intercept them.

"Captain Knox, four sailboats are coming towards us," a British sergeant shouted. Knox was standing near the helm station of the merchant ship being used as the escort ship.

Knox had prepared thoroughly for this mission. Anticipating that the pirates might use one, or even both, of the TVTS's motor boats in their operation, Knox had had two marine engines with heavy horsepower installed in this vessel. His ship had to have enough speed to overtake either the ADANG or the RAWI. For firepower, Knox relied on two Vickers M1 machine guns, one on the bow and the other one on the deck at the stern.

Knox had set the convoy on a course that would take it past Tarutao's western side. If the pirates attacked, they would have to come from the starboard side, the right flank of the convoy.

So Knox arranged the convoy in such a way that one ship would be leading the convoy and the other four ships would form two columns behind the lead ship. Knox's ship headed the column on its right flank in such a way as to be able to move up and down to protect the convoy.

"The ship leading the convoy must be the escort ship," Hawkins told Grant. The two of them stood on the deck of the SEA DRAGON, watching the convoy. "We're going to attack that ship as planned."

Three sailboats sailed ahead of the SEA DRAGON. Two of the sailboats carried five armed men, while the third boat had only one man in it. The SEA DRAGON headed for the left column of the convoy while one sailboat headed for the right column. The other two sailboats, including the one carrying the lone sailor, headed for the lead ship.

When his boat came within a hundred feet of the lead ship, the lone sailor lit a bonfire on the bow of his sailboat. As the boat caught fire, he directed the boat straight at the lead ship and prepared to jump overboard just before the collision.

Hawkins's plan was to cripple the lead ship by setting her on fire while the sailboat with five armed men dealt with the armed guards, if there were any, on the escort ship.

"They're going to knock off the lead ship thinking she's the escort ship," Knox said to the sailor controlling the helm. Then he shouted a command to the crew: "Start the engines and get the machine guns ready."

The engines roared to life, propelling the heavy ship through the waves. She headed at full speed towards the burning kamikaze boat, which was now about sixty feet from the lead ship.

Knox's gunners removed the canvas covering the machine guns. Quickly and efficiently, they installed the two Vickers, with hundred-round drum magazines, on steel tripods. They pulled back the cocking handles, loading the bullets into the firing chambers. Machine guns and gunners were now ready.

When the burning sailboat came into range, the British gunner on the bow opened fire. The .303 in. caliber bullets ripped apart the lone sailor and the wooden hull of the sailboat. It began to sink before it could reach the lead ship.

The men on the second sailboat fired on the lead ship with rifles and shotguns.

Knox's ship maneuvered to bring the second sailboat into machine gun range. The gunners took aim and opened fire, reducing the second sailboat to floating debris in a matter of seconds. None of the five pirates had survived.

Knox gave another command to the helmsman of his ship. The escort ship swung around and headed for the third sailboat, which was attacking the second merchant ship in the right column.

When the third sailboat came in range, the bow gunner fired repeatedly. The Vickers' bullets savaged the boat's wooden hull and cut down all five men on board.

While Knox was busy defending the lead ship and right column of the convoy, Hawkins took the opportunity to attack the two merchant ships in the left column. As the SEA DRAGON drew near the first ship, Hawkins was stunned to see several helmeted men emerge on the starboard side of the ship, submachine guns and rifles at the ready. Before Hawkins could react or could even shout a warning, the men on the merchant ship opened fire on the SEA DRAGON.

One of the pirates standing heedlessly on the bow of the SEA DRAGON was torn apart by bullets and fell into the sea. Hawkins and the rest of the pirates on the SEA DRAGON dropped to the deck as a hail of bullets whistled over their heads.

Grant raised his head just high enough above the railing to peer at the escort ship and shouted a warning to Hawkins, "Hawk, the ship that just finished off our three sailboats is coming directly at us. She's not a merchant ship, she's a patrol boat in disguise, and she's got a lot of speed and firepower. We better retreat now, Hawk, before we're in the range of her machine guns."

Hawkins remained silent, uncertain whether to fight or flee.

"Hawk, decide now, before we are caught in the middle between this ship and the one with the machine guns," Grant shouted. He tried to convince Hawkins to retreat. "Remember what you told me: one who fights and runs away may live to fight another day."

Hawkins finally made his decision. "All right. Let's abort the operation and return to Adang," he said to the captain of the SEA DRAGON, ordering him to divert her away from the convoy and head into the open sea towards Adang.

Luck was with Hawkins and Grant. Knox did not know that the two fugitives were on the ship speeding away from him. He thought that both of them were still on Adang, and that the pirates involved in the attack today were only guards and prisoners. He didn't know that Hawkins and Grant had personally participated in the attack.

"We're not going to pursue that pirate ship," Knox told his men. "Our mission is to protect the convoy and see to it that they arrive in Kantang and return to Penang safely. Their defeat today has taught them an expensive lesson. They'll have to think hard before they decide to attack another convoy again in the future."

Knox signaled the merchant ships to return to the original formation and continue their journey to Kantang.

From the limestone cliff that rose above Pante Bay, Khun Apipat and Cunningham observed the carnage with a mixture of awe and fear. Cunningham was so confident of his plan that he had invited Khun Apipat to come to watch the operation. He had also asked him to have a large number of prisoners standing by to unload the huge cargo he expected.

Both of them now realized that this was the beginning of the end of their pirating activities. The British authorities would certainly continue to provide armed escorts for the merchant ships, making future raids much more difficult.

Besides, they now had a problem with logistics. They had suffered unacceptable losses of ships, men, and firearms in this venture. All their small sailboats, used to intercept merchant ships, had been destroyed. They had lost four guards and seven prisoners, not including Nit, who had disappeared, and his four men who were killed almost three weeks ago. They had wasted almost half of the armaments that belonged to the TVTS.

Khun Apipat also faced the problem of justifying the loss of guards, prisoners, and firearms in the event of an investigation; the guards and firearms were the personnel and property of the government.

As for Cunningham, his main concern was to find a way to leave Tarutao safely with as much of their amassed loot as he could take with him. He had to do it without resistance from Khun Apipat. Cunningham was shrewd enough to have prepared his plan to escape from Tarutao with the treasure in advance.

Cunningham had recruited a guard and two prisoners with a promise to share the earnings from sales of the loot.

Earlier he had convinced Khun Apipat to set up a small base in Langkawi as a decoy to lure the Thai police away from Tarutao. He proposed that Khun Apipat periodically send the three men he'd recruited to Langkawi, ostensibly to take some of the less valuable items to store on the base. Khun Apipat had agreed to this plan.

But unknown to the TVTS director, Cunningham had instructed his men to also smuggle out valuable goods with them on their trips to Langkawi. Those goods were hidden separately in a cave far from the base where the less valuable merchandise used as a decoy was kept.

Under Cunningham's orders, his three men had gone to Satun and bought a sailboat with a single sail. Cunningham had the sailboat hidden in a stream that branched off from the main river flowing out to the sea at Pante Bay. The canal was also near the crocodile cave where all the booty was kept. If need be, the boat would be his means of escape from Tarutao.

Cunningham knew that the pirating activities would have to end sooner or later. The Thai Government and British authorities in Malaya would eventually recover from the war and regain control of the administration in Thailand and Malaya, respectively. Once that occurred, the parties harmed by piracy in Thailand and Penang would surely request that the authorities in their countries and put an end to the piracy.

When that happened, Khun Apipat would be the main suspect because there were many people who knew of Khun Apipat's direct involvement with the pirates of Tarutao. While Khun Apipat defended himself, Cunningham with most, if not all, of the treasure, would be free, rich, and far away.

CHAPTER 20

In mid-January 1946, Perowne summoned Knox to his office where he delivered a depressing, but not unexpected, piece of news, "Knox, the response we've received from the Thai Government about Hawkins and Grant is not very encouraging".

"What happened, sir?"

"Our embassy in Bangkok has been informed that Hawkins and Grant are no longer prisoners on Tarutao."

"That's impossible!" Knox exclaimed.

"Well, you should hear the whole story first," Perowne said. "The Thai Government had instructed Khun Apipat to confine Hawkins and Grant until they could be extradited to us. I have to admit that Khun Apipat is quite clever, he told his Government that all prisoners-of-war had been released when the war ended. He said they'd all left Tarutao, and he didn't know where they'd gone. Do you believe that?"

"Sir, the information I've received from my sources on Lipe indicates that Hawkins and Grant are on Adang and Cunningham is still on Tarutao.

"I don't doubt you, Knox, but the Thai government's response means that we won't be receiving any cooperation from them. I think we should try an alternative approach."

"Sir?" Knox's face brightened up a little.

"I'm going to suggest to Admiral Mountbatten that we undertake to suppress the pirates of Tarutao and capture Hawkins and Grant ourselves."

"Sir, are you serious?" Knox exclaimed. He paused a moment to bring his emotions under control, "I beg your pardon, sir!"

"I am serious, Knox," the Brigadier replied.

Knox believed him. Perowne, from 1943 to the war's end, had commanded the 23rd Indian Infantry Brigade in Burma, and had a reputation as a serious and tough soldier. He and his men, in a series of hard-fought battles, had driven the Japanese troops in Burma into retreat and eventual surrender.

"Sir, I completely agree with you, we cannot provide security for every merchant ship that sails in the southern Andaman Sea. During my years on Tarutao, I've come to know the characters of the men involved in this piracy, and they are all greedy, cunning, and ruthless. They won't stop just because we've spoiled two of their ventures and destroyed some of their ships."

"I see your point, Knox," Perowne said. "All we have to do next is go to Singapore and convince Admiral Mountbatten."

Knox and Perowne met with Mountbatten at the Allied headquarters in Singapore, and outlined their problem and the proposed solution. The Admiral listened carefully, occasionally nodding in agreement, but his response to their plan was measured and careful, "Gentlemen, your reasons are sound but there are certain procedures that we have to follow. First, I must ask our embassy in Bangkok to bring up the piracy issue with the Thai Government and propose a joint exercise against the pirates."

Admiral Mountbatten was a careful planner and decisive commander. His precise planning and implementation had ensured the success of the Allies' campaign to recapture Burma from the Japanese. However, in the postwar era, his position as SAC-SEA required him to take into account political and diplomatic considerations in relations with other countries in the region.

The Admiral continued as Perowne and Knox listened attentively, "As you may know, normal relations between Great Britain and Thailand were restored by an agreement signed on January 1. That agreement ended the war between the two countries, and we are under an obligation to respect their sovereignty by consulting them first. If the Thais aren't willing or able, then we'll do it ourselves."

Mountbatten smiled as he noticed the looks of anticipation on the faces of the men sitting before him. "Once I receive the consent of the Thai Government, I'll have to obtain the approval of our Cabinet in London."

"Sir, may I bring up a very important fact?" Knox asked.

"Please, Captain," the Admiral replied.

"The southwest monsoon usually begins in May and ends in October. In order to avoid having problems with the weather, we must put an end to the piracy before May."

"I'll include that information in my request to the Thai Government," the SAC-SEA said. Then he looked at Perowne and said, "Considering the political instability in Thailand, the frequent changes in government, and the conflict between political and military leaders, I don't think the Thai Government will be in a position to be involved in a military action, even against these pirates. Brigadier, I want you to start planning a minor deployment against the pirates on Tarutao and Adang, presuming that only our troops will be involved." Admiral Mountbatten believed in the 5 Ps: "prior planning prevents poor performance."

"Sir, you'll have the plan in one week," Perowne said decisively.

"Good, now that the war's over, our men are in high spirits and look forward to even a minor operation." Mountbatten said. Rising from his seat, he dismissed his subordinates, ending the meeting.

Eight days later, Knox was called into Perowne's office.

"Good news, Knox," the Brigadier said with a smile on his face. "The SAC-SEA sent me a radio message saying that the Thai Government has agreed to allow our troops to suppress the pirates, and will send a senior official to coordinate and observe the operation. He'll ask London right away for approval."

"I'm ready, sir."

"Good, be ready to implement our plan as soon as the Cabinet approves it."

Two days later, on February 20, 1946, the Office of the Cabinet in London received a coded telegram from Admiral Mountbatten in Singapore.

The telegram read:

" 1.   Coastal traffic in the vicinity of Penang has been considerably interfered with by pirates based on Langkawi Island in Malaya and Tarutao Island in Thailand.

2.   To date, British armed guards for coastal shipping have proved effective and a number of pirates have been killed. But with the gradual reduction of forces, the time will come when armed guards cannot be provided on a scale sufficient to prevent a recurrence of pirating activities.

3.   Therefore, I intend to carry out a minor operation

to suppress this nuisance. The Thai Government has given its full concurrence and is supplying an official to assist in the planning and indicate his Government's policy."

Two days after receiving the telegram, the Cabinet Officer sent a note to the Foreign Office seeking its view on Mountbatten's proposal.

"Sir, it has been two weeks since the SAC-SEA sent the request to London. Any reply, sir?" Knox asked Perowne.

Knox was getting restless. The men he'd picked and trained for the operation were ready and looking forward to the action.

"Not yet, Knox. Bureaucrats!" Perowne said with a sigh.

"Sir, it's fortunate that we're not fighting a war against an aggressive enemy," Knox said impatiently.

"Yes, I know. Anyway, I believe the approval will come any day now."

"Sir, Lek, my informant, has just returned from Lipe and he tells me that the situation on Lipe and Adang is getting worse. A few more Sea Gypsy girls have been abducted by Hawkins's men. Some Sea Gypsy families have decided to leave Lipe for other islands."

Knox paused to control his anger and frustration before continuing, "And, even more important, Hawkins has a three-masted ship standing by, fully provisioned and ready to sail away any day. It seems that Hawkins plans to leave Adang soon. Sir, may I make a suggestion?"

"Go ahead, Knox."

"I'm sure the Cabinet will approve the SAC-SEA's request any day now. If the operation isn't carried out very soon, it'll be too late to catch Hawkins and Grant. May I proceed to Lipe immediately with my team? We'll hole up there until the authorization comes from the SAC-SEA, then we'll move on Adang."

Knox paused. Perowne did not say anything, so Knox continued, "I would like to keep a close watch on Hawkins and Grant to make sure that they don't leave Adang too soon. If they do, I'll inform you by radio so that you can have our navy intercept them when they leave Thai waters."

Perowne thought for a moment, then said, "All right, Knox. You and your men can go to Lipe now. But remember, don't invade Adang and avoid any contact with Hawkins and Grant until you receive my authorization. Your move on Adang must coincide with the plan to invade Tarutao."

"Yes, sir, I understand."

"Good. Two days after you've either captured or disposed of Hawkins, Grant, and their men, I'll send our troops to raid Tarutao at Taloh Wow Bay. It means that you'll have one day to get from Adang to Pante Bay. Your task at Tarutao will be to guard the river at Pante Bay in case some of the pirates decide to escape by it. By the time you arrive at Pante Bay, my troops and I will be in Kuah on Langkawi. Any questions?"

"No, sir."

"Very well. Good luck."

Knox saluted, and left the room.

The next day Knox and his men left Penang for Langkawi, their only stop on the way to Lipe. Unbeknownst to him, that day, six thousand miles away in London, the British Cabinet Office received a note from the Foreign Office stating that it had no objection to the operation proposed by the SAC-SEA.

"Three small sailboats are approaching Lipe," a TVTS

prisoner serving as a lookout reported to Hawkins.

Hawkins and Grant were talking in front of their hut on the island of Adang. They had established their base on a small plateau located on the south side, halfway to the top of the highest mountain on Adang. When he'd explored the island almost a year ago, Hawkins had been particularly impressed with this plateau's advantages.

To their delight, Hawkins and his men enjoyed the luxury of an unlimited supply of fresh water. There was a pond on the plateau fed by an endless supply of water from the top of the mountain. The overflow from the pond trickled down through the rocks until, reaching the ground, it formed a small stream flowing into the channel separating Adang from Lipe.

The most favorable factor, however, was its high vantage point. From this plateau an observer could command a panoramic view of the Andaman Sea. In good weather, a lookout could see up to forty nautical miles away. The plateau overlooked Lipe across the channel, and Tarutao and Langkawi could be seen clearly on the horizon. Any ship approaching Adang could be easily spotted from a distance. In addition, there was only one trail leading up from the beach to the plateau, making it easy to defend against attacks.

"They must be Sea Gypsies returning from their fishing trips," Hawkins said.

"They might be coming for the birthday celebration of the village chief tomorrow," Grant added. "Do you want to go down there and look at some girls? There might be new ones coming from other islands."

"No, I'm getting tired of these Sea Gypsy girls," Hawkins said yawning with boredom. "They're not worth the trouble of walking all the way down there and then walking all the way back up here. I just want to take it easy for a while. You go ahead, Grant, if you want to, but don't cause any trouble. The last thing I want now is to antagonize those Sea Gypsies into burning down the SEA DRAGON. After all, she's our only way of getting off this island."

Hawkins paused to get up and stretch himself. Then he continued, "They may look gentle and harmless, but don't push them too far. I just want to leave here peacefully." He had begun to sense the Sea Gypsies' growing hatred for him and his men.

"Then why don't we leave now? You said you wanted to go to India," Grant asked.

"I've made up my mind, Grant," Hawkins said firmly. "But I want to hit a few more ships before we leave so we'll have enough money to last us a while."

The attack on the convoy of five merchant ships, which would have been their biggest conquest and satisfied their needs, had ended in disaster. Since then, not a single ship had passed through the vicinity of Adang. There had been two convoys of four ships each, but Hawkins, with only the SEA DRAGON left, dared not attack them. He had learned a costly lesson, and he did not want to risk losing the SEA DRAGON.

So everyday he had a man on the lookout watching for easier prey. But the only thing he'd spotted was three small, worthless sailboats belonging to Sea Gypsies.

The three small sailboats did indeed belong to the Sea Gypsies, and each man handling the tiller of the sailboats was a Sea Gypsy. However, the other occupants of the boats were not Sea Gypsies.

In the first sailboat were Lek, Knox, Malatee, and Prem. When Knox stopped in Langkawi to meet with Lek and his two Sea Gypsy friends, Malatee had asked Knox if she could come with the team. At first Knox had refused out of concern for her safety, but Malatee's persistent reasoning finally convinced Knox that she would be more of an asset than a liability. Malatee argued that her acquaintance with the Sea Gypsies on Lipe, her knowledge of the area, and her proficiency in the English, Thai, and Sea Gypsy languages would be useful if Knox and his men needed an interpreter. She also promised that she would not get involved in the operation itself.

The second sailboat was occupied by Rachan, Visnu, Chai, and a Gurkha corporal, with Teca at the tiller. In addition to the Indian troops, the British also employed many Gurkhas, a tribe from Nepal that produced first-rate soldiers, famed for their skill in the use of their fearsome short curved knives, called kukris.

The third sailboat, with Duwa at the tiller, had four Gurkha soldiers in it.

The special team had ten members: Knox, Rachan, Prem, Visnu, Chai, a Gurkha sergeant, two Gurkha corporals, and two Gurkha privates who acted as radio operators.

Knox had chosen all non-whites as members of the team. Because of their dark brown skin and Asian features, the four Indians and the five Gurkhas could, from a distance, pass for Sea Gypsies. The male occupants of the three sailboats sailed barechested as they approached Lipe, in the manner of Sea Gypsy men. Knox, whose skin was deeply tanned, but not dark enough to pass for a Sea Gypsy, had to lie down on the floor of the boat as they approached Lipe.

Knox had experienced considerable difficulty finding Gurkha soldiers to include in this special assignment. The Gurkhas were a mountain people, at home in jungles and mountainous terrains, and spending long hours in small sailboats was a dreadful experience for them, since most of them could not swim.

After endless searching, Knox had to be content with the five Gurkhas in his company who were just barely able to float for a short period of time. Besides, he expected no problems during the six hour sail from Langkawi to Lipe because March was considered to be among the calmest times of year in the Andaman Sea.

For the past two weeks, Knox and the members of his team sailed around Penang everyday in small sailboats to familiarize themselves with sailing in the open sea.

The three sailboats landed in the late afternoon on a long sandy beach on the south side of Lipe. Small hills, densely covered with trees, concealed them from onlookers, even the lookout in the pirate compound. After they finished setting up their tents, Knox sent Lek, Teca, and Duwa into the Sea Gypsy village to find out about Hawkins and his men. Malatee and his men, however, were under strict orders not to wander into the village.

Knox and Malatee walked together along the white sandy beach towards the eastern end of the bay where they climbed up some rocks. They sat down on the flat surface of a large boulder to watch the sunset on the horizon.

"This reminds me of the sunset we saw together at Pine Bay a year and a half ago," Malatee said. "I thought it was romantic then, but it's more so now." She smiled at Knox, a lovely, warm smile that, he'd noticed, she seemed to bestow only on him.

"I feel the same," Knox agreed. "Maybe it's because the atmosphere has changed. No more war, no confinement, no more anxiety about the future."

"But the next few days will also have a big effect on your future. Aren't you worried about that?"

"No, Malatee. It's not the same feeling. This is my job, a duty I have to perform. When we first met, the future was uncertain. Now that I've returned to the Army, I'm doing what I've been trained to do. And most important, I can see you more often, and without fearing that we'll be discovered by Khun Apipat."

Both of them laughed.

"Kevin, I have to tell you frankly. For you the end of the war has made you less anxious. But for me it has made me uncertain about the future."

"Why? I don't understand," Knox said with great concern.

"Because you are now free to go anywhere you want. The Army may send you somewhere so far away from me that we cannot see each other anymore. And you have to return to your own people." She paused and looked out at the sea. "You'll meet other women," she said softly, sadly.

"Malatee, you don't know how much you mean to me."

"No, I don't. You'll have to tell me."

"It's not only that you have saved my life and the lives of my men. It's you, Malatee. I care about you. I realize it more and more. During my days on Tarutao maybe I thought of you because I was lonely and there were no other women. But, Malatee, since the war has ended, I think of you more and more."

"Kevin, I'm glad we can talk like this. Since the war has ended you've been busy with your life in the Army. We haven't seen each other that often."

Knox sighed and breathed in the fresh air. He looked around with approval and said, "I remember once on Pine Bay you told me that someday you'd take me to visit four slands. It's unbelievable that we're here now, although not on holiday as I would have preferred. You were right. This place is beautiful, so quiet and peaceful."

"Until Hawkins, Grant, and the pirates came and ruined everything," Malatee replied, concerned for her people and their land.

"I promise you, Malatee, in a few days I'll return these islands to your people," Knox said clenching his right fist. "I envy the Sea Gypsies for having this island as their home, but at the same time I also feel happy for them. I really like this part of the Andaman Sea. You know, Malatee, I've thought about settling down on one of the islands in this area after I retire, or if I ever leave the Army. Now that peace has returned, I can plan my future."

"There's enough land on Lipe and Adang to build a home. But if you're thinking about having a rubber or coconut plantation, then it's better to settle down on Langkawi. It has more land and a better location."

"That's a good suggestion. I'll think about it."

She put her hand on his arm, reluctant to bring up her own worries, fearing that they might spoil the romantic night. Taking a deep breath, she began, "Kevin, the most important thing is that you complete your mission safely. I've been worried, I've been afraid, and that's why I pleaded with you to take me along. I wanted to be near you if...if...if anything happened. Please be careful, Kevin," Malatee said, smiling lovingly at Knox.

"Malatee, if I have you to come back to, I'll be extra careful. I want to share my future with you on Langkawi, or anywhere else that you choose to be."

Knox looked into Malatee's beautiful dark eyes and drew her closer, holding her gently in his arms, as the sun disappeared beyond the rim of the sea.

CHAPTER 21

The next morning Knox got up at daybreak. As he emerged from his tent, Lek and Teca approached to inform him that Hawkins and Grant were still in the pirate compound on Adang. Their ship, the SEA DRAGON, was standing by at the southeastern tip of the island. The pirates had no more than fifteen men with them, armed mostly with rifles, shotguns, and knives.

Knox wanted to spend the day scouting the area and devising the most effective plan to invade the pirate compound. He asked Teca to lead him to the north side of Lipe, which lay parallel to the south end of Adang. Accompanied by Rachan, Amar the Gurkha sergeant, and Lek, Knox followed Teca for about half a mile to the other side of the island. Kneeling on the ground, they chose a vantage point that provided an excellent view of the channel between Lipe and Adang. They concealed themselves behind the thick undergrowth and trees.

Using his field binoculars, Knox scanned the shore of Adang and to his right, spotted a three-masted vessel anchored near a white, sandy beach. It had to be the SEA DRAGON. On the shore beyond the beach stood a forest of tall pine trees.

To the left of the SEA DRAGON, Knox saw that the

beach ended at a small hill covered with dense forest running about six hundred feet along the shoreline. Clusters of rock lined the break between the forest and sea, and at the forest's edge stood another long beach. From the beach, the shore extended inland for nearly a thousand feet until it met the base of a large mountain covered with dense tropical rain forest.

"There's a path through that pine forest that leads to the pirates' base. It takes about an hour to walk up there," Teca said, pointing at the southeastern tip of the island. Lek translated Teca's words into Thai for Knox and his men.

"Is there another way up there?" Knox asked.

Teca pointed across the channel at the beach directly opposite them, and speaking through Lek, said, "Yes, there are two. One is a steep cliff that rises up from the sea on the eastern side. It's very difficult to climb. The other is to follow the water that flows down from the top of the mountain and comes out to the sea between those two big rocks."

With his binoculars, Knox saw a small stream coming out from between two large boulders at the left end of the beach.

"If we follow the stream up, how long will it take to reach the pirate camp?" Knox asked. He scanned the forest until, halfway up the mountain, he spotted some thatched roofs barely visible above the trees.

"About four hours," Teca replied.

"What are those boats doing near that ship?" Knox asked. In the distance, two small boats, sails down, floated near the SEA DRAGON.

"The Sea Gypsies are diving for spiny lobsters. They're abundant in that part of the channel," Lek replied. Teca remained silent.

Knox smiled. "We won't have to climb that mountain to get to the pirates. I have a plan that will bring them down to us."

He paused, looked at Rachan and Amar, and then continued, "When we begin the raid, Rachan, Prem, Visnu, a Gurkha corporal, and a radioman will take one boat with Teca. You sail near the SEA DRAGON, and pretend you're searching for a good place to dive for lobsters. Then, at the first chance you get, board the ship. I'm certain they won't have many guards on board. Dispose of them any way you like. Any questions so far?"

No one had any questions, they understood his orders. Knox continued, "Then set the ship on fire. After making sure that the ship is burning, all of you get back in the boat and land on the beach. Hide in the pine forest and ambush the pirates when they come running down to save the burning ship. At the same time Lek and I'll take the rest of the men in another boat, and cross the channel to the beach directly opposite us. We'll move across that hill, through the forest, towards the path that leads to the pirate camp. When they come down, we'll attack them from both sides."

Knox paused, reviewing the plan in his own mind, trying to find any flaws in it. He found none. He then said, "I'm certain that Hawkins and Grant will definitely come down to see that the fire's put out because that ship is their only way out of here. Any questions?"

No one spoke, apparently they understood Knox's plan. Knox fell silent for a moment, as if lost in memory, then said, "I don't want to say this because the last time I said it, I lost a man whom I loved like a brother. But in order to caution you, I have to say it again. Don't try to be heroes. Just stay alive. Make sure the pirates you hit don't rise up again to get you or your friends from behind.

Make sure your men understand this: those pirates are not assets to society. Most of them are condemned criminals and cold-blooded murderers, and after the things they've done, they don't deserve leniency. Just ask our friend, Teca, here."

Knox and his men looked with sympathy at the Sea Gypsy, whose fiancée and sister were still being held captive by the pirates.

Knox was pondering his plan when suddenly another thought struck him.

"After we return to the camp," Knox said to Lek, "you and your two friends move the three boats to this beach. Then the three of you take one of the boats and look for lobsters near that ship." Knox pointed at the SEA DRAGON. "When you get some lobsters, approach the ship and offer them to the pirates. I want to know how many guards are on the ship, and the types of weapons they have."

Lek nodded that he understood.

Knox and his men walked back to camp. Now that he had the tactical plan drawn up, he wished that the order to begin the operation would come. Arriving at camp, he checked with the two radio operators, but found no messages.

Knox had brought two radio sets so that his team could maintain constant communications with their base on Langkawi, even if one set broke or was destroyed. When they'd first arrived on Lipe, Knox sent a radio message that they'd reached their destination and all was well. Transmissions between the two islands went well, and Knox's message was subsequently relayed to the main base in Penang.

In the late afternoon, Lek and the two Sea Gypsies returned to the camp with enough lobsters for everyone. As Knox had instructed, they'd given some lobsters to the pirates on the SEA DRAGON and reported that there were four men on board. All carried knives, and Lek saw two single-barreled shotguns. Two men stood guard at all times, one on the bow and the other at the stern.

Knox congratulated the three men on a job well done, and asked them to do the same thing tomorrow in order to become friendly with the men guarding the SEA DRAGON.

Knox waited anxiously for one of the radio sets to broadcast the order to begin. He had no idea what was taking so long.

In London, the Foreign Office's note arrived at the Cabinet Office late in the afternoon on March 8, 1946, a Friday. The man in charge of the Cabinet Office felt that it was too late in the evening to send the telegram to the SAC-SEA in Singapore, which was seven hours ahead of London. It was late at night in Singapore anyway, he thought. Since the SAC-SEA's message was only designated IMPORTANT, with no other mention of its urgency, he decided to send the telegram out on Monday the 11th.

By the time the Cabinet Office finished encoding and transmitting the telegram to the SAC-SEA on March 11, it was eleven-forty in the morning in London, but six-forty in the evening in Singapore. The communications section of the SAC-SEA's office operated twenty-four hours a day and had been told to watch for this particularly important telegram.

Although it was after office hours, the communications section chief had the telegram decoded immediately. The message, which simply stated that the Cabinet Office approved the intention of the SAC-SEA to carry out a minor operation to suppress pirate activity in the Andaman Sea, was hand delivered to Mountbatten's residence at seven-thirty.

Mountbatten read the telegram in less than ten seconds, and instructed the communications section to radio Perowne in Penang immediately with orders to proceed with the operation.

Perowne received the message at eight-fifteen, and sent it on to the forward base in Langkawi to be relayed to Knox on Lipe at once.

Knox received the message, which simply stated, "Proceed as planned" at eight-thirty in the evening of March 11. He acknowledged the message and replied, "Operation commences 060012."

The next morning at six, Knox, Chai, and three Gurkha soldiers boarded a sailboat with Lek at the tiller, left Lipe, and headed straight for the beach on Adang.

At the same time Rachan and Prem boarded a sailboat with Teca, while Visnu and the two remaining Gurkha soldiers took the other boat with Duwa.

There had been a slight change of plan, Duwa was not to be left out of this operation. He had pleaded with Knox to use his boat.

Knox finally agreed, after realizing that six men with all their weapons and equipment would be too crowded in one boat. With two boats, they would have more room to maneuver, and could spread out and attack the SEA DRAGON simultaneously.

Knox's boat took thirty minutes to cross the channel. After landing on the beach at Adang, Knox and his men moved across the wooded hill towards the pine forest as planned.

Ten minutes after Knox and his men landed on the beach, the other two sailboats reached the SEA DRAGON. Rachan ordered Visnu and the two Gurkhas, Karbir and Rai, to board the ship. The three men threw large steel hooks with ropes tied to them at the wooden rail on the side of the ship. The hooks, wrapped in cloth to muffle the sound of contact, caught securely on the railing. Visnu, Karbir, and Rai began to climb up the ropes, as Rachan and Prem stood below with their pistols, equipped with silencers, aimed at the ship.

"A boat is approaching from the port side. I heard a noise. Let's take a look," a voice cried out.

As the three men climbed, footsteps clattered across the creaking deck, then suddenly, two faces peered over the railing and stared in astonishment at what they saw.

Before they could warn their colleagues on the ship or do anything to stop the assault, Rachan and Prem shot both pirates in the head, killing them instantly.

At that moment, Visnu and the two Gurkhas reached the railing and vaulted onto the ship's deck.

The two other pirates, asleep on the deck, were awakened by the thuds of their colleagues' bodies hitting the deck. Rising to meet the intruders, one of them reached for a knife and the other picked up a shotgun.

Visnu raised his silencer-equipped pistol.

Before the Indian corporal could fire a shot, a kukri flew out of Karbir's right hand and buried itself in the pirate's chest, killing him instantly. The shotgun fell from his hands.

The pirate with the knife, seeing what happened to his friend and realizing that the odds were against him, surrendered.

Remembering Knox's warning, Visnu approached the

remaining pirate and knocked him unconscious with the steel butt of his submachine gun. He took a small coil of rope from his pocket and tied the unconscious pirate to one of the ship's masts.

At the same time, Rachan and Prem boarded the ship with lit torches. As Visnu and the two Gurkhas retreated to the sailboat, they began to set fire to the sails and cabins. When they were certain that the fire had caught on, Rachan and Prem returned to their boat, and signaled Teca and Duwa to move the boats to the shore. When they reached the beach, they ran into the pine forest and positioned themselves along the right side of the path leading to the pirate compound.

Ten minutes later, Knox and his team appeared in the clearing. They ran into the forest and hid behind the pine trees on the left side of the path. There they waited for Hawkins and the pirates to come down to save the burning ship. Knox and his nine men were armed with Sten submachine guns, pistols, and knives. The five Gurkhas also had their kukris.

Hawkins and Grant woke to the sounds of shouting and urgent pounding on the doors of their rooms.

"Wake up! Wake up! The ship is on fire!" voices shouted repeatedly.

Hawkins and Grant hurried from their rooms and rushed to the lookout, where a group of men were already gathering and pointing down at the sea below. Hawkins's heart sank when he saw flames and smoke covering the deck of the SEA DRAGON. He knew immediately that the fire was no accident, and his first impulse was to blame the Sea Gypsies.

"What happened to those four damn guards!?" Hawkins asked himself furiously. They should not have allowed the fire to get started in the first place, and now the it was spreading all over the ship. He rushed back to his room to get his pistol and rifle, telling Grant and the remaining nine pirates to get their weapons and follow him down to see what had happened and whether they could save the ship.

Hurrying down the winding mountain path, Hawkins and his pirates took less than an hour to reach the pine forest. As they entered the forest, Hawkins became cautious. He told his men to slow down, move carefully, and spread out mong the trees instead of bunching together and becoming easy targets for anyone lying in wait.

Before the pirates could follow Hawkins's orders, firing erupted, killing five of them instantly in a hail of bullets. But the rows of pine trees partially blocked the ambushers' field of fire, so some of the pirates, including Hawkins and Grant, were saved. Hawkins and the rest of his men threw themselves on the ground, seeking protection behind pine trees and firing blindly into the trees ahead of them.

After a brief exchange of gunfire, some of the pirates began to lose heart as they realized that their rifles and shotguns were no match for the rapid fire of the submachine guns. Two of them got up and ran back towards the mountain. Hawkins and Chim, the guard who was the leader of the Thai pirates, tried in vain to call them back but the two pirates were cut down as they ran into the ambushers' line of fire. Besides Hawkins and Grant, only two TVTS guards, Chim and Karn, remained alive.

Hawkins looked around and sensed defeat, but he still did not know who the ambushers were. Judging from the weapons they were using and the way the ambush had been staged, he quessed that they must be well-trained professional men. Hawkins suspected that they might be

Thai security forces. He never thought that they might be British soldiers because this was Thai territory, and they would need permission from the Thai Government to be here.

Only when a familiar voice called out to them in English did he recognize the attackers.

"Hawkins, Grant, give up! You don't have a chance! You're outnumbered. We're taking you back to stand trial."

"It's Knox!" Grant exclaimed in astonishment. "How could it be?"

"Yes, it's him all right! I recognize his voice," Hawkins said grimly. "The Thai Government must have allowed the British to come after us. I won't surrender. If they take me back, I'll only be shot by a firing squad, so I might as well go on fighting. Even if I die, I might take some of them with me, maybe even Knox himself."

"What are we going to do now? We only have two men left," Grant asked. "We don't have a chance against submachine guns with these obsolete rifles."

"Let's retreat back to the camp. Adang is a big island, and we know the terrain better than Knox and his men. They won't have an easy time finding us, and we still have enough ammunition to pick them off one by one," Hawkins replied, confident that he would not be easily apprehended.

Hawkins motioned for Chim and Karn to follow them as he and Grant retreated quietly from the pine forest, up the narrow path to the camp.

Knox had anticipated Hawkins's strategy. It was his only way to escape the ambushers. To Hawkins's left was the sea, but he did not have a boat. To his right was the hill from which Knox and his men had come, and they were blocking him from reaching it. In front of him were the unknown and the unseen assailants. Therefore, Hawkins had no choice but to retreat up the mountain.

Knox led Chai and the three Gurkha soldiers as they ran alongside the path. Their plan was to keep Hawkins and his men from retreating up the mountain, thus denying them the advantage of the high terrain.

As Hawkins, Grant, and the two guards were making their way up a steep slope, they heard a volley of fire behind them. Hawkins heard screams of pain. He looked back and saw the blood covered bodies of Chim and Karn lying motionless on the path. He was certain that they were dead because Knox and his men shot to kill.

Knox and his men stepped over the guards' lifeless bodies, believing that they were dead. They were joined by Rachan and the rest of his team.

Five minutes after the British soldiers had disappeared in pursuit of Hawkins and Grant up the mountain, Chim slowly regained consciousness. He was wounded in the left arm and a bullet had creased his temple, knocking him out temporarily.

Chim pushed himself up and picked up a double-barreled shotgun that lay near him. He looked at Karn whose body was riddled with bullet holes, certain that he was dead. Chim examined his left arm considering himself lucky that the bullet had not hit the bone. Checking the shotgun, he discovered that both barrels were loaded.

Chim walked slowly through the pine forest, the shotgun in firing position, heading towards the beach. He passed dead pirates lying scattered on the ground, but because none of the ambushers was in sight, he presumed that they were chasing after Hawkins and Grant. He needed to find a boat so he could get back to Tarutao and warn Khun Apipat.

Chim smiled when he saw three Sea Gypsy sailboats

moored near the beach. Sitting against a pine tree were two Sea Gypsies looking out at the sea. Chim approached them silently and aimed his shotgun at the startled Teca and Duwa.

"Walk to the boat, you two," Chim said in the island language.

"What do you want with us?" Teca asked. He looked at Chim with hatred.

"You're going to take me to Tarutao. You'd better do as I say because this time I won't just hit you on the head; I'll shoot you in the chest."

"You! You were the one that knocked me out and helped the foreigner take Buruk!" Teca said fiercely, touching the scar on his right temple.

"Teca, let's do what he said," cautioned Duwa. He was afraid that Teca would lose his temper, attack Chim, and be killed.

Teca stood in silence controlling his rage, then walked from the pine forest to his boat, followed by Duwa and Chim.

"Hold it. There are three boats, but only two of you. Where is the other man?" Chim asked.

"He has gone with the foreign soldiers," Teca replied.

Chim got in the boat first and sat at the bow. He motioned with his shotgun at Teca and Duwa to push the boat out. Duwa picked up the anchor and put it in the boat. He helped Teca push the boat into deeper water, then climbed into the boat.

"Put the sail up and head for Tarutao," Chim said. As Duwa handled the tiller, Teca stood up, preparing to hoist the sail. With his back to Chim, Teca looked directly into Duwa's eyes. Duwa stared back, understanding the message in Teca's eyes.

Suddenly, Teca and Duwa threw their weight to one

side of the boat. Chim shouted a threat and aimed the shotgun at the two men, but had no chance to fire because the boat capsized, throwing the three men into the sea.

The shotgun was useless in the water. Chim let go of it because he needed both hands to stay afloat and swim. Struggling to swim up to the surface, he felt something holding down his legs. Soon his body became a dead weight, and he slowly began sinking to the bottom.

He looked down and saw Duwa holding to his ankles firmly with both arms. He tried using his arms to swim up, but suddenly someone grabbed his hands from behind and pulled him down. It was Teca.

Chim realized then that hijacking a boat with two Sea Gypsies in it threatened to be a fatal mistake. He was no match for these men in the water, and knew that they intended to hold him down until he drowned. Under water, he'd run out of air long before they did.

Chim struggled in vain, he could not shake himself free from the two men. He tried to hold his breath, but eventually reached the limit of his endurance. His nose and mouth unwillingly inhaled salt water into his lungs. Then Chim felt nothing and saw only blackness as his body slowly sank to the bottom of the channel.

Hawkins and Grant were halfway up the trail when Hawkins whispered to Grant. "We must try to get Knox first," he said. "Hide yourself in a bush here. I'll be the bait. When Knox follows me and has passed you, come out and take him from behind. How about it?"

"Sounds good. Let's do it," Grant replied eagerly.

Knox spotted Hawkins's back disappearing among a group of trees about one hundred feet ahead of him. He quickened his pace, hoping to catch up with Hawkins. He passed the bush where Grant was hiding without noticing him.

Grant smiled at his luck and quietly emerged from the bush. He stalked Knox from behind with his rifle raised, trying to find a clear field of fire.

Suddenly, Grant realized that he had made a mistake in stepping out from the bush without knowing exactly how many men Knox had with him. He'd only seen Knox, but it was obvious from the ambush and gunfire that Knox must have several men with him. Where were they?

Then Grant realized that he had been tricked into coming out from his hiding place to go after Knox, who was the bait.

Grant's sixth sense told him that someone was behind him. Quickly he turned around, ready to fire.

He saw something move in the bush in front of him.

Before he could fire a shot, he felt an excruciating pain in his chest. He looked down and saw the hilt of a knife protruding from his chest. The curved blade of a kukri was buried deeply, fatally, in his heart. Grant tried in vain to reach the hilt with his right hand, to pull it out, but found that he had lost all strength. He couldn't even raise his hand. He saw darkness, then fell noiselessly dead.

Hawkins retreated slowly up the path, expecting to hear a gunshot from Grant's rifle any second. He looked forward to Grant joining him with the news of the death of one of Knox's men, or maybe even Knox himself. But to his disappointment and irritation, there was no gunshot, no footsteps. An ominous stillness filled the forest.

What was that damn Grant doing? Where was he? Hawkins ground his teeth with impatience.

Suddenly, Hawkins saw an object hurtling through the air in his direction. It fell to the ground not far from his feet. Hawkins stood frozen in horror when he recognized what it was.

It was Grant's head, freshly severed from his body, blood still dripping from it. It lay on the ground staring up at him.

It was the most grotesque sight Hawkins had ever seen. He turned away and threw up behind a nearby tree, then shaking, leaned against the tree when he heard a voice coming from down the path.

"Surrender, Hawkins! Otherwise you'll end up like Grant!"

It was Knox's voice.

Hawkins looked in the direction of the voice. There, about sixty feet away, he saw his most hated enemy. Knox had a submachine gun in his hands pointing at Hawkins.

Desperation forced Hawkins to take a risk. With his left hand, he threw the rifle to his left as if he was going to surrender. Then suddenly, he dropped to his right knee while pulling a pistol from the waistband of his trousers. Hawkins aimed the pistol at Knox, while his right thumb released the safety catch. He hoped to fire the first shot, but Knox had anticipated the move. He squeezed the trigger of the Sten, and several 9 mm. Parabellum bullets ripped through Hawkins's chest, killing him instantly.

The long pursuit had ended.

Everyone in the Sea Gypsy village on Lipe, including Malatee, stood on the beach looking across the channel at Adang and listening to the periodic sound of gunfire.

Malatee was almost frantic with worry over the safety of Knox, Lek, and Knox's men.

The Sea Gypsies on Lipe were wondering whether the dreaded pirates would be destroyed once and for all so that peace and happiness could return to their little community.

Then Malatee saw three men walking from the pine forest to a sailboat. She knew that two of the men must be Sea Gypsies because they had no shirts on. But they were too far away to tell who the third man was. The sailboat moved out from the beach with the three men in it.

What was happening? Malatee asked herself, puzzled by what she saw.

Then the boat capsized, and all three men disappeared under the sea.

One minute later, two men came up. They pushed the capsized boat towards the beach and set it upright. The two men had no shirts on.

The exchange of gunfire lasted for about one and a half hours. Then it stopped completely.

Nothing moved on the shore or on the beach at Adang. From Lipe, nothing was visible but the charred bow of the SEA DRAGON and the three small empty sailboats moored near the beach. It was as though the green pine forest and the large mountain behind it had swallowed everyone.

Malatee could wait no longer. She waded into the knee-deep water, trying to see what was happening on the other side of the channel.

A few moments later, she saw a group of men emerge from the pine forest and board the three sailboats. However, Malatee was unable to accurately count the number of men in the group, nor could she see whether her Knox was among them, because they were all dressed in camouflaged combat uniforms.

Then she saw four figures run from the pine forest and get in one of the boats.

The three boats put up their sails and headed for Lipe.

As the three boats came closer, Malatee's heart filled with joy when she saw Knox sitting in the bow of one of the boats. She counted seventeen heads. She was puzzled because Knox and his nine men plus Lek, Teca, and Duwa would only make thirteen.

Who then, were the other four?

She looked again carefully and saw that the four were female. If they were Buruk, Lema, and the other two Sea Gypsy girls who had been held captive by the pirates, it meant that all the pirates, including Hawkins and Grant, must have been killed.

Malatee ran back up the beach to the assembled villagers and told them the good news that everyone was returning, including the four girls.

As soon as the three boats reached the beach, everyone rushed to greet Knox and his party and help them carry their arms and equipment up to the shore. Teca and Buruk, Duwa and Lema, and the other two girls were happily reunited with their families.

Malatee embraced Knox, tears running down her cheeks. She could not control her emotions, relieved that Knox had returned alive and unharmed.

Briefly, Knox told Malatee and the Sea Gypsies what had happened to the pirates. He also told them how they'd found the four girls, who'd decided to walk down from the pirate compound when they discovered that there was no one left there. They met Knox and his men after all the pirates had been killed.

Out of a sense of decency, Knox felt that the pirates should be buried rather than left to decay or be eaten by scavenging animals. Therefore he'd ordered his men to dig a large grave and bury the corpses.

Later, Knox sent a message to Perowne, "All the sharks, including two biggest ones, are dead."

"Congratulations. Trip to Tarutao 080015 confirmed. Be there on the 14th," was the return message.

CHAPTER 22

Late in the morning of March 14, 1946, Khun Apipat and his son, Sanoh, stepped off a motor boat from Satun at Taloh Wow Bay.

They'd gone to Satun on March 13 to attend a meeting called by the Governor of Satun to discuss the problem of the pirates in the Andaman Sea. The Governor and the police had been receiving complaints from merchants and ship owners in Satun and Kantang that their ships and goods were being lost to piracy. The meeting only lasted a day, but Khun Apipat had planned on staying another week after the meeting. He had been looking forward to a week of rest and relaxation.

However, Khun Apipat's plan was spoiled when a messenger arrived in Satun that evening with a message from Cunningham urging him to return to Tarutao at once. The messenger emphasized that it was a matter of life and death.

Khun Apipat knew that the American was serious. Cunningham had originally encouraged him to attend the meeting in the first place, saying it would be a splendid opportunity to learn how much the Thai authorities knew about the pirating activities and what their policy and plans were regarding the problem.

They hurried to Khun Apipat's office where Cunningham waited with a worried look on his face.

"Khun Apipat, something very important has come up," he said.

"What happened, Collin?" Khun Apipat asked.

"The men guarding the base on Langkawi went to Kuah two days ago to buy provisions. While there, they saw a sizable movement of soldiers and equipment on Kuah, and two British battleships anchored offshore, along with three or four smaller ships. Curious, they asked around and were told by some food vendors on the waterfront that the British were going to raid Tarutao in a few days to suppress the pirates. Fortunately, they had enough sense to realize how important this information was. They sailed immediately from Kuah and told me what they'd seen and heard. After questioning them about the movements of the British troops, I have come to believe that there's enough truth in the story for us to be alarmed. That's why I asked you to return at once. We need to talk about this."

"Collin, I'm not certain whether this time your assessment is correct. At the meeting yesterday, the Governor and other officials, including the police, didn't say anything about the pirates being on Tarutao, or any British plan to invade Tarutao. They concluded that the pirates were either former inmates who had already been released from Tarutao, or some desperate fishermen. Our men could have misinterpreted what they saw and heard."

"Oh, come on, Khun Apipat. You'd better think again!" Cunningham said. He was annoyed at Khun Apipat's gullibility. "Don't you see that the Governor called the meeting yesterday just to get you away from Tarutao in order to make it easy for the British to land here? They'd never mention this to you even if they did know about it."

Cunningham walked over to Khun Apipat, who was sitting behind his desk. He leaned over the desk to emphasize his point.

"In order for the British to be able to send their troops into Thai territory, they must have the consent of the Thai Government. If that's so, then the Governor must have been informed by the Government, but was told to keep quiet and not alert you. Don't you see that the meeting yesterday was part of their plan?"

"All right, even if you're right and the British come here with their troops, what do they expect to find? You know very well, Collin, that we don't keep the plunder here at Taloh Wow Bay. It's all at the crocodile cave." Khun Apipat smiled, confident that there would be no evidence that could connect him with the pirating activities.

"Don't be so sure, Khun Apipat," Cunningham said, shaking his head at Khun Apipat's stubbornness. "Not everyone on this island is involved in the piracy, but almost everyone knows about our activities. It's an open secret. Those who aren't involved and haven't profited from our piracy might be willing to act as witnesses in return for rewards or leniency in serving their terms here. They'll do anything, including pointing a finger at you as the leader of the pirates, or even selling out their best friends, just to get themselves off this island."

Frustrated, Cunningham walked back to his chair and slumped down in it.

Then he sat up again, looked at Khun Apipat, and said, "I don't think that our loot at the crocodile cave is a secret. Therefore, I strongly suggest that we move as much of the loot as possible either to our base on Langkawi or to Adang. And it has to be done right away, because the British may be here in a few days. Whatever we cannot move in time, we have to hide somewhere else on Tarutao."

This was the opportunity that Cunningham had been waiting for, and he was determined to exert as much control over the loot as he could. What he had suggested to Khun Apipat was logical. Best of all, it also fitted with his desire to find a way of taking the stolen goods out of Tarutao without Khun Apipat's resistance.

Sanoh, who had been silent throughout this discussion, spoke up, "I think that Collin's suggestion is reasonable, Father. In a situation like this it's best to trust as few people as possible. Because of your rank and position, you can't risk having the evidence found on Tarutao. We must be prepared for the worst situation. If the British really do come here, it means that our government must have enough evidence, or believe the evidence that the British have produced, in order to permit the British troops to enter our territory."

Sanoh stopped to think for a few seconds before continuing, "And another thing, Father, don't rule out the involvement of Knox and his men. I wouldn't be surprised if it was Knox who gave the British and Thai governments information about our activities."

"Sanoh is right, Khun Apipat," Cunningham said. "Last month orders came from Bangkok for you to confine Hawkins and Grant to await extradition to British Malaya. How did the British know that Hawkins and Grant were on Tarutao? Knox had to have told them."

"Yes, and you were clever to suggest a way out for me," Khun Apipat said. "So I informed Bangkok that all prisoners-of-war had been released when the war was over. It was a relief for me to be able to provide a logical answer for the government."

Cunningham smiled to himself when he heard what Khun Apipat had said. Actually it was a relief for Cunningham himself. He had now been officially recorded as released from Tarutao. Therefore, he could not be connected in anyway to the pirates. He had been looking for an alibi, and when Khun Apipat received the orders on the extradition of Hawkins and Grant, he had grabbed at the opportunity.

After listening to Cunningham and Sanoh, Khun Apipat became silent for a few moments, alone with his thoughts. Then he spoke, "All right, we'll do as Collin suggests, but let's do it as discreetly as possible. Use only the men whom we are certain can be trusted. We'll transfer the goods to the base on Langkawi. It's nearer than Adang. We'd need larger ships, which we don't have and can't find on such short notice, to carry all the stolen goods to Adang."

Khun Apipat paused again and sat in silence, then continued, "If Collin is right about the British, then they'll almost certainly invade Adang too, because of Hawkins and Grant. I've never underestimated Knox. I think he knows Hawkins and Grant are on Adang. If Knox is involved as Sanoh believes, then Hawkins and Grant will be the main targets. If that's the case, then Adang is not a safe place to keep our loot. Therefore, I think Langkawi is the most suitable place."

"Should we send someone to warn Hawkins and Grant?" Sanoh asked.

"I don't think that we should do that, Sanoh. We have Hawkins and Grant on Adang as our last way out," Cunningham said with a crafty smile.

"What do you mean by that, Collin?" Khun Apipat asked.

"When the British invade here and find nothing, we'll need a convincing decoy to divert their attention from our treasure on Tarutao and Langkawi. Hawkins and Grant are the best choice because they have been running from the law. We can inform the British that the pirates actually come out from Adang, not Tarutao, and that Hawkins is their leader." Cunningham paused when he saw a frown on the faces of both father and son.

He laughed before saying, "I know. You may think that it's ungentlemanly to do that to them. But we have no choice. It's either them or us, and I prefer it to be them, don't you?" Cunningham smiled when he heard no objections to his suggestion from either Khun Apipat or Sanoh.

While Khun Apipat and Cunningham were discussing their plans, thirty miles away, four small sailboats were leaving Lipe for Pante Bay on Tarutao. Knox, Malatee, and Knox's nine men were on the first three boats, with Lek, Teca, and Duwa handling the tillers. On the fourth boat were three Sea Gypsy men.

The Sea Gypsies on Lipe were grateful to Knox and his men for eliminating the pirates on Adang and freeing them from their predations. That night, they held a big feast for Knox and his men to show their gratitude and celebrate their own return to peace and happiness.

The next day, Knox and his men relaxed, checked their weapons and equipment, and went over the plans for the raid on Tarutao.

When the village chief learned of Knox's next assignment, he instructed three of his men to accompany Knox. The three men were familiar with the Pante Bay area, including the river that led to the crocodile cave. They had even hunted crocodiles there.

Knox welcomed their kind gesture. One of the benefits of having the Sea Gypsies around was the guarantee of a continuous supply of fresh seafood. They knew where and how to obtain food from the sea.

After six hours of sailing, the four sailboats arrived at the western side of Tarutao in the late afternoon. They anchored at a small secluded cove near Pante Bay and set up camp on the beach underneath two huge cashew trees.

Knox instructed one of his radio men to report to Brigadier Perowne that he and his men had arrived, and were ready for the operation tomorrow. The return message confirmed that Brigadier Perowne was on Langkawi and that the operation would go on as planned.

Knox instructed the three Sea Gypsies to enter the river at Pante Bay to see whether there was any activity there. Recalling his and Malatee's near encounter a year ago with Khun Apipat and Cunningham coming out from the river on the ADANG, Knox suspected that there might be pirate activity further up the river.

When they were in Penang, after he returned from Lipe, Lek had told Knox that some of the Sea Gypsies who fished near Pante Bay occasionally saw a few sailboats entering and leaving the river. The Sea Gypsies also knew about the crocodile cave at the end of the river. Although no one had ever ventured into the cave, they believed there was an opening at the other end because they could feel a breeze coming out from the cave.

Knox was certain that this information suggested the possibility that the pirates might store their loot in the cave. Another possibility was that the cave and the river could be a hideout and escape route for the pirates in an emergency.

Knox knew that men like Khun Apipat and Cunningham would not fight to the death, they would try to escape with their treasure and settle somewhere else.

Based on this assessment, Knox convinced Perowne to allow him and his men to position themselves at Pante Bay, in case Khun Apipat and Cunningham decided to escape through the cave and the river.

It was dark when the three Sea Gypsies returned to the camp.

"Did you see anything?" Knox asked, with Lek translating.

"There are two double-masted ships anchored in the river, halfway between the mouth of the river and the crocodile cave," one of the Sea Gypsies replied. "They can't go in any further because the river becomes too shallow for them. When we were there, we saw two rowboats carrying something from upriver to the ships."

"Did the two rowboats go back to where they came from?" Knox asked.

"No, it was dark by the time they finished loading the cargo onto the ships. All the men on the rowboats boarded the ships," the Sea Gypsy replied.

"Those two rowboats must be dinghies from the ships," Rachan commented. Knox nodded in agreement.

"How many men were there on the two ships?" Knox asked.

"We saw three in each rowboat, and four on each ship," another Sea Gypsy replied.

"That's fourteen altogether. I have a plan," Knox said. "Tomorrow morning I want the three of you to go back and watch the ships and the rowboats. When the rowboats leave, come back and let me know. Don't forget to count how many men go with the rowboats."

The next morning Brigadier Perowne and three hundred Gurkha soldiers left Kuah at six. They sailed on one frigate, which served as the command ship, and two landing craft. On board the frigate with Perowne was a senior Inspector General of the Thai Department of Corrections, named Vibul, who acted as a representative of the Thai Government. They expected to land at Taloh Wow Bay at eight.

At six-thirty, Knox, his men, the Sea Gypsies, and Malatee left the camp and headed for the river at Pante Bay. When they reached the mouth of the river, Knox sent the three Sea Gypsies up the river to see whether the rowboats had left the two ships.

The Sea Gypsies returned at seven-thirty to tell Knox that the two rowboats had left with three men on each boat. Knox ordered his men to get ready to board and take over the two ships.

"Collin! Wake up!" a voice shouted outside Cunningham's room, followed by a banging on the door.

"What's up?" Cunningham asked, as he opened the door and faced the man who woke him up.

It was one of the lookouts whom Cunningham had sent to keep watch at Taloh Wow Bay the night before. The American took the information that his men had told him about the British seriously. If the British did invade Tarutao, then he wanted to be the first to be alerted.

"Three warships are coming towards Taloh Wow Bay. They should be here in thirty minutes," the man said.

"So your information was right. The British really are coming. Did you happen to see how many men there were on those ships?" Cunningham asked.

"It's too far out. Do you want me to warn Khun Apipat and the others?"

"No," Cunningham said. "We have no time to do that. We have to get to the crocodile cave as fast as possible and load as much loot on our sailboat as we can. We'd better leave right now."

Knox and his men quietly approached the two ships on three boats. Malatee remained behind, on the fourth boat with the three Sea Gypsies.

Knox and his men commandeered the two ships without any resistance from the crew. The two vessels were merchant ships hired from Satun to carry the captured cargo to Langkawi. The crew were not pirates and were unarmed.

Knox inspected the cargo that had already been loaded on the two ships, and discovered that it was hundreds of burlap bags of rice. He and his men settled down waited for the rowboats to return with more cargo.

It was a bright, sunny morning. The weather was pleasant and a light breeze blew past the veranda of Khun Apipat's cottage, which was located on a small hill overlooking Taloh Wow Bay. From the cottage, Khun Apipat commanded a view of the entire bay and the prisoner compound. He had always enjoyed having breakfast on the veranda, under the shade of tall coconut trees.

Khun Apipat did not foresee any interruption in his routine this morning. He thought that maybe the news that Cunningham had told him about the British was only a rumor, or a misunderstanding on the part of the people on Langkawi.

As the two female prisoners he had assigned to perform maid duties at his cottage were about to serve him breakfast, Khun Apipat looked up towards the bay. He saw three military vessels, displaying British flags, cruising slowly into Taloh Wow Bay. The three ships were heading directly for the TVTS compound.

"Those must be the British ships! So Cunningham was right!" Khun Apipat exclaimed to himself. He was at a loss as to what to do for a moment. Then he finally got control of himself and told one of the maids to get Pradit, his deputy, immediately.

Five minutes later Pradit hurried into Khun Apipat's cottage.

"The British are coming! They will land here soon!" Khun Apipat cried to his deputy. "Find Cunningham and tell him to hurry to the crocodile cave to make sure that everything that can be is removed from the cave. What can't be moved to the merchant ships waiting in the river must be buried. I have a feeling that the British know about the crocodile cave. I'll try to stall them here so that our men will have time to remove all the evidence."

Khun Apipat walked down to shore, where the British ships were approaching. The British did not bother to use the pier to land their troops. The two medium-size landing craft came right up on the gravel bank of the bay. Their rectangular-shaped bows opened up, and hundreds of Gurkha soldiers in full fighting gear armed with rifles poured out of the two vessels. They regrouped into several squads that took off in different directions. One squad, led by a British Army captain, came straight to Khun Apipat as he hurried down to the shore.

"You must be Khun Apipat, the Director of the TVTS," the British captain said in English. He was looking at the photograph of Khun Apipat he was holding in his right hand. A Malay in British army uniform interpreted for him.

"Yes, I am Khun Apipat. What can I do for you?" Khun Apipat replied in Thai, with a forced smile.

"I've been authorized by the Thai Government and the British military command to place you under arrest," the captain said firmly and slowly through his interpreter. Ten Gurkhas surrounded Khun Apipat.

The reply stunned Khun Apipat for a moment, then he
recovered and asked, "On what charge and where is your
authorization? You are now encroaching on the territory
of Thailand."

The captain did not reply but instead pointed in the
direction of the landing crafts. Khun Apipat looked where
the captain was pointing.

To his astonishment and dismay, he saw Vibul, the
senior Inspector General of the DOC, walking towards
him, escorted by a high ranking British officer and a squad
of Gurkhas carrying submachine guns.

Khun Apipat greeted Vibul first in the Thai way with
a wai, bringing the palms of both hands together and
raising them to face level with his head bending down
slightly, because the man was senior to him.

"What's happening?" he asked. "Why are British soldiers
here? And why am I under arrest?"

"Khun Apipat, the Thai and British authorities have
considerable evidence that you and some of your guards
and prisoners have been involved in piracy in this area,"
the Inspector General replied. "The Thai Government,
after having seriously considered the evidence presented
to them, approved a British request to suppress the piracy.
I've been authorized to represent our Government in this
operation. I would like to advise you that, for your own
benefit, you and your men should give the British your
full cooperation."

The Inspector General paused to look around at the
TVTS compound. The guards and the prisoners stood in
groups watching the raid in fear and confusion. They all
waited for the order from Khun Apipat. As they searched
the buildings, the Gurkhas encountered no opposition.

The Inspector General spoke again, "Khun Apipat,
you'd better assemble your guards and prisoners here.

Names of the suspects will be called out. I would like to inform you that you and the accused will be entitled to a fair trial by Thai judges in Thai courts in accordance with Thai laws."

Khun Apipat was shaken, he had not expected to confront a situation like this. He barely managed to control himself as he told one of the guards nearby to do as the Inspector General had ordered.

Within twenty minutes all the guards and prisoners in the Taloh Wow Bay compound had gathered in front of the flagpole. Surrounding them were three hundred Gurkha soldiers, their rifles in firing position.

The Inspector General gave a list to a guard and told him to read out aloud the names of the guards and prisoners who were accused of involvement in the piracy.

The names of the guards, including Nit who had already been killed by Rachan, two policemen stationed on Tarutao, and the head of the fishery section, were read. Those who were present were told to walk up front and were handcuffed by the Gurkhas.

Five guards were missing. Khun Apipat explained to the Inspector General that Nit and two other guards had been killed in an accident while learning to sail. Chim and Karn had been sent to Adang with a detail of prisoners to get rattan.

Khun Apipat dared not admit that Nit had disappeared in a raid in December, and that the other two guards were killed while attacking the convoy of merchant ships in January. Khun Apipat was surprised and concerned that the names that were read out were all correct and that they were all members of his inner circle. But what astonished Khun Apipat the most was that the thirty prisoners whose names were called out had been actually involved in the plundering. Several prisoners whose names were called out were missing from the compound and Khun Apipat had to make up a story about how they were killed by malaria. The truth was that some of them were killed while trying to hunt down Knox and his men last August, four were killed with Nit, and some died while attacking the convoy of the merchant ships in January. Still others were on Adang with Hawkins.

Khun Apipat realized that Cunningham had been absolutely right. Someone on Tarutao had kept track of all the guards and prisoners who were involved in the piracy. The list was very accurate and almost complete.

Khun Apipat had no choice but to accept his fate.

Khun Apipat had no way of knowing that two of his guards were undercover Zone 9 policemen sent to collect evidence against the pirates and three of the prisoners were informants.

When the Thai Government was approached by the British Embassy in Bangkok about the problem with the pirates on Tarutao, it referred the matter to the Ministry of Interior, which in turn asked the Police Department for its views on the British request. The Police Department instructed the Zone 9 Provincial Police to supply it with any information or evidence they might have on the pirates of Tarutao.

The Zone 9 commander delivered the information he'd gathered from his informants on Tarutao, and recommended that the Thai government allow the British to send troops to Tarutao to suppress the pirates once and for all. Colonel Banchongsak stressed that Khun Apipat was unduly influential in government and business circles in the southern provinces, especially with the police in Satun and nearby provinces. Therefore, the Thai security forces, whether police or military, would not be effective.

The Police Department and the Thai government took Banchongsak's advice, and the British request was approved.

The two row boats, loaded with boxes of automobile spare parts and bags of rice, reached the merchant ships. A man on one of the boats shouted to the ships, announcing their arrival.

To their surprise, unfamiliar faces appeared at the railings of both ships. They were strange-looking men, dressed in what looked like military uniforms, pointing submachine guns at them.

Knox ordered the men in the rowboats to carry the cargo up to the ships. After they finished, they were tied up and reunited with their colleagues on the ship's deck. The captains of the two ships confessed that they had been hired by Sanoh to transport the cargo to Langkawi.

Knox now had enough material evidence and witnesses to connect Khun Apipat with the piracy.

"Good work, Knox. Everything is going according to plan at this end," Perowne said over the radio when Knox reported his results.

"Have you arrested Cunningham, the American?" asked Knox. He feared that Cunningham, with his slyness, elusiveness, and ability to manipulate people, would escape arrest.

"I haven't seen any foreigner among guards and prisoners here," Perowne replied.

"Sir, please ask around," Knox said with concern. "It's important that we get him. He is their mastermind. He is the pirates' strategist."

"I'll radio you back when I get word," Perowne said.

Five minutes later Perowne was on the radio again.

"Knox, Cunningham is not here. Everyone here says

that Cunningham was released after the war and left the island months ago."

"Sir, that's impossible! Just three weeks ago, my informant told me that Cunningham was still on Tarutao. I believe he's still on the island and they're covering up for him."

"If your informant is right, then Cunningham would probably head for the cave and the river you told me about."

"If he does, I'll be waiting for him."

Two hours later Perowne radioed Knox again.

"Knox, the operation at this end is complete. I'll have Khun Apipat and the other arrestees sent to Satun. The police are waiting to take them into custody. Anything at your end?"

"Nothing, sir."

"I'll leave fifty soldiers here on Tarutao under a captain to see that things are in order, but they won't stay long. As soon as Bangkok sends a new director here, we'll pull our troops out. I'm returning to Penang after Satun."

"With your permission, sir. I'd like to stay here until Cunningham is captured or it's confirmed that he really did leave the island."

"I'll give you two days. If you don't find him in that time, return to Penang. We've achieved our goals and you've contributed greatly to our success. But don't be too concerned with Cunningham. Unlike Hawkins and Grant, he's not our problem. I won't blame you if you don't get him. Besides, he's all alone now. I don't think he can do anymore harm. See you in two days, Knox."

"Collin, I'm glad to find you here," Pradit said as he rushed into the crocodile cave.

Cunningham and his two men were loading goods into a small sailboat.

"What happened, Pradit?" Cunningham asked, although he knew why Pradit had come.

"Hundreds of British troops have landed! The director has sent me to tell you to remove all the goods from this cave."

"I'm doing that now. Pradit, you should go back to Taloh Wow Bay now before you are found missing. You're the deputy, and Khun Apipat needs you at his side at a time like this. Please tell Khun Apipat that I appreciate his concern, and I'll look after all the treasure for him in Langkawi. I'll be waiting for him there."

"Yes, I'll tell him that, good-bye" Pradit said, as he left the cave.

Cunningham sighed in relief. He told his two men to stop loading and prepare to leave the cave for the river.

"Captain, there's a sailboat coming from upriver. There are three men in it," Rachan reported.

"That must be Cunningham and his men. Everybody keep down until they reach the ship," Knox said, pleased that he wouldn't have to wait long for Cunningham to show up.

Cunningham was glad to see that the two merchant ships were still waiting for him in the river. Although the sea was calm this time of year, and he could handle a sailboat adequately by himself, he didn't feel comfortable about sailing all the way to Langkawi in the small sailboat. He preferred to be in a bigger ship.

He was certain that luck was finally on his side, and that soon all the merchandise on the two ships would be his alone.

In his excitement, Cunningham failed to notice that the crews of the two ships seemed unusually inactive. As his boat reached the ship nearest him, a familiar face appeared above the wooden rail of the ship. It was too late for him to retreat or reach a weapon.

It was Knox, the last person on earth Cunningham wanted to see.

The Englishman smiled as he pointed a 9 mm. Browning automatic pistol at the American.

"Hello, Collin, it's been a long time. I've been waiting here just to greet you," Knox said. "Please remove the revolver from your belt and throw it in the river. Don't try anything. You are vastly outnumbered, and I don't want to shoot you. Hawkins and Grant didn't obey me and they're now dead and buried on Adang."

Cunningham believed Knox's threat.

"All right, Kevin. You win."

Cunningham threw his revolver into the river, and climbed up the rope ladder to the ship, followed by his two men.

Cunningham was well aware that Knox and his men were professional fighting men. Since he didn't have a chance of fighting his way out, he had to find another way to get himself out of this situation.

He smiled at Knox, Rachan, and the three Indian corporals, and finally at Malatee.

"Well, well, this is just like a school reunion. How are you, Kevin, Rachan, Prem, Visnu, Chai?" Cunningham greeted his former prison mates individually, and with genuine good feeling. Despite what had happened, he'd never had a personal conflict with any of them.

Knox and his men said nothing. They stood quietly, observing Cunningham and his two men.

"Where is Brown?" Cunningham asked, unaware that Hawkins had killed him.

"He's dead, shot by Hawkins when we were escaping from Tarutao last year," Knox replied, the anger and sorrow he felt at Brown's death returning to him. "Collin, I don't believe you didn't know that Brown was killed. I know you had a part in it."

"Kevin, I'm sorry to hear that. Please believe me. I didn't know what happened to him. He was a nice man," Cunningham said smoothly, then turning to Malatee, he inquired, "and who is this beautiful lady?"

"Her name is Malatee. She's a friend of mine," Knox replied, watching every move Cunningham made.

"That's a beautiful name. I am Collin Cunningham. It's nice to meet you," Cunningham said, smiling at Malatee while extending his right hand to her.

Her years in an English school in Penang and her custom of using the Western way of greeting, made Malatee instinctively raise her right hand to take Cunningham's.

Before Knox, who sensed trickery behind Cunningham's theatrical show of good manners, could warn Malatee or intervene, Cunningham suddenly pulled Malatee's towards him gripping her with his left arm. His right hand now free, Cunningham swiftly pulled a dagger from the inside of his right boot and pressed it to Malatee's throat.

His action took only three seconds, but stunned everyone. Knox cursed himself for being too careless and underestimating Cunningham.

"She has a beautiful neck, Kevin," Cunningham said. "So don't force me to put this dagger into it. Believe me, it's either her neck or mine, and I'd prefer it to be hers. But I don't want to hurt her or fight with you. I've never had anything against you, I just want to get away from here."

Cunningham paused to look around for a way off the ship. His own sailboat was blocked by the two merchant ships. Then he saw the four Sea Gypsy boats tied to the other side of the ship, facing out to the sea.

"Let me go, Kevin. You can keep all the treasure. I'll only take one of your sailboats," Cunningham said, slowly edging towards the railing with Malatee.

"Untie the boats now, all of them," Cunningham demanded.

Knox nodded at Prem who stood nearest the ropes that tied the four boats to the ship. Prem did as Cunningham demanded.

"Now, throw all your weapons into the river," Cunningham ordered.

Knox did as he was told. The four Indians followed suit.

"How are you going to get down into the boat, Collin? You can't do it holding Malatee like that. You don't have a chance. Better give yourself up," Knox said, trying to discourage the American.

Cunningham was silent. Looking around the ship, he glanced at the sandy riverbank and saw something there that gave him an idea. He had found a way to get off the ship safely and to divert Knox's attention away from him.

Still gripping Malatee, Cunningham moved across the ship back to the other side.

"Just watch me, Kevin," Cunningham replied with a mischievous smile.

Suddenly, Cunningham pushed Malatee overboard, aiming her at the riverbank he'd been watching.

Two full grown crocodiles basking in the sun were brought to eager life by the sound of Malatee hitting the water. They glided quickly into the river and headed directly for her.

Cunningham's frequent visits to the crocodile-infested cave had taught him to understand crocodile behavior. They would react to the sound of a heavy object dropping into the water near them, and would head for that spot hoping to find prey.

Knox and his men were caught off guard by this move, and their attention swiftly went to Malatee's plight. Cunningham was, for the moment, forgotten.

Cunningham ran to the other side of the ship and jumped into the river, as close to one of the four sailboats as possible. As he climbed onto the boat, he raised the sail quickly, hoping it would catch the wind. At the same time he stood up and thrust the sailboat's two long oars into the water with all of his strength. All Sea Gypsy boats had two long oars arranged as in a rowboat, but positioned high enough for a man to use while standing. Cunningham continued to row as a light wind filled the sail, propelling the small sailboat towards the mouth of the river.

Knox and his men stood stunned and helpless for a few seconds. All their weapons had been thrown in the river, so they had nothing to shoot the crocodiles. Malatee saw the crocodiles coming in her direction, and began swimming towards the nearest rowboat.

The shouting caught the attention of the five Gurkha soldiers aboard the other merchant ship. They heard the commotion, ran to the side of the ship, and saw what was happening to Malatee. They raised their Stens, but dared not fire at the crocodiles because Malatee was also in the line of fire.

Finally, Knox sprang into action. He shouted for Rachan to untie the rope that moored the two rowboats to the ship, then jumped into the river very near a rowboat.

Instead of trying to untie the rope as Knox had told him to do, Rachan saved a valuable few seconds by pulling his jungle knife from its sheath and cutting the rope with one powerful stroke.

Knox quickly climbed into the rowboat. He picked up an oars, placed one end against the hull of the ship, and pushed with all his strength. The rowboat surged towards Malatee, who was swimming for her life.

Knox moved quickly to the bow of the boat. With all his remaining strength, he pulled Malatee into the boat just seconds before the strong jaws of the nearest crocodile could reach her.

"Shoot Cunningham! Shoot at the sailboat!" Rachan shouted frantically at the Gurkhas in the other ship while pointing at the sailboat which was moving faster as the sail fully caught the wind.

The sound of five Stens echoed between the mangrove forests lining the riverbanks as the Gurkhas followed Rachan's order. The first volley of fire whizzed over Cunningham's head. Cunningham dropped to on the floor of the boat, one hand still firmly grasping the tiller. Cunningham hoped that the wooden hull of the boat was hard enough to protect him from the hail of 9 mm. Parabellum bullets. He heard the sound of bullets hitting the hull, but none of the bullets hit him.

The sound of gunfire grew fainter and fainter, disappearing once the boat was finally out of range.

Cunningham sat upright again and directed the small sailboat towards the open sea. He sighed in relief, certain now that he had miraculously escaped from Tarutao without a scratch. He looked up at the sky and laughed aloud thankful that luck was still on his side. The British, with their hundreds of troops, could not capture him. Knox with all his men could not stop him. Fate had brought him to Tarutao and fate had guided him out of Tarutao safely. He knew in his heart that he was born to be a survivor.

However, Cunningham had not yet realized that some of the bullets from the five Stens had penetrated the hull below the water line. The small bullet holes began to slowly let water into the small boat. But by the time Cunningham realized that his boat was leaking, he would be far from shore.

Two weeks after the raid, a small, bullet-riddled Sea Gypsy sailboat with a broken mast and wooden hull washed ashore on the beach at Pine Bay on Tarutao. No body was found in the wrecked boat or anywhere else. The occupant of the boat was presumed lost at sea.

EPILOGUE

On a sunny afternoon in early December 1975, a 44 ft. Carbineer yacht coming from Langkawi stopped in front of the headquarters of Tarutao National Park at Pante Bay. Her white fiberglass hull gleamed in the sunlight as her three occupants, two men and a woman, busily lowered her two sails and anchor. Then they lowered a dinghy with an outboard motor into the calm sea and prepared to go ashore.

One of the men and the woman stood at the bow, looking at Pante Bay with excitement.

"I can't believe it! It has been almost thirty years!" said Kevin Knox, now a physically fit sixty-year-old man. Although his once thick brown hair had turned gray and grown a little thinner, he did not look his age. His long stay in the tropics and constant exposure to the sun had made his skin very tan.

"Twenty-nine years and eight months to be exact," Malatee said. She, too, looked younger than her fifty-one years. Nor had the births of her two sons spoiled her figure. Her long black hair was now cut short and flecked with only a few gray hairs. She wore white knee-length Bermuda shorts, instead of the traditional sarong, and a white short-sleeve sports-shirt.

Knox turned his eyes away from the shore and looked approvingly at Malatee. He told her, "You always look great in shorts."

"Oh, Kevin, you've been saying that for the past ten years, ever since you bought me my first pair of shorts," Malatee said laughing softly.

"And it's more practical than a sarong on a ship."

"Kevin, I still remember how often you've told me that you loved to see me going into the water with a sarong on and coming up soaking wet. You said I looked sexiest with a wet sarong clinging to my body."

"Well, that was before we were married. That was all I had to look forward to then," Knox said. They laughed and embraced comfortably.

"Are you two coming or not?" shouted a male voice from the stern of the yacht.

Knox and Malatee walked towards the stern and looked down at a young man in his mid-twenties standing in the dinghy. He was Charles, their oldest son.

"Your father and I were reminiscing about the old days," Malatee said, looking adoringly at her son.

Charles Knox's features resembled his father's but the dark hair, dark eyes, and darker complexion were Malatee's contribution. He had an athletic figure which reminded her of Kevin in his younger days. Kevin was a few years older than Charles when they first met and he rescued her from Hawkins and Grant. His chivalrous act touched her deeply. Her feelings for him began with admiration, developed into affection, and finally, love.

Knox and Malatee were married in 1948 in Penang when Knox was promoted to major. Later that year, Knox resigned from the Army and moved to Langkawi, where he bought a rubber plantation.

Malatee gave birth to Charles in 1950 and Peter in 1953. Both Charles and Peter received their primary education in Singapore and were sent to a university in England. Charles came back two years ago with a degree in Business Administration and was helping Kevin run their plantation and their import-export business. Peter was in his last year at the university studying International Relations, and looking forward to a career in the British Foreign Service.

"I don't understand why you older people like to talk about the past," Charles said, shaking his head as Kevin and Malatee sat down in the dinghy.

"Remember this sentence thirty years from now," Knox said, smiling. "If it were not for the old days on Tarutao, Charles, you wouldn't be here today."

"Dad, Mom has always said that everyone has his own destiny. If I was destined to be born to you two, it would have happened no matter what."

"Oh, Charles, you sound like your father. You always find reasons to support your argument," Malatee said. The three of them laughed.

Charles pulled hard on the motor cord, and the engine instantly came to life. He pushed the dinghy away from the yacht and turned it towards the beach.

"Welcome to Tarutao National Park. You are our first foreign visitors since it opened to the public a month ago," a park officer said in English. Kevin, Malatee, and Charles had walked first into a one-story wooden building with the signs RECEPTION and TOURIST INFORMATION on its front door.

"I know that this island was once a prison. When did Tarutao become a national park?" Knox asked in Thai.

The officer gave him a surprised look, then a pleasant smile. "Oh, you can speak Thai. The prison was abolished in 1948. The Government made Tarutao a national park in April, last year. The area of the park also covers the islands of Adang, Rawi, and Butang, but excludes Lipe, which belongs to the Sea Gypsies."

"We'd heard that Tarutao has become a park; that's why we're here," Knox said.

"There is an entrance fee," the park officer said.

"How much is the fee?" Malatee asked, also in Thai.

The officer smiled at her, believing that she was a Thai because of her perfect accent.

"Ten baht for you as a Thai. Fifty baht each for these two farangs (Westerners)," the officer replied, handing Malatee three tickets and three brochures on the park. Malatee laughed as she paid the officer 110 baht, the equivalent of US$5.50, while Knox scratched his head at a loss as to what to say.

"I thought the pirate days were over years ago. It's a strange regulation. One fee for the locals and more expensive ones for the foreigners," Knox said, shaking his head in disbelief as they walked out of the building.

"Kevin, this is Tarutao, remember? They make their own rules here," Malatee said. She handed Kevin and Charles one brochure each.

"Dad, the brochure has a section on the history of the island, including the pirates. It has the name of the prison director who was sentenced to fifteen years imprisonment for involvement in the piracy," Charles said excitedly. They were sitting on stools made of coconut logs underneath the shade of pine trees.

"The sentence was a light one, considering what Khun Apipat and his men had done. He was quite influential in government circles. What else does the brochure say?"

"It mentions the suppression of the pirates by the British troops in 1946. However, it doesn't say anything about prisoners-of-war here, only the political prisoners, including the five who escaped to Langkawi in 1939."

"I had a part in that escape, Charles," Malatee said, recalling the past.

"Yes, you've told me about that. Dad, how come there was no mentioning of the prisoners-of-war? You said you were one of them?" Charles asked.

"The presence of the prisoners-of-war on Tarutao had never been officially recorded by the authorities in Bangkok. We were sent here from Alor Setar by the order of General Yamashita. Anyway, it was too small an affair to be included in the brochure," Knox explained, then asked, "Does the brochure say anything more about the political prisoners? What happened to them?"

"They were granted amnesty by the Thai Government in 1944," Charles replied. "After the war, several of them entered politics and were elected to parliament. The names of Praya Sarapai, Praya Surapan, Prince Sittiporn, and Luang Mahasit are mentioned. They were also members of the cabinet at that time."

"The first two were among the five prisoners who escaped to Langkawi," Malatee interrupted.

"And Luang Mahasit was the one who taught me Thai," Knox added.

"Kevin, what did really happen to Cunningham?" Malatee asked. "You've never told me about it."

"There is nothing to tell," Knox replied. "He just disappeared after he threw you into the river and sailed away. For the next five years I asked our armed forces in Malaya, Singapore, Burma, and even India to look for him. We sent similar requests to our embassies in Bangkok,

Jakarta, and Manila. Cunningham used to live in the Philippines and Sarawak. But no one ever heard of or saw him, which I thought was impossible. So after five years I gave up."

"It was a good thing that you did, Kevin. I know you blamed him for Brown's death, but it was time to let bygones be bygones. Besides, you once told me that there was no warrant for his arrest."

"You're right, Malatee. Let's forgive and forget. We're too old to hold a grudge. If I were to run into him now, I think we could become friends."

"Will you be spending the night here? Do you need a bungalow?" asked a park officer who approached them.

"No, thank you. We'll be camping on the beach at Pine Bay," Malatee replied.

"Are there still crocodiles on the island?" Knox asked. Malatee shuddered at the mention of those ferocious reptiles.

"Very, very few. After the prison was abolished, many people came here to hunt crocodiles. Now, they're almost extinct. Have you ever seen crocodiles before?"

"Well, I have. But want my son here to see them," Knox replied, pointing at Charles.

"I'm sorry, but it's now very difficult to find one," the officer said.

"Kevin, my last experience with crocodiles has lasted me a lifetime. I still shudder every time I think of how close I came to having my body snapped in half. Charles, your father saved my life."

"Otherwise I wouldn't be here, I know," Charles said. "Here comes more talk about old times."

"I'll leave you two lovers alone with the memories of

how you spent your time here. I wasn't here to intrude then; so, I'm not going to be here now," Charles said. They had set up two tents in exactly the same place Malatee chose every time she came to see Knox years ago. "I'll go have a look around. Maybe I can find some treasure hidden by the pirates."

"You do that, Charles. Don't come back before dark," Malatee said, laughing. She threw an orange to her son who deftly caught it with his right hand. Charles waved at his parents and walked away towards the sea.

"Dad, Dad, come with me quickly!" Charles shouted repeatedly across the stream. Kevin, who sat in front of the tents watching Malatee preparing dinner, looked up when he heard the excited shouting.

"What is he up to now?" Kevin asked Malatee. He stood up and saw Charles standing on a rock, shouting at him.

"Hurry, Dad! Bring a flashlight! I've found something!" shouted Charles again.

"I'll go see what he's found. It better be something worthwhile," Knox said, as he picked up a flashlight and a Bowie style hunting knife.

"Don't be too long, Kevin. Dinner is almost ready," Malatee said as Knox waded across the stream towards his son.

"What have you found that has made you so excited, Charles?" Kevin asked as he reached his son.

"I've found a body, or rather the remains of one. Follow me, Dad. It's not that far," Charles said as he headed along the ridge that led up the mountain. Kevin followed behind him.

"And I thought you'd found a treasure," said Kevin

shaking his head. "You have me walking up the hill just to see the remains of an unknown person! There were hundreds or close to a thousand bodies on Tarutao during those days."

"There might be treasure around. This man was probably left by the pirates to guard it."

"You've seen too many pirate movies. This is Tarutao, not Treasure Island."

"We'll see, Dad. Here we are," Charles said as he stopped in front of a shaft about seven feet in diameter.

Knox knelt down carefully on the edge of the shaft, not sure whether the earth would hold his weight. He motioned Charles to move back from the edge; their combined weight might cause the earth to collapse. Knox was relieved when he felt the ground was solid. There must be limestone rock underneath, he decided.

Knox looked down to the bottom of the shaft about ten feet below. There was enough light to see the object lying there.

It was a complete set of human bones. It must have been lying there undisturbed for years.

Then Knox noticed that there was also light coming in from the direction of the sea. He looked up towards the sea.

"It's a cave! There's an entrance from the sea. We should enter from there. It's too high to jump from here, and anyway I don't feel like jumping abruptly into a strange place. We don't know what else is down there. Do you want to have a look now?"

"Why not, Dad? You have a flashlight with you. I feel adventurous," Charles said eagerly.

Knox did not say a word. He traced his steps back to the cluster of rocks that formed the shoreline. A tangled mass of bamboo rods littered the ground, washed ashore

by the waves. Kevin and Charles each picked up a rod
for walking. Kevin, who was agile for a man his age,
jumped from rock to rock as Charles followed.

Ten minutes later they were staring in disbelief at a
cave at the base of the cliff. The cave was large enough
for four men abreast to enter comfortably.

"I'd never noticed that there was a cave here. Look
at the water mark. At high tide the sea almost covered
the entrance," Kevin said. He pointed to an even patch
of dark green where moss grew on the wall.

"Let's go in before the tide comes up," Charles urged.

"Take the knife, Charles. You're stronger," Kevin said,
handing the hunting knife to his son. "Tarutao is still a
wilderness. We have to be ready for any animal that might
be hiding in the cave."

Charles took the knife out of the sheath and held it in
his right hand. The bamboo rod was in his left. Kevin
had the flashlight and a bamboo rod in each hand. He
turned on the flashlight as he and his son entered the cave
together.

Once in the cave they discovered that the limestone floor
of the cave was as even as if it had been paved by human
hands. It was the wondrous result of the tide's diligent
grinding, year after year. The floor inclined as Kevin and
Charles went in further, until the water mark was visible,
indicating how high the tide would reach.

Above the water mark lay the remains that they'd seen
from the edge of the shaft. The body was stretched out,
lying near a cave wall. Pieces of fabric, which used to
be clothing, hung on the bones. No shoes were visible.

"He, let's assume it was a man, must have either fallen
down into the shaft or come in from the sea. But why
did he allow himself to die like this?" Kevin asked.

"Maybe he fell in through the shaft, and broke his legs. He couldn't crawl out through the cave's entrance, because it was either high tide at that time or he was too weak to move," Charles suggested.

"That's a logical deduction. Another guess is that he could have been the victim of a shipwreck and the tide carried him into this cave. He might have been alive, and crawled up until the tide couldn't reach him. You might be right, Charles, about the injury part. He must have been seriously injured and lost the strength to move out of the cave. It looks like he died of starvation and injury," Kevin said. He felt sorry for this unknown man.

"What a terrible way to die!" Charles said.

Kevin shone the flashlight on the body and looked closely, trying to find something that could identify the person. Then both of them were stunned to notice a dagger, with a seven inch blade, lying among the bones that once formed the corpse's right hand.

As Kevin knelt down to examine the dagger more closely, his eyes noticed some writing on the wall of the cave.

Kevin moved closer to the wall. The words must have been there for years, but they were still clear enough to read. The dying man, using the last of his strength, had carved a message on the wall with his dagger.

"Oh, my God! It can't be!" Kevin exclaimed in horror as he saw the writing clearly. His face became pale and he seemed to age suddenly.

The message was four very short lines:
BOAT CAPSIZED   LEGS BROKEN
NO FOOD   NO WATER
WEAK   DYING
DAMN YOU, KNOX!

THE END